Praise for Carla Laureano

LONDON TIDES

"In *London Tides*, Carla Laureano shows how fear and grief can hold us captive—unable to love ourselves and others. Yes, Laureano has written a beautiful reconciliation romance, but she also delves into deeper themes of identity and acceptance. The character of Grace Brennan, in spite of her unconventional life, speaks to all of us."

> **BETH K. VOGT**, author of *Things I Never Told You* and *Moments We Forget*

"Achieving an aching depth and a resounding trueness within a heated yet baggage-ridden romance, author Carla Laureano has proven herself a storyteller who is not afraid to take her characters into the darkest regions of their own hearts. An excellent follow-up to *Five Days in Skye*, *London Tides* tugs and churns every emotion . . . right up until the lovely, hope-buoying end."

> **SERENA CHASE**, author of *Intermission* and the Eyes of E'veria series

"At times lighthearted; at times heart wrenching. Laureano has penned a delightfully romantic tale about the importance of finding home. If readers weren't already smitten with the MacDonald brothers, they will be after *London Tides!*"

> **KATIE GANSHERT**, award-winning author of *No One Ever Asked*

"Another captivating story! *London Tides* is as compelling and engaging as Laureano's award-winning *Five Days in Skye*. It's deliciously romantic and filled with tension, wonderful characters, and vivid scenery. A must-read this summer!"

> **KATHERINE REAY,** author of *A Portrait of Emily Price* and *The Austen Escape*

"War photographer Grace Brennan is the kind of character I love to read about—she's savvy, fearless, and damaged, yet is determined to carry on. Returning to London means making amends with Ian MacDonald, the fiancé she left behind, and author Carla Laureano knows how to make the most of their chemistry. But a chance at love for Grace also means facing the realities of PTSD, a subject Laureano handles with great sensitivity and care. Vividly written and deeply felt, *London Tides* will sweep readers away."

> **HILLARY MANTON LODGE,** author of *A Table by the Window*

FIVE DAYS IN SKYE

"Sweet and scathing, lush and intimate. . . . This story has guts and heart as well as the depth and heat necessary to satisfy any romance reader's palate."

> *USA TODAY*

"From page one, *Five Days in Skye* captured my imagination and every minute of my pleasure-reading time. With enviable finesse, author Carla Laureano weaves romance, hope, healing, and faith into a spunky and sparkling tale that made me sorry to say good-bye to the characters and the alluring Isle of Skye. I look forward to reading more from this author."

TAMARA LEIGH, author of *Splitting Harriet* and *The Unveiling*, book one in the Age of Faith series

"After reading *Five Days in Skye*, I wanted to pack my bags and catch the first flight to Scotland to discover Skye for myself. In her debut novel, Carla Laureano brought Skye alive with vivid detail, drew me into the main characters' budding romance, and kept me turning the pages late into the night. I'm looking forward to more books from Carla!"

BETH K. VOGT, author of *Things I Never Told You* and *Moments We Forget*

"*Five Days in Skye* swept me away to Scotland! Against the craggy beauty of the Isle of Skye, author Carla Laureano weaves a story . . . of love between an American businesswoman and a Scottish celebrity chef. Fans of the movie *The Holiday* are sure to enjoy this contemporary romance. Laureano's voice is deft, seamless, and wonderfully accomplished. An exciting newcomer to the world of Christian fiction!"

BECKY WADE, author of *My Stubborn Heart* and *Undeniably Yours*

THE SATURDAY NIGHT SUPPER CLUB

"A terrific read from a talented author. Made me hungry more than once. I can't wait to read what comes next."

FRANCINE RIVERS, *New York Times* bestselling author of *The Masterpiece*

"Bright, jovial, and peppered with romance and delectable cuisine, this is a sweet and lively love story."
    PUBLISHERS WEEKLY, starred review

"Romance aficionados and fans of stories about overcoming obstacles and the role of faith in everyday life will eagerly await the next entry in this sweet food-centered series."
    LIBRARY JOURNAL

"Laureano's latest novel, the first in her Supper Club series, is a delight for foodies! There's a delectable amount of behind-the-scenes restaurant and cooking detail . . . that will literally have readers' mouths watering for a taste."
    ROMANTIC TIMES, 4 ½ star Top Pick

"This romance nurtures the balance between following one's dreams and embracing the moment."
    FOREWORD MAGAZINE

"Writing charmingly about faith, love, friendship, and food, Laureano will leave readers hungry for the next installment in the Supper Club series."
    BOOKLIST

"You don't have to be a foodie to enjoy *The Saturday Night Supper Club*, but if you are, you're in for an extra treat. Carla Laureano has written a delicious romance you'll want to devour in one sitting. Filled with sugar and spice, *The Saturday Night Supper Club* will leave you hungry for more from this talented author."

IRENE HANNON, bestselling author and three-time RITA Award winner

"At turns devastating and delightful, this novel contrasts the heartbreak of instant infamy against the charm of a budding attraction. Highly recommended!"

SERENA CHASE, author of *Intermission* and the Eyes of E'veria series

"An absolute delight with compelling characters, a rich sense of place, and food that lingers on your palate long after the final page."

KATHERINE REAY, author of *A Portrait of Emily Price* and *The Austen Escape*

"Smart, funny, romantic, hopeful—the perfect starter for Laureano's scrumptious new series."

CANDACE CALVERT, bestselling author of *Maybe It's You* and *The Recipe*

"*The Saturday Night Supper Club* is a riveting read, crafted with sophisticated characters, delicious settings, and a satisfying romance that will leave readers breathless and anxious for the next book in the series."

JEN TURANO, *USA Today* bestselling author of *A Change of Fortune*

Brunch at Bittersweet Café

"With fun food scenes and organic spiritual elements, Laureano's book will be relished by sweet-toothed inspirational readers."

PUBLISHERS WEEKLY

"Realistic romance and spiritual message make *Brunch at Bittersweet Café* an exceptional pick."

MIDWEST BOOK REVIEW

London Tides

London Tides

CARLA LAUREANO

Tyndale House Publishers, Inc.
Carol Stream, Illinois

Visit Tyndale online at www.tyndale.com.

Visit Carla Laureano's website at www.carlalaureano.com.

TYNDALE and Tyndale's quill logo are registered trademarks of Tyndale House Publishers, Inc.

London Tides

Previously published in 2015 by David C Cook under ISBN 978-1-4347-0822-9. First printing by Tyndale House Publishers, Inc., in 2019.

Designed by Eva M. Winters

Edited by Sarah Mason Rische

Published in association with the literary agency of The Steve Laube Agency.

London Tides is a work of fiction. Where real people, events, establishments, organizations, or locales appear, they are used fictitiously. All other elements of the novel are drawn from the author's imagination.

For information about special discounts for bulk purchases, please contact Tyndale House Publishers at csresponse@tyndale.com, or call 1-800-323-9400.

Library of Congress Cataloging-in-Publication Data
Names: Laureano, Carla, author.
Title: London tides / Carla Laureano.
Description: Carol Stream, Illinois : Tyndale House Publishers, Inc., [2019]
   | Series: The MacDonald family trilogy
Identifiers: LCCN 2018060357 | ISBN 9781496426253 (sc)
Subjects: | GSAFD: Love stories. | Christian fiction.
Classification: LCC PS3612.A93257 L66 2019 | DDC 813/.6—dc23 LC record
   available at https://lccn.loc.gov/2018060357

Printed in the United States of America

25   24   23   22   21   20   19
 7   6   5   4   3   2   1

To all my sisters who feel unseen and insignificant—
You are loved. Your stories matter.

And for Camille Lepage (1988–2014),
whose life and work helped shape Grace.
Rest in peace.

Acknowledgments

MY TYNDALE TEAM—thank you for giving me the chance to once more put this story out into the world, this time as close to my original vision as I could make it. Books don't often get a second chance, so I'm eternally grateful.

My agent, Steve Laube—I'm going to start calling you the Author Whisperer, because you somehow always know just what I need to hear. Thank you.

My new editors, Jan Stob and Sarah Rische—thank you for understanding what this story means to me and where I wanted to see it go. You make this process all worthwhile!

The book's original editor, Rachelle Gardner—the road was rocky, but without you, this would have never made it to press the first time. I won't ever forget that.

My "Usual Suspects"—seriously, though, you guys are the only thing keeping me focused and somewhat sane (please stop laughing)—my family, Laurie Tomlinson, Elizabeth Younts, Brandy Vallance, Evangeline Denmark, Serena Chase, Beth Vogt, Jen Turano, and Halee Matthews.

My beta readers, Evangeline Denmark, Elizabeth Olmedo, Laurie Tomlinson, Brandy Vallance, and Sarah Varland. You might not recognize this book when you read it again, but I so appreciate you taking time out of your lives and writing to give me your honest feedback.

I couldn't end without naming the photojournalists whose work and lives inspired me while writing Grace, particularly Lynsey Addario, Deborah Copaken, and Camille Lepage. Their risks give a look into a world the rest of us might never imagine. I owe their photographs great thanks for opening my eyes and heart to people and places I've never considered. I'm sure I got some details wrong, but in the end I hope my admiration and respect for the discipline shines through.

A Note from the Author

LONDON TIDES WAS FIRST RELEASED in summer of 2015, but it was a slightly different version from the story you're about to read. Novels are often shaped by individuals other than their authors: editors, publishing executives, retailers. At the time, certain elements of my original story were deemed too edgy for the market and I was asked to revise the last quarter of the book. And while I was proud of the finished project, I always felt that Grace's character arc had somewhat suffered from the changes.

The series was then acquired by Tyndale House Publishers, who graciously agreed to take a look at the first version of the book—and liked it as much as I did. What you have here is a combination of the best of both versions—a true collaborative effort—with some brand-new material worked in. And despite the amount of hair-pulling required to get to this version, this story remains the one that is nearest to my heart. I hope you love it as much as I do.

CHAPTER ONE

SHE SHOULDN'T BE HERE.

Grace Brennan snapped several pictures of the fog-shrouded river, forcing down the tide of anxiety that threatened to rise up and engulf her. Chances were he wouldn't be here either. People changed in ten years. She certainly had. What kind of man stuck to such a rigid schedule for over a decade?

She ambled down the cement embankment to where the muddy waters of the Thames lapped the bank and raised her camera once more. Even in the dim morning light, her telephoto lens captured every detail of the boats rowing against the ebb tide, from the markings on the shells to the club crests on the rowers' kit. Grace had photographed enough

1

regattas in her career to recognize the different clubs and schools by their colors, to distinguish the casuals from the competitive rowers. To know from a distance she hadn't seen him yet.

It was a mad impulse that brought her here anyhow. Her regrets should have stayed in the past, where they belonged, with the rest of her mistakes. Back then, her fears had clouded her judgment, skewed her perspective. And no matter how far she'd come, there might always be parts of her that were broken. What would coming back here do but remind her of what she'd given up?

She was about ready to move on to some street-level shots when a sleek red eight glided with precision toward the bank on which she stood. Again the camera came up to focus on the crew, and her heart rose into her throat when her gaze landed on the man in the stroke seat nearest the stern.

His dark hair was short now, thick waves cropped into submission, but she would have recognized him anywhere. He radiated capability and confidence with an oar in hand, and even his rowing waterproofs couldn't hide a physique that was as lean and muscular as a decade before. Clearly she'd had good reason to believe things hadn't changed.

Grace's hand tightened convulsively around the column of the thick lens as she let the neck strap take the camera's weight. Her muscles tensed, her heart pounding. Should she call to him? Would he even speak to her?

Then he turned her way and stopped, the oar frozen in midair. He saw her, no mistake. She held her breath, waiting to see what he would do.

Just as quickly, he turned away, his movements brusque

and businesslike as he removed his oar from the lock. Her hopes rushed away as quickly as the tide.

Ten years wondering how she'd feel if she saw him again. Ten years convincing herself that time and distance would change things. Pure rubbish, all of it.

She still loved him. And he still hadn't forgiven her.

Grace wound her way into the Regency Café, ignoring the irritated looks from waiting patrons. Even at eight in the morning, the greasy spoon was packed with diners, the queue stretching out the door, voices raised in a hum just short of deafening. She scanned the crowded room until her gaze landed on a beautiful Indian woman staking out a corner table.

Asha held up her arm and pointed to her wristwatch with raised eyebrows.

"I know, I know, I'm late."

Grace grimaced as she approached the table, but Asha pulled her into a bone-crushing hug before she could get out the rest of her apology.

"Only by about two years! When did you arrive in London? Before you called this morning, I didn't even know you were coming."

"Landed last night." The tightness in Grace's chest eased as she slid into a chair and placed her gear bag between her feet. "It was a last-minute decision. Did you order for us?"

"Of course. I didn't queue for an hour for tea. I got your usual. It *is* your usual, right? You didn't go vegan on me or anything . . ."

Grace laughed. "Absolutely not. I live on bacon. Besides,

3

Paris hasn't been as much fun since they stopped sautéing everything in a kilo of butter. You know you're in trouble when even the French turn health conscious."

Asha laughed too, her expression radiating happiness. Since they'd met on a medical mission in Jaipur twelve years ago, Dr. Asha Issar had become her close friend and confidante. Grace had no doubt that her joy was genuine.

"So tell me, why *are* you back in London?"

"To see you, of course." At Asha's disbelieving look, Grace smiled and amended, "It was time, Ash. I couldn't avoid an entire country forever. I'm considering moving back."

"I'd love that. But you said you'd never leave the field. What happened?" Asha's attention settled on Grace's right arm, where it rested on the table. "Does it have something to do with the new tattoo?"

Grace touched the tiny green dragon that curled around her wrist like a bracelet, melding seamlessly into the design of colored flowers and wrought iron above it. It was good work—artistic work—but she should have known Asha would understand this was no more a whim than the other tattoos that covered her right arm to the shoulder.

"Brian is dead."

"Oh, Grace, I'm so sorry. What happened?"

Grace swallowed hard while she brought her voice under control. "You hear about the incident in Syria?"

"That was him?" Understanding dawned on Asha's face. "That was you. You were the other photographer who survived the blast. Grace, why didn't you tell me?"

Because she hadn't told anyone. Because the grief was too fresh. And deep down, she felt responsible.

Sure, she'd not been the one to fire the grenade. She'd

warned Brian that their position was too exposed, had been trying to get them out. But he was so young and eager to get the shot, and it had been her responsibility to rein in that reckless enthusiasm, just as her own mentor Jean-Auguste had done for her.

She'd failed miserably.

"So that's why I'm here," Grace said at last. "I'm supposed to be in Aleppo, but I couldn't get on the plane."

Asha reached for her hand across the table and squeezed it hard. "I understand; I really do. But you love the work. Surely you don't want to quit."

"Come on, Ash. You know shooting conflicts was supposed to be a short-term plan, not the past ten years of my life. Everyone with half a brain is out, onto something safer."

"But you've worked for this since you were nineteen!"

"And look where it's gotten me."

"Achieving a level of success most people never imagine. *Newsweek* and *National Geographic* have you on speed dial. You were listed as one of the most influential photographers of the decade, for heaven's sake."

"One of the most influential photographers of the decade." Grace gave a short, humorless laugh. "Had I died along with Brian, would anyone have missed me besides you and Jean-Auguste? I'm thirty-four, Ash. I can pack up my entire life in three cases and a duffel bag. My parents don't talk to me anymore, and the only person to send me a birthday card was the president of my photo agency."

Asha's gaze drilled into her. "You're back for Ian."

"When you say it that way, I sound completely pathetic."

"Not *completely* pathetic. Just a little bit."

"It was daft," Grace said. "If you could have seen the look on his face—"

"You saw him? What did you do? What did he say?"

"I don't know. I didn't stick around to find out."

"Grace—"

"I know, I know. But what do you say in that situation? 'Hi, I'm sorry I ran out on you six months before our wedding. How have you been?' Besides, for all I know, he's married and has half a dozen kids now."

"He's not married."

The pronouncement stunned Grace into momentary silence. "You've seen him?"

"He and Jake go out for a pint on occasion. He dates, but as far as I can tell, nothing serious. It leads one to believe he's waiting for something. Or someone."

Grace's heart jolted at the words, but she shook her head. However much she might want to put things right, what she had done to him was unforgivaable. What kind of woman left the man she loved without a proper good-bye? What kind of man forgave that sort of betrayal?

"You should talk to him, Grace. Even if it's just to put him behind you."

As Grace opened her mouth to reply, the woman behind the counter shouted a familiar order. "That us?"

"Yeah. I'll get it." Asha pushed back the chair.

"Bacon, egg, mushrooms, tomatoes, two toasts! You comin' to get it, or you want me to fax it to ya?"

Grace chuckled. "Let me. Least I can do after you saved me the hour wait."

She pushed her way back to the counter, relieved to escape her friend's scrutiny. Maybe Asha was right, but she'd been trying to put Ian behind her for ten years. What made either of them think she'd be any more successful now?

By the time Grace returned with their breakfasts, she'd steeled herself for more analysis, but Asha didn't bring up the subject again. Instead, she asked, "Where are you staying?"

"Hotel."

Asha reached into her handbag and slid a key across the table. "You know the address."

"Ash, I couldn't—"

"Nonsense. Of course you could. How long will you be here?"

"At least through the end of August. A friend is putting together a showing of my portraits at his gallery in Putney. After that, I'm not sure."

"You just got here, and you're already looking for an excuse to leave." A smile softened Asha's words, though, and she reached out to squeeze Grace's hand again. "I'm glad you're back."

"Me too." To stave off further discussion, Grace dug into her breakfast and barely stifled a groan of pleasure. Paris might be the culinary center of Europe, but nothing beat an old-fashioned fry-up from this landmark diner. She allowed herself to savor a few more bites before she shot a stern look at Asha. "So. Jake. Don't think you're going to slip that one by me. Did you finally say yes?"

Asha shrugged. "After five years of asking me out, it seemed only fair to give the bloke a chance."

"It's about time. I've always thought you two would make a great couple."

She laughed. "It had crossed my mind over the years. But one or both of us were always seeing someone else. He was busy with work; I was splitting my time between here and India . . . It wasn't the right time for a relationship."

If anyone understood that, it was Grace. Still, after Asha had broken off a tumultuous romance with a fellow physician, Grace had wondered if she would ever take a chance on another man. "We should have dinner, then, the three of us. I haven't seen him in ages."

"You haven't seen anyone in ages," Asha countered, but it was without heat. She glanced at her watch and grimaced. "I have to go or I'll be late for my shift. Move your things to the flat, yeah? I'll be back later tonight."

"Thanks, Ash. It means a lot to me." Grace gave her a quick hug, then watched her stride from the restaurant. Of all her friends, Asha was the most dependable, the most understanding. But then, she had a better perspective on what Grace did for a living, having spent much of her early career in conflict zones herself. It took firsthand experience to understand how it felt to live day-to-day in varying degrees of danger.

She turned back to her plate, but her mind returned to Ian. She should have stuck around and talked to him, told him the conclusions she'd reached in the three months since Brian's death. After all these years, he deserved to know why she had run away. Deserved to know it hadn't been because she'd stopped loving him.

And maybe he deserved to know that leaving him had been the biggest mistake of her life.

CHAPTER TWO

"YOU ALL RIGHT THERE, MATE?"

Ian MacDonald stared at the place Grace had occupied moments before, his limbs frozen. It took several seconds for Chris's words to sink in. "Fine. Someone I thought I knew."

Chris followed Ian's gaze, but the space between the club's boathouse and the neighboring building was now vacant. "Nice one today. Still set a good rhythm."

"If by good you mean sadistic," Marc muttered from the back of the boat.

Ian grinned at their coxswain, who also happened to be an old Cambridge teammate. "Sadistic? That was barely twenty-five."

"Thirty-two on the push," Marc shot back.

Ian's smile widened. By today's standards, thirty-two strokes a minute was barely a race pace, but it was close to what they'd managed back in the day. The crew for his weekday outings was made up of men like him—former Oxbridge and British Team rowers whose competitiveness hadn't diminished with their available training time. Still, seeing the younger crews on the water made him realize how much time had passed since he was in his prime.

Back then, the only thing that had mattered to him more than rowing was Grace. He'd abandoned his career, his sponsorships, his dreams of Olympic gold. And she'd disappeared without a word, taking every last possession but her engagement ring.

"Waist, ready, up!"

Marc's command cut through the memory, and in unison, the eight-man crew lifted the boat to waist level. At the cox's next command, they pressed the boat upside down over their heads. The familiar routine gave Ian something to focus on, but he barely avoided banging the stern on the doorframe as they carried the shell back to the club's boathouse.

After that, he managed to keep his mind on his actions, but he still showered and dressed in a daze, letting the jokes of the other men in the changing room flow around him until Chris stopped behind him.

"Coming to breakfast? Or do you have someone waiting?" Chris waggled his eyebrows suggestively while Ian stared in confusion. "Your date last night?"

He finally followed the insinuation. "Ah . . . no. We wrapped it up early. Not that I'm in the habit of taking home women I've just met."

"You're not in the habit of taking home *any* women. I've

set you up on three dates and none of them have made it past dinner. What's wrong with this one?"

"Nothing's wrong with her. She's a perfectly lovely woman—"

"She's gorgeous!"

"—who is about as interesting as watching paint dry—"

"So? Did I mention she was gorgeous?"

"—and did nothing but talk about the last case she won." Chris shot him a reproving look. "You're a lawyer too."

"I used to be a lawyer." Now he didn't quite know what he was. "I don't know why you keep insisting on setting me up."

"At this point I'm not sure either." Chris heaved a sigh that made it clear Ian's lack of interest in casual dating was a disgrace to men everywhere. "Anyhow, breakfast?"

"Brunch at Mum's. We're taking out the quad on Tuesday?"

"I'll be here."

Ian hiked his kit bag onto his shoulder and clambered down the stairs to ground level. Instantly, his unanswered questions crowded in. What was Grace doing back in London? Had she been looking for him? Or had he imagined the petite blonde standing on the bank? The woman he'd seen had much shorter hair than his Grace—

His Grace. The words, even spoken in his head, made his stomach clench. She had made it clear she had no interest in being his Grace when she left. They'd shared a life, a bed, a home for two years, but when it had come time to make it permanent, she'd run. Even in retrospect, there'd been no signs it was coming.

No. He wasn't going to do this today. He'd already wasted far too much of his life rehashing what went wrong with Grace. Regardless of her location, he was better off without her.

———❦———

Forty minutes later, Ian knelt on the cold cement of an underground car park in Emperor's Gate to unlock a heavy chamois cover. A smile came to his face for the first time since leaving the club. If he were honest, his dutiful attendance at his mother's monthly garden brunches had far less to do with the overly fussy food and pretentious conversation than his method of transportation.

A 1966 Austin-Healey BJ8, a classic piece of British automotive history and the one car he'd dreamed of owning since childhood. It had taken him two years and considerable expense to restore her, from the rusted-out two-tone paint job to the ripped black leather interior. The classic car always served as an excuse to avoid the gossip and slip away with the other auto enthusiasts, including his uncle Rodney. In fact, Rodney was solely to blame for the vehicle's existence. He'd been the one to take Ian and his younger brother, James, to races at Silverstone and the occasional classic car meet. James had never latched on to the idea, but those outings had been the highlight of Ian's childhood.

Now that he owned his dream, the trouble was finding time to enjoy it. London's traffic and its congestion zones made it hardly worth the effort to drive, and work and rowing kept him well tied to the city. Maybe he should take another trip to Scotland and check on the progress of the Skye hotel. Completely unnecessary, of course—Jamie and his fiancée, Andrea, had matters well in hand—but it would be a useful excuse for a short escape.

The twenty-five-minute drive to Hampstead went much too quickly, and he'd barely managed to settle the tension from Grace's unexpected appearance before he turned off to his mother's estate. He punched in the gate code and waited for the wrought-iron gates to swing inward. Somehow the opulence of the house struck him as even more excessive than usual as he navigated through the newly landscaped allée to the front of the spectacular Georgian-style manor, all heavy red brick and mullioned windows. He might have spent school holidays here while at Eton, but he'd never dared call it home.

He left the car beside several other expensive vehicles, shrugging his suit jacket on as he went, and headed to the center of the parterre, where several tables had been set up. At least a dozen people milled about, glasses already in hand. Almost immediately, an elegant, dark-haired woman in a cream-colored suit and matching hat caught sight of him and made her way over.

"Ian, darling!"

"Mum." Ian accepted her embrace and kissed her on the cheek. "You look lovely."

"And you look quite dapper yourself, Son." Marjorie took a surreptitious look around. "You didn't bring anyone, did you? Good. I want you to meet Rachel Corson. You remember the Corsons, don't you? The father is in shipping, and the mother—"

"Mum, stop." He cut her off before she could go further in her description. Knowing her, she already had them married in her mind. She'd been fairly vocal about his inability to accomplish it himself. "The last time I met one of your friends' daughters, it was a disaster. Let's not repeat history, shall we?"

Marjorie leveled a look at him that managed to fall short of motherly concern. "Five minutes."

"No."

"I knew you'd see it my way. Don't go anywhere. I'll be right back."

Ian sighed and tugged on his tie, which had already begun to feel too tight. Twenty-five minutes in the Healey did not in any way make up for this.

"Run, while you still have the chance."

Ian twisted toward the voice at his shoulder. "Rodney, you startled me."

"Bloody Mary?"

Ian took a glass from his uncle and looked him over. If Marjorie was impeccably put together, her younger brother always had a studiously mussed air, as if he had been rudely summoned away from a game of snooker. His suit was expensive but rumpled, and he might have forgotten to comb his hair that morning. His eyes, however, missed nothing. Unfortunately.

Ian sipped the cocktail and barely covered his cough. "Might you add some tomato juice to the vodka next time? It's not yet noon."

"Only way I can get through these events of your mother's. And you'll need it if you plan to stick around for her latest matchmaking attempt."

"That bad?"

"Pretty, but insipid."

Ian took another drink, intending to fortify himself for the inquisition, but the trail it burned down his throat convinced him to set the glass on a nearby table. He decided to cut to the chase. Rodney would get it out of him eventually anyway. "Grace is back."

"Ah."

"That's all you've got to say? 'Ah'?"

"What do you want me to say?"

"That I'm mad to be thinking about her after what happened."

Rodney shrugged.

"You don't think so?"

"You were happy with Grace right up until she disappeared."

"We were too different. Look at Mum and Dad. They were happy for a while; then Mum left."

"There's much more to that story than a few differences." Rodney tossed back the rest of the cocktail, then set his glass down beside Ian's. "And you are not as much like your mother as you think. You drive the Healey?"

"Of course."

"Let's go have a look, then."

Ian cast a glance back at Marjorie, but she had been waylaid by a group of her guests, none of whom could possibly be Rachel. He hoped. A judge with his family, or maybe an MP. They all looked alike to Ian. He followed his uncle back around the side of the house to the drive.

"How's work?" Rodney asked.

"Work is . . . work." It wasn't that Ian disliked his job exactly. His brother, Jamie, was a renowned chef who had built his first restaurant into an empire that now included six locations, several cookbooks, and a recently completed television cooking program. There was no way he could handle the details himself, and Ian was good at details. But it wasn't exactly the career Ian had envisioned for himself.

Fortunately Rodney didn't press, instead stopping next to the Healey to give it an admiring once-over. "Beautiful car, this is. Shame the only time you bring it out is for your mum's brunches."

Ian crossed his arms over his chest. "Say what you really want to say."

"Am I that transparent? Fine, then. I want to know when you're going to give yourself permission to do what *you* want to do."

"I am doing what I want to do."

"Are you? Just because Grace left doesn't make your mother right. Not about who you are, what you do, who you love."

"You're telling me that I should give Grace another chance."

"I'm telling you that you don't need anyone's permission. Your life is between you and God. And don't give me that look. I know I'm a drunk. God loves me anyway." Rodney circled the car, squatted down to examine the grille.

Ian shook his head and repressed a smile. No matter what other family members might think about the conflict between Rodney's professed faith and his drinking habit, Ian couldn't disagree with the sentiment. God knew he and Jamie had given Him plenty of reasons to despair about their life choices over the years.

Rodney stood up again and winked at his nephew. "If a beauty like that belonged to me, I wouldn't be spending my Saturday here with the rich and boring."

Rodney wasn't entirely talking about the car. Ian loosened his tie and strode resolutely back to the gathering, hoping his mum wasn't yet looking for him. She'd more willingly excuse murder than rudeness. A sign of poor breeding, she'd say, which was ironic considering most of her English friends thought Ian's Scottish upbringing made that a foregone conclusion.

Sure enough, his mum wore a look that told him his escape had not gone unnoticed, and she unleashed the full force of her glare as soon as he got within shouting distance. Fortunately, one of her staff drew her off before she could head his direction. A reprieve, if only temporary.

Outdoor brunch at Leaf Hill was distinguished from indoor brunch only by the location: the china, crystal, silver, and linen were simply transported onto the patio in their entirety. Ian followed the flow of guests to the patio table and found his designated spot to Marjorie's left. The judge stopped on his mum's other side. When the older man leaned down to whisper something in her ear, Ian's eyebrows reached skyward. Was this more than just a political connection?

"Ah, I should have known." A pretty young woman—ginger hair, pale skin, warm brown eyes—appeared beside him. She held out a hand. "Rachel Corson. And let me apologize in advance for however my matchmaking mother set this up."

This was Mum's mystery woman? He briefly shook her hand, then pulled out her chair. "Ian MacDonald. And I rather think we have *my* mother to thank for it."

"Or they're in collusion together." A hint of wry humor lit her eyes. "Mum's been after me to give her grandchildren, and she'll take any excuse to foist me off on an unsuspecting bachelor. Embarrassing, isn't it?"

At least Rodney had been wrong about one thing. Rachel wasn't insipid. She chatted amiably about various topics as they devoured the impressive brunch spread: scrambled eggs with salmon, eggs Benedict, and truffled brioche with sautéed mushrooms. Only when she began talking about her studies at the London School of Economics did he figure out she must be nearly twenty years younger than him. Mum must have been getting desperate if she was thrusting girls not even out of uni at him. As if that wouldn't make him feel ancient.

By the end of the meal, he just wanted to make a quick escape. Climb into his car and drive, watch the speedometer climb and enjoy the wind-up of the roadster's throaty engine. But he knew he would sedately navigate the traffic back to the garage in Emperor's Gate and walk the handful of blocks home to his flat.

"What did you think?" Marjorie asked when he said his farewells.

"She's practically a child, Mum."

Marjorie fixed him with a reproving look. "I'm trying to help."

"I know you are. But this is the sort of thing a man needs to work out for himself. Right?"

She didn't answer, a sure sign the subject was far from dropped, but she made him bend so she could kiss his cheek. "Don't work too hard."

"I won't," he promised, aware it was somewhat of a lie. Besides rowing, what else was there?

He turned the Healey back to west London, but he couldn't even take his usual pleasure in the trip. By the time he let himself into the first-floor flat of his historic Gloucester Road building, his resigned mood had turned downright foul.

It was completely irrational, of course. The brunch at Leaf Hill had been fine. His mother's meddling had resulted in a rather pleasant conversation, even if Rachel hadn't sparked the least bit of interest besides the acknowledgment that she was a very pretty girl.

Why exactly was that? Age aside, she was one of the more interesting women he'd met recently. And yet it hadn't even crossed his mind to get her phone number.

The beginnings of a headache throbbed in his temples as he crossed the modest reception room into the kitchen. He poured himself a glass of orange juice from the refrigerator and stood in the wash of cold air, his fingers clenched around the tumbler. Blast Grace. He'd been doing fine before she'd showed up on the bank this morning with her camera, looking . . .

. . . like Grace. The mere sight of her was enough to bring up long-buried memories—the smell of her skin, the taste of her mouth, the way her body fit against his. The brogue that her years away from Ireland hadn't completely eradicated, a lilt that surfaced when she was angry or upset.

Those last months, her eyes had lost their haunted look. She had smiled more freely, laughed more often. And then she had simply disappeared without a word. How could he have been so wrong about her?

Let her go.

As if he had any choice. No matter how hard he'd tried to move on, the past still held him by the throat.

Ian went to the shallow drawer by the sink and lifted out a stack of publications. Ten years of newspapers and magazines, Grace's career documented in print. Photos from the *Times* and the *Guardian* that had been picked up from the AP wire. Beautifully composed essays on African farmers or bush hospitals from the magazines of humanitarian organizations. The *National Geographic* story about Ugandan child soldiers being treated in trauma counseling centers, an essay as powerful as it was heartbreaking.

Grace possessed the rare ability to capture the humanity in any subject, whether it was the unemployed worker angry with the establishment or the hollow-eyed boy wielding an automatic weapon. In the last several years, her work had gotten more daring, the settings progressively more dangerous. Only someone who had endured her own share of tragedy could see beneath the surface of the story to the hurting souls beneath.

Now she was back—not in Los Angeles, where she'd begun her career, or Dublin, where she'd been raised, but London, where she'd once intended to make a life with him. That had to mean something.

Jake would know where Grace was staying, especially now that he was dating her friend Asha. Ian had his mobile phone out of his pocket and a number on the dialer before he realized what he was doing and slammed it back down on the counter.

No. He wasn't going to run after Grace and beg her for an explanation. If she wanted to talk, she obviously knew where to find him.

CHAPTER THREE

ASHA LIVED ON THE THIRD FLOOR of a typical redbrick mansion block in Earl's Court, a transitional neighborhood in central London not far from the museums and Hyde Park. Or it had been transitional once. As Grace hefted her cases and bags out of the black cab at the curb, it was clear more things had changed in ten years than just her. This little neighborhood was no longer a haven for broke students and immigrants, if the shiny new Jaguar parked a block down was any indication.

Grace paid the driver through the open front window and palmed the key Asha had given her, the pile of belongings in front of the stairs making her wish she had packed more lightly. Even so, she'd brought hardly any personal items. The stack of black hard cases held her camera bodies and lenses, her lighting setups, and most importantly, her film archives.

Four trips up and down three flights of stairs later, Grace collapsed against the door marked *14*, shoved the key into the lock, and pushed. Nothing happened. She held down the latch and threw her shoulder into the door until it opened with a crack. Grace grinned. The door had stuck for as long as she could remember—only worsened with every coat of new paint—but Asha refused to have it shaved down. An extra layer of security for a woman living alone, she said.

The interior of the flat, however, had changed, the warm jewel tones that her friend had once favored now painted over in shades of cream and white and gray. There was a new pullout sofa in the living room that would serve as Grace's bed, and photography hung on the walls. Grace didn't need to look to know they were the framed shots of India she had sent Asha for her last birthday. Their prominent positions warmed her.

It took nearly as much work to get her things into the flat, where she stacked the cases neatly in the corner, taking up as little of the tiny space as possible. Then she wandered into the kitchen, which featured a table and four chairs, a two-burner hob, and a small refrigerator. Grace opened the door and smiled when she saw the fridge was empty but for a bowl of fruit and a half-finished carton of milk. So maybe Asha's quick offer of hospitality hadn't been completely unselfish. They'd once lived together, and Grace had quickly discovered that Asha's idea of cooking was heating up takeaway.

Tandoori chicken for dinner it was.

Grace double-checked the pantry and freezer to see what ingredients she would need to buy—all of them—and then plopped down on Asha's sofa with a notepad. This was one of her favorite dishes, learned on the trip to India during which she'd first met Asha. It also happened to be one of Ian's favorites. She and Ian's brother, James, had tinkered with the recipe in Ian's kitchen, arguing over the right proportions of cinnamon and black pepper and ginger. The memory, fond as it was, made her insides clench. When she'd left Ian, she hadn't just abandoned the man she loved; she'd abandoned her adopted London family as well. James . . . Ian's sister, Serena . . . all their mutual friends. Naturally, when it was clear Grace wasn't coming back, everyone but Asha had rallied around him and shut her out. She'd been arrogant to think it didn't matter, naive to think they'd come around.

She sighed and tossed the pad onto the sofa next to her. Thinking about the past was pointless. Ian's reaction had told her all she needed to know: her return was an unwelcome surprise. If she really wanted to make a life for herself in London, she would have to do it without him. It had been only nostalgia and grief that made her believe she could change things.

Grace's mobile pulled her out of her introspection. She fished the phone from her jacket pocket and pressed it to her ear. "Grace Brennan."

"Grace! You're here!"

The clipped London accent of her friend and gallery owner Melvin Colville, brought a smile back to her lips. "You got my message."

"I did. Are you free to come by the gallery today?"

"Of course. What time?"

"Four this afternoon? And bring your slides if you have them."

"I do. See you then." Grace clicked off the phone, her spirits rising, then glanced at her watch. It was barely eleven, which gave her plenty of time to buy groceries and get the chicken marinating for dinner, then dig out the slide negatives that corresponded to the scans she had e-mailed Melvin before she left Paris.

At least there were still some people in London happy to have her back.

Grace climbed the stairs from the Underground platform and emerged to a street-level cloud of diesel fumes over musty river water. Her stomach immediately began to do backflips. It was one thing to have her photos printed in magazines, picked up on the AP wire. That was her job, her calling even. But this collection of portraiture, taken as a personal mission and the fulfillment of a promise . . . that was something entirely different. Her job as a war photographer was to show other people's tragedies, but this collection hit far too close to her own.

She'd never been a coward, though, and if she could trust anyone with her work, it would be Melvin.

Her steps slowed before a glass storefront beside a corner pub, an elegant black sign with gilt letters proclaiming *Putney Bank Gallery.* Kraft paper obscured the view through the windows, but a brick propped open the door to let in air and let out the sound of hammering.

Grace stepped inside, pausing by the door so she could watch the activity unnoticed. Several men with tool belts were securing false walls faced with plasterboard to chains from the ceiling joists, and a ginger-haired woman rolled a layer of new white paint on the permanent walls.

"Grace!"

She turned from the preparations to the man striding across the polished concrete floor toward her. Midsixties and trim, with a shaved head and neat beard, he seemed far more comfortable in his prestigious London gallery than he ever had in an editorial office. Even then, his taste had been impeccable and his influence wide.

Grace accepted his hug and quick kiss on the cheek. "Melvin, this looks amazing! Who is it?"

"Gordon Wright. Abstract oils. We'll be cutting it close for Friday, but we'll make it. We always do. How about you? How does it feel to be back in London?"

"Like home, surprisingly. It's changed a bit since I spent any real time here."

"It always does. Come, I've something to show you in my office."

Grace followed him around piles of tools and paint buckets into a small office at the back of the gallery, sparsely furnished with a desk and two inexpensive chairs, its walls covered with whiteboards and pin boards and light boxes. It was a nod to his former life as a photo editor at *Londinium Monthly*, one of the first publications to print Grace's photography. Her long and eccentric friendship with Melvin had spanned years and multiple changes of career direction, but it was the only reason she had considered his request to open her archives.

He unbuttoned his blazer as he settled behind the desk and gestured for Grace to take one of the chairs. "I have to admit, Grace, you shocked me. What you sent me was not at all what I expected."

Grace's stomach immediately took a nosedive into the soles of her green Doc Martens. "I told you, Melvin, it's a personal project. I didn't shoot them to be exhibited—"

"No, you misunderstand me." He leaned forward and folded his hands on top of the desk. "They're fantastic. I've only seen your editorial work, your war photography, which is very good. Poignant, painful, often shocking. But these . . ." He stood and slid a whiteboard out of the way of a wall-mounted corkboard. "These are incredible."

Grace twisted around and then rose, amazement swelling in her chest. He had printed two dozen of the photos she'd sent him as black-and-white four-by-sixes and pinned them out in what she assumed was the order he'd want to display them in the gallery. She'd taken the photos, scanned the slides, viewed them on a screen, but somehow seeing them this way gave them heft. Importance even.

"See what I mean? These are art, Grace. I can't believe you've never shared them before."

She stepped forward to view each of the photos close up. Men, women, children from around the world, captured in the midst of their normal activities. Mourning. Celebrating. Living. Even she could admit there was a melancholy beauty to them, a common thread between composition and style that seemed to unite people across cultures and countries.

"Hope," Melvin said softly. "Even in the ones that show someone's worst moments, you somehow captured hope."

Grace flicked her gaze to his face, then away, too embarrassed to see the admiration in his expression. "Are these your final selections?"

"No. But I thought we'd start here. Which of them must you absolutely have exhibited?"

"I trust your editorial vision."

Melvin rubbed his bearded chin thoughtfully. "You did these on an M3, yes? Thirty-five millimeter?"

"You know I did."

Melvin's expression softened then. "How are you doing? I heard about Brian. It must be very difficult for you, especially coming on the anniversary of Aidan's death."

Grace swallowed hard and bit her lip in a vain attempt to stem the swell of tears. Each time she thought she'd made peace with the incident, the grief came back in full force. The irony of the timing had not been lost on her. Every year, she commemorated the day her photojournalist brother had been killed during a Northern Irish nationalist riot, and every year, the grief rushed back as keen and sharp as the day it happened. To lose another young man on that day—especially one close to Aidan's age—it had felt like God was trying to tell her something.

Maybe He was.

She forced a watery smile. "Let's just say it will never be my favorite day."

"I can understand that." Melvin seated himself behind the desk again and slipped on a pair of black-rimmed glasses. "Did you bring me the slides?"

Grace fished a small box from her rucksack and pushed it across the desk to him. He lifted the top and thumbed through the mounted negatives, then placed the box in his drawer. "I'll take good care of these, Grace. I'll start on some tests this week and then we can fine-tune the final prints. Eight weeks feels like a long time, but I can guarantee you we'll be working up until the last minute. What are you doing with the photos once the exhibit is over?"

"I hadn't thought that far ahead. I'm still trying not to hyperventilate over the thought of people viewing work I've hoarded for the last decade or two."

"Oh, I wouldn't worry about that." A peculiar glint in Melvin's eyes raised warning flags. "You should sell them. Especially if you never plan on exhibiting or printing these again."

"I'm not interested in selling them. Besides, who would want something like this hanging in their home?"

He stared at her in disbelief. "I don't think you understand quite how well-known you've become. A one-off print from the renowned Grace Brennan could bring in a fair bit of money."

"I'm not interested in the money."

"Who says you have to keep it?"

That stopped Grace's next protest before it could form.

"I know you, Grace. You've never been about the money. As long as you could afford a bed, food, and film, you were happy. I also know that you're not exactly hurting for funds these days, despite the fact you've been wearing those same blasted steel-toed boots for the last ten years. But can you think of what one of those charities could do with, say, two hundred thousand pounds?"

"No one would pay ten thousand pounds for one of my photographs," she said, but she knew Melvin caught the doubt in her words. Even after Melvin's commission for the showing and the cost of production, that was a massive amount of money that could be put to good use. "May I think about it?"

"Of course. I know what these mean to you, and I'm honored you'd trust me with them. You've become quite an artist. Aidan would be proud."

It felt like a dismissal, so she pushed her chair back from the desk. But Melvin's eyes traveled instead to a spot over her shoulder. "Ah! You got my message. You're just in time."

Grace twisted in her chair and blinked in surprise at the tall, blond man standing in the doorway. "Henry? What are you doing here? When did you get back to London?" She looked between the two men, scowling halfheartedly at Melvin. "Did you set this up?"

Henry laughed and pressed Grace into a friendly squeeze. "Hey, Grace. In answer to your questions: I heard you were here, I moved back to London a year ago, and yes, of course he set this up."

Melvin was grinning at both of them, evidently pleased at her reaction to the impromptu reunion. She took a seat in the far chair, leaving room for Henry to sit in the one she'd just vacated. "I don't understand. I didn't even know you two knew each other."

"Melvin knows everyone," Henry said. "But it was actually one of my old editors who called me. Melvin told him you might be moving back to England, he gave me a call, I got in touch with Melvin, *et voilà*, here I am."

"So, you quit too. You're out."

"Seemed like a good time. Ella is having a baby in the fall, and these days conflict isn't the safest place to make a living when you have a family to support. Not that it ever was."

Now Grace understood. This wasn't just a visit; this was an impromptu intervention. Henry had been one of the last foreign correspondents from her batch to stay with the job, but he'd spent the last several years in Eastern Europe while she covered the Middle East. "I can hardly believe it. I thought you'd be the last one standing. What are you doing now?"

Henry exchanged a look with Melvin. His expression turned a little sheepish. "I just took a position in communications with Children's Advocacy Fund."

Grace let out a laugh of disbelief. "You're working for an NGO. After all the times we said that was the last job we'd ever take?"

"Times change, Grace. You of all people should know it's not so easy to let go of your life's work. Besides, I believe in this organization. They're actually doing things right. And it lets me use my experience doing something other than sitting behind a production desk."

"Well, I'm glad you've found something that makes you happy. And Ella has to be thrilled."

"She is. So am I." He paused long enough to fix her with a serious look. "That's why I want you to come work for me."

Grace blinked at him. "Work for you in what way?"

"I need a creative director, someone with experience in the field who has a strong editorial eye. I've been following your work for years, Grace. These photos here—" he waved at Melvin's board—"prove your talent doesn't just lie in conflict. These are the kinds of photos our donors need to see."

"So you want me to be a fund-raiser?"

"No, I want you to be a journalist. The marketing collateral coming out of London right now is slick. Commercial. It doesn't tell a story. It's all smiling African children and happy farmers. It doesn't communicate our needs, or why donations are important. I think you're the perfect person to change that."

Grace sat there, stunned. Yes, she had come back to London wanting to make big changes to her life. But she'd been thinking she might go back to commercial photography.

Working for a charitable organization had never occurred to her. She'd always had the impression of the head offices being filled with do-gooders who had never put a foot on the ground, who had absolutely no idea what the program directors in the far-flung reaches of the earth went through. Westerners came to Asia and Africa and India, mucked up what was actually working in the villages, and left them worse off than before, all in the name of charity. And now he wanted her to be one of them? Melvin's earlier words began to make sense.

"See what we're about first and then decide." Henry pulled out a heavy square of vellum from his inside pocket and passed it to her. "We're having a fund-raising dinner on Friday. Come, see the presentation, talk to the board of directors. You know me, Grace. I'm not going to be involved in something that isn't making a difference to the people we're trying to help."

Grace turned over the invitation in her hand. The Savoy hotel. Possibly the poshest venue in London, and the last place she wanted to spend a Friday night. But she couldn't bear to dash the hopeful looks on both men's faces. "Okay. I'll go. But I'm not promising anything."

"Fair enough." Henry gave Grace's shoulder a squeeze, then rose to shake Melvin's hand. "Nice seeing you, Melvin. I'll see you Friday, Grace."

Grace nodded as he left the room, then turned an accusing stare on her former editor. "You set me up."

"What? I've known you forever, Grace. You're not going to be happy shooting weddings and births and skyscrapers for a living. You need more meaning to your life than that. What's wrong with having a little security at the same time?"

Grace shook her head and shouldered her rucksack as she rose. "You meddle more than a little old lady."

"So my wife says. You can thank me later."

A reluctant smile crept onto her face. "We'll see about that. Call me when you have the test prints started."

"Will do, Grace. Don't cause any trouble in the meantime."

It sounded like a challenge, but that was because she felt backed into a corner. She wound her way back out through the construction zone and took a deep breath of exhaust-filled air. Of all the nongovernmental organizations she'd interacted with, the Children's Advocacy Fund was one of the better ones. Asha volunteered with the organization for part of the year, claiming it was one of the few that focused on local development rather than handouts. Still, Grace had spent her life being an observer, a dispassionate reporter, a watchdog of sorts. It was her job to record the truth, to witness the things that no one wanted to acknowledge.

And look where that's gotten you.

She plugged her earphones into her ears and started back the way she had come. Melvin might think her return to London was assured, but he'd unintentionally given her more reasons to doubt. *"You need more meaning to your life than that,"* he'd said. Even he didn't understand the whole truth of it. It wasn't just about meaning. It was about identity.

If she wasn't a war photographer anymore, then who was she?

CHAPTER FOUR

GRACE WOKE WITH A CRY as a grenade shook the ground beneath her feet. For several terrified moments she scrambled for protection, something to shield her from the next one, but she came up with a handful of blankets and a mangled pillow instead of dirt and rubble.

A dream. Thank You, God, just a dream. She reached for a lamp just as Asha burst out of the bedroom.

"What's wrong? What happened?"

"I'm sorry. A nightmare. I'm . . . I'm really sorry." Grace pressed her hands over her racing heart and realized her T-shirt was drenched in sweat.

Asha deflated like a balloon. She sank down on the arm of the sofa that served as Grace's bed and pushed her tousled hair from her face. "Are you all right?" She didn't ask what the dream was about. She already knew.

"I'll be okay. I didn't mean to wake you."

Asha squinted at the clock. "I have to be up in twenty minutes anyhow. I'll go make some tea."

While Asha stumbled to the kitchen and began banging about in the cupboards, Grace sank back against her pillows and tried to banish the memory of the dream.

Brilliant light shone down on her from an unnaturally blue sky, seeming to amplify the oppressive heat. Explosions rocked the ground around her, and she ducked behind a stone wall beneath a shower of dust and debris. The photographer beside her—as green as any twentysomething she'd ever met—huddled over his camera, his eyes terrified. He yelled something at her, but the automatic-weapons fire drowned out his words.

When there was a break in the barrage, Grace poked her head up over the wall and raised her camera again. "Now or never!" she said to Brian, who she assumed was still hunkered behind her. But a quick look revealed nothing but empty space.

She swore loudly as she saw him running in a half crouch toward a broken-down section of the wall. Before she could call him back, a flash of light burst in her vision, followed by a deafening explosion that threw her back to the ground. The scene swam around her: colors, muted sounds, a ringing in her ears. Dazed, she lifted her head.

Brian was gone. Or at least in any form recognizable as a man.

Grace pressed her fingertips to her eyes as if that could erase the dream. That wasn't even how it had happened.

Brian had been killed three months ago in Syria, but her memory had superimposed the violence in Misrata, Libya, where two of her more experienced colleagues had died in the period they now called the Arab Spring.

Syria or Libya, she'd witnessed enough violence to last a lifetime.

She fingered the small Celtic cross tattoo on the inside of her right forearm, the one she'd had inked with the dates of Brian's birth and death. It was a replica of a larger one he'd had on his arm, at least as much as she could remember from the one night they'd compared tats. His had had more detail, though. Maybe she should add some shading to the cross and the lilies behind it . . .

But she knew very well that the design was just a record. Proof. It did nothing to change the reality of what she'd seen and experienced. It did nothing to bring him back. That's why she had chosen to finish the sleeve with the green dragon before she left Paris, a symbolic ending not just to her career but also to the things she'd done to cope.

"That part of your life is over," she murmured to herself, unsure whether it was supposed to be reassurance or warning.

"What did you say?" Asha called from the kitchen, her voice more alert.

"I just asked if the tea was ready."

"Almost. You bought croissants?"

Grace climbed off the sofa bed, then wandered into the kitchen, where Asha was staring at the kettle. The normalcy of the act relieved the pressure building inside. "They're for you. I don't know how you manage to keep your figure with all the junk you eat."

Asha grinned and waved a hand over her hip. "Jake likes me with some curves."

"On you, the weight goes to all the right places. On me, it gets lost in the middle and meanders about aimlessly for a bit."

"Oh, don't make me laugh. It's too early."

Grace threw her a grin and retrieved a carton from the refrigerator. "You eat the pastries. I bought yogurt for me."

"So, from the looks of the refrigerator, I owe you an apology," Asha said. "I had no idea you were making dinner or I would have come home early."

Grace waved off the apology. "Busy night at hospital?"

"Understaffed, as usual." The kettle clicked off, and Asha poured water into each of their mugs. "How about you? What did you do?"

"Dropped by the gallery to see Melvin. Who apparently thought I needed an intervention, because he brought in Henry Symon to see me."

"What?" Asha plopped into the seat across from Grace and shoved a mug of tea toward her. "The journalist, right? The one who nearly got you killed in Kandahar."

"He nearly got *himself* killed in Kandahar. I was just along for the ride." Despite the dodgy situation the journalist's bad intel had gotten them into, she could look back on the incident with a chuckle. They'd gotten out with their lives and relatively whole, even if she'd ended up losing a thousand euro in equipment. "Besides, I think that experience is what soured him on his career choices. He is apparently now living a quiet and very safe life in London as the communications director for CAF." Grace sipped her tea and watched Asha over her mug. "And he wants me to come work for him."

"Are you considering it?"

"I don't know. Possibly. He invited me to the benefit on Friday."

"Oh good. That saves me from having to scrounge you up a ticket." Asha tore into her croissant, then paused with a piece of the pastry halfway to her mouth. "You're actually doing it, aren't you? Moving back. Quitting."

"I don't know, Ash." Grace had spent most of the previous night turning that very question over in her mind, and she was no closer to an answer than she had been before. "It all depends, I guess."

"On Ian?"

Grace let out a harsh laugh. "Hardly. He made it pretty clear he has no interest in talking to me. If I'm staying, it will have nothing to do with him."

Asha didn't look convinced, but she didn't argue as she finished the rest of her tea and croissant. "You mind if I take the bathroom first? I have to be at work in forty-five minutes. No, scratch that. Thirty-five." Asha put her mug in the sink and headed for the bathroom, turning when she reached the door. "Grace, if you need someone . . . call me, all right?"

Grace nodded, glad that Asha didn't feel the need to elaborate. "I will."

As soon as Asha closed the door, Grace tossed the barely touched yogurt into the bin and turned to packing her gear bag with the lenses and filters she would need for the Sunday morning flower market. A few minutes later, Asha emerged from the bathroom in a pair of slacks and a button-down blouse, her damp hair fastened into a knot at the back of her head. Even without makeup, she was one of the prettiest women Grace had ever seen.

Asha grabbed her handbag from the hook by the door and fixed Grace with a serious look. "I mean it. Call me."

"I will."

The first strains of sunlight peeked through the louver shades, nudging Grace in the direction of the washroom. If she waited too long, she'd miss the peak lighting for the stalls. Shower first, though. If you could call it a shower. The claw-foot tub had never been plumbed for a showerhead, so she had to settle for a handheld sprayer attached to the tub filler by a rubber hose. But she wasn't complaining. Considering all the places it was standard practice to fill a bucket in order to flush the toilet, London's reliable municipal water supply seemed nothing short of a miracle.

Fifteen minutes later, she was bounding down the building's staircase to the pavement, wearing a light pullover, jeans, and a newsboy cap pulled on over her cropped hair. The short walk to the Earl's Court Tube station helped clear the last ghosts of the nightmare, building anticipation for her morning outing. Of all the locations in London she'd shot, the flower market and neighboring Brick Lane were among her favorites.

She plugged her earphones into her mobile while she waited on the platform, staring at the bills pasted to the opposite wall. Somehow she'd always loved the dusty, dank underground smell of the Tube, the rush of warm air and the clatter of rails as the train approached.

Only a few people waited on the platform this morning, older people dressed for church, younger ones looking like they were dragging themselves in from clubbing the night before. Grace climbed into the nearest carriage—heeding the warning to "mind the gap"—and settled into one of the gaudy-colored seats. The Rolling Stones blared through her earphones. Perfect. She tapped her foot along to the music until it was time to hop off at the next station and change lines for the last leg of the trip.

Her mood was lighter and her nerves more settled when she emerged onto street level and headed toward the short, packed street that was the Columbia Road flower market. She backed into the shelter of a shop awning to unzip her gear bag and affixed a 20mm lens to her Canon camera body before she let the crowd swallow her again. Flower vendors lined each side of the street, leaving barely enough room for pedestrians to squeeze by, their squares marked out by rolling racks and open barrels, awnings both solid and striped. Around her, the hum of voices made a pleasant counterpoint to the deep, harsh shouts of the vendors hawking their wares.

"Fresh roses!" one shouted. "Peonies. Two for a tenner!"

Grace smiled at the vendor to her left and wove her way to his stall. Tall and beefy with sunbaked skin, he looked more like a dockworker than a purveyor of delicate blooms.

"Morning," she said. "Lovely selection. Have you any tulips, or is it too late in the season?"

His weathered face cracked into a smile. "No tulips, dear, but I've Belgian roses. Come have a gander."

Grace squeezed between a barrel of carnations and two gawking women. She looked over the cellophane-wrapped bouquets for a moment before she selected a small bunch of yellow roses streaked with red. They'd be lovely on Asha's kitchen table. "I'll take these."

The vendor pulled the bunch from the water and dropped them into a cone-shaped bag, which Grace tucked into the string sack over one shoulder. She handed over a five-pound note and asked, "Do you mind if I take some photos?"

"Go right ahead."

Grace smiled her thanks as she backed away and knelt for a different angle. The Columbia Road vendors had a reputation for being unfriendly to photographers, but they really just wanted to be treated with respect. Photographing their stands without permission would be like walking into a shop and snapping pictures without asking. She'd never been turned away, and she always came home with a string bag full of flowers and a memory card full of images. It was more than a fair trade.

"Cheers." She waved to the vendor and moved on, getting swept up in the relentless flow of pedestrians amid the perfume of thousands of flowers and blooming plants. She'd forgotten how much she adored London. The sights, the sounds, the jumble of accents. And yet, despite a handful of visits in the last decade, she'd never stayed long, moving on instead to assignments on the continent or in Asia, Africa, the Middle East. How strange to find it was still the only city that felt remotely like home.

She continued to shoot market stands and street scenes until the sharp angle of the morning light forced her to put her camera away for the day. Her rumbling stomach reminded her she'd never finished her breakfast or managed to get herself a cup of coffee. She wandered toward Hackney Road and her favorite Parisian-style café, tucked between a shoe store and a used bookshop. Coffee and a pastry—regardless of what she'd told Asha about swearing off the croissants—would be just the thing to finish off her morning before she headed back to the flat.

Patrons holding paper cups of coffee and glassine pastry bags jostled her on her way into the tiny shop. Apparently, she wasn't the only one in desperate need of a midmorning pick-me-up: the queue wound haphazardly through the space, twenty patrons deep.

Grace found a spot behind an elegant-looking blonde in high-heeled boots and a trench coat. The woman spoke rapid-fire French into a mobile phone, her voice occasionally rising in pitch above the hiss and puff of the espresso machine behind the counter. Something about a winter issue and a certain Jacques's inability to make a deadline.

Québécoise? Her accent wasn't Parisian, even if her style was. Grace bit her cheek to keep from smiling when the woman let loose a particularly creative string of insults, then ended the call midsentence to order.

Grace perused the pastry selection through the glass-fronted case until the woman began to rummage frantically through her satchel.

"*Oh là là!* I can't believe I left my wallet in the hotel."

The cashier gave an impatient sigh and snatched the woman's coffee off the counter.

Grace stepped forward. "Just ring us up together, please. I'll have a café au lait and one of those chocolate croissants."

The woman looked at Grace, startled. "Please, that's not necessary."

"Morning caffeine is very necessary. Besides, it's the least I can do for teaching me a few new phrases in French."

The woman chuckled. "I'm Monique. And *merci.*"

"Grace. *De rien.*" The woman behind the counter exchanged the coffees and pastry for a handful of pound coins, and Grace took hers. "Have a lovely day, Monique."

Monique scooped up her coffee and fell in with Grace, dodging oncoming patrons as they wound toward the door.

"Won't you sit with me for a moment? I can at least offer you a few more amusing French phrases."

"I'm heading back to the Tube if you'd like to walk with me."

"Which way?"

"Bethnal Green. Do you know London well?"

"Well enough. I'm in town for a conference, but I like to come here if I stay over on a Sunday." Monique indicated the paper-wrapped bouquet sticking out of her shoulder bag.

"So do I," Grace said.

"You're clearly a photographer. What's your *spécialité*?"

"Conflict. The street photography is just for fun."

Monique's eyebrows lifted. "Impressive. Do you have a business card?"

Grace retrieved one from the outside pocket of her bag. Monique smiled and tucked it into her purse. "It was a pleasure to meet you, Grace. Stay safe. And thanks for the coffee." Monique turned on her heel, her boots clicking on the pavement as she walked away.

What an odd woman. Grace shrugged and proceeded to the Tube station, already thinking through her morning's shots. She would spend the rest of her day on her computer, processing images and uploading the best shots to her online portfolio and social media accounts.

Stay safe. Monique's words came back to Grace as she descended to the platform. The most danger she faced at the moment was pricking herself on the thorns of her roses. Why had she identified herself as a conflict photographer? Why hadn't she corrected herself?

Maybe she wasn't as ready to give up her old career as she thought.

CHAPTER FIVE

IT WAS ONLY 10 A.M., and he already had a headache. Ian dragged off his wire-rimmed reading glasses and massaged his temples with his fingertips. He'd skipped his outing this morning, choosing instead to do his workout at home, then headed to the office just after seven. Mondays tended to be busy, especially considering Jamie hadn't been back to London in well over a month. The hotel renovation in Skye was finally drawing to a close, in time for Jamie and Andrea's summer wedding. Unfortunately, that meant Ian was left to take up the slack in London. As usual.

He sighed and slipped the glasses back on. That was an excuse. He never let anything dissuade him from taking out the single scull he kept racked at the club's boathouse. The river was his favorite spot to think, a way to work through his troubles without having to worry about the technical skill his crewmates expected from him. But he'd done enough thinking for one weekend.

And part of him didn't want to know if Grace would show up looking for him.

He didn't want to see her, plain and simple. He hated how quickly she'd taken over his thoughts. How she'd invaded his dreams the past two nights. It had taken the mere knowledge she was back in London to dredge up uncomfortable questions. Why had she left, and why was she back?

Maybe if they'd done more talking ten years ago, he wouldn't have been blindsided when she left her engagement ring on their kitchen counter while he slept.

"Sir, you have a visitor."

Ian jerked his head up to the pretty blonde woman standing in the doorway. "Yes, Eva. Who is it?"

"Oh, um . . ."

Ian repressed a sigh. How was it that Jamie could maintain the same efficient assistant for seven years, and he seemed to be retraining a new one every three weeks? Apparently, he didn't have any more luck keeping employees than he did keeping fiancées. And considering the current assistant had managed to forget the name of his visitor between her desk and his door, he suspected he'd be searching for a replacement in about a week.

"Never mind. Send him—or her—in."

"No need. I'm here." Jake Hudson appeared in the doorway, holding up two paper cups while he wove around the still-gaping Eva. "Coffee delivery."

Ian waited for a moment, and when the girl didn't move, he said, "Thank you, Eva. You may leave us now."

Thankfully, she got the hint and scurried out of the office. Ian rubbed the side of his nose ruefully. Make it thirty-six hours.

"Another new assistant?" Jake folded his lanky frame into the chair across from Ian's desk and shoved one of the cups toward him. He wore jeans and a battered canvas jacket with a woven scarf looped around his neck. He looked every inch the foreign correspondent, never mind the fact he covered political news in London. Hard to believe he'd once been a green, overeager writer reporting on local sporting news.

Ian took an experimental sip of the coffee. Strong and black, the way he liked it. He lifted his cup in salute. "God has a special reward for you in heaven, Jake."

"If you stopped hiring the pretty ones, you might get someone who could make a pot of coffee."

"She's not that pretty. What are you doing here?"

"I've a favor to ask."

"Sounds ominous. Especially when it requires a trip to my office and a coffee bribe."

"I tried to call, but—Eva, is it?—disconnected me three times. It seemed easier to show up."

Ian almost spit coffee onto his desk blotter as Eva's job expectancy plummeted to twenty-four hours. So much for the staffing agency. He wanted his money back. "All right then, what's the favor?"

"You wouldn't happen to have an extra ticket to the CAF fund-raiser on Friday, would you?"

"As a matter of fact, I do. Why?"

"Asha gave away my ticket because I thought I wouldn't be able to make it, but I'm now free and she's a bit miffed at me."

Ian chuckled. Asha was one of the most good-natured

women he'd ever met, but she had little patience for ineffi-
ciency. "I'd thought I might bring a date, but . . ."

"None of them lasted that long?"

"Something like that."

Jake sat thoughtfully for a few moments. "By now you
know Grace is back."

"Yes."

"Asha said she came to the club to see you."

"She did."

"So . . ."

Ian tapped his pen against the edge of the desk. "So
what? She ran off without saying anything. Seems to be her
speciality."

"You know she's staying with Asha, right? You don't want
to see her?"

"No. We have nothing to say to each other."

"Even if she wants to apologize?"

Ian's eyes narrowed. "Did Asha put you up to this?"

Jake didn't say anything. He didn't have to—his guilty
expression said it for him.

Ian stopped his tapping and tossed the pen onto the desk.
"Listen, if she wanted to apologize, she's had ample opportunity. England is not the only country with phones, post, and
e-mail. If she wants to talk to me, she clearly knows where
to find me."

"Okay. Consider the subject dropped. I just never understood what happened between you two."

Me neither. "If you don't mind, I've got five hours' worth of
work to fit in before lunch, which is in about ninety minutes.
I'll messenger you the ticket. I don't have it on me."

"Cheers, mate." Jake raised his cup in half salute, half

wave, then slipped out the door, almost bumping into Eva on his way out.

"Sir, your ten thirty is here. Waiting in the conference room."

"I don't have a ten thirty." Ian frowned and brought up his schedule on his computer. His morning showed an empty block between the nine o'clock with marketing and his two o'clock with Jamie's publicist.

"Okay, sir, I'll tell him we need to reschedule."

"No! Please don't. Who is it?"

Eva scrunched up her nose, as if it would help her recall the correct name. "Um, a Mr. Barnett? Barnes?"

"Barrett? Andrew Barrett?"

"Mr. Barrett, yes! That's it!" His assistant beamed as if he'd unraveled an impossible equation.

Ian repressed a sigh, rose from his desk, and reached for his suit coat. "Mr. Barrett is one of James's solicitors. And you have his appointment on the schedule for tomorrow at one." He took one last sip of his coffee and steeled himself for the unpleasant conversation to come.

Some days he actually did hate his job.

And at the rate she was going, Eva would be lucky to last the day.

Twenty minutes later, Andrew Barrett left the offices of MacDonald Enterprises looking considerably less smug than he had when he'd entered. Ian couldn't find it in himself to feel bad about firing the law firm. Ever since the elder Barrett had retired and passed responsibility for the firm on to his son, their work had been shoddy and overbilled. Only after

Barrett botched two contracts had Jamie finally signed off on a change.

Ian had never been so aware of the fact his power was a sham. He might be chief operating officer of this company, but it was his younger brother's business. His brother's image. His brother's name on which he traded.

For someone who had once been half a second behind an Olympic gold medal, it was a galling reminder.

Ian pushed down the thought as he strode from the conference room to his office. Pure pride. He'd known when he took the position that there was little glory or recognition in it. Only lots of responsibility and an obscenely large paycheck to make sure Jamie could focus on his cooking, his celebrity, and soon, his new wife. Most days, it seemed like a fair trade. Regular office hours and the freedom to take holidays when he wanted, whether or not he actually took advantage of it . . . and yet it in no way resembled the life he'd once envisioned for himself.

He passed Eva, who was staring intently at her computer screen, then stopped abruptly in front of his desk. "What is this?"

The woman popped up from her desk and appeared behind him. "Your lunch. Egg salad on wheat, as you requested."

Ian blinked at her. "I didn't—never mind. I'm eating out today. Help yourself." He turned on his heel and strode toward the exterior door of the office suite, hoping by some miracle she'd be gone when he returned and save him from firing yet another person today.

CHAPTER SIX

ASHA PROMISED TO BE HOME early on the night of the benefit, exacting from Grace a solemn vow that she would wait so they could get ready together. Even though she didn't say it outright, Grace suspected her elegant friend wanted to vet her clothing choices. Not that three hours gave them many options should Asha find Grace's wardrobe unsuitable.

Grace waited with her laptop at the kitchen table, eyes tracing a constant triangle between the screen, the invitation, and the clock hanging on the kitchen wall. She wasn't nervous, exactly. She'd been to her share of formal events, particularly in Paris, where even a minor thing like a dinner party was elevated to an art form. But this was different. While she was evaluating CAF to see if she wanted to work for them, they'd be doing the same. Call it an unofficial interview with formal wear and an open bar.

Put that way, maybe there was an advantage to these kinds of "interviews." People, she could deal with. People, she liked. It was simply offices, suits, and the associated restrictions that made her edgy.

But as the clock hands swept by half three and toward four without any sign of Asha, she began to wonder if she'd somehow misunderstood. At last, the key turned in the lock at ten after five, and Asha rushed in.

"So sorry, Grace. I got hung up at work and the Tube was simply awful. Did you make it to the cleaners?"

Grace chuckled. Anyone else stumbling in harried and apologetic would be disheveled, but Asha still managed to look as poised and beautiful as ever. "Your clothes are on the back of your bedroom door."

"You are an angel." Asha gave her a quick squeeze around the shoulders on her way through the kitchen. "I feel bad having you run my errands. First the groceries, then my cleaning—"

"The groceries were a matter of self-preservation, but you know I'm glad to do it. Call it repayment for letting me crash on your sofa."

"That was the plan behind offering, of course. I knew you'd cook, clean, and shop for me. I need a housewife."

"As long as you don't expect me to meet you at the door in heels and red lipstick."

"Oh, I know better than to part you from your ugly green Docs. You aren't planning on wearing those with your dress tonight, are you?"

Grace laughed at Asha's expression of genuine alarm.

"No, of course not. Besides, who said anything about a dress? I haven't worn a skirt since I was ten, and that was for my confirmation. I looked like I was being eaten by a wedding cake."

"You do have something to wear, right? I might have something that would fit you."

Grace snorted. Asha was inches taller than her. Anything she owned would swim on Grace's petite frame. "I have formal wear. I am an actual grown-up, you know."

Asha cast a dubious glance toward Grace's battered duffel bag.

"Okay, so it needed some pressing."

Asha grinned. "I'm going to start getting ready. The car will pick us up at six."

Fortunately, with Asha on the job, Grace had no time to feel nervous as they dressed and styled and applied more cosmetics than Grace knew existed. She even managed a pretense of calmness until the sedan's driver opened the door for them at the River Entrance of the Savoy just before seven. Instantly, her stomach felt as if she had swallowed a handful of broken glass. Tonight might set the course for the next phase of her life. The fact she hadn't decided whether she wanted the job made no difference—simply considering the possibility made this move to London real for the first time. She smoothed down the front of her slim tuxedo trousers, then buttoned and unbuttoned her jacket.

Asha looped her arm through Grace's and dragged her toward the brass-studded glass doors, merging into the steady stream of guests disembarking from their own cars. "Will you stop fidgeting? You look gorgeous."

"No, *you* look gorgeous. I'll be lucky if I don't trip in these blasted heels. Why did I let you talk me into these?"

"Because that outfit demands stilettos. You look like a celebrity, Grace. Haven't you noticed everyone trying to figure out if they should know you?"

As they entered the opulently decorated lower lobby, filled with guests in tuxedos and floor-length designer gowns, Grace was suddenly happy she'd taken her friend up on her offer to do her hair and makeup. The other woman was beautiful on an average day, but in her fuchsia evening *salwar kameez*, she was stunning. The sequined and embroidered full skirt swirled around the ankles of her matching trousers, making her look like she belonged at a red-carpet Bollywood premiere.

They followed the trickle of elegantly dressed guests to a smaller space outside the ballroom, where others already mingled with drinks in groups of two or three. As soon as they set foot on the patterned rug, a tuxedoed man raised a hand and headed their way.

Grace blinked. "Is that Jake?"

"Shines up nicely, doesn't he?" Asha grinned before she lifted her face for a greeting kiss.

Then Jake turned to Grace. "All the rumors are true, I see." Heedless of the event, he put an arm around her and kissed her cheek. "Welcome back. We've missed you."

"Still a liar, but that's what I've always loved about you." She laughed, her heart suddenly light. From the corner of her eye, she saw a man glimpse Asha and make his way toward them. "I'm going to the bar while I still can. Do you want anything?"

"House white," Asha said, while Jake shook his head.

Slipping away before the man was close enough to require introductions, Grace navigated the spongy floor carefully in the unaccustomed high heels. She slid up to an empty space at the bar and caught the bartender's eye. "A glass of your house white and a tonic with lime, please."

"Sure you don't want some gin with your tonic? These evenings can get pretty long."

Grace chuckled when she realized the lad was flirting with her, despite the fact she had more than a decade on him. "No, the tonic will be fine."

"Suit yourself." He winked at her and set the drinks in front of her on the bar. She bit back a smile and turned, nearly bumping into the man behind her.

"Smart woman. Hit up the bar before you're subjected to the inquisition." Henry leaned past to order a Scotch on the rocks and then turned back to her. "You ready?"

"I was. You know, I'm usually the one asking the questions."

"So ask the questions." Henry took his drink and gestured with his head for her to follow. "Come, I'll introduce you round."

He led her back over to where Asha and Jake stood conversing with the man from earlier. Grace handed Asha her drink and put on a friendly smile as Henry made introductions.

"Grace, this is Kenneth DeVries, the vice president of communications at CAF." *And my boss,* his significant look said.

"A pleasure to meet you. I'm Grace Brennan."

"I know who you are." His eyes rested briefly on the tattoos exposed by her pushed-up jacket sleeves before he grasped her offered hand. "I'd venture to say everyone knows who you are. Henry tells us there's already some Pulitzer buzz about you."

"This is the first I've heard of it," Grace said. "But Henry stays much better connected in the journalism world than I do. I'm just a photographer."

"Grace is far too humble." Henry's message was clear: she needed to play up her experience with the man so he thought he was stealing her away to work with CAF. While she appreciated the thought, the idea still went against the grain. Either DeVries shared her editorial vision, or he didn't. Whether or not she'd been shortlisted for a Pulitzer nomination—a long shot if she'd ever heard one—was irrelevant.

But it didn't seem to matter. Mr. DeVries gave her a knowing smile. "I'm far more familiar with Ms. Brennan's work than she probably thinks. Henry, I see a few board members over there by the door. Introduce her, will you?"

"My pleasure. If you'll come with me, Grace. Dr. Issar, Mr. Hudson, it was nice to see you." Henry pressed a hand lightly against her back.

Grace shook Mr. DeVries's hand once more before Henry steered her toward another group of tuxedo-clad men. "I take it that's his tacit approval?"

"Absolutely. I mentioned you to him this week, and while he knew your name, he wasn't familiar with your work. I'd say he's done his research."

"Who are we impressing now?"

"Board of directors, at least a few members. They'll be the ones who have the final vote on your hire. Assuming you decide you want the job, of course." He put on a smile and injected himself into the conversation with the ease of a politician.

Henry quickly made the introductions, and Grace repeated their names to fix them in her mind. Dr. Philip Vogel, director of international programs. Dr. Leonard Cho, medical adviser. Harvey Kinlan, chairman of the board.

Kinlan cut straight to the chase. "Symon here says that you're giving up fieldwork and coming back to London."

"It's a possibility, yes," Grace said carefully. "I've spent ten years covering conflicts, though. It's not an easy thing to leave behind."

"I imagine it isn't," Kinlan said. "Yet there are advantages to a steady, less dangerous job, as Symon will tell you."

"What I've appreciated," Henry said, "is that I've been able to spend time with program coordinators and local volunteers. Being based out of London doesn't mean being handcuffed to a desk."

Henry knew her far too well, neutralizing her number one objection before she could voice it. "I imagine in addition to the creative director position, you have a director of photography."

"We do," Vogel said, "along with staff photographers and freelancers. But I imagine Henry would want you to spend some time in the field if that's where your interest lies. He tells me you've freelanced for other NGOs over the years."

Grace shot Henry an amused look, which made him grimace. Those experiences had been exactly why they said they'd never work for an international nonprofit. Apparently, he'd left that part out. "I'm curious to hear how you administer your programs locally. Far too many organizations stop at relief, and any further rehabilitation or development fails because they are too arrogant to learn from and understand the local culture."

Eyebrows raised at her bluntness, but Vogel answered easily. "We're well aware of the problems, and I think you'll find CAF very sensitive to these issues." His eyes flickered to a point over Grace's shoulder. "Ah, MacDonald, there you are. I want you to meet someone."

Immediately, all her incisive, intelligent questions fled, her attention focused to one single point. Surely it couldn't be. MacDonald was a common Scottish surname. She was being paranoid. When she turned to prove it, though, the smile slipped from her face, turning instead to a grotesque twitch.

Ian seemed not to notice her discomfiture, or maybe he was enjoying it. "Grace and I know each other already," he said. He took the hand that she didn't remember offering, and his piercing blue gaze collided with hers. She went cold in an instant.

In the past week, she'd managed to convince herself that her brief impression of him at the river had been flawed, that he had to have changed in the last decade. And he had—for the better. If he'd been good-looking before, maturity had made him even more appealing, the fine lines at the corners of his pale-blue eyes and the hint of early gray at the temples adding interest to his handsome face. He also seemed taller and broader than she remembered, his perfectly tailored tuxedo emphasizing both the breadth of his shoulders and his impressive height. No matter which way she considered him, he was heart-stopping.

Only then did she realize she had gaped at him for a full minute without saying anything. She opened her mouth and still nothing came out. He smiled coolly at her as he released her hand, then looked past her to the men. "I'm very familiar with her work, in fact. She would be quite an asset to CAF. I'm sure the rest of the board will agree."

The three men leveled curious looks at them. *Say something,* she commanded herself, but shock washed away coherent speech. What was he doing here? Why hadn't anyone told her he was involved in this charity? Had Asha known they would run into him, or was this all a big coincidence?

Fortunately the ballroom doors opened at that moment, and the hum of quiet conversation escalated to a roar. Vogel smiled in her direction. "We've an empty seat at our table. Please, you must join us."

At last, Grace's voice made a reappearance. "Thank you. I'd be honored." And yet, instead of drawing her off with them as she'd hoped, he and the other men moved into the crowd themselves, leaving Grace standing there dumbly with Ian.

The slight twist of his mouth said he wasn't any happier about the arrangement than she was. "Shall we?"

Grace moved automatically, even though the light press of his hand at her back sent a tingle straight up her spine. She needed to get a grip on herself. "Wait, what did you mean 'the rest of the board'?"

"I was elected to the board of directors a couple of years ago. I assume you didn't know, or you wouldn't be considering the position."

A spark of anger finally burned through the glacier that seemed to have formed over her on his arrival. "This has absolutely nothing to do with you. Henry Symon recommended me for the job, and if I'm coming back to London for good, there are far worse career directions."

"Are you?"

"Am I what?"

"Coming back to London."

She blinked at him. "I don't know yet. I guess that still depends."

"On the job?"

On you. The words surfaced in her mind and were halfway to her lips before she arrested them. But from the searching look he gave her, she wondered if she'd voiced them aloud.

And then the wondering expression vanished, replaced by the perfect, polished composure he wore with as much pride as his tuxedo. He nodded toward the ballroom. "After you."

Ian let out a long breath as Grace passed through the ballroom doors. Thirty more seconds alone with her, and he'd make a complete fool out of himself in front of her, his colleagues, and half of London's elite. When he'd glimpsed her holding court among the rapt members of CAF's executive staff, he'd flown through dread and anger to something he didn't even want to name. Considering how the attention of every other male in her vicinity had obliterated his determination to avoid her, it certainly wasn't the indifference he'd been hoping for.

Not that anyone would really blame him. In a sea of conservative wool and sequins, she looked like a rock star, from her short-cropped blonde hair and sultry eye makeup to her form-fitting tuxedo, the sleeves of which were pushed up to show the tattoos on her right arm. He'd always pictured her as she'd left him—young, wild, and avant-garde—but now he had to add beautiful, sexy, and unapproachable to the list. He certainly hadn't been able to take his eyes off her.

Which was the entirely wrong thing to be thinking as he

escorted her to a table full of his colleagues, especially when her mere proximity made his mouth go dry.

Grace faltered just inside the double doors, her brows furrowing as she took in the opulence of the expansive room. Glass chandeliers dripped light from above, while roses and crystal decorated the white-robed tables.

"Seems strange to have all this luxury to raise money for children who are dying of disease and starvation."

He dipped his head to speak low into her ear. "You don't think this food actually costs five hundred quid a person, do you? Besides, it's always good to show donors the lives of the less fortunate when they're wearing four-thousand-pound suits."

"Like you?" Grace raised an eyebrow, taking him in from head to toe in a way that didn't at all feel complimentary.

Ian rested his hand on her back long enough to steer her toward a table near the front of the room. "You know, Grace, we aren't all heartless corporate raiders. Some of us actually feel our success gives us an obligation to those without the same opportunities."

Grace looked embarrassed. "I've lived lean for so long, all this makes me uncomfortable."

"I know. That's why CAF needs you. I meant what I said, Grace. You would bring something valuable to the organization."

Surprise lit her expression, but he purposely didn't look at her as they approached the table. Of course, the only two chairs left were next to each other. She unbuttoned her jacket when she sat, and he automatically helped her out of it, hanging it on her chair. The back of her sequined top revealed a pink-and-white peony inked above her right shoulder blade.

That was new. He barely restrained himself from brushing a finger across it. Given Grace's propensity for symbolism, what did the image represent?

Artfully shaped eyebrows lifted at the sight of Grace's tattoos, but the women quickly masked their expressions. He wondered if that was the reason she'd chosen to remove her jacket in the chilly ballroom, a sort of litmus test for the board's tolerance for unconventionality.

Ian settled beside her and made the introductions of the wives and daughters sitting with the board members she'd already met. When he got to the man sitting on Grace's other side, a French doctor named André Marchal, he realized he should have switched their seats. Marchal immediately took Grace's hand with a brilliant smile.

"*Enchanté.*"

"*Tout le plaisir est pour moi,*" Grace replied immediately with a nod.

"Ah, you speak French so beautifully. Do you spend much time in France?"

The doctor's gaze never wavered from Grace. The slow flicker of irritation built in Ian's chest. Marchal was always charming—and perpetually bored, it seemed—so the intense interest in his expression was doubly disturbing. Ian casually laid his arm across the back of her chair as he leaned forward. "I understand Grace lives part of the year in Paris. Is that right?"

She gave him a puzzled smile. "I'm based in Paris, yes, though I spend very little time there. Most of this past year I worked in the Middle East."

"Ah, very nice." Dr. Marchal gave a vague smile and a nod toward Ian, as if to acknowledge that he'd made his point.

"I hope you spend the best part in France. Our winters can be so dreary."

Ian leaned back but he didn't remove his arm.

Grace reached for her water glass and took a sip before she murmured to him, "Are you quite done?"

He leaned over to whisper in her ear, "Not even close. Marchal is—"

"I know what Marchal is. I live in France, remember?" She pulled away and gave him an amused smile as if he'd said something funny. Oh, Grace might pretend like she didn't fit in with this group, but she played the game better than any of them.

"So, Ms. Brennan." Kenneth DeVries caught her eye over the elaborate centerpiece. "Henry tells me you've had the chance to look over our most recent publications. I'd like to hear what you think."

"They're very well produced."

It was a diplomatic answer, and DeVries's smile said he knew it. "I get the impression you don't believe that's a good thing."

When Grace hesitated, Ian finally dropped his arm from the back of her seat. "Please, go ahead. We'd like to hear your opinion."

She shot him a look that told him exactly what she thought about his interference, but then she leveled her gaze at DeVries across the table. "Quality is always important, and there's no doubt you have that. But they come across as impersonal."

"We don't wish our communications to be manipulative," Vogel put in from Ian's left.

"I understand that, but there's an element of manipulation

in all art and commerce. It's as much your job as it is mine to elicit an emotional reaction from donors."

"As fund-raisers," DeVries said.

"As human beings," Grace countered. "We relate to each other as individuals, not statistics. A single person can't help 900 million hungry people. Even the figure is too much to comprehend. But a family of seven children, two of whom may not survive past age five, simply because they lack access to food and clean water? That's something everyone can feel."

"And that's what you do with your photos."

"Exactly. It's one thing to look at people as a colored region on a map, but another to see them as mothers, fathers, brothers, sons. That's what journalists do, and that's what CAF needs to do as well."

As the conversation veered into more specifics of how she would overhaul the organization's creative branding, then into Grace's own work, Ian couldn't help but be impressed. The woman he remembered would never have been able to hold her own at a table full of suits, let alone talk philosophy, art, and politics with equal confidence. Like the others, he found himself hanging on every word, rapt at the thoughtful conclusions she'd come to in over a decade of photographing the world's war zones. She had changed drastically from the twenty-four-year-old he remembered.

Twenty-four. Had either of them ever really been that young? For the first time it struck him how laughable it was to have carried a flame for this woman for the last decade. They were not remotely the same people they had been. He'd been a cocky athlete, she as much a thrill-seeker as a humanitarian. This Grace Brennan, as impressive as she might be, was a complete stranger to him.

"Didn't we, MacDonald?"

"I'm sorry?" He'd missed the shift in conversation, and Kinlan's amused glance said he knew why.

"I was telling Grace that her insights are exactly why we decided to hire someone with experience in the field, as opposed to a marketing director."

"Yes, indeed we did." Actually, Ian only vaguely remembered that discussion, and when Henry Symon had pitched his vision to the board, Grace's name hadn't come up.

Fortunately, the lights came up on the stage then, and the emcee for the evening's event took the podium. Ian settled back in his chair to listen.

As the evening progressed with speeches, videos, and a beautiful performance from the African Children's Choir, Ian watched Grace work the table. She'd been slightly aloof and awkward as a younger woman, especially around what she liked to call "posh society types," and that had suited him fine. After all, he'd spent most of his twenties trying to outrun his association with his mum's wealthy and powerful family. But like him, she'd seemed to come to the conclusion that it was useless to lump people into categories based on income or postcode. She chatted as easily with the jewel-bedecked wives as she had with their husbands, drawing out discussions of their own hobbies and charitable pursuits. He found his determination to stay cold toward her slipping in the face of her passion and enthusiasm.

When the program ended and the attendees began to rise from their tables, Kenneth DeVries paused with his wife and handed Grace a business card. "Call me for an appointment when you're ready. Between what I've heard tonight and Symon singing your praises, I'd like to talk with you more."

Grace turned over the card in her hand. "I'll think about it. Seriously."

"Excellent. Good night, MacDonald."

Ian nodded to Henry and said good-byes to the others as the table slowly drained of people. Grace studied the card for a moment longer, then tucked it into her tiny handbag.

"Are you really considering the job?"

"Maybe. I'm intrigued. But it still depends."

As Ian repressed the urge to again voice the obvious question, he wasn't sure what bothered him more: that he couldn't bring himself to ask or that he actually might care about the answer.

Grace's nerves returned in force as the ballroom emptied of guests. The benefit had been grand—the food exceptional, the program moving, and the company surprisingly enjoyable. But she could no longer avoid the inevitable conversation that had been a decade in the making.

Nor could she avoid the truth that a decade had not diminished her attraction to Ian. Never mind the fact that he'd become the polar opposite of her usual type, that had she seen the bespoke suit–wearing executive ten years ago, she wouldn't have given him a second look. His observation while she tucked DeVries's card into her clutch lit up every nerve ending and intensified the flutter in her chest.

She should have been prepared. Chemistry had never been an issue between them.

She gathered her courage. "Ian, we need to talk."

"Not here." He gently guided her back through the ball-room doors, ever the gentleman, his stiff posture seemingly meant to cut off any possibility of conversation.

"Then somewhere else. Let me buy you a drink upstairs at the bar."

Ian stopped and looked seriously into her eyes, unsmiling. "You don't have to play me, Grace. I meant what I said. If you come up for consideration at CAF, I'll vote in your favor. I think you would be excellent in that role."

"You think that's what I'm doing? Trying to make amends so I can get a job? Clearly you don't know me at all."

"Clearly I never did."

His composure cracked for the briefest time, and in that moment, she saw the hurt that lingered behind his eyes. He might not have spent the last decade pining over her, and he was obviously mature enough to separate their past from his business considerations, but that didn't mean the wounds she'd inflicted had completely healed. "Ian, I'm sorry. I . . ."

His eyes flicked uncomfortably to an approaching couple, who smiled and nodded at him. He was right. This wasn't the place to have this discussion, but as reluctant as he was to even have a conversation with her, she might never get another chance. She glanced around and pulled him into an intersecting corridor, pushing her way through the first door she came to. It was a meeting room of some sort, empty but for the stacks of chairs around the perimeter.

"Grace, this isn't necessary," he began, but she cut him off.

"It's absolutely necessary." Her heart pounded in her chest, and despite the fact it had been her idea to have it out, she suddenly had no idea what to say. "Ian, I'm sorry. I know it's a shock to have me show up after ten years. I should have stayed and talked to you at the club. I panicked."

A faint, humorless smile crossed his lips. "Somehow I don't believe that."

"Believe that when I realized how much anger you still harbor toward me, I'd have rather faced a firing squad than you."

"I wasn't angry; I was stunned. Ten years, Grace. Ten. Not a phone call, not a letter to say you were okay. If it weren't for your photo credits, I wouldn't have known you were alive."

"You've followed my work?"

"Of course I have. Unlike you, I can't cut people out of my life that easily."

He knew where to strike to inflict the deepest wound. She closed her eyes for a moment, absorbed the impact of the blow. "I deserved that. I'm sorry. I shouldn't have done it like that."

"You shouldn't have done it at all, Grace."

The words came out low, barely audible, and against all reason, sent a little shiver down her spine. She tried to gather her dignity around herself again, but she only succeeded in blinking away tears before they could do more than swell on her lashes. "You're right. And by the time I realized the mistake I'd made, it was too late."

She didn't stay to see the impact her words had on him, just pushed blindly by him and back into the hallway, nearly plowing over a woman draped head-to-toe in sequins. Grace mumbled an apology and threaded her way toward the crowded entrance doors, where she got caught in the throng of people waiting for drivers and taxis at the curbside rank.

That whole exchange had been pointless. Nothing she

said could ever change that she'd promised to love him forever and hadn't stuck around to prove it. Not even the fact she had, in her own way, kept her promise. A man had his pride, after all. That he could still be cordial—and even more shocking, recommend her for a job—was a sign that he possessed far more character than she'd given him credit for.

Wrapped in her musings, she nearly jumped out of her skin when a hand touched her elbow. "At least let me see you home."

Grace jerked her head up and looked directly into Ian's face. He didn't look angry. If anything, his slight smile seemed self-deprecating. She swallowed while her mouth caught up to her brain. "That's not necessary. Asha should be around somewhere."

"I believe Asha left with Jake." He nodded toward a flash of fuchsia as it disappeared into a hired sedan. Asha probably thought she was doing Grace a favor, leaving her to work things out with Ian.

"Even so, London is far safer than most of the places I've lived."

"Will you stop arguing, please? I'd feel better knowing you made it home safely."

She found herself nodding her agreement, even while her mind whirred through questions. Why was he going to this trouble for her? Were there things he wanted to say without an audience? Or did his gentlemanly streak really run that deep?

The latter, she decided. Even as a cocky, boisterous twenty-something athlete, he'd opened doors for her, pulled out her chair, and helped her on with her coat. To do anything less would have been unthinkable. She imagined he would probably make sure a murderer got home safely, just so he didn't have to have it on his conscience. He certainly didn't seem all that interested in making small talk now.

When they came up next at the taxi rank, he climbed into the cab after her and immediately gave the driver Asha's address.

"How do you know where I'm staying?"

He didn't look at her. "Jake told me."

So he had known where she was, but had chosen not to pursue the conversation she'd run away from at his club. She supposed she couldn't blame him. But as the taxi pulled away from the curb, an uncomfortable silence enveloped them. She had spent her career interacting with victims and witnesses who had experienced things she couldn't even fathom, conversing with varying degrees of fluency in French and Arabic and Urdu. Yet now, facing a man with whom she'd once shared everything, the only thing that came to mind was stark terror.

Ian broke first. "You impressed them tonight, you know. You impressed me. And I think I understand now."

It was the last thing she expected from him, this gentle, resigned tone. She frowned. "Understand what?"

He threw a wry smile her direction. "When I heard you talking tonight, I realized you weren't running away from me; you were running toward something you needed more. I suppose that's why I don't understand why you're back in London."

Grace wanted to tell him the truth, but she didn't know the answer. Tonight had reminded her that her work mattered. The people whose stories she told in photos mattered. How could she weigh her own pain more heavily than theirs? And yet how could she not, when the results of her experiences were taking her apart a bit more each day?

And so the only thing that came out was a canned answer, a pitiful ghost of the truth. "Looking for a new direction, I suppose. It's time."

His expression closed as if he recognized the evasion, and even though his disappointment shouldn't have wounded her after all this time, she still winced. Mercifully, the cab slowed and pulled to the curb in front of Asha's building before the silence could turn awkward again. She pressed the fare through the window to the driver, then slid out of the backseat, aware of Ian following. She fumbled for the key in her sequined clutch.

"Grace."

She turned to where he stood on the pavement, his expression raw as he watched her. "I forgave you the moment you left," he said quietly. "But that doesn't mean I've forgotten."

Grace couldn't find her voice, couldn't do anything but nod. Still he didn't move. It took several seconds to understand he was waiting for her to get inside safely. She shoved the key into the lock on the third try and burst into the foyer. By the time she turned back, the cab was already pulling away from the curb.

"That doesn't mean I've forgotten."

Neither had she.

CHAPTER SEVEN

"DO YOU EVER SLEEP?"

Grace looked up from the hob to where Asha stood in the doorway. "Sorry, did I wake you? I thought you might like some breakfast before you head to hospital."

"I would, were it not my day off. I'd kind of hoped to sleep in past six." Asha pushed a messy handful of black hair out of her eyes and stumbled to Grace's side. Despite her grumpy tone, her face perked up a bit at the contents of the pan. "Is that chorizo?"

"*Longganisa.* You eat it with rice and eggs. Think of it as a Filipino fry-up."

"Mmm." It wasn't quite acknowledgment or appreciation, but at least Asha was being a good sport about being awoken early on her day off. She stifled a yawn and flipped on the kettle before collapsing into a chair at the table. "When were you in the Philippines?"

Grace paused midway through giving the garlic fried rice a stir. "Fifteen years ago, maybe? After I left Los Angeles, I traveled with a friend who was shooting freelance stories on prostitution. We rented a room in Manila from this sweet little *lola* for a few months, and she taught me how to make this."

"Sounds cheery."

"You know how it is." Most of Grace's subjects had been fairly distressing, but there had been lightness too. The Filipino people were welcoming and hospitable, and their devotion to their Catholic faith reminded her of home—if she could still call Ireland home, considering she'd not been back since she turned eighteen.

"All right, give this a go." Grace packed rice into a little bowl, then upended it on the center of each of their plates. A sunny-side-up egg went on top, with several of the longganisa links on the side. She plopped into the seat across from Asha and slid one of the plates toward her.

Asha took one bite and sighed. "Okay. This might have been worth waking up for."

Grace grinned. "Aren't you glad I cook to work out my problems?"

"Very glad. You know, times like this I wonder if you didn't go after the wrong MacDonald brother."

"That would have been too many cooks in the kitchen. Literally. Besides, back then James was 24-7 about work. Ian was the one who liked to have fun."

"So, I take it my breakfast is due to a blue-eyed rower sort of problem?"

Grace popped up out of her chair. "Hold that thought. Tea's ready."

"You're avoiding."

"And you're pushing."

"Well, I butted out last night, and look where it got us—you're taking a culinary stroll down memory lane. Not that I mind being the beneficiary of your angst, but what happened?"

Grace poured their tea, then brought the mugs back to the table. "Nothing happened. Ian was nice. Reserved. Saw me home. He might not exactly be sticking pins into my voodoo doll, but he's also not thrilled to see me. He's . . . indifferent."

Asha chewed, her expression thoughtful. "He saw you home?"

"Said he wanted to make sure I was safe."

"That doesn't sound indifferent. Had he merely been concerned for your safety, he would have put you in a cab. This is London, not Lebanon or wherever you just came back from."

"It would almost be easier if he shut me out, instead of telling me he's forgiven me and then leaving. You know him better than I do these days. What do you think?"

"He's cautious. Can you really blame him?"

"Cautious. That doesn't sound like the man I knew at all." Her Ian had been impetuous, daring, spontaneous. Yes, there was discipline involved in his rowing, but he and his crewmates had shared the same kamikaze attitude: leave it all on the water, no matter what. Better to die than to let your teammates down. Give everything for the people who depended on you.

Give everything for those you loved.

Grace let out a groan and buried her face in her hands.

"I did this to him, didn't I? He gave up rowing for me, and then I left him, and he decided it wasn't worth taking risks anymore." She lifted her head. "I'm right, aren't I?"

"I don't know, Grace. Ian's never been the sort to blame other people for his own decisions. And he doesn't mince words. If he said he's forgiven you, then he's forgiven you."

"But he hasn't forgotten what I did to him." Grace pushed her food around on her plate, no longer hungry. "What do I do?"

Asha folded her arms on the tabletop and leaned over them, a sure sign she was going into doctor mode. "What do you want? I mean, honestly. If you just want to make amends, I'd say you've done what you can. Leave it alone and move on with your life. He has."

"And if I don't want to move on?"

"Then you need to show him that you've changed, that you're not going to run away this time if he gives you another chance. Just be sure you're doing it for the right reasons, yeah?"

The right reasons. She wasn't sure she even knew what those were anymore. After ten years, it was ridiculous to think she knew anything about him. Foolish to think they even had a hope of rekindling what they once had. But they'd never find out if they didn't have the chance to get to know each other again, and Asha was right: he'd never take that chance if she didn't show him she had changed.

The first step would be to not run away.

Of all the things Ian expected to see when he climbed out of the boat, Grace was the least likely. In fact, he was fairly certain he'd imagined it, a sort of visual déjà vu, or maybe early senility. Given Grace's usual avoidance of confrontation, it certainly couldn't be her.

But no, when he flicked a glance over his shoulder, she was still there, her hands thrust into the pockets of a black army jacket instead of holding a camera. When she saw him looking at her, she raised a hand in tentative greeting.

"Got a fan, MacDonald?" Marc asked from the stern end.

"I have absolutely no idea." He didn't look her way again. Maybe if he didn't acknowledge her, she'd give up and leave. An admittedly childish plan, but it was better than acknowledging the way his pulse had accelerated at her arrival.

No, much better that she leave of her own volition.

When he exited the clubhouse half an hour later to find his plan had worked, he didn't feel even the slightest prick of disappointment. Not at all.

Then he rounded the corner and saw her sitting on a green wooden bench, earphones plugged into her ears while she scrolled through something on the screen of her mobile.

"What are you doing here?"

Grace removed the earphones and quickly shoved her phone into one of the jacket's pockets. "Hoping you might let me buy you breakfast."

His *no* stalled on his lips. What had caused the deviation from the regular script? "Where?"

"Your choice."

"All right, then. This way."

She didn't even blink, just fell into step with him on the pavement. "Was that Chris I saw down there?"

"It was."

"How much of the old squad rows here?"

"Only a few. Chris is a regular, rows bow in my four a few

days a week. Marc coxes for us on the weekends for kicks with the other lads. We see Nikolai around the boathouse, but he's still competitive, so he rarely joins us. He's a dentist now, if you can believe that."

Grace's smile flashed, and it did strange things to his gut. "Nik, a dentist? That's the last thing I would have expected. I thought he'd read accounting at Cambridge or some such."

"Well, he turned out to be rubbish as an accountant, but I'm not exactly sure of the thought process that brought him round to teeth as a career option. I suspect he did it so he could set his hours around his workouts."

"I'm glad to see you stuck with it," Grace said softly. "Or rather, went back to it. Do you compete?"

"No. I don't have the time to stay in race shape. But I've done too much damage to my body over the years to stop, and it's more entertaining than physical therapy."

"Your physical therapist probably thanks you. You were always a terrible patient, and somehow I doubt time has changed that much." She threw him a wry grin, and he returned it despite himself. In the light of day, side by side on the pavement chatting like old friends, the awkwardness of the night before disappeared. She might be able to pull off the evening wear and stiletto heels with aplomb, but the regular Grace—the one in faded jeans and boots with a newsboy cap pulled low over her eyes—was still there.

When they stopped in front of his choice of restaurant—a greasy spoon near Putney Bridge—she broke into a laugh that was as damaging to his distance as her smile. "You can choose anywhere, and you pick this dive?"

Ian held the door open for her. "Best fried slice on the West End, as you well remember. And I'm starving."

He saw her amusement fade to curiosity, but he didn't delve into the reason he'd chosen one of their old haunts. The interior was still the familiar polished ceramic tiles and cheap Formica tables, not a surprise since they hadn't changed since 1972. She flicked a glance to the corner booth, her teeth pulling the edge of her lip. That had been their table, the site of hours of laughter and conversation and more than a few stolen kisses. After they placed their order at the counter and took their mugs of tea, Grace made a beeline for the opposite side of the café, as far from their usual spot as she could get.

Probably a wise idea, if he still thought of the table as their spot.

Ian leaned back against the booth and draped an arm over the backrest while he studied her. "So what's this really all about? I'm thinking you didn't wander down here on a whim for breakfast."

She toyed with the salt and pepper shakers for a moment, then set them firmly on the table in front of her and looked him in the eye. "Last night, you asked me why I was back in London."

"I did. And you lied to me. Not very convincingly, I might add."

She flinched and fidgeted with the zipper of her jacket. "I didn't lie, exactly. I just didn't tell you the whole truth."

He said nothing, just continued to wait.

"You said you understood that I was running toward something, not away from you. You're right about that. At the time, I was young and idealistic and not a little bit stupid. I thought I had an obligation to change the world."

"Which you have."

"Have I?" Doubt swam in her green eyes. "Or have I been

riding on others' coattails, exploiting their good work and claiming it for my own? I didn't establish those schools and hospitals, but everyone's whispering Pulitzer. All I did was take some pictures."

"I've seen those photos, Grace. They're stunning. Whatever accolades you get for them—for your body of work—they're well deserved. I don't understand why you're doubting your talent now."

"It's not my talent I'm doubting. Just my . . . effectiveness. That photo we're all chasing—the one that's going to make the world stand up and take notice—it doesn't exist. At some point, it's time to move on. Get out while we still can."

It was the slightest break in her voice, and the way her hand went back to the dragon tattoo on her wrist, that alerted him this wasn't just an existential crisis, a questioning of her career path now that she'd achieved success. "Who did you lose?"

She didn't meet his eyes this time. "I've lost eight colleagues over the last ten years. Good photographers. Good journalists. They knew the risks in this job, and they accepted them. It's what made them effective. But Brian was different."

Something sharp and painful twisted in Ian's chest before he could arrest his emotions. "He was special to you."

"I was responsible for him. When I was his age, Jean-Auguste took me aside and told me the truth. He saved my life more than a few times. I wanted to do that for Brian, but I failed. He got killed, right in front of me, and since then, it hasn't been the same."

Her grief tugged at his sympathies. To lose a friend—a protégé—in such a horrific way . . . No wonder she wanted to make a change. No wonder she doubted the risks were worth the payoff.

"Grace, you've experienced something horrible. It's normal to question if it's all been worth it."

"I know I can't change anything," she said softly. "But I wonder if I gave up the best thing in my life for no reason."

Two plates thunked down in front of them, startling him out of the spell her words had woven around him. The server looked between them. "You need anything else?"

"No, thank you." Grace smiled politely and picked up her fork.

But Ian couldn't tear his eyes away from her. She couldn't make a statement like that and then pretend it had never happened. The best thing in her life? Did that mean she was back for him? "I don't know what to say."

"You don't have to say anything. I didn't mean to put you on the spot. I just thought you deserved an honest answer."

Ian fell back against the booth, his shock overcoming his appetite while he tried to reconcile the woman sitting across from him with the one he remembered. Her eyes had always held that slightly haunted look, the recollection of terrible things in the past buried just below her gaze, but she was different now. Wiser. Sadder. Warier. He supposed they both were, forced to accept that sometimes life didn't turn out the way they'd envisioned it. He couldn't deny any longer that her decision to leave had changed everything for him. And yet ten years later her smile could still take his breath away. What was he to make of that?

"Are you going to eat?" she asked, still not meeting his eyes.

He picked up his fork and then set it back down with a clank. "What exactly do you want from me?"

Clearly, she hadn't anticipated a direct approach. Two

spots of color bloomed on her pale cheeks. "I guess I was hoping that we could at least be friends."

"No."

She blinked rapidly, clearly struggling against hurt. "I see. I suppose I deserve that."

"Not merely friends. I think we both know where that ends up."

Her lips parted on a half exhale, half laugh, and God help him if his mind didn't go straight to what it would be like to kiss them again.

"We do?" she asked.

"We do."

"Then where does that leave us?"

You're an idiot, his better judgment chanted in the back of his mind. He shoved it away. "Dinner."

"Tonight?" When he nodded, she narrowed her eyes. "What if I already have plans?"

Was that a hint of coyness in her tone? "Cancel them. Unless, of course, you're not interested."

"No," she said slowly, "I'm interested."

"I'll pick you up at seven, then." Ian retrieved his utensils, his appetite back with a vengeance now that he'd made a decision. It was rash, reckless, utterly ridiculous to be even considering getting involved with her again. In all likelihood, they wouldn't make it through dinner before discovering that the embers of whatever they had shared were too cold to ever be fanned back to life.

But it was better than spending another ten years wondering what would have happened had he taken a chance.

CHAPTER EIGHT

A KNOCK CAME AT THE DOOR at precisely 6:55 and set Grace's heart hammering. She leaned over the sink to give her lips one last swipe of pale-pink lipstick, then thrust her feet into a pair of black leather ballet flats. She hadn't any idea where Ian was taking her, so she'd opted for a safe casual look: skinny jeans and a slinky top beneath a blazer with a gauzy scarf wrapped around her neck. In the last two days, she'd pretty much exhausted all the date-appropriate clothing stuffed in her duffel bag. She hadn't exactly thought this through when she left Paris.

The knock came again and she rushed to the door, yanking it open without checking the peephole. Ian stood there with an umbrella in hand, drops of water flecking his dark hair and sparkling on the shoulders of his trench coat. "Are you ready?"

She looked down at her casual clothing, then back at the perfectly creased trousers showing beneath his coat. "I'm underdressed."

"No, you look beautiful."

The sudden warmth in his voice made her heart stop for a second. She grabbed her handbag from the coatrack and stepped into the hall with him. "Where are we going exactly?"

"I don't know yet. I guess we'll see. Shall we?" He smiled mysteriously and swept a hand toward the staircase. Out on the stoop, he extended the umbrella and held it over her as they dashed for the black cab waiting at the curb.

Once they were safely inside, the driver turned. "You know where we're headed yet?"

Ian pushed up his sleeve to check his watch. "A few minutes more."

"Suit yourself. Meter's still running."

Grace sent him a quizzical look. "What's this about now?"

As if on cue, Ian's mobile beeped from his pocket. He dug it out and checked a text. "West Croydon."

The driver made a sound that might have been exasperation, then pulled out onto the street. Grace stared in bafflement, though Ian looked unperturbed about the unconventional start to their evening.

"Did you have a nice afternoon?" he asked. "What did you do?"

"Wandered around Putney and took photos. You?"

He waved a hand. "This."

"You're really not going to tell me what this is about?"

"Not at all. It would spoil the surprise."

"But it took you all afternoon to set up?"

He gave a single nod, clearly not going to give away any details. She leaned back against the seat in bewilderment. This was nothing like she'd expected. She'd been thinking casual dinner, maybe at one of James's restaurants, followed by cocktails or coffee. Not crossing half of London in Saturday night traffic in the pouring rain to a mystery location, apparently sent to him via text message. He had put in some effort to not be predictable.

When they pulled up on a nearly deserted block in front of an abandoned warehouse, though, a little quiver of nervousness began. The brick storefronts were shuttered for the night, graffiti scrawled across the metal roll-up doors. Grace took Ian's hand and stepped out into the fine mist of rain, her heart slamming into her ribs. It took all she had not to look around for potential ambush sites. This was London, and she was with Ian. He would never bring her anyplace dangerous.

"Don't look at me like I've suddenly become an ax murderer," Ian said with a wry smile. "I know that's what you were thinking."

"It did cross my mind," she murmured.

His answering laugh was so warm and amused, though, it unclenched her stomach and calmed her heart. He squeezed her hand as they approached an orange-painted door.

A burly man in a black shirt stepped from the shadow of the building. He would have been threatening if he hadn't been holding a tablet computer and wearing an earpiece.

"Welcome, sir, ma'am. Your names?"

"Smithson."

The man checked his tablet and then reached to open the door for them. "Enjoy your evening, Mr. Smithson."

They stepped into darkness. Grace hesitated as her eyes adjusted to the surroundings. Black screens and drapes cordoned off a reception area and a temporary cloakroom that seemed to be made of . . . trees? Or coatracks that looked like trees. Strains of live flamenco music drifted from somewhere inside.

"Welcome to Seek." A gorgeous woman with dark curls tied back in a kerchief and dressed in colorful full skirts greeted them. "Right this way, Mr. Smithson."

Grace cast an intrigued look at Ian and followed the woman around the screen into the massive warehouse space. But rather than the concert venue she'd begun to anticipate, they stepped into a Spanish town square, complete with cobblestones underfoot and a splashing fountain in the center. Festive paper lanterns strung from tree to tree—live trees this time, Grace realized—lit the space with a dim, romantic glow.

"What is this?" she asked as the hostess led them to a spot at one of the long, rustic tables.

"If I had to guess, I'd say Basque Country. Sometime in the past."

Grace laughed in surprise. She climbed over the bench at their place, wide enough for two and adorned with an embroidered red cushion. More details filtered in: a glittering canopy of stars overhead, a group of musicians with guitars and percussion boxes in the corner. In fact, had she not just come in from the London streets, she'd be convinced she'd somehow been transported to a plaza in Spain.

Ian watched her, a slight smile on his lips. "It's a pop-up restaurant. It's kept completely secret until the night of. No one knows where it will appear next or what the theme will be."

"I don't know what to say." She looked at him in wonder. "You didn't have to go to this trouble for me."

"First dates should be memorable."

"This is more like our five hundredth date, Ian."

"It's our first date," he said firmly before he reached for the jug of sangria on the table in front of them. "Of course, considering it was a last-minute first date, I'm happy I managed to pull it off. This usually requires some advance booking."

"How advance?"

He shrugged, but his eyes twinkled in the low light. "Four months, give or take."

"The advantages of working in the restaurant business?"

"The advantages of having a food critic owe you a favor." He raised his glass to her. "Hence the fact I get to be Mr. Smithson for the evening. To surprises and starting over."

"And secret identities," she said, clinking her glass to his. He was trying to impress her, and she found it completely endearing. More than that. Humbling. Her heart twinged with something painful and unfamiliar. She had practically begged him for a second chance, and yet he was acting like he was the one who needed to prove himself.

Ian shifted so he was facing her on the bench. "So, the obligatory first-date questions."

"What do I do for a living?" The sangria was already making her feel a little warm and flirtatious, so she set the glass down on the table and folded her hands primly in her lap.

"I think we have that one covered. But since we're being somewhat adventurous . . . what's the maddest thing you've done in the last few years?"

"Maddest or most ill-advised?"

"Either. Though it makes me wonder that you have to draw the distinction."

Grace laughed. She had plenty of both to choose from, but she also had enough practice to steer away from the truly heart-wrenching stories to the ones people wanted to hear. The ones that sounded far more glamorous in the retelling than they had felt at the time. "Riding in a NATO chopper on a rescue mission in Iraq."

"Really! That was not what I was expecting. What happened?"

Maybe she did need another sip of the sangria to tell the story. "I won't go into the why, but when we approached the landing zone, we took fire . . . Why are you looking at me like that?"

"Like what?" he asked, smiling.

"Like I did something brave. I was holding on for dear life. I really thought I was going to die. I was so terrified I didn't even get any shots off."

"Somehow I don't believe that."

"Completely true. I've been held at gunpoint, robbed multiple times, locked down in hotels because of bomb threats, but that was the most scared I've ever been in my life. I don't see myself getting back onto a helicopter for any reason anytime soon."

"And yet you can tell the story so easily."

"It's a good story."

"It's a very good story. You really think you can leave all the good stories behind?"

The question hit close to home on a night when she just wanted to enjoy herself and get to know a very handsome man. She went for lighthearted instead. "Who needs all that when I can visit Basque Country right in the middle of London?"

He didn't say anything, but looked at her in that intense way that caught her breath and made the twinge turn to a quiver. The serving plates began to go down all along the tables, placed by men in embroidered white trousers and red berets. It began with the Basque version of tapas called *pintxos*: goat cheese and green olive tapenade on toasted bread, thinly sliced smoked fish wrapped around fruit, something that tasted like ceviche piled on a peppery cracker.

"This is amazing," she said with a happy sigh. "When's the last time you were in Spain?"

"With you. Do you remember? Barcelona?"

"Ah yes, Barcelona. I remember. Your squad won."

"Yes, we won. But that's not what stands out most from that trip."

Grace flushed as she followed his memories. They'd been there for his rowing competition, but they'd found more than enough time for strolls hand in hand through the Barrio Gótico, the Gothic Quarter, steeped in history and romance. There had been one particular bar decorated like a fairy wood, complete with trees and strong sangria—

"Wait. Did you . . . ? Is that why you chose this? Because of Barcelona? I thought no one knew the theme?"

He shrugged, but his smile over the rim of his cup gave away the answer. "I told you. Advantage of being owed a favor by someone in the know."

Something about the fact he'd specifically tried to re-create one of their romantic moments made her breathless. She'd taken his words last night about not having forgotten as a warning, a reminder that his trust would not be so easily won. But had he also meant that he hadn't forgotten what they once were to each other?

The server was back again, removing the pintxos plates and trading them for enameled pottery bowls of fragrant lamb stew. Despite the fact that there must have been two hundred people in the room, the darkness, the sensual flamenco music, the aromas of exotic, unfamiliar food wound around them like a cocoon. It would have been the perfect seduction scene, but now it was even more romantic because she knew he intended nothing of the sort. In fact, despite being nestled together on a single bench, eating with their fingers, he didn't touch her. Just looked at her with those unsettling clear-blue eyes as if she was something wondrous.

"If you keep looking at me like that," she murmured, "I'm going to think you like me." It was a stupid thing to say, but she had to do something to lessen the magic that wove steadily around her with each moment.

"If I didn't like you, we wouldn't be here. Besides, first date. Remember?"

"Right, first date." And from the lack of suspicion in his expression, she could believe he meant it. Could almost believe it herself.

They finished their night with *gâteau Basque*, a shortbread cake filled with a fragrant pastry cream and brandied cherries, just about the most delicious thing Grace had tasted in years. When Ian took her fork and fed her a bite of it with a wicked little smile, she almost changed her mind about the seduction.

"You're dangerous, do you know that?" she said when he helped her on with her coat, the end of the evening coming much too soon. "You certainly know how to make an impression."

Ian smiled mysteriously and guided her into the crowd making their way to the front of the warehouse, where a line of taxicabs waited to pick up the departing guests. He put up the umbrella against the steadily falling rain and pulled her closer beneath its shelter. Her heart gave a little hiccup.

It turned to a full-fledged stutter when they slid into the humid backseat of a cab and he turned the full force of that intense gaze on her. "Did you have a good time?"

"And then some. This morning, I would have said it would be impossible for you to surprise me, but I'm surprised. Thank you. This was . . . lovely."

"It was entirely my pleasure."

As the cab slid through the dark, Grace fell silent, aware of the mere inches that separated them. She could practically feel the heat from his body, imagined the electric current spanning the space between their hands on the seat, achingly close but still so separate. She shifted her handbag into her lap so she wouldn't be tempted to give in to the mad impulses rushing through her veins. She was feeling the magic of the night, the allure of the unexpectedly perfect surprise. His romantic streak hadn't dissipated with time.

By the time he handed her out of the cab in front of Asha's building, she felt as jittery as a schoolgirl anticipating her first kiss.

"Don't you need it to wait?"

"Tube's still running. Or I can walk. I'm close by."

"In the rain? I doubt you live that close."

"I own a flat on Gloucester Road."

"Of course you do." Grace felt a little silly to have thought he was still living in his second floor flat in Islington.

"Here, allow me." Ian gently took her key and opened the

door, making her realize she'd been staring at him like an idiot on the building's stoop.

As she climbed the stairs, her heart thudded harder than the exertion warranted. Outside the flat, she took back her keys and flipped through the ring with a tremor in her normally steady hands.

He closed his hand over hers to stop her fumbling with the lock. "Wait."

She froze, suddenly aware of the small space that separated them, the kindling warmth in his eyes, and realized there was nothing she wanted more in that moment than to kiss him. Which was a spectacularly bad idea when the way his gaze skimmed her face shot her pulse into overdrive.

Then again, she'd always had an affinity for bad ideas. She stepped into him and lifted her face to his.

It was all the invitation he needed. His hand went to her waist automatically, but he didn't pull her closer. Instead, he limited the touch to the merest brush of lips, the mingling of breath. She lifted her hand to his neck to caress the bit of skin that showed above the collar of his coat, her thumb tracing the edge of his jaw.

His fingers tightened on her waist just before he pulled away. "Good night, Grace."

"Good night, Ian."

He paused at the top of the stairs while she fitted the key to the lock and let herself in with a crack of warped wood. She fastened the latch and chain and took a long moment to catch her breath with her forehead pressed against the door.

Heavens have mercy. If she'd had any doubt whether their chemistry had survived a decade apart, it was long gone.

He'd cast a spell around her all night long, and that was even before the kiss.

She needed to be realistic, though. Just because they had one date—a magical, sensual date—didn't mean anything had changed. She had to remember that. As soon as she managed to wipe the stupid smile off her face.

After the previous morning's blunder, Grace purposely stayed in bed so she wouldn't wake Asha. When she finally pried her eyes open to a brightly lit reception room, she was met with the unmistakable crackle and aroma of bacon frying.

"Am I hallucinating, or are you actually making breakfast?" Grace blinked sleepily from the doorway, aware of the irony in this role reversal.

Asha picked up a crispy piece of bacon draining on the plate next to the hob and took a bite. "I'm not making breakfast. I'm frying bacon. There's a difference."

Grace laughed and nudged Asha out of the way. "Go get the eggs for me. If you're going to bait me with bacon grease, you could at least make my tea."

"On it." Asha pulled a mug from the cupboard. "So . . ."

"So what?"

"The date? How was it?"

Grace felt it coming, tried to stop it . . . but no, the stupid smile came right back to her face. She'd done so well putting her expectations in line last night, only to have her hopes flare right back to life. "It was good."

"Just good?"

Grace bit her lip. "Fine. It was amazing. Incredibly romantic."

Asha squealed and hoisted herself up on the counter, looking far more like a giggly coed than a thirty-seven-year-old
doctor. "Tell me everything."

"Tea?" Grace prompted.

"Right. Here. Now, you go."

"Well, he took me to a pop-up restaurant called Seek. I'm
not really allowed to give details because they swear you to
secrecy when you leave."

"That's no fair. How can I live vicariously if you won't
tell?"

Grace smiled at the recollection. "Let's say it re-created a
romantic moment in our past."

"That's a good sign," Asha said. "Should the eggs be
smoking?"

"Blast." Grace twisted down the heat, then flipped the
eggs over in the pan. A little brown but not scorched. "It's
eggs over-well this morning, Ash."

"Completely worth it. Did he kiss you?"

The smile came back.

"He did." Asha sighed. "This is really good, Grace. Is it
bad if I'm a little jealous?"

"Not as long as you don't let Jake hear you say it."

Asha chuckled. "Jake has nothing to fear. You realize this
proves my theory all along."

"Which is?"

"That he was waiting for you. None of those other women
had a chance with him. He went through the motions until
you showed up. Do you think he's put anything like that
together for anyone else?"

He had called in a fairly significant favor, thanks to his
connections. But reading into it too much would only set her

up for disappointment. She changed the subject. "So what are you planning for today?"

"Meeting Jake this afternoon. I'm on at six tomorrow, so it will be an early night. You could come along, you know. He'd love to see you again."

"Some other time. I'm not going to barge into your Sunday afternoon plans. Besides, three's a crowd."

"Then invite Ian." Asha's sweet smile hid a hint of the devil.

Grace laughed. "I don't think we're at double-date status yet, but thanks."

"Suit yourself. I think you might be surprised at the time he could free up if you rang him."

Grace grinned and put their plates on the table. She managed to divert the subject from her and Ian until they finished breakfast and Asha was out the door. She even managed to keep him out of her thoughts while she booted her laptop and opened the folder that contained her raw files still to be processed. She paused at one of the mist-shrouded bridge shots she'd taken that first morning she had found him at his rowing club and had to press down the anticipation that welled up inside her.

That had been some date. And brief as it was, the kiss hadn't been half-bad either.

She chewed her lip against the smile that once more surfaced unbidden. The amount of effort Ian had put into surprising her seemed to express his feelings pretty clearly . . . or at least his willingness to give them a shot.

Grace plugged her earphones into her mobile and scrolled through her usual choices—the Rolling Stones, the Kinks, the Clash—but none of them suited her mood. She finally landed on the Beatles and smiled. *Abbey Road.*

Perfect. She and Ian had listened to it endlessly on road trips to his regattas, sharing one set of earphones like teenagers. She couldn't deny the lift in her spirits when "Come Together" blasted out. The perfect blend of nostalgia and energy.

Inspired by her musical choices, she plowed through her editing in record time, uploading files to her portfolio, then checking her e-mail.

The phone cut off George Harrison singing "Something," and she jerked it up with her heart in her throat before she noticed it was not Ian's name on the screen, but Melvin's.

"Hello, Melvin. Let me guess. The first prints are done?"

"That they are. Are you busy?"

She glanced at the clock—3:23. Asha was out with Jake. Grace checked her phone for text messages or voice mail. Nothing on the status bar. "No. Just finishing up for the day. Shall I come over?"

"Please do. I can't wait for you to see these."

It was better than passing the time hoping Ian might call and waffling over whether she should call him. She grabbed her camera bag out of reflex, stuffed the phone in her pocket, and headed out the door.

Half an hour later, she entered the gallery to find Melvin speaking with an elegantly dressed couple before a large abstract oil painting. Without missing a beat of his pitch, he gave her a little tilt of his head to indicate she should go back to his office.

Several minutes later, Melvin entered. "Grace, beautiful." He kissed both cheeks, then held her back at arm's length. "My. You look pleased with yourself. Finding London to your liking?"

"Something like that." She shrugged, but the bloom of heat up her neck gave her away faster than any words could.

"Ah, must be a man. Don't worry, I'm not going to grill you about it. Come on back and see what I've got so far."

Melvin led her down the hall to a space adjacent to his darkroom, humming to himself in a way that made her think he wasn't about to drop the subject completely. A twelve-by-eighteen had been affixed to the whiteboard. Grace moved closer to take in the details of the print from inches away. It was the best of a series of shots she'd taken in a Sudanese village, witnessing the rebuilding that was taking place after its destruction years before. She'd impulsively switched from her Canon to the Leica to capture the image of a farmer squatting in his field, his hands cupping new growth springing from the ground.

"You burned this area round the seedling," she said. The highlighting drew the eye to the sprout, emphasizing the detail's symbolism.

"I think this is one of my favorites."

"Mine too." She still remembered the conversation she'd had with the farmer through an interpreter. The farmer had lost most of his family and yet he stayed, saying he wouldn't give anyone the power to force him from his rightful place. She had promised she would come back to see his progress the next time she passed through Sudan.

That would probably never happen now.

"Grace?"

She lifted her head and realized she'd been staring blankly at the photo for some time. "It's perfect."

"Harder to leave behind than you thought?"

She drew in a long, deep breath before she could answer. "How can you hate and love something simultaneously?"

"Because hate and love are flip sides of the same coin. It would be impossible for you to feel indifferent. Have you thought any more about the job?"

Kenneth DeVries's business card was in the outer pocket of her gear bag, but she'd not yet decided whether she was going to call. "I have. I'm still not sure an office job is for me. I've spent ten years in the field, Melvin. Settling down feels like—"

"Settling." He favored her with a sympathetic smile. "You're not the only one who has had to go through this. Everyone comes to a turning point in their lives eventually, especially people like us. We have to decide what's more important: work or the people we love. For me, the most important thing was saving my marriage and seeing my children grow up. I finally realized that there would always be another story, another emergency demanding my attention. But there might not ever be another chance at this life."

Their perspectives might be slightly different from opposite sides of the same editorial desk, but she felt the truth of his words. "If I didn't know better, I'd say you have the heart of a romantic."

"Just don't tell my wife. She'll expect roses when I get home tonight." Melvin rose from his perch on the edge of the table. "Come, we have three more prints to review. I'll have another batch by Wednesday, I think."

"Thank you, Melvin."

"Hey, I'm as invested in making this show a success as you are."

"That's not what I meant."

Melvin squeezed her shoulder as he brushed by. "I know."

CHAPTER NINE

WHAT NOW?

Ian tapped his pen on the edge of his desk, stealing a look at his mobile before he shoved it into his drawer. Ten o'clock on Monday morning. Not even thirty-six hours since he'd left Grace at the door of Asha's flat. It was too early to call her for another date, wasn't it?

He was rubbish with these kinds of rules.

It wasn't as if he and Grace had ever gone in for tradition, anyway. They'd sped from first date to inseparable to living together in the space of two months, and after that, they had spent every waking nonworking moment together. Yet he couldn't help but wonder if it had been that mad rush to intimacy, that break with tradition, that had left their

97

relationship on such a shaky foundation that she could justify disappearing without a word. He wasn't willing to make the same mistake a second time.

Even if he was fairly certain the only thing that could get her out of his head was a lobotomy.

He pulled his mind back to the computer, where an in-box full of e-mails still demanded attention before his first appointment. Eva hadn't lasted a week, and not having an assistant had gone from annoying to concerning. A small business it might be—at least in terms of employees—but the sheer volume of paperwork necessitated a full-time position. He hoped that a capable replacement was waiting somewhere in today's interview schedule.

Instead of tackling the steadily building in-box, though, he found himself thinking about how much he had missed the feel of Grace in his arms. How that kiss good night had been much too brief—

"Ian, your ten o'clock is here."

Ian jerked his head up. Jamie's assistant stood in the doorway in all her tweed-suited glory, a young woman standing uncertainly behind her. "Yes, thank you, Bridget. Ms. Marusic, please come in."

The candidate smiled shyly and took a seat in front of his desk. She was younger than he'd thought from her CV: perhaps only twenty-five. Brown hair in a no-nonsense ponytail, dark-brown eyes, a suit every bit as conservative as Bridget's. In fact, were he to choose a word to describe her, *brown* would be the only logical answer.

He shuffled papers until he found her CV. "You have worked for two very large corporations since you graduated university four years ago. Tell me why you want to work for us." Ian always asked this question, more for his own amusement than any real insight he gained. Mostly it was a way to filter those without enough common sense to keep their mouths shut.

"I'm an excellent assistant. You need an assistant."

"Fair enough. You type sixty words per minute; you're proficient in all the software we use. Are you comfortable setting up conference calls and taking notes in meetings?"

A single nod. "Of course."

Well, she wouldn't be bothering him with useless chatter, at least. He quizzed her on the rest of her qualifications, which she answered quietly and succinctly. "Do you have any questions?"

"Do you conduct random drug testing?"

Ian blinked at her and then rose smoothly to his feet. "Thank you for coming, Ms. Marusic. We'll be in touch."

His day's other interviews weren't much better. Either the candidates didn't have the skills, or they had odd requirements like the inability to work every other Wednesday or the need to bring their puppy to the office. A headache began to throb behind Ian's left eye, joining the increasing pain in his muscles from this morning's punishing outing in his single scull. By four o'clock, his in-box was still piled high, and he was no closer to finding an assistant than he had been that morning. Fortunately, he only had to suffer through one more disaster.

He was clearing his desk, shoving paperwork into his briefcase, when a light knock sounded on the glass partition door. He glanced up to find a petite, black-haired woman standing in the doorway. Dressed in a conservative navy skirt suit with an ivory silk blouse and low-heeled shoes, she looked every inch the corporate assistant. His hopes lifted. "Ms. Grey, I presume?"

"And you would be Mr. MacDonald," she answered in a pronounced Scottish accent. Her eyes flicked over his desk and the half-packed state of his briefcase. "Did I come at a bad time? I'd be happy to reschedule."

"No, not at all." He held out a hand to the chair across from the desk and seated himself again. "You're Scottish."

"I am." Her mouth turned up slightly. "As are you."

Ian chuckled, sifted through the remaining paperwork, and found her CV. "Based on your schooling, I'd expected you to be American. You did your undergrad work at Yale and then completed a master's degree in financial economics at Oxford."

"I hope that won't be a problem for you. Cambridge man and all."

So she'd done her homework as well, even if her slight smile said she was teasing. "Not unless you happened to be on the men's rowing team." He returned to her qualifications. "You've held positions at some of the largest consulting firms in England, where most likely you hired your own assistants. So tell me, what are you doing here, Ms. Grey?"

"I have all the requisite skills. I'm capable of handling multiple projects simultaneously, but I don't find ordering your lunch or picking up your dry cleaning beneath me. I speak fluent French and German, which may come in useful as the company expands—and I expect it will, given the aggressive rate of growth the corporation's restaurant side has shown in the last several years."

"That's not what I was asking."

"I understand that." Ms. Grey swallowed, the first break

in her confidence since her arrival. "I'm in need of a job, Mr. MacDonald. I left my last position for personal reasons, and all my employers but that one will give me glowing references."

"Ms. Grey, you are overqualified for this position."

"I understand that as well."

Ian sighed. He would regret this. He knew better than to hire someone who would want to move on to bigger and better things. Then again, his last several hires hadn't worked out so well. "Well, I have no doubt you're capable of handling the job. I have several more interviews to conduct this week, and then I'll make a decision. Are your references attached?"

"They are." Ms. Grey rose and gathered her handbag. "Thank you, Mr. MacDonald."

"Please, call me Ian."

Her smile froze. "If you don't mind, sir, I'd prefer to call you Mr. MacDonald."

"Very well, Ms. Grey. I'll be in touch." He watched her walk precisely out the door, handbag tucked under her arm. She might not be willing to admit it, but he had an idea why Ms. Grey had left her last job.

But that wasn't his concern, and despite the fact he'd managed to ignore what really *was* weighing on his mind all day, he couldn't any longer. He picked up his phone and dialed.

CHAPTER TEN

FOR FIVE NIGHTS, Grace dreamed about London, Ian, and photography. On the sixth, she dreamed about war.

She sat straight up, strangling in her blankets and drenched in cold sweat. The thin blue light through the louvers suggested early morning, but the fact she heard nothing from the bedroom meant either Asha was already gone or for once Grace had made it through a nightmare without screaming.

Grace fell back against the pillows and lifted her watch in front of her face to read its glowing dial—7:30. Asha had left hours ago, and she wouldn't have to put on a happy face. She'd hoped her streak of flashback- and nightmare-free nights might be a sign that coming to London was loosening her memories' hold.

She should have known it wouldn't be that easy.

As her heartbeat slowed and she concentrated on the air moving in and out of her lungs, the nightmare's grip loosened enough that she remembered why she'd been anticipating this day.

Saturday. Her "second date" with Ian.

A smile came to her lips, banishing the rest of her lingering dread. It seemed he'd developed a taste for surprises, because even though he had called on Monday to ask her out for Saturday, he'd refused to give any hint as to what they were doing. His only instructions had been "Dress warmly and comfortably and bring your camera."

Grace had spent the next four days trying to figure out what he might have in mind, while Asha nagged Jake to wheedle the information out of Ian. But Ian was apparently being tight-lipped even with his mates, because Asha turned up nothing helpful.

By the time Ian buzzed the intercom at 10 a.m., Grace's stomach had rejected butterflies in favor of stampeding water buffalo. She pressed the button to let him up and spent the next two minutes lecturing herself on how silly it was to feel nervous. When the knock finally came, she counted to five to gather herself, then opened the door. "Hi there."

Ian shut the door behind him and automatically flipped the knob on the latch. He was wearing his weekend uniform of chinos and a light pullover, the clingy knit emphasizing his lean, muscled physique. Grace tried not to linger on the thought as she breathed in his spicy aftershave. He'd probably come straight from his club. She barely resisted the impulse to run her fingers through his hair to see if it was still wet. Why it should matter to her if it was, she couldn't fathom.

His eyes swept over her, his expression appreciative, though she didn't know what he could find to appreciate in her faded jeans and plain T-shirt. Then his gaze was back on her face, and he smiled. "Ready to go?"

She pulled on a cabled sweater draped over the back of the sofa, settled her cap on her head, and picked up her camera bag. "Ready if you are. Where exactly are we going?"

He opened the door for her. "Not telling yet. But I hope you don't mind a drive."

"A drive? When did you buy a car?"

His smile widened. "A few years ago. Just wait."

They emerged from the front door of her building onto the pavement, and Grace stopped short, her mouth dropping open at the roadster parked at the curb. "No. You didn't."

"I did." He positively oozed satisfaction. He probably thought she'd forgotten.

She circled the car with a slow smile, trailing a finger along the glass-like surface of the pristine black-and-silver paint job. "Sixty-six, right? Like we always talked about? Wherever did you find it? There can only be a handful of these left."

"It had been sitting in a farmer's barn in Yorkshire for thirty years. Took it off his hands for a song, even though it cost me half my savings to restore."

"Somehow I doubt that. Unless you plated it in gold."

"Once again you overestimate my net worth."

She laughed and went back to her giddy examination of the restored roadster. When she finished her circuit, he had the passenger door open for her. She slid into the seat and flashed him a smile. "She's a beauty, all right. Let's see how she runs."

When Ian climbed into the driver's side, she raised her eyes significantly to the soft-top roof. "Aren't you forgetting something? Roadsters are not made to be driven with the hood up. Everyone knows that. It's a universal rule."

"Still my Grace," he murmured, the sudden light in his eyes out of proportion with the statement, but he climbed out and retracted the top, clipping it into place behind the narrow rear seat. Then he was sitting beside her again, twisting the key in the ignition, and the engine rumbled to life.

"Nothing like these old carbureted beasts, huh?" Grace ran a hand reverently across the dash. "They may be a little short on horsepower by modern standards, but they make up for it in character. You're going to let me drive it, right?"

"Not a chance. I've seen you drive."

"I'm an excellent driver! I learned on the LA freeways."

"And if that weren't reason enough to keep the keys from you, you perfected your skills in developing countries where the concept of lanes is optional. Don't count on it."

She wrinkled her nose at him, but as he navigated west through the London streets, she had to admit it was both a spectacular car and a beautiful day. This was the type of trip she'd always envisioned when they'd talked about restoring a classic. If he were to have a car in London with all the associated expenses, he'd said, it must be purely frivolous. No saloon or estate or petrol-sipping subcompact, only pure British muscle, something with enough thrill to make it worth the time and effort.

Earlier, seeing him in his tuxedo mingling with London's high society, she'd wondered if that man still existed. The surprise dinner date had been her only indication that he'd not gone completely staid and conservative on her.

His positively wicked smile when he "accidentally" grazed her thigh while reaching for the gear lever was another.

"So this is how you impress the ladies these days?" She wasn't particularly easy to impress, but so far he'd managed it rather well.

"You are the first lady who has been in this car. Except for Mum, briefly, and she was less than enthralled."

"That's to be expected. She doesn't seem like the convertible type. Besides, you're not dating your mum."

"I'd certainly hope not." Then he sent her a teasing glance. "Is that what we're doing? Dating?"

"Considering this is the second surprise trip you've concocted and you kissed me good night last time, what else would you call it?"

"Showing you all London has to offer?"

Something in his eyes, even in the brief moment he looked away from the road, made her insides go jittery again. But she put on an understanding expression. "I see now. So this is all just a public service."

"Exactly."

"Then I suppose it's a good thing you're not in charge of the tourist board. You wouldn't be able to keep up with demand."

"Winning you over that quickly, am I?"

You have no idea, she thought. She swiftly changed the subject. "So, I'm curious. You asked me all about my job, but you never said how you ended up working for James."

"Well, you knew I was getting my graduate diploma in law. After that, I did a postgrad degree for my law concentration and went to work for a multinational firm for a few years. Then Jamie opened the restaurant and got the cookbook deal.

At first he just wanted some advice on business structure and legal matters. Eventually, he opened more restaurants and got the BBC program, so he needed someone reliable to oversee the corporate aspects. That's when I came on as his chief operating officer."

Grace watched Ian's face as he delivered the summary as if it was an explanation he'd given over and over. His tone was calm, but she saw the tension in his jaw, the way he held the steering wheel a bit too tightly. "If you hate it so much, why do you keep doing it?"

He seemed legitimately surprised. "I don't hate it. What gave you that idea?"

"Ian, I know you better than that. I remember how you used to talk about rowing as if it were the most fascinating topic on earth. Obviously, this isn't what you would have chosen for yourself. So why do it?"

"For the money. I'm grossly overpaid."

"I don't believe you."

"It's true. Jamie would feel far too guilty about it otherwise. Lots of zeros." His casual smile felt put-on, forced, despite his light tone.

"No, I don't believe you're in it for the money. You've never cared about that, and you always said you'd rather scrape by on what you could earn honestly than cave to your mum's demands. So why?"

"Because it makes Jamie and Mum happy."

"What about what makes *you* happy?"

"You made me happy, Grace." His tone was low, barely audible. "The rest was just something to do."

He might as well have struck her—it would have knocked the wind from her all the same. "Ian, you know I—"

"Shh, Grace, no. I didn't mean . . . Can we start over?" He reached for her hand and squeezed it before bringing it to his lips, an unconscious gesture that still managed to feel natural after all these years. "I wasn't trying to pick a fight, especially not today."

The vise eased up a degree, and she managed to take a breath. "You know you don't have to go to all this trouble for me."

"This may come as a surprise to you, but I like you. I want to spend time with you. And if I get to take the Healey out at the same time—"

"It's a win-win situation."

"Precisely." He grinned at her, the dark mood of moments before sliding away like thunderclouds before a brisk wind. "You can begin guessing at any time, by the way."

"No idea yet. Obviously we're leaving London." She stretched her hand out the window and let the wind slide through her fingers. "Do I get a hint?"

"This is your hint. Tell me when you've figured it out."

Grace paid more attention to the road signs and realized they were headed southwest. By the time they gained Basingstoke and kept going, the most logical possibilities were Southampton and Salisbury. When they passed the turnoff to Southampton, she murmured, "Salisbury it is."

"Indeed. Your online portfolio had photos of the cathedrals at St. Paul's, Canterbury, and Salford, but no Salisbury. You've never been here, have you?"

"No. I had a print of the Constable painting in my reception room at one time, though."

"I know. I remember. Framed in that awful red metal frame, above that equally awful brocade sofa."

"That was twelve years ago! I can't believe you remember that. I barely remember that."

"We had some good times, didn't we?"

"We did." She smiled at the recollection. "Some young and foolish times too."

"Does that make us old and wise now?"

"Speak for yourself," she retorted playfully. At his raised eyebrow, she said, "I'm still waiting on that wisdom."

"Aren't we all?" He delivered the last with a smirk, and for the first time, she thought they might be able to truly be free from the specters of the past.

CHAPTER ELEVEN

SALISBURY WAS A CHARMING medieval village that com-
bined the old architecture of the city with the typical English
high street storefronts—many upscale and modern, with a
handful of chain stores. After finding a spot in the multistory
car park at Old George Mall, they emerged into the throngs of
people covering the pavements around Market Square. Grace
paused occasionally to take photos, snapping quick candids of
pedestrians or kneeling down to change the perspective of the
frame. Ian waited patiently, not speaking, but she felt his eyes
on her. Her skin prickled, not unpleasantly, from the attention.

At last they were in front of the cathedral, its expanse of
manicured green lawn stretching out around the towering
Gothic structure, so much taller than it looked from a distance.
More photos from different angles, and then they entered into
the nave of the church with a handful of other Saturday visitors.

The inside possessed a hush, a sense of history undisturbed by time, broken only by soft whispers and the click of shoes on the stone floor. Grace had photographed cathedrals from the Vatican to Notre Dame, all as much tourist attractions as churches, but this magnificent structure also served as a neighborhood place of worship. She stepped aside to switch lenses and clean the glass before she began taking shots of the soaring ceiling, then the left transept. When she lowered the camera, Ian took her hand and tugged her out the door into the cathedral's cloisters, where a long series of Gothic arches formed a repetitive geometric vista down the corridor. More pointed arches framed the garden close in the stone square.

"This is my favorite part," Ian said as the camera went back to her eye, the shutter clicking softly in the quiet.

They made their way around the square, much of the same view, but Grace took advantage of the varying lighting to frame more shots. When Ian lowered himself onto the low ledge that supported the pillars of the arches, she turned the camera on him. "Stay right there."

He leaned back against a column, clearly uncomfortable being the subject of her shot—strange, considering how he had once welcomed the press's attention. She focused on his face, her heart beating a little harder in her chest. She never got used to how handsome he was. It only seemed to highlight their differences. He belonged on that side of the camera, while she preferred to stay behind it. And yet the way he looked back at her now, even through the separation of the lens, made her feel special. Valued. Wanted.

Grace lowered the camera, surprised by the strength of those feelings. She couldn't be thinking this way already, getting invested so soon. She cleared her throat. "Thank you.

This was a lovely surprise. It's been years since I've done something like this. I've been working in war zones for so long, this feels like a holiday."

Ian took her hand as they headed back around the cloister to the cathedral, and rather than feeling strange, it seemed comfortable. Right. "Tell me how exactly you ended up photographing wars."

"You know I always felt pulled to documentary as a career like my brother. It wasn't as easy to break into back then as it is now. These days, journalism students show up on the fringes of war zones with iPhones and manage to sell shots to major news outlets. But when I started out, you had to have an in. I built my portfolio doing editorial work in southeast Asia and India, but the Middle East was where freelancers were making their careers. So I developed my contacts in England, waiting for my chance. And when I got the call from a friend to go to Israel for the summit talks, I couldn't pass it up."

He seemed to be putting together the timeline, the pieces of the story. "That's why you left London."

She nodded, then moved on before they could dive back into uncomfortable topics. "I tagged along with him for a couple of years, shooting on the fringes before I felt ready to be in the thick of things. That's when I met Jean-Auguste."

"Your mentor."

"Yes. He was the one who taught me I had to be measured and careful if I wanted to live long enough to build a career in conflict."

Ian flinched, once more reminding her of the difference in their lives. To anyone accustomed to a normal existence, her attitude must have seemed callous. How could she explain that the need to capture the truth only increased with the danger? That the only way to change what happened in the world was to shine light on it amid the predictable, safe lives of people back home? At least that's what she'd believed.

"He helped me make the leap to serious journalism, introduced me to his contacts. Taught me both the craft and the business. I don't think I realized how much I owed him until I started seeing other young photographers show up, rash and reckless, hell-bent on getting themselves killed. Until then, I didn't understand what I—what all of us, really—were chasing after."

"And what was that?"

"Meaning. A reason God put us here on earth."

Surprise flickered over his face, she assumed because she'd never been particularly religious in her younger years, depending on the brash assurance of youth and stupidity rather than the care of an almighty Father. The pain that quickly followed took her aback, though, and too late she realized what he must think—that she had left because she wasn't happy with him, because he wasn't enough.

She stopped walking. "Ian, you know what Aidan's death did to me and my family. I left Ireland with something to prove, and I couldn't go back until I'd done it. I thought that was something I couldn't do in London."

"So, this was all because you had to prove your father wrong?"

"Maybe a little. But I saw what Aidan did. He believed the truth was important enough to die for. And at some point it became less about proving Dad wrong and more about proving Aidan right."

Ian nodded quietly. He wouldn't push. He never had, just accepted her, neuroses and all. It was no wonder she'd fallen for him. It was no wonder she was dangerously close to doing it again. She felt suddenly light-headed and sank down onto one of the wooden benches against the cloister wall.

"Grace, I'm sorry. I didn't mean to pry." Ian's hand stretched out, but instead of taking hers, his fingertips gently traced the inked designs on her forearm. She yanked her sleeve back down.

"You've never tried to hide them from me," he said quietly. "Why now?"

Because it was a catalog of things she wanted to forget and yet couldn't let herself forget. "I've never understood why you were so fascinated with them. I always figured someone like you would think they were repulsive."

"Someone like me," he murmured. His fingers slid beneath the cuff of her sweater and caressed her skin. His touch sent a shiver straight up her arm and back down her spine. "It's a way to know you, Grace, to understand the things you won't speak of. I know they're not merely decorative."

"No. But I'm done with that. They're from part of my life I need to leave behind if I'm going to move forward."

He studied her face as if he was trying to discern the truth in her words, then stood and held out his hand. "Come on."

She took his hand automatically, and the warm strength in his fingers as they closed around hers did something strange to her chest. They backtracked through the cathedral into the cool afternoon air, where a breeze ruffled their clothing. Clouds had begun to slide over the clear blue sky. Grace itched to take out the camera and snap a few shots.

"Go ahead. I know you want to."

"How do you—?" She broke off when she realized her free hand was already curled around the camera grip.

He made a gesture to proceed and stepped back, his arms

crossed over his chest. With an abashed smile, she knelt so she could vary the angle of the clouds and the trees in the viewfinder. When she glanced up again, he was watching her with a thoughtful look that made her stomach turn flips.

But he only asked, "What do you think? Lunch now?"

"Sure."

He led her across the cathedral lawn and back into Market Square, where he guided her into a two-story restaurant. The hostess led them through the clubby bar area and up a narrow staircase into the half-filled dining room above, where they took their seats at a table that overlooked the market below.

"I have to hand it to you, Ian. You're really good at this."

"At what?" he asked innocently.

"This." She waved a hand. "Twice now, you've managed to put together the perfect date. It's not really fair. How is a girl supposed to resist you?"

"I wasn't under the impression you wanted to." Ian gave her a mischievous expression that was more dangerous than the outing itself. "Seriously, Grace, you deserve a little fun. A reminder of why you loved England in the first place."

"So it's a public service again?"

"No. This is all quite personal."

She suppressed a smile and opened the menu, scanning the offerings before she closed it again. "Old standby. Fish-and-chips."

"Ale?"

"Pass. I think I proved with the sangria last week that my tolerance has gotten shockingly low."

"So that's why you were flirting with me."

"I was not flirting!" She chuckled at his raised eyebrows. "Okay, I might have been flirting a little. But I can assure you, it had nothing to do with the wine."

A server came to take their order, then disappeared again. Grace watched the people milling about below, buying fresh fruit and vegetables from the farmers' stands, looking over handcrafted art pieces and garden ornaments. "This is why I love photography."

"Because you love squash?"

Grace made a face. "Look at it. This moment will never happen again. All these people, together in one place. Change a single thing and it wouldn't be this moment. Wait five minutes and everything is different. But a photo—it's the only way you can stop time. It's proof of a moment you can never get back."

"You have a unique way of looking at the world, you know that?"

She shook her head, embarrassed. "Too much time alone, thinking. Too much time looking through a viewfinder."

They moved on to other topics, nothing too serious, nothing significant. All the while, Grace's thoughts were spinning. This was lovely. Normal. Utterly unremarkable. She felt more relaxed and happy than she could remember being in years. Even in Paris, she'd always felt on edge, like she was waiting for the next excuse to leave. It might have been headquarters, but it had never felt like home.

When their meal was at last finished, Ian paid, and they made their way down the stairs to the pub below. As they wound between the polished oak tables, a scatter of newsprint caught her eye.

She paused and lifted a section, the blood draining from her face. On the front page, above the fold, a photo and headline proclaimed an outbreak of violence in Syria. She automatically checked the photo credit. Sergio Medina.

Ian peered over her shoulder. "What is it?"

She swallowed. "I would have been here. This was supposed to be my assignment. Sergio took my place."

Ian's brow furrowed. "Why didn't you go then?"

Because I froze. I had a panic attack in the airport and couldn't even get past the ticket counter. It was the first time she'd admitted it to herself, even in her head.

"Grace?"

She realized he was still waiting for an answer. She dropped the paper on the table and sidled away from it. "It doesn't matter."

"Clearly it does. Why won't you tell me?" Ian caught up with her in a few long strides as she broke out onto the pavement. "What am I missing?"

Grace swallowed down the lump in her throat and rounded on him. "I'm not quitting because I want to. I'm quitting because I have to."

"I don't understand."

"I'm not capable of doing it anymore." Until now, she'd almost believed if she avoided saying it aloud, it wouldn't be true. "I thought I was dealing with it. Thought I could go back. But I couldn't get on the plane."

Ian's expression softened to one of sympathy. "How long has this been going on?"

"Three months." Ever since Brian died in front of her. She started walking again to avoid seeing the look on Ian's face, whether sympathy or disappointment. She didn't want either.

His hand found hers, and she didn't pull away, even though she didn't grip it back. "Have you seen someone about it?"

"You mean a shrink? Or a priest? Because I've seen both. Neither were any help. The first put me on a bunch of medication that made me feel worse. The other told me I would get over it when I had enough faith for God to heal me. So I did the only thing I could do. I ran away."

"Surely you don't blame yourself. Grace, after all you've experienced—"

"You don't understand. I'm a war photographer who can't photograph wars. What does that make me?"

"It makes you exactly what you've always been. Your talent is in your way of looking at the world. It doesn't matter if you're shooting conflicts or market scenes. Just because you've always photographed war doesn't mean you can't do something else."

"What if I don't want to do something else? It's not like I'm giving up some boring office job to go to another boring office job. What I did was *important*. It had meaning. And now . . ." She shook her head. "You couldn't possibly understand."

"So what? Everything you said to me was a lie? All the talk about doubting your path, questioning the cost? That was what you thought I wanted to hear? Tell me, Grace, because I feel like I'm seeing two different people here."

She realized their raised voices were drawing attention and tugged him down the street. "No. That's all true. I've questioned it for years. I've wondered if the sacrifices were worth it."

"Then I don't understand why it hurts you so much to think about leaving it behind."

Grace pressed her fingers to her eyes, trying to find the words to explain. "If I quit, it's like they've won. They killed Aidan and they killed Brian and they made me leave. And no matter what I do from now on, I'll feel like a failure."

Too late, she saw the hurt in his eyes, realized how it must sound to him. She'd built him up, made it seem like she was back for him, and now she was telling him once more he was not enough. "Ian, I didn't mean—"

"No. You meant it. You meant it now, just like you meant it when you left." He released her hand, a muscle pulsing in his jaw. "I may not know what it's like to live in a war zone. But I know what it's like to let go of something I loved. For someone I loved more. And that's apparently what *you* can't understand."

A flush of shame heated her cheeks. "Ian—"

"Come on. I'll take you home." He didn't reach for her hand this time, and the foot of space separating them might as well have been a mile. By the time they reached the car park, Grace felt as cold as the wind that whipped around them. Ian unlocked the Healey for her and opened the door, but he left the top up. Grace clasped her hands in her lap, staring blindly through the windscreen.

They spent the drive back to London with only the drone of the radio and the snap of the wind against the roadster's soft top for company. When he pulled up outside her building, they both sat silently.

"Ian, I'm sorry. I didn't mean—"

He silenced her with a slight shake of his head. "I'm not mad at you, Grace. Not really. I just thought—" He cut himself off with another annoyed shake. "You need to decide what you want. I'm not going to try to convince you. I'm not going to chase you."

It was so much kinder than she deserved. She swallowed and chewed her lip to keep the tears from coming. "Thanks for the trip. The car's a beauty."

"Yes, she is."

Grace gave him one more nod, then climbed the steps to the door without looking back. She heard Ian put the roadster into gear and pull away from the curb into traffic.

He may have said it was her decision, but somehow it felt like he had made it for her.

Ian returned the Healey to the car park, the tension in his clenched jaw making his face and neck ache. He drew the cover over the roadster, careful to let only the chamois lining touch the mirrorlike paint job.

Looking at the car had given him hope that not all damage was permanent, that broken things could be restored with time and love and attention. Maybe that only went for cars, not people. The attraction between him and Grace was still there, but maybe that was all it was, the gleam of varnish over a rusted shell of a relationship.

He should have expected as much. Maybe Chris and his mum were right. Maybe his refusal to date normal, ordinary women was just a refusal to commit. If he really wanted a relationship, wouldn't someone like Rachel or the lawyer be a better choice? No drama, no traumatic past, no need to prove her worth. With that sort of woman, he could have a perfectly happy life. Pleasant. Undemanding. Safe.

And yet in the two weeks since Grace had returned to London, he'd felt more alive than he had in the past ten years.

He walked back to his Gloucester Road flat, where he changed into a pair of shorts and headed straight for his spare room, which housed his weights and rowing machine. Despite his furious energy, he forced himself through stretches before he climbed onto the ergometer.

With every pull, his mind felt a little clearer. Maybe Grace had it right. He had lost something of himself, too, but maybe that something wasn't her. He'd abandoned all his own goals, first for Grace, then for Jamie and his mum. And for what? To end up almost forty years old and alone, in a job that more than paid the bills but bored him to tears?

Grace's words came back to him, diffusing some of his anger. She had been searching for meaning too, the reason she existed on this earth. Rather than stay in London and let herself stagnate, she'd gone out and found her sense of purpose. He could have used her departure as a challenge to do the same, but instead he'd let himself be smothered in a meaningless, rote existence. Wake up, row, go to work, lift weights, go to bed. Repeat, maybe with an occasional trip to the pub or a family visit. It was as if the uniformity of his rowing had permeated every part of his life. Precise. Measured. Do everything the same way each time. Get the results you expect by the technique you put in. No room for uncertainty or creativity or thought, no room for anything but perfection.

Grace wasn't perfect. She was messy, passionate, unpredictable. That's what he'd always loved about her. That's why his life had never felt complete without her.

Ian stopped abruptly after the monitor registered one kilometer, then collapsed onto his back on the floor. The sound of his own panting and the whir of the erg's fan as it slowed closed in around him. He stared at the ceiling as if some divine answer were written there.

Maybe Grace had been right to leave. Had she stayed, she would have been smothered by his boring, bleak existence, doing nothing of importance. The niggling feeling grew to a crushing weight, squeezing out a bitter laugh.

Ironic. Stay or go, Grace was once more in the center of the wreckage of his life.

CHAPTER TWELVE

ASHA'S FLAT WAS FAR TOO QUIET. Grace flicked on the television for company, then turned it right back off. She paced a few times between the door and the kitchen, a sick feeling in her stomach.

She'd screwed it up. No doubt about it. Yes, she was still ambivalent about giving up conflict photography—okay, heartbroken. But the dream this morning had said it all. Her issues weren't going to resolve themselves anytime soon. Her therapist had been useless, and as she told Ian, antidepressants and antipsychotics only made her alternately anxious and suicidal, the two things she'd been trying to avoid.

Likewise, church hadn't helped. It had only made her feel

more broken and alone. Not because of God—there was comfort in the familiarity of Scripture, the childhood faith she'd retained even through her wild youth and begun to return to in the past few years—but because of the parishioners and the priests. They'd looked at her tattoos and her career choices and concluded she was to blame for her own trauma. There was no way they could possibly understand what she'd been through or how it had affected her.

Like it or not, that part of her life was over. The sooner she accepted it, the sooner she could begin building a new one. A life she had hoped might include Ian.

And it could have, had she not so artlessly conveyed that he wasn't reason enough to leave her former life behind.

In the past she would have sought to relieve this terrible feeling in a self-destructive way. But it wasn't an option. That life was dead, even further in her past than the death of her career. It was one thing she didn't want back.

Her eyes fell on her duffel bag, which lay open from her preparations this morning. Near the top was an ugly green-and-yellow tote bag, from which peeked an even uglier ball of red, blue, and white yarn.

Therapy. Or at least that was the idea. She'd picked up the yarn and needles on a whim and never looked at them again, even though her Irish grandmother had taught her to knit as a girl. God only knew why she had brought them.

Well, maybe that was exactly right. She climbed under a fuzzy blanket on the sofa and dragged the tote onto her lap.

That was how Asha found her hours later, holding the beginnings of a sock from which pointy sticks jutted in all directions. Asha tossed her keys on the table and hung up her coat. "What on earth are you doing?"

Grace looked up and forced a smile. "What does it look like I'm doing? I'm wrestling an octopus by one leg."

Asha chuckled and flopped down on the sofa beside her. "I never took you for a knitter."

"Makeshift therapy," Grace said with a grimace. "It's supposed to help control the impulse toward stupidity."

"I can see that. What I can't understand is why you'd choose wool that looks like clown vomit."

"It's patriotic! The color is called Union Jack."

"You're not British."

"Would you rather I have gone for my own patriotic colors of orange, white, and green?"

Asha pretended to shudder. "No, thank you. Color choices aside, why the sudden need for wool therapy?"

Grace lowered the porcupine in her hands to her lap. "Ian took me to Salisbury this morning."

"How'd it go?"

"Complete disaster. They could write self-help books about this relationship. Not that there is a relationship."

"Oh, there's a relationship, whether you want to acknowledge it or not. That tends to happen when two people are still in love with each other but refuse to admit it."

Grace picked up her needles again and focused on the tiny stitches. "I don't think admitting it is the problem."

"Then why are you sitting here and torturing yourself with your knitting, pining for a man you could have if only you weren't so stubborn?"

"It has nothing to do with being stubborn. I screwed things up. It was a beautiful day, everything was going great, and then I basically told him he had nothing to do with my return to London—that I was only back because I was forced to retire."

"Oh, sweetie. Why didn't you tell me that's why you came back?"

Grace held up her knitting in response. Asha sighed. "So, what now?"

"With Ian? I don't know. He wants a guarantee, some sort of commitment, and I don't know if I can give that. I'm still figuring out where to go next, what to do with my life."

"Did he tell you that?" Asha asked, eyes narrowing. "Or are you assuming?"

"It's pretty clear he wants me to commit to staying in London."

"Well, of course he does. Why wouldn't he?" Asha abruptly pushed off the sofa and wandered to the kitchen. She returned with an open bag of crisps and tilted them in Grace's direction.

Grace shook her head.

"Listen, I don't know if all this ridiculous back-and-forth is your twisted courtship ritual or what. But two weeks ago, you were desperate for him to give you a second chance, and now that he gives you one, you sabotage it?"

Grace didn't look at her. "I thought you'd be on my side."

"I'm on the side that's going to make you happy, Grace. I love you."

"You're acting like I'm not trying. I am. But how can I reassure him I'm going to stay when I don't even know myself?"

Asha perched on the edge of the seat and took one of Grace's hands. "Sweetie, tell me what you're really afraid of here."

A lump rose in her throat. What was she afraid of? Why was she so reluctant to give her life here a second chance? "I already ruined things with us once. What if I try again and it's not enough? I can't do that to him again. I can't do that to me again."

"Grace, if I know Ian, he's not asking you for forever right now. Why are you overthinking this?"

Asha made it sound simple.

Well, why couldn't it be?

Asha smiled, obviously seeing that she was getting through to her. "I tell you what. I'll get takeaway and then we'll combine our feminine wiles and figure out the best way for you to grovel your way back into his good graces. Which do you want, fish-and-chips or shawarma?"

"Shawarma, definitely. I've had enough fish-and-chips for one day."

"I'll be back, then." Asha grabbed her coat and pocketbook and paused near the door. "It'll work out, Grace. You'll see."

Grace picked up her mangled knitting, then tossed it aside. Yes, she'd take a chance. But after what happened today, would he?

The next day, Grace hesitated outside Ian's flat, her hand poised inches from the door. Maybe she shouldn't have come unannounced. He was usually home on Sunday evenings, but who was to say he hadn't gone out?

Cowardly thoughts, all of them. She rapped on the door with more confidence than she felt, shifting the heavy, insulated containers to her other hip. She and Asha had decided dinner was safest. He would never turn down her cooking.

But no scrape of chains or rattle of dead bolts came on the other side. She'd never been to his new place—had she gotten the address wrong? She knocked harder the second time. Nothing.

She was a fool, not just for coming unannounced, but for thinking he was sitting around waiting for her. She turned back to the stairs, but before she could set foot on the first step, the door opened behind her. "Grace?"

She turned and paused midstep on the landing. Ian stood in the doorway, shirtless and breathing hard, his mobile phone strapped to one arm and earphones dangling from his hand.

She stared at him for several seconds before she could manage words. "Am I interrupting you? I knocked a few times."

"I was on the erg. I didn't hear you right away over the music. What's up?"

Grace's stomach did a backflip. He wasn't acting as if he harbored any ill feelings toward her, but she wouldn't have called his tone welcoming either. She held up the containers. "I brought dinner. Call it a peace offering."

He frowned as if considering, then straightened and nudged the door all the way open. She stepped inside.

Their place in Islington had been the typical bachelor pad with its mismatched furniture and bare walls. The Gloucester Road flat, on the other hand, was elegant and sophisticated, decorated in a spare, clean-lined Scandinavian style—grays, whites, and black with pops of color here and there. Framed photography and modern art decorated the pristine ivory walls. Somehow, it surprised her. Not that his tastes had matured, but that a traditionalist like him would favor such a restrained, contemporary style.

"Nice flat," she said. "Not what I expected."

He was still looking at her with that same cautious expression—neither angry nor open. "You didn't come to admire the flat. Why are you really here?"

He was going to make her say it, standing in the foyer while holding two hot bowls of food. She looked around for rescue and finally off-loaded them onto the small table that held a stack of mail. "I came to apologize. You did something nice for me, and I ruined it. I was insensitive and didn't think about what I said before I said it."

He wiped a hand over his face in what could have been weariness or exasperation. "Here's the thing, Grace. I'm not angry with you. I told you that yesterday. But I don't want to be anyone's consolation prize. I don't want you to be with me just because you can't do the thing you love most. I deserve more than that. *You* deserve more than that."

The words pierced as they struck. "Ian, I could have gone anywhere in the world to start over, but I came to London. Because of you." Her heart thumped so hard she was pretty sure he could see it. "I'm still figuring out what my life should look like now, but you're not my consolation prize."

His eyes darkened, and he took a step toward her. He'd only kissed her once, but the anticipation was enough to send her pulse into overdrive. She closed her eyes as his head dipped toward hers, aching for the proof that reality was as good as her memories.

But the kiss never came. Instead, the latch of the door clicked near her ear.

Grace's eyes snapped open. "What—?"

"We're going to finish this conversation, but first I need a shower." He flashed a wry twist of a smile. "And proper clothes."

"You're a tease."

He bent again, and this time, his breath brushed her cheek, raising a shiver on her skin. "Not a tease. Just not in a hurry. Make yourself at home." He stepped away from her, then strode toward his bedroom.

She chewed her bottom lip to stop her grin, allowing herself an appreciative look before he disappeared. No, he wasn't nearly as staid and conservative as he liked to pretend. But the hot-blooded athlete she remembered would have pushed her against the wall and kissed her senseless after that declaration. And they probably wouldn't have gotten round to dinner at all.

Maybe it was good they'd both developed some restraint. Their first relationship had progressed so quickly, it had become easier to fuel their connection with the physical rather than own up to the emotions beneath it. Clearly, if they were going to have a second chance, it had to be based on more than chemistry.

She moved into the small, modern kitchen, taking stock of the space, then opened a cabinet above the dishwasher. Sure enough, the plates and glasses were there, just as they'd been in the Islington flat. That would mean the flatware was to the right of the sink. She smiled when she found the neat array of cutlery. Some things didn't change.

Grace set the table and unpacked the two containers of food onto ceramic trivets, then wandered back into the reception room. A short hallway led to the bedrooms and bath. She bypassed Ian's room and wandered into the spare he had set up as a gym. A weight bench with a rack of free weights stood in one corner, while his rowing machine took up the center of the room. On the far side lay his trophy wall, displaying a collection of shadow-boxed medals and framed photos.

There were several pictures of Ian with his Cambridge crewmates in their iconic light-blue blazers, along with framed newspaper articles showing the outcomes of the five Oxford and Cambridge Boat Races he'd rowed in—four wins, one loss. Five world championship gold medals from his time on the British national team, one in the juniors and four more in men's and veterans' classes. And in the place of honor in the middle, his framed Olympic silver medal.

Grace remembered when he had won that, or lost the gold, as he regarded it. Three full boat lengths ahead of bronze, and yet it was the half-second behind gold that had haunted him. He felt he'd let down his teammates, even though it had been years since Great Britain had won an Olympic gold in rowing.

He'd been brilliant back then: driven, confident in his own skills, maybe a little cocky. But he'd also understood how fortunate he was to succeed at something he loved. And then he'd proposed to Grace and decided he needed to do something steady and responsible. The nonstop training wasn't conducive to a happy marriage, he'd said, as if he weren't giving up something he'd worked for his entire life.

Had it not been for her, there might be an Olympic gold on that wall.

"Ready to eat?"

Grace started at Ian's voice over her shoulder. She'd been so enwrapped in her thoughts that she hadn't heard the shower turn off or noticed him enter the room. He put a tentative hand on her waist, and she leaned back against him, the faint, masculine scent of his favorite soap and aftershave enveloping her. It instantly brought back the memory of late nights years ago when he'd slip into bed after she'd fallen asleep, wrapping his arms around her beneath crisp sheets. She closed her eyes and inhaled the memory.

But that was another life. She straightened abruptly and turned to him. "Dinner?"

"Sure. Dinner." He followed her back to the kitchen, pausing to turn on the stereo on the way to the dinner table. Grace lifted the lids on the containers of rice and stew as he came up behind her.

"Smells wonderful. What is it?"

"My famous tikka masala."

Ian took the serving spoon from her hand. "You don't pull punches, do you? I've been to every Indian restaurant in London trying to find something this good and failed miserably."

"It's the cardamom. Most restaurants don't use enough." She watched him as he served their food. In a simple T-shirt and tracksuit bottoms, his hair wet from the shower, he looked worlds away from the executive in the bespoke tuxedo. This was the Ian she remembered—casual, relaxed, smiling. Almost unbearably handsome. That didn't change with his wardrobe.

"You and Jamie used to drive me mad, trying to deconstruct every dish when we ate out."

"I remember. He was more insufferable than me by far, but he was usually right."

Ian smiled. Then his expression grew serious. "I think I owe you an apology, Grace. I know how much you love your work. I know how hard it must be to leave it behind." He hesitated. "I also know people suffering from traumatic stress have an even more difficult time adjusting to a normal life."

She combed her fingers through her hair, bowing her head against the acute prick of embarrassment. "You've been reading mental health websites."

"Grace, I care about you—"

"I know. But just like you don't want to be my consolation prize, I don't want to be your rehabilitation project. Whatever my issues are, they aren't *me*. I'm not a victim. My decision to leave the field has been a long time in coming. Even Jean-Auguste always warned me about staying too long." She held out her wrist to display the detailed green dragon that encircled it. "His favorite quote is 'He who fights too long against dragons becomes a dragon himself—'"

"'And if you gaze long enough into the abyss, the abyss will gaze into you.' It's Nietzsche. You think your work has changed you?"

"I know it's changed me," Grace said softly. "You can't see all the suffering and violence and hatred without wondering if there's still good in the world. Most of my colleagues see evil as proof that God couldn't exist. But despite all the bad, there are still people who help others when their safety, their very lives are at risk. When I see that, I know without a doubt He has to exist. I think without God the good that remains couldn't survive."

Ian reached for her hand across the table and brushed his thumb over her tattoo. "If you can still see the good, why fear the dragon?"

"Because I realized Jean-Auguste is right. Every day, the abyss looks back a little longer." She held his eyes, willed him to understand that even as she mourned her old life, she was embracing something better, something that wouldn't chip away at her belief in hope and happiness.

Something that, deep down, she wanted to share with him.

He released her hand, the absence coming sharp like a physical pain. But he simply circled round to the chair beside her and took her face in his hands. "I know you are not a victim, Grace. You are a strong, caring, talented woman."

The way he was looking at her made her chest seize. She reached for humor out of reflex. "You forgot beautiful."

A smile flickered across his lips and put a new light into his eyes. "Oh no, I didn't forget beautiful." He brushed the lightest kiss across her lips. "Or sexy." Another kiss at the corner of her mouth. "Or tempting." He pulled back long enough to stare into her eyes, his intensity making her breath hitch and her insides twist with longing.

Without a doubt, she still loved him. And for the first time since her return, she believed there was a chance he could love her again too. She tipped her head to his forehead, breathing him in, embracing the hope that there might be something to salvage from the wreck of their past. And then he was kissing her again, while the stew cooled on the table and the years between them slipped away.

CHAPTER THIRTEEN

IAN WAS LATE TO WORK for the first time in years.

Last night, he and Grace had finally gotten back to their supper when it became clear how little it would take to reignite the flicker of desire into a full-fledged bonfire. Their reunion was too new and too fragile to endure the temptation. Instead, they had stayed up late, music turned on low while they talked with her feet in his lap, as if no time had passed. Then he'd insisted on seeing her home, which led to a rather lengthy good-bye in the hall outside Asha's flat.

All only tangentially related to his lateness, except that he'd been too distracted to set his alarm. He'd slept through his morning outing and woken at half eight, with just time enough to throw on clothes, comb his hair, and hail a taxi, which had been a mistake considering the London morning traffic. The Tube would have been faster.

Fortunately, his morning schedule was relatively clear, allowing him to begin calling Ms. Grey's references personally. Of all the candidates he'd seen the previous week, she remained the most qualified and the most stable. Still, there was an element of danger in hiring because of Jamie's celebrity status. It was Ian's job to fully vet anyone who would have any contact with Jamie, his finances, or their family. But every supervisor he spoke with said the same thing. Ms. Grey was dependable, logical, and dedicated to her work in a way that bordered on obsessive. A creative problem-solver, good with people, the type that should have been well on her way to an executive position. What had happened to make her leave a managerial position at one of London's largest firms without a reference?

He certainly wouldn't get a straight answer from the firm itself. Instead he sorted through his contacts. He didn't know anyone at Walker and Brown, but he had gone to university with the vice president of the independent auditing firm that worked with them and every other major financial services company in London.

"Ian!" Alexander picked up on the second ring in his syncopated London accent. "Long time, mate. How are you?"

"Good. Yourself? Finally made VP, I hear."

"Long time in coming, that. You calling for business or just to catch up?"

"Actually, I was hoping you could get me some information on a potential hire. Abigail Grey, most recently at Walker and Brown. She left about six months ago and won't say why."

"Grey, right. Senior financial examiner. Sharp woman.

I worked with her on the last two audits, but I hadn't realized she left. Want me to see what I can find out?"

"If you would." Ian paused. "Heard you got married recently. How's married life treating you the second time round?"

"Good. Hoping this time it will stick, you know? The hours aren't exactly conducive to romance. What about you?"

Ian let himself smile a little. "Dating someone."

"Past time you settled down. We're getting old."

"Yeah, I'm aware of that. Let me know what you find out."

Ian hung up, then began to go through his overflowing e-mail in-box. His mobile phone beeped beside him. A text message from Grace.

Lunch today? Miss you already. (Lame, I know.)

He grinned and texted back: Wish I could. Dinner later?

A few seconds later, her reply: Asha's working late. Come by and I'll cook.

That was something to look forward to. Grace clearly knew his weakness for her cooking.

He went back to his in-box with slightly more enthusiasm. The weekend's new mail was about finished when his direct line rang.

"Ian, Alexander here. I talked to my friend at Walker. No one really knows what happened. Abigail Grey was a private woman."

"Surely there were rumors."

"Rumors, yes. Sounds like she's a single mother and her daughter has health problems, so she definitely didn't leave by choice."

"So . . ."

Alexander hesitated. "No one is saying anything, but no

other female executive has lasted in that department more than two years. Everyone has quit or been transferred. Ms. Grey lasted more than twice that time, but . . ."

Definitely suspicious, and it hinted at some sort of harassment. Just because there were laws against these things didn't mean they still didn't happen. "Nothing to indicate impropriety or criminal behavior or anything like that?"

"Not remotely. Everyone suspects she was driven out."

"Fair enough. Thanks for the help."

"Anytime, mate. Nice to talk."

Ian hung up the phone. His instincts said she was the right hire, and this information seemed to confirm it. He hesitated over her CV before he picked up the phone and dialed her. She answered on the third ring.

"Ms. Grey, I'd like to offer you the job. I'm e-mailing you a formal offer letter now, but I'd like to have you start as soon as possible."

"May I review the offer and get back to you?"

"Of course." She was cautious, and Ian couldn't blame her. "I'll look forward to your decision."

Which was an understatement, considering she was the only candidate who had a chance of lasting more than a week. Maybe people assumed working for the company of a celebrity chef would be glamorous, when in reality, it was mostly boring, dry business details. Clearly Ms. Grey hadn't gone into finance for the excitement.

He sent off the letter, then turned to another stack of paperwork, hoping his offer had been aggressive enough to snag her.

Alexander was right. They were getting old, and his workaholic tendencies weren't conducive to maintaining a relationship. He would do what it took not to lose Grace again, and that included getting help in the office.

Once the workday was over, he resisted the urge to skip his workout and forced himself through a grueling weight circuit that made him wish he'd gone straight to see Grace after all. By the time he made it to Asha's place, he could barely contain his anticipation.

She let him up when he buzzed at the intercom, but he found the door on the latch when he reached the flat. Cautiously he entered.

The low pulsing thrum of electric bass filled the interior as music poured from a small set of speakers in the living room. He paused at the edge of the kitchen, a smile twitching his lips as he watched Grace stir something at the stove while she sang along with "Bullet the Blue Sky."

"U2, huh?"

She glanced over her shoulder with a mischievous expression that melted his insides. "They're Irish. Which automatically makes them brilliant."

He stepped up behind her and slid his arms around her waist. She shivered as he dropped small kisses from her ear to her shoulder. "Hold that thought," she said. "The risotto's almost done."

He leaned against the counter while she added grated Parmesan and gave it a final stir. "There. Mushroom risotto with sautéed shrimp."

He stepped closer. "Am I allowed now?"

"No." She stretched up on tiptoes to snatch a light kiss and then darted out of reach. "Risotto is only good while it's hot. Take a seat."

"Yes, ma'am." He watched her while she served their food,

every bit as comfortable in the kitchen as she was with a camera. "You know, a man could get used to this."

"Don't get *too* used to it. I'm not exactly the domestic type."

"You could at least let me dream." He dug into the risotto—a touch gummy but still delicious—and asked, "What did you do today?"

"Very little, actually. Had breakfast with Asha and spent the afternoon with Melvin at the gallery."

"Lady of leisure."

"Indeed. It was nice. What about you?"

"I found an assistant. Assuming she accepts my offer."

"Oh? Is she pretty?"

"She's very professional." Ian studied her. Was Grace jealous? That was completely unlike her. Then she broke into a grin and he relaxed.

"Just having a laugh. And I'm sure she's pretty, but I also know that you are far too serious to notice those things."

"Am I?" He grabbed the support rail beneath the seat of her chair and dragged it over to him to put her lips within reach. Only when she wrapped an arm around his neck to steady herself did he draw back. "Because I noticed that you've gone shopping, and you look pretty fantastic in those jeans."

Pink tinged her cheeks, but she held his eye. "Risotto, remember? Getting cold."

"Right." He hid his smile when she scooted her chair to its proper place. "I do love risotto. It's a little labor intensive for a weeknight, isn't it?"

"I needed a distraction. I've got an interview tomorrow."

"With CAF? When did that happen?"

"I finally dug up the business card and called Kenneth DeVries today. He wants to see me tomorrow morning."

"So you're really doing it." Even though it was just a preliminary interview, the decision had significance, especially coming on the heels of their tumultuous weekend.

"I'm not entirely sure CAF is the right fit for me, but staying in London? Yes. I'm giving it a go." She looked at him, breath held, and he realized she wanted his approval, an acknowledgment of the decision she was making.

He reached for her hand and squeezed it hard. "They'd be lucky to have you. If they're smart, they'll make as good a case for the organization as you will for yourself. And it doesn't hurt to be in a relationship with a member of the board of directors."

She laughed, her green eyes sparkling in a way that made his chest clench. "Is that what this is? A relationship?"

"What do you think?" He lifted her hand and kissed her palm, gratified by the sudden quickening of her breath.

"I think someone is trying to wheedle seconds from me."

"Well, if you're offering . . ."

Grace laughed and took his bowl back to the range. "Any tips for tomorrow?"

"Grace, you're a shoo-in. You impressed everyone at the benefit—and don't think winning over their wives doesn't work in your favor. All you have to do is reiterate what you already told them, and I suspect the job is yours."

She nodded, but the way she worried her lower lip was a sign of anxiety. Surely a simple job interview didn't make her nervous. Maybe she wasn't sure CAF was the right place for her.

It was far more comfortable to believe her uncertainty centered on the job rather than on him.

CHAPTER FOURTEEN

"WHY ARE YOU NERVOUS?"

Grace didn't meet Asha's eye as she discarded the third blouse of the morning. Ninety minutes until the job interview, and she still hadn't decided what to wear. She reached for choice number four. "I'm not nervous exactly, just . . . Okay, fine, I'm nervous. What if I completely muck it up?"

"What if you do? It's not like you need the money right away. And you can still set up shoots for the autumn if you need to."

Grace slid a white silk blouse over her head, noting the wrinkles across the front, and slipped her black suit jacket back on. "It's not that, Ash, it's just—"

"You're making an effort for Ian. Isn't that what this is

about?" Asha slid from the bed and came up behind her in the mirror.

Asha was always too perceptive to slip anything by her. "His life is here in London. If we're going to make a relationship work, it would help to spend more than a few days at a time in the same city. And that means I get a real job. I don't want to spend the rest of my life shooting weddings. I want to be involved in something that makes an impact. CAF seems to be the best of both worlds."

Asha put both hands on Grace's shoulders. "They would be crazy not to take you. But this blouse? It's not happening. You might as well go in with a noose wrapped round your neck." She bent and rummaged through the open duffel bag that still served as Grace's wardrobe and pulled out a plain green T-shirt. "Here."

The cotton replaced the silk, with the jacket over top. Asha handed her a necklace made of multiple strands of glass beads. "Jewelry, then roll up the sleeves so you can see the watch."

"Don't you think I should cover up the tattoos?"

"That ship sailed at the benefit." Asha grinned and smoothed down the necklace. "There. Now you look like the artistic type who's going to take them into the twenty-first century. I'd say it's an improvement."

Grace glanced in the mirror and blinked. Asha was right. She looked more casual, but still put together, a conservative black suit paired with the T-shirt, Asha's fashionably chunky watch, and the flashy necklace. She reached out and slid her arm around her friend's waist. "Thanks, Asha. I probably should go. Being late won't make a great impression."

She slid her feet into her single pair of dress shoes, low-heeled patent leather, grabbed her oversize bag and portfolio, and headed for ground level. She found herself praying as the heels of her shoes clicked against the concrete of the road outside.

God, please don't let me mess this one up. You know how hard I want to make this work. Please, just . . . help me get through this with my dignity intact.

She chuckled as she descended the stairs into the Tube station, realizing that not once had she asked God to help her get the job. If that wasn't ambivalence toward the situation, she didn't know what was. She needed this job, of course. It was an essential step in making a more settled lifestyle work, in making this relationship work. She would not be the bohemian photographer wife of a rich executive—

Wife? Where had that come from? She and Ian had been back together for less than two weeks. They'd done some kissing and catching up, but they hadn't delved into anything more serious. After what she had put him through, she wouldn't blame him if he never fully trusted her again.

And yet that single word—*wife*—could fill her with a longing for something she hadn't even known she wanted. For a lifestyle she wasn't sure she was capable of maintaining.

She plugged in her headphones while she waited for the train, the platform filling in around her. At a high-enough volume, the Ramones worked well to drown out the thoughts in her head. Before she could think better of it, she pulled out her phone and texted Ian: On my way to interview. Think I'm gonna be sick.

Make sure you sick up in the potted palm then. Kenneth DeVries wears expensive shoes.

Grace grinned at Ian's complete lack of sympathy. Thanks so much for the support.

No problem. You'll be brilliant. I promise. Just tell him why this means so much to you.

She bit her lip against her smile and tucked the phone back into her pocket, his support—flippant as it may have been—thawing the cold lump of anxiety in her chest. When was the last time she'd had someone in her corner? Someone who was as invested in her happiness as he was his own? She'd had relationships over the years, but they'd been more out of convenience and mutual necessity, formed in the chaos of conflict when the only thing that had anchored her to reality was a warm body next to her in bed. War photographers could be an odd lot, alternating between solitary and overly trusting, but they were terrible at commitment when they knew each assignment could be their last.

Maybe that's why Grace made a phenomenal journalist but a crummy fiancée.

She let the flow of people carry her onto the carriage when the train stopped at the platform and wrapped her fingers around a sticky rail as it jolted forward. Things were going to change. She could get a job that utilized both her experience and her passion and put behind her the nomadic lifestyle that had made attachment so difficult.

At Westminster, she made the change to Jubilee, which dove beneath the Thames and emptied out at her destination, Canary Wharf. As she rode the escalator up to street level, her heart started thumping again. Even now, she thought she would be less nervous in the deserts of Iraq than in this jungle of concrete, steel, and glass that made up London's second-biggest financial district.

But the bright sunlight streaming in through the arched glass canopy of the Tube exit comforted her, as did Jubilee

Park's unexpected swath of green. When she at last reached her destination—an enormous, intimidating skyscraper in Canada Square topped with a pyramidal glass roof—she was a full twenty minutes early. She took a moment to gather herself on the pavement outside before pushing through the glass doors into the building.

Acres of marble, glass, and brass surrounded her. She didn't look around, just made her way steadily through the trickle of suited businesspeople to a bank of lifts, where she climbed on and punched the number for her floor. It seemed odd for a charity to be housed in one of the premier business buildings in the financial district, but considering the amount of money that flowed through the organization each year, perhaps it made sense.

CAF's bright and open reception area, however, was far less posh than the building itself would have led her to believe. An Asian woman with a long ponytail draped over one shoulder smiled at her as she entered. "May I help you?"

"Grace Brennan to see Kenneth DeVries."

"Of course, Ms. Brennan. If you'll take a seat, Mr. DeVries will be with you shortly."

Grace nodded, then wandered back to a comfortable grouping of armchairs, but she didn't sit. Her insides were still too jittery to trust. When her eyes lit on a large palm in a ceramic planter, she barely stifled her grin. So Ian wasn't just having a laugh at her expense.

"Grace!"

She turned. Rather than Mr. DeVries, it was Henry Symon who came to greet her, positively beaming.

"Good morning, Henry. I didn't expect to see you here."

"I'm joining you and Kenneth today. Make sure he knows

exactly why he needs to hire you." He shot her a puckish grin, and Grace laughed, her nervousness dissolving as he beckoned her. "Come on through to the back."

Grace followed Henry through the reception area and down a plainly decorated hall to a large office. Behind a gleaming wood desk piled high with folios and stacks of paperwork sat Kenneth DeVries. After their introduction at the benefit, she'd been anticipating a suit, not this ordinary-looking man in chinos and a windowpane-check dress shirt.

"Ms. Brennan, welcome." He rose to shake her hand, then gestured to one of the seats opposite his desk. "Have a seat. You too, Henry."

DeVries studied her for a moment and then smiled. "I'll admit I never thought we'd succeed in getting you here."

"That makes two of us. Thank you for seeing me on such short notice."

"Of course. Now, what do you have for me?"

Grace reached into her bag for her book and handed it over. He flipped open the cover and immediately his eyebrows rose. "This is gorgeous. Until I did my research, I hadn't realized how many of your photographs I'd seen. These were where, Nigeria?"

"Cameroon."

He kept turning pages. She watched his facial expression and body language until he finally closed the book. "There's no doubt you're an extraordinary talent. You're still in high demand for conflicts. Why work for an NGO now?"

A loaded question if ever there was one. But he wanted the surface-level answer. "Times change. People mature. Quite frankly, I'm feeling like it's time to settle down, but somehow shooting weddings and births doesn't feel like a viable option."

"I'd think not. Well, there would be some travel involved, but the creative director primarily works with our marketing and publicity team, reporting to Henry here. I trust you had a chance to review the job responsibilities my assistant e-mailed you?"

"I did. I've worked with publications in one capacity or another for fifteen years, even if it was from the other side of the desk, so I'm familiar with the process. I'm certain that I'm more than capable of doing the job."

"I have no doubt that you are." DeVries set her book aside. "Do you have your CV?"

She found the double-sided sheet inside a folder in her bag and handed it to him, cursing the little tremor in her hand. It was not that she was ashamed of her life's work—quite the opposite, in fact—but her qualifications were much better displayed in a portfolio than on a sheet of paper.

"Ah, it says here you attended Leeds College of Art. Good photography program. No graduation date, though?"

"No. I left to work as a photographer's assistant in Los Angeles. It was an opportunity I couldn't pass up." He didn't need to know that leaving school to travel with her photographer boyfriend was the thing that had separated her from her family, and that the "job" had lasted as long as it took for him to find a new assistant/girlfriend once they reached California.

DeVries nodded slowly, but the way he didn't quite meet her eyes made her heart sink. "I must level with you, Grace, this could be a problem. I know you're more than qualified, but when I invited you to come in, I thought you'd completed university."

"Kenneth, you've seen her work." Henry leaned forward

in his chair. "You don't learn those skills at uni. Which would you rather have: someone with a brilliant eye and an understanding of what we do here, or a piece of paper?"

"I'm not the one we have to convince," DeVries said. "This is a management position, and all London managers have to be vetted by the board. There are a few members who might balk at the fact Grace is a woman, let alone one who dropped out of university."

An ache began in her temples. This was why she hated office jobs: the politics, the prejudices, the ridiculous rules. Up to this point in her career, no one had cared where she went to school. No one had even asked. You earned your stripes by doing, not by writing papers and taking exams. But she had committed to Ian, and to herself, that she would make a go of London. That meant she couldn't let this slip away without a fight.

"They would be making a mistake then, Mr. DeVries. I'm the best person for this job, and I am one of the few people who has seen firsthand the needs that this organization addresses. It's easy enough to spout platitudes about Christian charity and feeding the hungry, but when you've seen mothers fall weeping in the dirt because their children will have full stomachs for the first time in months—that's what people need to see. That's what will move them to action. Not pretty designs or feel-good slogans. If a diploma is the most important thing to your board of directors, there's not much I can do about that. But you're looking for something that can't be taught in any school."

DeVries stared at her for a long moment, then gave a nod. "All right then."

"Excuse me?"

"I said all right. I'll put you through for consideration at the board meeting next month. Your passion is what we need here. I suspect you won't have any trouble winning over the board with a speech like that."

Relief rushed through her, followed by a giddy sense of victory. "Thank you."

"There is one thing." A smile tipped up the edges of DeVries's mouth. "Exactly how close are you and Ian MacDonald?"

She felt a flush creep up her neck. Apparently, they hadn't been as discreet as she thought. "We're currently dating."

To her surprise, he smiled. "I suspected as much. Best we keep that little detail between the three of us, though. There's nothing in organization policy against board members dating employees, but I don't see the need to muddy the waters further."

"You want me to lie?"

"Of course not. Just don't bring it up unless you're asked." DeVries rose and offered his hand again. "Next board meeting is set for the end of August. One of us will call you to confirm the exact date and time."

"Thank you." She shook his hand vigorously, unable to hold back her smile. "I appreciate the chance."

"You're welcome. One more thing." DeVries leaned over and shuffled through paperwork on his desk until he found a single form. "I need your approval to conduct a background check."

"Background check?"

"Strictly routine. It's mostly to assure ourselves that you haven't been involved in any financial impropriety or committed a felony. That sort of thing."

"No, of course, I understand." Grace took the sheet and hurriedly scrawled her signature across the bottom before thrusting it back at him. "I'll look forward to your call."

"Thank you again, Ms. Brennan. Henry will show you out."

She walked with Henry to the reception area, said the expected good-byes and thank-yous, then strode from the office. Not until she stepped onto the lift did she draw a full breath. She'd done it. It sounded like the board's approval was a formality, and both Kenneth DeVries and Henry Symon wanted her for the job.

There was only one person with whom she wanted to celebrate.

CHAPTER FIFTEEN

WHEN IAN STEPPED OFF THE LIFT onto the second floor, Ms. Grey was waiting in a perfectly pressed suit, an attaché case on the ground next to her feet.

"Ms. Grey, you're early," he said. "Reception doesn't come in until nine."

"I wanted to get a start on setting up my desk, sir. I hope you don't mind. I arrived a few minutes ago."

"Not at all. Welcome to MacDonald Enterprises." He unlocked the door and stepped inside the office space, flipping on the lights as he went. The hum of fluorescents followed them through the empty reception area.

Ian stopped outside his office. "This is your desk. Paperwork is already waiting. If you can fill that out straightaway, I'll have you set up with a code for the computer system by midday."

"Code?"

Ian smiled. "Considering the kind of media attention James receives, we keep information under fairly strict control. As my assistant, you'll be privy to most of that anyhow. That's why there's a confidentiality agreement in the pile."

Ms. Grey looked completely unperturbed. "That makes sense. Before I start, what can I do? Should I turn on the copier and make a pot of coffee?"

"I would appreciate that, thank you." Ian crossed into his glassed-in office and set his briefcase on the desk. Could it be true? A capable assistant? What were the chances he could actually keep her?

After sorting through the hundred messages in his e-mail in-box, he went straight into a marketing meeting. Ms. Grey handed him a sheaf of completed forms when he returned. "I'm ready when you are, sir."

"Give me a moment, then, and we'll go over your duties." Ian returned to his office, hung his coat on the hanger on the back of the door, and grabbed his coffee mug.

He seated himself in front of Ms. Grey's desk. "All right. As you might have already guessed, we're a small operation. Five full-time employees, including you and me. James's assistant, Bridget, does reception and phones. She reports directly to him. Douglass is our graphic designer and de facto IT guy. Then we have Elizabeth, the marketing manager, who works with his publicist—who of course has other clients and works from her own office."

She nodded, taking notes, though Ian expected she memorized every word.

"You will be assisting me with the company's operational duties. All financial information comes through me, whether it be royalties and residuals or the monthly P and L from the restaurants. My brother works directly with his head chefs and front-of-house managers on menus, ordering, and accounts payable. I make sure all the information is properly gathered and in line with previous months. It's redundant, but since James isn't as involved as he was in the beginning, having an extra set of eyes on the restaurants' books keeps everyone honest. Still with me?"

"Of course."

"Good. Let me show you the network. We're paperless, so any statements or reports get scanned in and then shredded immediately. I'll log in." He leaned across the desk for the keyboard, pretending not to notice Ms. Grey's flinch. So his speculations had been correct after all.

He walked her through the network filing system and software, and then sat back. "Pretty straightforward for you, I'd think. What we do is relatively boring."

"It all seems perfectly reasonable, sir. I'll get started and let you know if I have any questions."

Ian nodded, then returned to his own desk. In truth, he had handed off several of his own daily tasks as a test, which left his day significantly lighter than usual. When his mobile phone beeped from his desk drawer, he pulled it out and found Grace's text message waiting. He smiled to himself as he texted back a rather unhelpful suggestion for dealing with her nervousness. Her immediate sarcastic response elicited a chuckle.

It wasn't like Grace to text him just because, though. She probably was legitimately nervous. He keyed in a more serious response.

You'll be brilliant. I promise. Just tell him why this means so much to you.

The office intercom buzzed and he punched the flashing light. "Ms. Grey?"

"Mr. MacD—that is, your brother, James—is on line two for you."

"Thank you." He switched over to the active line. "Good morning, Jamie."

"Morning. Another new assistant?"

Ian caught the thread of amusement in his brother's voice. "Hopefully my last for a while. Ms. Grey can transfer calls and make coffee, and her eyes didn't glaze over when I explained the computer system."

"That sounds promising."

"Quite. So, what's up? You're usually too busy gazing lovingly into your gorgeous fiancée's eyes to call me here."

"That's still on the agenda for later after Andrea finishes with the contractor. He made the mistake of lying about why we're a week behind schedule. It didn't go over well."

"I can imagine."

Jamie had originally met his American fiancée when Ian hired her to consult on the renovation of the family hotel on the Isle of Skye. Now that she'd moved to Scotland and formed her own hospitality consulting firm in Inverness, they were using the renovations as the first project in her portfolio. From what Ian had seen on his last trip to Skye, Andrea was running the job with equal measures of charm and intimidation.

"You still haven't told me why you're calling," Ian said.

"Right. I didn't get your reply to the wedding invitation."

"You didn't?" He shuffled papers in his in-box, then opened several drawers of his desk until he laid hands on an ivory vellum envelope. Still unopened. "It's sitting right here. I must have forgotten to post it."

"I already know you're coming, since you're the best man. I just need to know if you're coming by yourself or bringing a plus one."

Now Ian remembered why he hadn't opened it. There was nothing worse than attending your younger brother's wedding alone, and he'd fooled himself into thinking that avoiding the matter would make it go away.

He tilted the envelope back and forth between his fingers before he placed it firmly on the surface of his desk. "I'm bringing someone."

"Really? You're seeing someone?"

"Something like that. Just don't mention it to Mum."

Jamie paused on the other end of the line. "Why not?"

"You know how she is. If she knew, she'd have a private detective on the case in thirty seconds flat. When will you be back in London? There are a few things we need to go over in person, and I'm not about to interrupt your wedding with business."

"After the honeymoon. We'll stay in the flat for a few weeks before we head back to Scotland."

"Fair enough. Let me know the dates and I'll put it on the calendar." Ian said his farewells and hung up the phone. He was certainly capable of going to the wedding alone, but now Grace was back in his life.

A woman that his mother had once thrown out of Leaf Hill for daring to challenge Marjorie's treatment of her.

No, there was no way this could go wrong.

He was following that thought to its inevitable conclusion when his phone beeped again. Done! Heading through Westminster. Lunch?

He glanced at the clock. It had been little more than an

hour since the last text message. Did that mean it went well or poorly? Wouldn't miss it. I can get out of here in 30.

They decided on a little café not far from the office, and Ian turned back to his work. As he went through the third statement, he dragged off his glasses and pinched the bridge of his nose. What he'd told Ms. Grey was true. Most of what he did all day was mind-numbingly boring. He essentially preserved his brother's income streams and played babysitter to all the various employees, vendors, and contractors who worked for Jamie. He was quite literally his brother's keeper.

But that was the way the world worked. A perfectly fulfilling career was a myth perpetuated by television and self-help books. Wasn't it?

When he met Grace in the narrow cafe, she was already seated with a glass of sparkling water in hand, head bent over her mobile. His eyebrows lifted. He was used to seeing her in jeans and Doc Martens, but now she wore a slim-cut black suit with several strings of glittering glass beads around her neck.

The hostess saw him, but he waved her off and maneuvered himself behind Grace. He bent to murmur in her ear, "Mind if I join you, beautiful?"

She turned her head just enough for him to see the mischievous glint in her eye. "I don't know. My athlete boyfriend might object to me having lunch with a handsome stranger in pinstripes."

Ian chuckled and took the seat across from her. "Is that what I am? Your boyfriend?"

"Do you want to be?" She gave him a sultry little smile that made his wool suit jacket suddenly feel a bit too warm.

He reached for her hand across the table as the waitress arrived to take his drink order.

"Sparkling water for me as well." When they were alone again, he said, "I take it the interview went well?"

"I think so, yes." She recounted the conversation, from Mr. DeVries's praise of her artistic vision to his reluctance to put her forward to the board for consideration.

"So he's hesitant because you didn't finish university? That's mad! Henry thinks you're a lock for a Pulitzer nomination!"

"Well, in the end, I convinced him that my experience more than makes up for my lack of education. He's going to put the application up at the next board meeting."

"That's fantastic," Ian said. "I know you'll be perfect."

"And the potted palm isn't even the worse for wear. What about you? How is your day so far?"

"Fine. Ms. Grey started work today."

"Shouldn't that please you? You said the last several assistants didn't work out."

"Let's just say I'm feeling uncharacteristically contemplative. I was explaining my responsibilities to my new assistant and realized how dreadfully dull it all is." He leaned forward across his folded arms. "I'm going to be forty years old, Grace. What am I doing here?"

"Besides having a midlife crisis during your lunch break?" Her teasing smile coaxed one in return from him. "What's this really about?"

He leaned back and drummed his fingers on the table. "I don't know. Pathetic whinging. Forget I said anything. I don't want to ruin our celebration."

Grace studied him for a minute, then rose and tossed a banknote on the table. "C'mon. Let's go."

"But we'd planned—"

"Hang the plans. Are you coming?"

Ian shrugged apologetically to the server and followed Grace out of the café. Once out on the pavement, he looked to her. "Where to?"

"I don't know. Let's just walk for a bit."

"I really do need to get back."

"Why? James isn't around, so you're the boss. And your capable assistant has things well under control, right?"

"Yes, but—"

"Then loosen up that tie and let's go. How often does London get sunshine, even in July? It's criminal not to enjoy it." She took a small digital camera from her bag and slipped its strap around her wrist. Then she threaded her fingers through his and tugged him down the street.

Their progress was slow, in a pleasant, unhurried way, punctuated every few blocks by Grace raising her camera and snapping shots of passersby or buildings or a cluster of birds. What there was about the typical cityscape to inspire her, he didn't know, but gradually he managed to stop thinking about the work awaiting him back at the office and let himself enjoy watching her. There was something unreasonably sexy about her careless confidence, the easy but competent way she handled the camera.

"You're gorgeous," he said.

"You're delusional." She smiled at him, though. "Maybe delusional isn't so bad. Oh look, shawarma. Let's eat here."

"This place is good," he said. They stepped up to the little shop wedged between a news kiosk and a leather tourist shop and ordered lamb shawarma. Then they found a nearby bench on which to perch while they ate.

"Shall we take bets on my ability to keep tzatziki off my trousers?" Ian asked while he peeled back the foil wrapper.

"You should stop wearing suits."

"For greater ease of shawarma eating?"

Grace chuckled and took a sip of her fizzy. "Because they suck the life out of you. It's like cuff links are your Kryptonite."

"Cuff links keep my sleeves together. Besides, that would make me Superman."

"Well, then, Superman, you should kiss me."

"Excuse me?"

"Kiss me. You didn't seem to have a problem with it anywhere else. But you weren't wearing a suit then."

"That logic is completely mental." He laid his arm across the back of the bench, then leaned over and pressed a light kiss to her lips.

She cocked her head and considered. "Point proved."

"Hey!"

"You call that a kiss?"

"In public? Yes."

"That is pathetic."

He gave her a mock scowl. "Are you trying to make me angry now?"

"No, I'm trying to make the point that you are two different people, and I wanted to have lunch with the one who would kiss me like he meant it." Her eyes glinted with challenge.

He wrapped his hand around her jacket lapel, then pulled her close enough to press his lips to hers again. She smiled against his mouth before she softened to him, sliding her hands beneath his jacket so her fingernails could trace shivery trails down his back through his shirt.

It was Grace who pulled away first, a little breathless, but utterly self-satisfied. "Well."

Ian cleared his throat. "I win."

"No, I'm pretty sure I win." Grace gave him a naughty little grin before she turned back to her shawarma. "That was a rather impressive public display of affection. Next thing you know, you'll be wearing a pullover to work. Of all the horrors."

Ian laughed and nudged her leg with his knee. The grin she shot back unexpectedly wormed into his chest and gave his heart a firm clench. He pulled off his tie and draped it around her neck. "You've made me see the error of my ways. I might even go back to work tieless."

"You're so very brave."

He reached for her hand and laced his fingers with hers. Before he lost his nerve or she shifted the topic to a joke again, he said, "I have something to ask you."

"Yes?" she said slowly. No fear, but the caution in her voice was unmistakable.

"Will you come to Scotland with me for Jamie's wedding next month?"

"His wedding?"

"What did you think I was going to say?"

"I had no idea," Grace said with a self-conscious laugh. "Of course I'll go. But what will your family think? Won't your mum be there?"

"Jamie and Serena have always loved you. And Mum . . . well, she'll have to get over it. What do you say?"

"I say yes." She stretched up and stole a kiss. "As long as you let me keep this tie."

He grinned at her and loosened the top button of his shirt. "It looks better on you anyway."

CHAPTER SIXTEEN

"SPILL IT."

Grace cracked an eye open before diving back under the warm duvet, ignoring Asha's expectant look as she perched on the arm of the sofa. But the lure of fresh, hot tea was too strong to resist, wafting through the layers of down and cotton over her head. With a sigh she threw the duvet back and accepted the mug while she blinked sleep out of her eyes.

"Spill what?" The first sip—milk, light sugar, just how she liked it—woke her marginally. The second pried her eyes open to somewhat resemble alertness. "And what time is it anyway?"

"It's ten after nine. You're lucky I let you sleep in at all after that cryptic text message you sent me."

The text message. Grace had sent it late last night after she'd tired of waiting for Asha to come home from dinner with Jake. The excitement of the interview—and admittedly, the lunch with Ian—had driven away sleep for hours, which explained why she felt like she'd been hit by a lorry this morning.

Asha was still waiting, so Grace filled her in on the interview with DeVries and his promise to take her application to the board of directors at the next meeting.

"But Ian's on the board, right? Surely this is a formality."

"I hope so. DeVries asked about my relationship with him. Didn't seem too disturbed over it, but he also didn't want it to become common knowledge."

"Right." Asha's eyes sparkled, and she nudged Grace aside so she could climb beneath the covers with her. "How's all that going?"

Grace took another sip of her tea so she didn't have to answer right away. What was she supposed to say? That she felt giddy at the mere thought of him, as smitten as a schoolgirl with her first crush? Or that he could light up every nerve ending in her body just by looking at her? That was far too confessional for a morning when she'd barely consumed a quarter cup of caffeine, so she settled for "Good. He asked me to go to Scotland with him for James's wedding."

Asha squealed. "That's great! You're going, right?"

"Of course. But that was the reason for the text message. I need your shopping expertise. I have to find a dress."

"Say no more." Asha gripped Grace's shoulder with mock seriousness. "I knew this day would come. My little girl has become a woman."

Grace snorted, but Asha's enthusiasm warmed her. No

questions about what it meant that Ian was bringing her to a function where his mother would be present. No prodding about what this indicated about their relationship.

"So . . . does that mean you're going to have to play nice with his mum?"

Spoke too soon. Grace shrugged, unwilling to let the matter dampen her spirits. "He didn't seem to care, so I'm not going to worry about it."

"I'd say that's a big step. After she kicked you off of her property that time, the fact he's willing to risk her ire says he's serious."

Her tea again served as an excuse not to answer, even though she'd thought the same thing. Ian was nothing if not a dutiful son, though to his credit, he'd not stood by and allowed his mother to insult Grace. But she wasn't sure she wanted to be the reason for more family discord.

Why not? You're the one who broke up your own family.

She discarded the thought before it could take root and poison her mind. She was not responsible for the actions and reactions of others. "So. Dress. Where are we going?"

"Oh, don't worry about that. I've got you taken care of. Wear comfortable shoes."

In retrospect, Grace should have known what the glint in Asha's eye meant, but four stores and six hours on Oxford Street later, she wondered if she should have gone to Marks & Spencer and picked the first black dress she could find.

Now, as she shimmied the twentieth option over her head, she was beginning to think Asha was torturing her on purpose.

"Let's see it, then," Asha called from outside the dressing cubicle.

Grace walked slowly from the tiny space to the full-length mirror. The dress was a pretty color—a vibrant royal blue— and the long sleeves covered both arms to the wrist. But when she turned to view the plunging back in the mirror, she immediately swiveled back toward the cubicle.

"Where are you going? It's perfect!"

"I don't think so."

"But it shows off your tattoo so beautifully! When did you get this one?"

Grace twisted to look over her shoulder. The V-shaped opening exposed her back almost to the waist, revealing most of the Celtic Tree of Life inked there, its roots and branches braided into an endless circle. She'd gotten it shortly after she'd left London, when she'd finished her first assignment and she was so homesick for Ian that she'd nearly hopped the first plane home. At the time, it had symbolized the interconnectedness of humanity, one person's responsibility to another, but now she wondered if she'd just been trying to justify choosing her career over Ian. She ignored Asha's question. "Trust me, this is not the kind of attention I want at James's wedding."

Asha looked unconvinced, but she flopped back down in the upholstered chair to wait while Grace went back to try the next option. Her voice followed Grace into the cubicle.

"You know, sweetie, have you ever thought that maybe the things you're so afraid will draw attention are the things that Ian likes about you? Lord knows all the proper English businesswomen have never had a shot with him."

Grace paused with the dress halfway over her head.

Ian had always been fascinated with her tattoos. But this wasn't about Ian or her. The day was supposed to celebrate James and his new wife. There was no reason to draw attention to herself when all eyes should be on the bride and groom.

But she underestimated Asha's persuasiveness. When they headed up to John Lewis's third floor café for a late lunch, she was in possession of both the blue dress and a pair of coordinating heels. Unfortunately she also had the niggling sense that what she had seen as a straightforward trip to Scotland might be fraught with more drama than she was ready to handle. Ian's family—at least the Scottish side—were good people. They didn't need the turmoil that Grace would bring into their family, whether it was for a weekend or longer.

Yet when her phone rang, she scrambled for it like a teenager waiting for an invitation to prom.

"Hello, beautiful." Ian's low, quiet voice sent shivers straight down to her toes.

"Hi. I'm having lunch with Asha. Can I ring you back?"

"No need. Chris invited us to a film tonight. Do you want to go?"

Us? There was already an *us*, that his best mate would assume she should be invited? "Do *you* want to go?"

"If you do. We're supposed to meet at that old Indian place in Piccadilly at half past six if we're joining them."

"Sure. Meet you there?"

"No, I'll pick you up at Asha's place." His voice dropped another octave, which meant he was calling from work. "I can't wait to see you."

"Me too." She clicked off and dropped her phone back

in her pocket, then scowled at Asha's searching expression. "What?"

"That was Ian." Her eyes widened as if she'd suddenly worked out a puzzle. "You're in love with him."

Grace swallowed but said nothing.

"I don't mean you *still* love him, like you always have. I mean you've fallen for him all over again."

Her heart gave a brutal twist. She couldn't deny Asha was right. But what was she supposed to say? That in the space of a couple of weeks, she couldn't imagine being without him? That he was never far from her mind? That at times she wanted him so badly she couldn't breathe? It was all true, but it made her sound pathetic and obsessive, so instead she settled for a noncommittal answer. "He makes me happy, but I'm being cautious."

"Just don't 'cautious' yourself into another decade of misery because it scares you. There's a reason why neither of you settled with anyone else. I pray you both figure it out before one of you gets stupid again."

"Well, in the meantime, we're going to the cinema with one of his mates tonight, so you will have to do with Jake for company."

"Good. Grace, I want you to be happy. No one deserves it more."

Grace smiled in response, but Asha's words left her feeling unsettled. She wanted to believe it was true, needed to believe it was possible. But for the first time, it wasn't Ian's heart she feared for. It was her own.

CHAPTER SEVENTEEN

ASHA LEFT THE FLAT FIRST, giving Grace enough time to wash and change before Ian arrived. Tonight, she'd made an effort to dress nicely in new jeans, metallic sandals that showed off her polka-dotted pedicure, and a light mesh sweater. She was putting on a coat of mascara when the downstairs buzzer rang.

A minute later, she opened the door to find Ian equally casually dressed in his typical chinos and fine-gauge pullover. She barely had the door closed behind them before he lifted her around the middle and gave her a hello kiss that made her glad she wasn't standing on her own feet.

"Hi," she said, breathless.

He set her down with a grin that was almost as devastating

to her balance as the kiss. "I've been wanting to do that all day. Are you ready to go?"

"Let me get my bag." She found her much-neglected shoulder bag, into which she loaded her keys, her wallet, and her tiny digital camera.

"You're bringing a camera?" he asked as she looked up. "Don't you have one on your mobile?"

"It doesn't take great photos in low light. You never know what you're going to come across."

They descended the stairs to the foyer, and Ian held open the front door. "I like that way of approaching life."

"Which way? Always be prepared? Like the Boy Scouts?"

"No, with anticipation of something new and worth remembering."

That was unexpected. What had gotten into him tonight? "Had you given up on spontaneity?"

"Maybe I just didn't have anyone to appreciate it with." He squeezed her hand, then flagged down a passing taxi when they reached the corner.

Grace's enthusiasm waned the closer they got to Piccadilly Circus, the irony of which was not lost on her. Dinner with Ian's friends was the least frightening thing she'd done in a decade, including seeing him again. He seemed to pick up on her mood and pulled her aside before they entered the building.

"Grace, relax. You'll like Sarah. You already know Chris."

"I'm fine. Really. I'll be on my best behavior."

Ian gave her a little nudge, and his grin surfaced. "I certainly hope not. What fun would that be?"

They climbed the narrow staircase to the restaurant a floor up, an open space with the spare formality that seemed to characterize Indian restaurants. They waved off the host and crossed the room to where Chris waited at a window table for four, his hulking form standing out in a roomful of normal-size people.

"Ian." He greeted his friend first, then turned to Grace, his smile widening. "Grace. It's been donkey's years! You look great! How are you?"

Grace accepted his awkward, side-arm hug, chuckling at the effusive greeting. "Nice to see you, Chris. You haven't changed a bit."

"And you are as good a liar as you ever were. This is my girlfriend, Sarah."

Grace shook her hand while they exchanged the expected pleasantries, and she took the seat Ian held for her. Sarah was not the kind of woman Grace had anticipated. She was pretty in a natural, accessible way, with a shoulder-length brown bob and almost no makeup—nothing like the overly styled groupies Chris had dated in his British Team days. When Sarah smiled, her dark eyes sparkled merrily. Grace instantly liked her.

"I have to say, Grace, you are not at all what I expected."

"Oh? How's that?"

"When Chris said you were a war photographer, I didn't expect anyone so . . . well, pretty."

Grace felt a surprise flush rise to her cheeks. She'd been called many things by other women, but pretty usually wasn't one of them. "I'll admit, after knowing Chris years ago, I didn't expect you to be—"

Sarah grinned. "Normal? Trust me, I know."

"Hey!" Chris protested.

Grace stifled a laugh and flipped open the heavy cardboard menu to scan the listings. The banter flowing around her lifted her spirits. Despite her earlier reservations, the normalcy of the evening was irresistible. She was accustomed to being crowded around a table with a group of journalists, their cameras within easy reach. No need to listen for air raid sirens or wonder if the slam of a lorry's cargo door was an RPG hitting a nearby building.

She could actually *relax*.

After they placed their order, Grace folded her hands atop the table. "So, Sarah, I know Chris is an investment analyst. What do you do for a living?"

"I'm a bookkeeper for an office-cleaning firm." Sarah's freckled nose scrunched up. "Sounds dead dull, doesn't it?"

It did, but Grace could hardly say that. "Not necessarily. Do you like it?"

Sarah shrugged. "It's all right. Chris and I live together, so it's for mad money, really. Pays for the trips back to see the folks and take holidays and all that. Besides, with all the time he spends at work and at the club, I've got to do something with my time."

Grace smiled, though inwardly, Sarah's attitude fascinated her. She really had no problem with her live-in boyfriend paying the expenses or working a boring job to pass the time? "Do you have any hobbies?"

Sarah leaned forward, a conspiratorial look on her face. "I tap-dance."

"You . . . tap-dance?"

"I do. It's brilliant fun, even if I have two left feet at times. You should try it, Grace. You might like it."

"Well, I—" She glanced at Ian, who was watching them with an amused expression. Clearly he wanted to see how she'd get out of this gracefully. "Why not? Maybe it would be fun."

Chris and Ian exchanged a look, then simultaneously burst out laughing.

"What?" Grace and Sarah demanded in unison, which only made them laugh harder.

"Sorry," Ian said. "The idea of you in tights and tap shoes with little bows on them—"

Sarah gave the men a mock scowl. "Philistines. No appreciation for the arts."

"The arts?" Chris choked out, spurring on another round of laughter and earning him an elbow in the side from Sarah.

Grace settled back in her chair, her grin making her cheeks ache. Chris and Sarah were good-natured, fun-loving people. Normal people. Their easy inclusion of her made her heart swell. Ian slipped an arm around her and pressed a quick kiss to the top of her head, which only added to the warm feeling in her chest.

"But really, Grace, tell us about your work. It must be fascinating." Sarah seemed enthralled by the very idea of her career.

"It's not nearly as glamorous as it sounds," Grace said, shaking her head. "I spend loads of time bored in a hotel waiting for something to happen."

"Go on," Ian murmured, giving her a little nudge. Their expectant looks said she wasn't getting out of it anytime soon.

For every bad memory she had, there was at least one good story, like the one she'd been telling Ian at the Basque pop-up restaurant. Her experiences sounded exciting and breathless in the retelling, even when in reality they had been boring or terrifying. She told stories of interviewing and photographing families while local militia were pounding down doors in villages. Going inside modern-day harems where no men would ever be allowed. And then she decided to tell them a story she'd not told anyone.

"Syria, about three years ago. Usually, journalists are careful not to go out early in the morning because that's when most kidnappings happen."

"Why early morning?" Chris asked.

"Easiest time to grab someone off the street, and there's less chance of getting stuck in traffic on the getaway."

"Really," Ian murmured. "I wouldn't have thought."

"Mostly, they're opportunists looking for ransom," Grace said. "Until recently, there were more kidnappings for money and political bargaining power than ideological statements. So on this particular day, I had a meeting with a source, a little earlier than I'd usually be out. But things had been quiet, and my fixer had gone to quite a bit of trouble to set it up."

Grace fell silent for a moment, her heart thudding heavily as she recalled that morning. "It's not required or even common for women to cover their heads in Syria, especially not Damascus. But I'd been warned that my contact was a conservative, older Muslim, so I'd decided to wear a *hijab* for the meeting.

"I was walking out of the hotel, and my driver was parked down the street. I was halfway to the car when one of the pins popped out of the fabric and fell onto the pavement. When I bent over to pick it up, I saw another car pull up at the curb behind me, and two men jumped out of the backseat."

"What did you do?" Sarah asked, her eyes wide.

"I ran. And they ran. Just before I reached the door of the hotel, one of them caught up to me and grabbed me." She paused. "All he caught was the loose hijab—which wouldn't have been loose had I not lost the pin—and I got away."

"That's some story," Ian said, his tone low. He squeezed her hand under the table.

"The thing is, I've pinned a headscarf hundreds of times. There's no reason that pin should have come out on its own. The only thing I can think is that God intervened directly."

"Couldn't it have been a coincidence?" Chris asked.

Grace had asked herself that very thing. At the time, she hadn't truly believed that God manifested Himself so distinctly in anyone's life. If He did, why wouldn't He have stepped in and made Himself known in any number of other horrible situations?

And yet somewhere, deep down inside her, she'd known it wasn't mere luck or coincidence. She'd been saved for some reason, even if she was still trying to figure out why.

But none of that she could say aloud. She shrugged. "I never made it to my appointment, and the next day bombs started going off around the city. Where would I have been if I'd been kidnapped? I guess I'll never know."

The food arrived at the table, pulling everyone out of the story.

"Either way, it's a bloody good yarn, Grace." Chris lifted a glass to her, clearly not convinced. But from the way Sarah watched her, Grace could tell she was mulling the possibilities.

Her heart still thumping from the recollection, Grace reached for the bowl of rice. She'd not been paying attention to what they'd ordered beyond her tandoori masala, so as the conversation turned to other topics, she spooned a little of each dish onto her plate.

Lamb vindaloo, she decided when she tasted the first one.

The second, tandoori masala, was unmistakable. But when she tasted the third one, she froze. "What is this?"

Ian peered at her plate. "That's the karahi beef. It's—"

"Pakistani, I know."

"You don't like it? I'll eat yours if you don't."

Grace couldn't answer. Her heart, which had already been beating hard from the adrenaline of her memories, felt like it would burst out of her chest. Sweat broke out on her forehead. She set her fork down firmly before they could notice her hands were shaking. "Will you excuse me for a moment?"

She threw her napkin on the table and raced to the toilet cubicle at the front of the restaurant. It took all her control not to slam the door behind her, but she managed to shut and lock it before the trembling in her knees got too bad to stay upright.

She collapsed on the stool by the little tower holding toilet tissue and air freshener. It was good that she noticed that. Usually if she were heading for a flashback, she wouldn't notice anything but the narrowing of her vision.

A run-of-the-mill panic attack, then.

She pushed herself up from the stool, flicked the faucet on, then splashed cold water on her face. She'd never had a food trigger an episode. This was new.

Maybe she should have expected it. The last time she'd had that dish had been in the home of a Christian Pakistani family, one of the many families in Peshawar who feared for their lives, one of the few who would talk to a Western female journalist and her entourage. They'd been kind and talkative, their daughter fascinated by her camera, the two younger sons playing in the back room. None of them knowing in twenty-four hours, they would be dead.

Because of their hospitality. Because of Grace.

A sob escaped from her lips as she bent over the sink, tears dropping into the swirl of water down the drain. She desperately tried to get control of her breathing, but her lungs got tighter and tighter the more she fought against it.

Dead. All dead. God, why had it happened that way? Why had she pushed? Even worse, she had taken the photos. Afterward. Like a vulture, picking over the remains of people who had been kind to her.

A knock shuddered the door. "Grace? Are you all right?"

She jerked upright and wiped her face with her sleeve. Ian. "I'm fine. Give me a minute."

"Grace, open the door."

He was going to draw attention to them with all the noise he was making. She disengaged the lock and stepped back, dragging her wrist across her eyes. Ian stepped inside.

"What's going on, Grace?" He took in her tearstained face, her trembling body, and seemed to put it together. His expression shifted and he opened his arms.

She stepped into them without hesitation. He wrapped his arms around her and held her tight, his hands stroking her hair while she sobbed. When her tears subsided, he whispered, "I'm sorry, sweetheart. If I'd have known—"

"You couldn't. How could you have?" She pulled away. A quick glance in the mirror showed the wreckage of her mascara. "I'm so sorry, Ian. I've ruined the evening."

"You haven't ruined anything. Though the longer we stay in here together, the more speculation there'll be about what we're doing."

Grace choked on a watery laugh. "You're awful."

His smile faded. "Do you want to beg off the film and go home instead?"

He was serious. She thought about it for a moment and then shook her head. "Let's go anyway. It will be a good distraction."

"Are you sure?"

"I'm sure. I . . . I'm terribly sorry. It doesn't happen often, but I can't control it when it does."

"Shh, I know. It's not your fault." He took her face in his hands and wiped away a smudge of mascara with his thumb. "What do you want me to do?"

"Just . . . go back out and smooth things over?"

"Done." He leaned down to place a gentle kiss on her mouth, then turned toward the door. "Take your time."

Grace drew a breath and put herself back together the best she could. Cold water to take down the puffiness in her eyes. Tissues to erase the mascara stains. A little lip gloss—well, that didn't help much of anything. She still looked like she'd had a meltdown in a public toilet, but there was nothing to be done about that except steel herself against the embarrassment and go out.

When she returned to the table, Ian and his friends were chatting while they finished their food. Grace's plate had been removed, along with the offending dish. She looked at Ian in surprise, but he gave her a reassuring smile.

"Grace, we're sorry," Sarah said. "We wouldn't have pushed if we'd known."

"No apologies necessary, please. What am I missing?"

"Chris and I were just talking about the time we bet part of the squad they wouldn't strip down on the side of the road—and then we drove off without them." Ian grinned at his mate across the table. "I still remember them running after the van in the snow, bare as the way they entered the world."

"Freshers never have any idea what they're in for," Chris said, barely getting the words out before he dissolved into laughter again.

"It's a good thing these two grew up a bit in the last twenty years," Sarah said, but she seemed just as amused.

"Marginally." Ian winked at Grace, but underneath the table, he gripped her hand hard. She squeezed back gratefully.

They kept the topics light—mostly stories of their misdeeds, to which Grace could add a few Sarah had never heard—but through it all, Ian held her hand. Strong, steady, reassuring. He let her go only long enough to pay the bill, and then they were back out on the street.

He held her back in the swiftly deepening twilight. "Are you sure you don't want to call it a night?"

"No. I like Chris and Sarah. It'll be fine."

Ian squeezed her shoulder, letting his thumb brush her neck for a moment, then gave a nod. She drew a deep breath of gratitude and plunged into the crowd beside him, trying to keep Chris's blond head in sight over the other pedestrians.

Even on a weeknight, Piccadilly Circus was glutted with people: tourists with cameras capturing the neon lights and swiftly changing signage; locals pushing through without irritation or concern on their way to their destinations; the babble of voices in a dozen languages melding with buskers and boom boxes and car horns. Ian threaded a path for them through the crowd with one hand firmly on her waist, shifting himself to block her from the occasional drunken reveler or clueless holiday-goer. He was almost too good to be true. Chivalrous, sensitive, understanding. How long had it been since someone had taken the trouble to look after her? Not because he thought she needed it—he'd made it clear that he knew she could take care of herself—but because he actually cared about her?

For that matter, how long had it been since she'd truly cared about someone in return?

Her insides gave a clench, twisting up her heart and lungs all at once and forcing the thrum of her blood into her ears. She only realized she'd stopped when Ian slowed and cast a puzzled look in her direction. "Grace?"

"I think I love you," she murmured.

He frowned, then bent down so he could hear her. "What did you say? It's too loud."

"I said, I think I love you."

He jerked back. "In Piccadilly Circus?"

"No, everywhere." A smile burst onto her face, a new lightness bubbling up inside. "In Piccadilly Circus. In Earl's Court. I suspect I would feel the same way in Scotland, though we'll have to test that theory."

His expression rippled from consternation to pleasure as he processed what she was saying. At last it settled on something she could only name as joy. He took her face in his hands and kissed her hard, stealing her breath with the intensity of his reaction. And then his kiss gentled, exploring as if they had all the time in the world, as if they weren't standing in the middle of a crowded public space. The jostling of bodies around them only forced them closer together, and he wrapped his arms around her as if to shield her again from the crowd. From her memories. And for that moment, pressed as close to him as they could possibly get, she actually believed he could do it.

When he lifted his lips from hers, he didn't release her. He moved his mouth to her ear and whispered, "I feel like I've been waiting my entire life to hear that, Grace. I love you too. I've not said anything because I didn't want to frighten you away."

She stretched on tiptoes to kiss him again. "I'm here. And I'm staying." She looked around. "And we've lost your friends because of that extremely impressive PDA."

Ian smiled at her and kissed her one last time. "Not really thinking about them right now. Besides, we'll catch up with them at the cinema."

But they barely made it more than a half dozen steps through the square before running into Chris and Sarah, who were grinning like mad fools.

"Get distracted?" Sarah asked.

"You saw that, did you?" Ian said.

"Well, Chris did. I'm too short." Sarah looked between the two of them, eyebrows raised. "Are we on to the cinema then, or do you want to take a rain check?"

Grace looked up at Ian, trying to gauge his reaction. All the emotion and adrenaline rushing through her made it hard to concentrate. "No, I've been looking forward to the film. We should go."

They fell back in together toward the cinema, its facade illuminated with neon strip lighting. Grace barely noticed when Ian bought their tickets or when they found their way to their designated screen. When they settled into their seats, Grace was thankful to be on one end beside Ian so she didn't have to make small talk with Chris or Sarah. She wasn't sure she was capable of it.

The film slipped by without penetrating her brain while

she turned around what she'd said, over and over in her mind. She had told Ian she loved him. And he loved her too. This should have made her panicky and unsettled. She should have been questioning whether it was the emotion of her earlier episode, the catharsis of the unaccustomed tears that had made her say it. But even she couldn't find it in herself to tear apart and overanalyze what had just happened.

She'd told him she loved him, that she was staying. And she meant it.

Sarah and Chris said something about heading to a club for live music, but Ian begged off, for which Grace was grateful. She'd not seen any of the film, and from the way Ian had periodically brought her hand to his lips, he hadn't been any more focused on the screen than she had.

They climbed into a black cab just after eleven, where he immediately reclaimed her hand. "So. Did the night turn out all right after all?"

"You know it did." She smiled at him in the dark. "I've always liked Chris. And Sarah is delightful."

"I thought you'd like her. And she doesn't invite just anyone to tap-dance, you know. She liked you."

Grace threw him a doubtful look. "Maybe before I had my meltdown."

"Chris's brother is in the military. He understands. Believe me, no one is thinking anything about it. Other than thinking you're amazing and brave."

"You're biased."

"That I am." He slid an arm around her shoulders and

pulled her to his side. She leaned against him and let out a long sigh.

Ten years after she left him, she still loved him and he still loved her.

What now?

"Stop thinking," he whispered in her ear, nuzzling her neck for a second. "We don't have to make any decisions tonight."

She let out a low laugh. He'd never struck her as particularly perceptive, but in this, he had her bang to rights. Had their roles reversed so much? He was the planner. She was the free spirit. He'd had his life laid out in front of him practically since birth, even if he'd refused to follow the script for a while. She was a drifter in all senses of the word. And yet there was a beautiful symmetry in the idea of one day at a time.

When at last the taxi dropped them at the curb, he leaned forward to pay the driver, then followed her into the building to Asha's flat. Grace unlocked the door—suddenly nervous. She turned to him. "Ian—"

The look on his face obliterated whatever she had been about to say. As if of one mind, they closed the space between them in a crushing embrace, lips finding lips, drinking in each other in a mad rush of emotion and desire. Her back hit the door without her fully registering it—she was too focused on his fingers digging into her hips, his mouth devouring hers. She groped behind her for the knob, and they practically fell through the door, breaking contact only long enough to slam it behind them.

"Grace," he murmured as his lips left hers to travel along her neck. She raked her hands through his hair. This she remembered. This never changed. All the pent-up emotion of the night bubbled to the surface, screaming for release.

And then the reality of what that meant washed over her. "Wait," she whispered. "Ian, stop."

Her words seemed to hit him like a bucket of cold water. He froze and dropped his forehead against the wall behind her. "I'm sorry, I—"

"No. Don't say anything for a second." She was breathing as hard as he was, and it took her several moments to gather her thoughts enough to speak. "There are some things we should talk about."

He pushed away from the wall, and that little bit of distance felt like a mile. Still, the look he gave her was filled with tenderness. "You don't have to explain anything. We just got . . . a little carried away."

Did he actually look abashed? That was not something she would have expected from him. She stretched up on tiptoe and pressed a kiss to his lips. "It's been an emotional night—"

"And we shouldn't take advantage." He passed a hand over his face. "Grace, really, it's okay. I didn't come here expecting anything."

"Will you hush?" She softened the words with a rueful smile and hooked a finger through his belt loop to pull him closer again. "And if you could, stop looking so ruddy attractive so I can think for a minute."

That earned a smile. "I'm listening."

She let out a breath. This wasn't anything she had expected to be discussing right now, but it had to be said. "Ian, there's something you need to understand. My life over there—it was different."

His eyebrows drew together slightly, but he didn't say anything.

"You're in danger much of the time. People you know and respect die. For that matter, strangers die, and rather than helping, you keep your distance through the lens and keep shooting. And sometimes, at the end of the day, it's just too much to go back to your hotel room alone. You know?"

He exhaled slowly. "Grace, I never had the expectation that you lived like a nun. If you think that bothers me—"

"No. It's not something I'm proud of, but it's not something I can change, either. I just . . . I don't want this—us—to be out of reflex or habit. You mean more to me than that, and now that we have a second chance, I want to do things right. Does that make sense?"

He trailed a finger down her cheek, and even now, the tingle of that simple touch put cracks into her resolve. "I love you, Grace. And I think you're right. We could benefit from taking things slowly this time." His mouth twisted into a wry smile. "I just seem to forget how hard it is to keep my hands off you."

"Well, you're not that easy to resist yourself."

His hands closed on her waist, and his head dipped to kiss her softly. It took an effort not to move closer. "I promise you, there is no pressure, no expectation. And if the right time involves a wedding ring and a white dress—"

She let out a breath in a puff. "That's even more terrifying than getting shot at. Did you have to mention the w word?"

"That's supposed to be my line, remember?" He lifted her hand to his lips, his expression turning serious. "I've spent most of the last ten years wondering what my life would have been like with you still in it. I'm not about to ruin our chance to find out. No need to rush decisions—about anything."

His expression was so tender it made her insides ache. "I love you, Ian."

"And I will never get tired of hearing that." One more kiss, just a touch too heated to be called sweet, and he was backing away from her. "Good night. Get some rest."

"Not a chance."

Grace smiled as he let himself out. She locked the door behind him, then took a moment to sag against the wall before she pushed herself up and retrieved her T-shirt and flannel shorts from her duffel. She didn't regret sending him home or explaining her reasoning behind it. It was what she needed—what they needed—to make sure they didn't follow their previous path. They'd already seen where that ended.

Still, even after she climbed beneath the soft, well-worn duvet and flicked off the light, sleep didn't come. The sofa bed felt cold and empty without him, even if what she craved was simply his presence beside her, pillowing her head on his shoulder as they fell asleep.

But she knew herself well enough to recognize it wouldn't end there, and she didn't want Ian to be just another regret. They needed a chance to have a real relationship, without . . . distractions. She needed time to see if Ian was the one, beyond her physical connection with him.

Grace had already confessed her mistakes to God. She had vowed that she would be different, that she would honor the second chance she'd been given. And she wanted to keep that promise. She was determined to keep that promise.

But she had never felt so weak.

CHAPTER EIGHTEEN

"So, WHAT WAS ALL THAT about last night?" Chris sat down on the changing room bench after their outing, dressed in a navy-blue suit that seemed incongruously polished on his large body.

Ian shrugged and fastened his shirt cuffs with a pair of onyx links, a slight smile surfacing as he remembered Grace's suggestion that they were his Kryptonite. "I don't know what you mean."

"You kissed her in the middle of a crowd. I've never known you to even hold a woman's hand in public."

"Psychoanalyzing me now?"

Chris pushed himself up. "Come on, I'll buy you breakfast. Surely you have time for breakfast."

"For some posh investment analyst, you don't seem to spend much time in the office."

"I spend all my time in the office that I'm not here."

"Which I'm sure Sarah is thrilled about."

Chris winced. "Coming or not?"

Ian glanced at his watch. Nearly eight. Technically, the office didn't open until nine, and with Ms. Grey in charge, it hardly mattered as long as he arrived by his ten o'clock conference call. "All right. If you're buying. Where to?"

They ended up where they always ended up, the greasy spoon at Putney Bridge where Ian had brought Grace the morning of their first date. It was crowded today, packed with locals and holiday-goers filling up on EBCB—eggs, bacon, chips, and beans.

"Should have known this was where you'd go if you were paying," Ian cracked when they took one of the few remaining tables.

"Where else?" Chris dumped half the sugar shaker into his tea and stirred it with a clank of cutlery against ceramic. He seemed to be choosing his words carefully. "You know I like Grace. I always have."

"I sense a *but* coming."

"*But* surely you can see the effect that job had on her. I know PTSD when I see it. She had a flashback because of the food last night, didn't she?"

Ian stared at his friend. Chris was clearly speaking out of concern, but the things that Grace had told him were confidential. How much was too much to reveal? "I know what Grace is going through. She's dealing with it."

"I don't think you do. And I don't think she's dealing with it at all. My brother served in the Balkans, and you know how long ago that was. Still has nightmares. Can't walk down the street without checking his sight lines and escape routes. Sleeps with a knife under his pillow. Craig's wife hung in there for a while, but after a few years, she couldn't take it anymore. The drinking, the women—"

"That's combat stress," Ian said. "Grace hasn't been in combat. She hasn't killed anyone."

"Do you think that's any better? The things she's seen— even soldiers don't deal with that sometimes. You only have to look at her pictures, mate. She's carrying around some heavy baggage."

"So what are you saying?" Ian stuffed down the anger that threatened to spill into his voice. "Are you saying she's damaged and I should write her off? You know me better than that."

Chris leaned back against the booth and spread his hands wide. "I'm not telling you what to do. I'm telling you that these things don't disappear overnight. You need to understand what you're getting into."

Before he got too attached to cut her loose. The subtext was clear. Completely understandable, and yet the wrongness of it all made him feel a little ill. Grace herself had said she didn't want to be his rehabilitation project.

Was Chris right, though? So far she'd referred to her problems as "issues" and "episodes." She'd refused to go to another therapist, didn't think she needed one. And yet she was self-aware enough to recognize her own destructive coping mechanisms, to not want to repeat the same mistakes. That had to be a sign of progress.

Chris could evidently see his comments had thrown Ian into a tailspin. "Listen, you know I'm behind you whatever you do. But I've seen it firsthand, and I thought you needed to be prepared."

Ian gave him a slow nod.

"Anyway, that's not what I wanted to talk about today. You hear about Nik?"

"No. What about him?"

"Fractured his collarbone playing rugby with his boys in the garden. He's going to be out indefinitely."

Ian winced. There was a reason they had avoided playing contact sports while rowing. The training scheme took its own toll on the body without adding the possibility of major injury on top of it. Recovery was a solid eight to twelve weeks for a fractured collarbone. "So Henley's out. Pairs too. What about it?"

"There was some talk about you as a replacement."

"I'm no longer competitive. You know that."

"I don't know that. You could have been stellar, you know, one of the best, had you just stuck with it. Your name would be up there with Pinsent and Searle. You don't lose those instincts."

"But you lose the hunger," Ian said.

"So you're not interested."

Of course I'm interested, he wanted to say, but he had to be sensible. No matter how flattering it was to be considered to sub for a rower like Nik, he'd have to dedicate himself completely to training for the next several months. And for what? A chance to relive the glory days? Stroking a veteran boat in a second-string race? He pushed back his unfinished meal and stood. "No, sorry. Thanks for breakfast, though."

"You would have done it a few months ago, wouldn't you?"

"Whether or not I would have is irrelevant."

"Yeah, that's what I thought." Chris gave him a wry look. "Listen, some of the lads are having supper and a pint at the local after workout tonight. You might as well come along. And bring Grace."

It was Chris's way of asking if they were still okay. Ian gave a quick nod. "I'll ask her."

"Good. And don't be too hasty on that decision. I still think you'd make a good sub for Nik."

"I'll think about it." But his mind was made up. He'd already spent too much time living in the past.

An hour later, Ian made his way back to the Tube, kit bag on one shoulder, briefcase in hand, while Chris's words tumbled over in his mind. What he had said about Grace and her issues, the offer to sub on the veteran crew: things he would have once given serious consideration.

But he'd meant what he said. His rowing career was over. And he wouldn't abandon Grace because of what she'd endured for the sake of what she believed was right. The two were linked somehow in his mind. Once, he'd had as much passion for his rowing as Grace had for her photography, but somewhere along the line it had become rote. Something to fill the time, a way to keep his mind busy and his body active. Something that defined him beyond the daily routine of going to his brother's office, minding his brother's business. When he was on the water, his problems seemed distant. The familiar clunk of the oars in the locks, the swish of the water against the hull, metaphorical barriers against his regrets.

But now that Grace was back, he could see how empty his life had been.

Actually, it had started earlier than that, watching his

brother fall in love with a woman he hardly knew, seeing the changes that Andrea's presence had made in Jamie's life, small at first, and then greater. Jamie had always been driven, successful, outgoing. But now he actually seemed happy. A little sickening at times, but more settled than Ian had ever imagined seeing him.

It made it harder to claim that some men just weren't suited to the domestic life.

It was why Ian had made the cursory attempts at dating, even when he knew at first sight none of those women would ever elicit more than vague affection and admiration. They had never stolen his breath, never kept him up nights, and he would have said that was a good thing. Look what his passion for Grace had done to him once before.

He'd been lying to himself.

Which is why rather than head to the office as he should have, he found himself returning to his flat. When he emerged from the Underground onto street level, he pulled his mobile from his pocket and called the office.

"Ms. Grey, it's Ian." Even if she refused to call him by his first name, he wasn't about to get into the habit of referring to himself as *mister.* "I'm going to take my ten o'clock at home. Will you please conference me through when it comes in?"

"Of course, sir. I'd be happy to. Should we expect you later?"

"What's on my calendar?"

"Just a three o'clock status update with Bridget. I can reschedule it for tomorrow if you'd like."

"Hold off on that. I'm not sure how my day is going to play out yet. I'll let you know if I'm not coming in."

"Yes, sir. I'll talk to you at ten."

When he pushed through the door of his flat, he tossed his kit bag in the foyer, dropped the briefcase on the hall table, and went straight to the old-fashioned address book he kept in the drawer with Grace's clips, a remnant of days when mobile phones were the size of bricks. He flipped through to find the one contact he'd been fairly certain he would never call again. Then he dialed.

"This is Ian MacDonald. I'd like to make an appointment with Mr. Segal for today if possible."

"Of course, sir," the faintly German-accented voice said on the other end of the line. "Mr. Segal would be pleased to meet with you. Design or purchase?"

"Design. Or I suppose I should say redesign. Mr. Segal made a piece for me a number of years ago."

"I understand, sir. Would half past two at the Old Bond Street boutique suit you?"

"It would, thank you." He said his good-byes and clicked off, his pulse feeling oddly unsteady.

He went to the walk-in wardrobe in his bedroom and knelt before the small safe bolted to the floor. It was empty but for his passport, a small stack of banknotes, and the insanely expensive gold Patek Philippe watch his mother had given him for his thirtieth birthday but he hated too much to actually wear.

Plus a small, gray velvet box.

He took the box out and flipped open the lid. He hadn't looked at the engagement ring since Grace had left it on his kitchen countertop. Even when he'd moved house, he'd left the box closed, simply shoving it back into the safe and not questioning why he couldn't bear to let it go. Now, looking at the cushion-cut diamond set in a flashy pavé band, he wondered why he'd ever thought she would wear something so ostentatious.

He snapped the box closed and returned to the living room, where he intended to prep for the conference call with the first of the law firms he was considering to replace Barrett. No matter how much he tried to concentrate, that gray box drew his attention. It was rash, coming so soon after they'd revived their relationship. It wasn't as if he planned on asking her to marry him right now. He simply believed in being prepared.

Prepared to do whatever it took to convince her to stay this time.

CHAPTER NINETEEN

THE NEXT DAY PASSED MORE SLOWLY than any other day of Grace's life. She'd always prided herself on her good sense and her independence, but now she checked her phone every three minutes to see if she'd missed a call or text from Ian. It made her feel pathetic and clingy. Melvin had asked her to come by the gallery in the late afternoon, but that gave her hours in which to mark every single minute until the clock turned over to three thirty.

Melvin greeted her with a smile. "Grace—I'm glad you came. I wanted your opinion on this particular photo."

Curious, Grace followed Melvin back to the workroom, where a single print was pinned out. Grace smiled when she saw it. It was one of her favorites, a Sudanese woman standing before a burned-out building, cradling a tiny baby. Despite the background's gloomy subject matter, the photo had captured the woman's total adoration for her infant. To Grace, it perfectly summarized the theme of the collection.

But she could also see why Melvin had singled it out as problematic. The balance between the woman's dark skin and the brightly lit background would be difficult to get right. She moved closer to the photograph, inspecting it, noting the areas where the contrast was too low or the print too light.

Melvin came up beside her. "I can dodge the woman in the foreground and expose the rest a bit more. You have some time to join me in the darkroom?"

"Sure." Grace gathered her gear and followed him through the connected doorway.

The small, ventilated room was barely large enough for both of them, so Grace pressed her back against the wall while Melvin refilled emulsion trays and checked supplies. He turned off the lights, and a red overhead came on in their place.

"I'm surprised you didn't want to do these yourself," he said. "This used to be an interest of yours."

"I'm out of practice. A darkroom necessitates a permanent address. Besides, why would I go to the trouble when I have you?"

Melvin chuckled. "When you have time, I'll show you some large-format platinum prints I'm working on. The platinum gives the images a depth you just can't get with silver."

"I'd love to." She smiled as she watched him expose the negative through the enlarger, wishing she had been able to shoot some of these portraits medium format. But the larger camera didn't lend itself to trekking into the villages and up the mountainsides where she'd taken most of these. Besides, part of the appeal had been using Aidan's Leica on a project he'd always talked about but wasn't able to attempt before he died. The practicality of printing 35mm for gallery exhibition had never occurred to her.

Melvin was putting the paper into the developer tray when Grace's phone trilled in her pocket. She pushed an earphone into her ear, then clicked the microphone button. "Grace Brennan."

"Am I interrupting something?"

Ian's voice sent a pleasant hum of energy through her. She turned away and lowered her voice, though the room's size hardly allowed for privacy. "I'm in the darkroom with Melvin, fine-tuning a print. I was just thinking about calling you."

"Oh, really?"

Something about the way he uttered those two words made her flush to her toes. She cleared her throat. "I missed you."

"Then we're even. How about dinner? A pint and a light supper at the Plucked Goose, maybe?"

"Are we dining alone?"

"With Chris and some of the other lads, probably."

First dinner with Chris and Sarah, now a pint with his mates. That was some sort of girlfriend initiation, even if she knew most of them from the old days. "What time?"

"Half eight?"

"I'll be there."

"See you then, love."

Grace clicked off and tried to wipe the smile from her face before she turned. She didn't need Melvin to know she'd become a complete fool over a man.

Too late. Melvin was grinning at her over the developer tray. "That him?"

"You heard everything, didn't you?"

"Of course I did. Who is he? Anyone I know?"

"Do you remember Ian MacDonald?"

"Your ex?" His eyebrows arched into where his hairline should have been. "I liked him."

"You never met him!"

"True, but I liked how you were when you were with him. Happy. You used to laugh, Grace."

"I laugh!"

The dubious look he sent her said it all. Then he shrugged. "I suppose I don't blame you. I'd be more worried if you weren't affected by everything you've seen and experienced. You should have someone who gives you as much as you give everyone else. You deserve some happiness."

When she didn't immediately answer, Melvin transferred the print carefully into the fixative, then said, "Stop worrying, Grace. Stop waiting for the other shoe to drop and just live for a while, will you?"

He knew her too well. "I'll do my best."

"Good. A couple more minutes and we can take a look at this."

His words trailed her through the rest of the afternoon, through talk of exposures and burning and dodging. It was after six o'clock before they had gotten a print that pleased them both. Fourteen more to go, but she knew the process would be a pleasure. Melvin shared her vision, and he was always careful to guide without imposing his own expectations.

But their discussion stayed with her through the trek

home and her preparations for supper with Ian. If she stayed in London, she would have the freedom to explore whatever creative endeavors she wished. She could have a darkroom. She could experiment with other kinds of photography besides conflict.

Maybe if she could stop focusing on the misery of the world around her, she could embrace the happiness that was in front of her.

CHAPTER TWENTY

THE NEXT FOUR WEEKS TOOK ON their own rhythm. Grace photographed London while Ian rowed and worked, and they met for dinner almost every night. She and Melvin made their way through the remaining prints, some of which they got on the first try, others requiring multiple days of fine-tuning and numerous reprints. All the while, James's wedding in Scotland came nearer. And surprisingly, the idea of seeing Ian's family again held more anticipation than fear.

When Ian called and said he would pick Grace up at Asha's flat at 6 a.m., she expected him to arrive in a cab. Instead the sleek, shiny roadster pulled up to the curb, the hood already tucked back.

Grace straightened from her perch on the front steps. "I thought we were taking the train."

He climbed out and circled around to the pavement. "Change of plans. Are you disappointed?"

"Not at all. Driving to Scotland in what might be the coolest car ever built? That's the good kind of spontaneity."

"And so is this." He grabbed her hand and pulled her into a long, lingering kiss. When he let her go, she was fairly certain she had a dumb, dreamy look on her face. He eyed her suitcase on the steps. "That's all you're bringing? Could you have fit enough shoes and clothes for the weekend in that?"

She gave him a withering look.

"I'll take that as a yes." He lifted the suitcase and grimaced. "What's in this? Every pair of steel-toed boots you own?"

"That's my camera equipment, so be careful. It's worth as much as your car. Almost." A wild exaggeration, but it was worth it for how gingerly he placed it in the boot.

"Where are your clothes, then?"

"Rucksack." She turned so he could see the sizable pack on her back.

"You're something else, Grace. Come on. We've got six hundred miles to cover in one day."

Grace climbed into the passenger side and placed her rucksack behind her seat. "You could have been slightly less spontaneous and decided to leave yesterday. When exactly did this idea hit you?"

"About two hours ago." He twisted the key in the ignition, then pulled a pair of sunglasses from his jacket pocket.

"I changed my mind. You look like James Bond, not Superman."

"*That* I can live with."

Grace settled back as he pulled into light morning traffic,

enjoying the coolness of the air, even if it came with London's signature fragrance of damp concrete and diesel fumes. Twelve hours straight in a car would have been a horror with anyone else, but she selfishly loved the idea of having Ian all to herself.

"What are you thinking?" he asked after several minutes of silence.

About you. Out loud she said, "I was wondering if you'd finally let me drive her."

He threw her an unreadable look—he really did look like James Bond in those shades—and then said, "Maybe."

"That's an improvement. I've graduated from 'not a chance' to 'maybe.'" She grinned and went back to her observation of the London cityscape. By the time they were out of London proper, though, the nerves were already encroaching.

"What do you think they'll say when you show up with me?"

"Jamie will probably pat me on the back and tell me it's about time. Serena will ask me if I'm happy. And if she's smart, Mum will keep quiet."

"I told you before, I don't want to cause any problems."

He lifted her hand to his lips without taking his eyes off the road. "They'll have to get used to it. But let's not borrow trouble. If there's one thing of which I'm absolutely certain, it's that Andrea will adore you."

"The American?"

"Yes, the American. And if Mum reconciled herself to the fact Jamie is marrying an American . . ."

Grace accepted the statement, even though she knew it wasn't the same thing. Marjorie might dislike the idea that James was marrying an American on principle, but she hated Grace in particular. Besides, from what Ian had said, Andrea was a successful, educated businesswoman who had moved to Inverness and started her own company. Grace was a drifter, making her living by her camera, owning only what was small enough to pack in a duffel bag and a few hard cases. In fact, the exact phrase Marjorie had used was *Irish gypsy trash*. Grace almost didn't blame her for thinking she wasn't good enough for her son. But the son thought she was good enough for him, and that was the only thing that mattered. Wasn't it?

As they continued west and then north, Ian sensed Grace settling in beside him, even though she shot him searching looks. Did she think he'd gone completely mad, binning their train tickets in favor of the slower and more tedious drive to Scotland? It was something he might have done in younger, rasher days, which was probably where the urge came from in the first place. Being back with Grace felt like it had erased those years they'd spent apart, loosened the rules and the practicality that had governed his life for a decade.

It seemed that Grace was thinking along the same lines, because she said, "Did you ever think we'd be here together, doing something like this?"

"Going to Jamie's wedding in Scotland? No, I was pretty sure he'd be a permanent bachelor." He chuckled when he remembered the lecture he'd given his brother, about how Andrea was too good for him if he was just trying to get her into bed. He'd underestimated both the change in Jamie's values and the effect that their consultant had had on him. The fact that Jamie had found her at her sister's home in Ohio and flown halfway across the world to get her back had proven that he was serious about her. And for the first time, Ian thought he and Jamie might have something in common.

"You know very well that's not what I'm talking about. I mean me, giving up my life on the road. You giving up rowing to be a big-time lawyer."

"I'm hardly a big-time lawyer. More like a small-time solicitor who keeps up his practising certificate out of habit rather than any real need. Frankly, I do little other than babysit my brother's money and shuffle paperwork. And now that I have Ms. Grey, I do far less paperwork shuffling."

She cocked her head, picking up what he'd left unsaid. "You told me all this is just something to do. What would you do? If you didn't have any responsibilities to family or the business?"

"If I could walk out of Jamie's company and never come back?" He thought for a minute. "I don't know. Once, I might have said I'd go back to rowing competitively, assuming I still had the ability, but I recently realized it doesn't hold the same appeal for me."

"Technically, you don't have to do anything." Grace raised an eyebrow significantly at him. "You could . . . I don't know . . . travel. That's the advantage of a wealthy family and a trust fund."

"Unfortunately, I'd have a guilty conscience. Not sure I could look at myself in the mirror if I weren't doing something. I never wanted to be one of the idle rich. None of us have."

"Most men don't choose contract law for fun."

"I didn't actually study contract law. My degree is in public international law. That's part of the reason I came on with CAF when the board position opened. I already had some expertise in the area." He glanced at her, frowning. "I never told you that?"

"You never told me that. I assumed you were drawing up wills and trusts and the like before James stole you away. Why that speciality?"

Ian remained silent, trying not to take the simple question as an indictment. He'd ignored that part of his life for so long he'd almost forgotten it existed. "Maybe I had the notion that I could change the world too. You were the one who actually did."

Grace flinched, and he realized his blunder too late. "Grace, I'm sorry, I didn't mean—"

"No, I know you didn't. I knew it would be hard to leave that behind. Some days are harder than others."

Not for the first time, a little kernel of doubt sprouted in Ian's heart. "Are you sure this is what you want to do? I don't want you to have any regrets. I don't want you to resent me."

Honest surprise surfaced on her face. "I could never resent you. You have to understand, this is who I've been for so many years, I'm not sure who I am without the camera in my hand." She hesitated, then added softly, "I'm not sure who I am without their pain."

Ian stayed quiet for a moment, letting the statement rest, afraid to breathe lest it would pull apart like tissue paper. "I wish you would let me help you with . . . all of this you're carrying."

"You already have." She laced her fingers with his and squeezed hard. "After I left you, I felt like I was looking for something. Someplace to call home, maybe. And nothing has ever felt right. Until now. I have to believe you're the reason for that. Is that . . . a lot of pressure?"

"No. Not pressure." He took off the sunglasses and looked away from the road long enough to let her see he meant it. "It's a gift."

CHAPTER TWENTY-ONE

SCOTLAND WAS BEAUTIFUL. There had been a time in Ian's life when the wide-open spaces of green and the craggy face of the Highlands had represented a life Mum hated, and one by extension he was supposed to hate too. It had been easy enough to avoid his home country when he went away to Eton, spending term breaks at Leaf Hill or at his wealthy schoolmates' country estates. It wasn't so much contempt for the less-refined aspects of Scotland, but that it was simply easier to do as Mum wished. He'd chosen her over his father, Jamie, and Serena. To admit he missed Skye would have been tantamount to admitting he'd made a mistake, and no one could afford for him to do that. It was only when Duncan MacDonald's death three years ago transferred the hotel to his children's hands that Ian realized the connection he still had with his birthplace.

Now, as he and Grace bumped down the gravel road to the hotel, he could own up to what he'd not told Jamie. Sometimes even one who loved the city as he did felt his soul stretch in the presence of Skye's natural beauty, as if awakened from a long slumber. Even in the dark, it was good to be back.

"You may not recognize the place," he said as he made the turn down to the hotel. In the last rays of twilight, the bay and the lighthouse were cast in shades of silvery blue, an ethereal landscape of light and shadow. On its edge, illuminated by pools of light from new fixtures, stood the renovated MacDonald Guest House.

"It's lovely," Grace said. "Changes to the facade?"

"Several." Ian pulled in beside a handful of cars—all wedding guests, since they'd not yet officially begun booking travelers—and put the roadster into park. He jumped out and circled to open Grace's door. A delighted smile played on her lips as the breeze off the sound ruffled her hair. "Come through and I'll show you about."

If he'd ever been skeptical of Andrea's expertise, he was no longer. The addition of new rooms and a kitchen off the back had been integrated seamlessly, the new masonry indistinguishable from the old 1800s stone facade. The bar addition had an attractive solid-oak door and antique windows, while the sunroom on the far side was positioned to bring light into the breakfast room and restaurant. Ian could barely remember what it had looked like before.

"Seems they're already setting up for tomorrow," Grace observed, crunching past him to peek at the meadow beyond, where crates of folding chairs and tables awaited deployment for the ceremony. "What a lovely site for the wedding."

"Andrea insisted," came a deep voice behind them. "And if you've met Andrea, you know she almost always gets what she wants."

They turned to find Jamie grinning at them, his hands thrust into the pockets of his jeans. Ian crushed his brother into a hug, picking him up off the ground for a moment. "Last night as a bachelor. How do you feel?"

"Fine. And anxious to get this whole event on its way." Jamie looked past him, and his expression shifted to one of shock. "Grace?"

"None other."

To Grace's credit, she didn't look the least bit uncomfortable as she smiled and extended her hand. "Hi, James."

"None of this." Jamie hugged her almost as enthusiastically as Ian had done to him. Then he slung an arm over Grace's shoulder like he would have done with his own sister. "So this was Ian's big secret? I can understand being back in London, but you're back with him? Why?"

Considering Jamie's words were accompanied by his usual mischievous grin, he could hardly be angry. Ian let him have his fun, then asked, "May I have my girlfriend back now?"

Jamie lifted his arm and stepped away, hands up. "By all means. Let me show you to your rooms, and then we can go up to the house. Andrea and Serena are seeing to some last-minute details."

"You've been busy finishing the interiors before the wedding," Ian said as Jamie led the way to the front entrance.

"Andrea has. The contractors are frightened to cross her.

That woman is fierce." The way he said it made Ian think he'd enjoyed the show immensely. "Here we are. The new foyer. Your rooms are on the first floor."

Ian admired the newly renovated interior while Jamie paused to retrieve two room keys from the cabinet beside the desk. They followed him up the stairs to the left, where he unlocked the door to room twelve. "Grace, I think you'll enjoy this one. Best view in the house."

It was indeed a stunning view of the sound, or it would be when the sun rose in the morning over the water. The restrained decor was luxurious without detracting from the natural beauty outside. Andrea and Jamie had truly outdone themselves. Grace disappeared into her room as Jamie continued down the hall.

"Andrea insisted your guest get the best room," Jamie murmured. "We put you in eleven, across the hall."

Ian's room was slightly smaller but equally lavish, this one overlooking the meadow where the wedding would take place the next afternoon.

"So." Jamie gave Ian a questioning look. "Grace. This is really happening again?"

Something in his brother's tone made Ian vaguely uncomfortable. "You don't approve?"

"Not for me to approve or disapprove. I like Grace— I always have. Suits you better than some London coed."

"You talked to Mum."

"Of course I did. You didn't think she'd keep that to herself, did you? I heard all about your stubborn refusal to let her matchmake."

"Mum's the last one I want involved in my love life."

"Plan on hiding Grace in a broom cupboard tomorrow, do you?"

"No, boot of the car." Grace's voice came from the hallway behind them. "You lads really need to work on your whispering."

Jamie swaggered forward and slung his arm around her shoulders once more. "See, this is why I have always liked you, Grace. Let's go find Andrea. You two will get on famously, I can tell."

Grace shot Ian an amused look over her shoulder, but she looked comfortable beneath Jamie's arm, so Ian didn't interfere. For once, he blessed his brother's annoyingly effusive charm for defusing what could have been an uncomfortable situation.

"So tell me about this woman who overcame your permanent vow of bachelorhood," Grace was saying as they walked down the stairs. "An American no less! That explains the dour expressions on the faces of all the Englishwomen in London. They thought one of their own would snag you."

Ian grinned. He needn't have worried. Grace could always hold her own.

Once they reached the foyer, Jamie asked, "Luggage now or later? You missed supper at the house, but I can make something for you if you're hungry."

"I forgot how much I missed that about you." Grace looked to Ian. "I'm not hungry, but the luggage can wait if you want to go straight up."

Jamie was already guiding Grace toward the passenger seat of his silver Audi. Ian called after them, "If you weren't getting married, I'd be concerned by all this."

"If I weren't getting married, you would have to be." Jamie

winked at Grace, who laughed. His brother was an incorrigible flirt, but toward Grace, his manner was downright brotherly.

Ian climbed into the spacious backseat, folding his long legs into an area that still managed to be too small for them. Grace and Jamie were already onto discussions about the wedding tomorrow and Andrea's insistence that they have a proper Scottish ceremony, complete with kilts and a piper.

"Did you pack your kilt?" Grace asked over her shoulder.

"Of course I did. I'm the best man."

"Now that, I can't wait to see."

"I'd venture that I wear a kilt more often than you wear a dress."

"And you'd be right."

Up at the house, little had changed. The garden plot was in full leaf under Aunt Muriel's care, with bright flowers in the window boxes off the white clapboard house. Ian opened Grace's door and led her up the macadam steps to their aunt's house before Jamie could claim her again.

The front door opened to warmth and laughter and the smell of baking—a sure sign Serena was busy in the kitchen. He guided Grace inside and closed the door behind them.

"Uncle Ian!" Emmy jumped up from her spot at the table where she was making paper roses and threw her arms around his waist.

"My gorgeous girl!" Ian picked up his seven-year-old niece and gave her a squeeze before plopping her back down. A toddler flew at his legs and nearly knocked himself over with the force of the collision.

"Ah, Maxie." He settled the two-year-old comfortably on his arm. "Say hi to my friend Grace."

Max held his arms out to her. "Bup."

Her eyebrows lifted, but she took the toddler, who immediately started poking her tattoos, presumably to see if they'd rub off. Grace laughed. "Built-in entertainment."

"He's gotten over his shy phase," Serena said as she entered the reception room, a tea towel in hand. Then she stopped. "Grace!"

"And here I thought you might not remember me."

"Nonsense." Serena strode forward and squeezed Grace into a hug around the child. "You're hard to forget. Maxie, leave her alone."

"It's fine," Grace said, but she surrendered the little boy to his mother. He immediately twisted his fingers through the end of her bob.

"Little monkey, this one," she said. "Em, go get Aunt Andrea."

"No, I'm here." A beautiful dark-haired woman passed through the doorway and went straight to Ian. He kissed her cheek, and she squeezed his arm before she held out a hand to Grace. "I'm Andrea. So pleased to meet you."

"Likewise. I'm Grace." She shook Andrea's hand. "Congratulations on your marriage."

"Thank you." She looked back to Ian. "Are you two hungry? Serena and I are baking for breakfast tomorrow, but Jamie's getting restless, knowing there's cooking for the reception going on without him."

"I am not," Jamie protested, but the doting look he gave Andrea before he kissed her a little too long said it hardly mattered what she said. He was undoubtedly smitten with his fiancée.

Grace smiled up at Ian in a way that made him guess she

was thinking the same, and he drew her back against himself automatically. "Hold up. Where's Aunt Muriel?"

Serena's expression turned serious. "She wasn't feeling well. Overworking herself with wedding preparations, I think." But something in her voice, the worry in her expression, made him think the excuse was for the children's benefit. She looked to Grace. "What do you say? Up to some batter-mixing?"

"Go on if you want," Ian murmured in Grace's ear before dropping a kiss on her temple. "I need to get the third degree from Jamie now."

"While I get the female version." She gave him a mysterious smile he couldn't quite interpret before she followed his sister and soon-to-be sister-in-law through the doorway.

Jamie clapped a hand on his shoulder. "Let's have a talk, you and I. Fancy helping me bring some wine back down to the hotel?"

"You purposely left that for last, didn't you?"

"Of course I did. Plus I want to check on Jeremy."

"Ah, you brought him up from London to do the food?"

"Seemed like an appropriate trade, since I'm going to invest in his restaurant."

Ian stopped. Jeremy Davis was the head chef at Jamie's Notting Hill restaurant, and the most reliable and responsible of all the kitchen staff. "When were you going to tell me about this?"

"I'm telling you now." Jamie raised his voice. "Andrea, love, we'll be back."

"All right, Jamie, love," she called back in perfect mimicry of his Scottish accent. "Try to be gentle."

"I love that woman," he said with a grin before propelling

Ian out the front door. "Took me long enough to convince her to marry me. Not as long as some, however."

"I deserved that."

"So let's get straight to it. Is there a reason you didn't mention it was Grace you were bringing? For that matter, is there a reason you didn't tell us she was back?"

Ian winced, though he had no reason to feel guilty. "I wasn't sure how you would react. It's Grace."

"It is. The woman who basically destroyed you, your rowing career, and every plan you had for the future."

Ian climbed into the car. "That had nothing to do with her."

"It had everything to do with her." Jamie started the car and backed down the drive. "Question is, what happens now that she's back?"

"What's it to you? Since when do you involve yourself in my love life?"

Jamie raised an eyebrow. "That answers my next question. I was going to ask if it was serious."

Ian realized his brother had been baiting him, much as he'd done to Jamie when he was pursuing Andrea. "It's Grace. It's automatically serious."

"That's what I thought. But something's different this time, isn't it?"

"God, I hope so." It was as much a prayer as an answer. He shifted topics. "What's up with Muriel?"

"I don't know. She's not herself. We've been trying to get her to see her doctor, but you know Muriel."

"Doesn't do anything she doesn't want to do, I know. She's exactly like Dad."

"We've hired a new manager for the hotel so she won't have to work so hard. He's taking over the labor-intensive tasks and managing the bar. He's also under strict instructions to keep an eye on her."

"I don't like it."

"I don't either, but what else can we do? You're in London. Serena visits when she can, but Em has school in Inverness. And Andrea and I—"

"Right. How are you working that?"

"We just bought a home in Nairn and she's set up office nearby. I'm still traveling back and forth between there and London. Let's be honest. The restaurants may run themselves, but I can't leave them for more than a few weeks at a time. We can't live on Skye."

"This manager is trustworthy, you think?"

Jamie pulled up to the hotel, something in his face telling Ian he wouldn't like the answer. "Raised here. Just moved back. He's an engineer."

"A . . . what?"

Jamie got out and walked round to the boot. Ian followed. "Listen," Jamie said, "he's responsible, he needed the job, and he's good with the reservation system. You know as well as I do that people come to Skye for their own reasons. They don't tend to want a lot of questions."

Jamie was right. If his siblings trusted this manager, he would too. "I just hate the idea of no family being here if Muriel is unwell."

"I know. Me too. Grab one of those cases?"

Ian took the wine bottles and followed Jamie around back to the kitchen entrance, where the light and heat and clatter spoke to preparations still under way. Jamie went straight to the industrial walk-in refrigerator and placed the box on the floor next to the others like it.

"This is an improvement," Ian observed. "A far cry from the little cottage kitchen."

"We'll see. Restaurant opens for its first dinner seating next month."

Ian scanned the kitchen, where several men in white chef jackets prepped the ingredients for the next day's reception. It was all gleaming tiles and stainless steel, the same standards as Jamie's restaurant kitchens. He offered his hand. "You've done a good job. You *and* Andrea."

"Thank you." Jamie shook his hand. "Let's check in with Jeremy, and then we can get back to our women."

Of course he would deliver the last bit with a wicked, knowing wink. He was enjoying this turn of events.

To be perfectly honest, so was Ian.

CHAPTER TWENTY-TWO

GRACE LET HERSELF BE DRAWN into the kitchen with Serena and Andrea. The smell of baking breads coming from the oven and the mess spread over the countertops said they'd already been at it for some time. "Who's all this for?" she asked, accepting a mixing bowl from Serena.

"Wedding guests," Serena said. "The restaurant at the hotel isn't open yet, and there isn't much nearby. Mix that together, will you? A dozen or so strokes is all."

"Serena also seems to think that I need entertainment on the night before my wedding," Andrea put in, spooning already-mixed batter into muffin tins. "Apparently sleep is overrated in this family."

"Always has been." Grace smiled. The easy manner between the two other women said that Andrea had been readily accepted into the family.

"You seem pretty familiar with the MacDonalds," Andrea said, a twinkle in her eye. "You've known Ian for a while, then?"

"Oh, I think you know the answer to that." Grace stirred the batter carefully, scraping flour off the sides of the bowl as she went. "Who's the designated interrogator?"

"Since I'm technically not a member of this family until tomorrow, I'll give that honor to Serena." Andrea winked at her soon-to-be sister-in-law and whisked the muffin tin to the countertop beside the oven.

Grace reached for the floured pan Serena nudged across the counter. "All right. I'm ready. Go."

Serena laughed. "I haven't even had time to think up proper questions! Which is probably why Ian didn't warn us you were coming."

"Well, if Serena isn't going to take advantage, I will." Andrea returned to the island, wiping her hands on a tea towel. "What do you do for a living, Grace?"

Andrea couldn't have known she'd started with the hardest question. "I'm a photographer, though I'm considering a change. The travel doesn't appeal to me like it once did."

"I hear that," Andrea said. "What discipline?"

"I do some occasional commercial work, but mostly conflict."

Andrea's eyebrows lifted. "You're a war photographer? That's impressive. Not many women in your field, are there?"

"No. Bit of a boys' club, that."

"So, does that mean you're settling in London, Grace?"

Serena's tone was pleasant, but there was no doubt about the underlying implication.

"That's exactly what it means. I'm in the interview process for a job right now, but if that doesn't work out, I'll have to look for other options in the city."

"So you're serious about my brother?"

Grace placed the spoon carefully in the bowl. "I know you're aware of what went on before—"

"Actually, Ian never said a word," Serena murmured. "Didn't speak of it. Just said that the wedding was off and you had gone, and he didn't want to talk about it."

"Sounds like Ian." He wouldn't have said anything negative about her, even if he thought it. Maybe it was because he thought she would someday come back, and he didn't want to taint her relationship with his family. But more likely it was because that was the kind of man he was. Kept his thoughts close and his hurts closer, never spoke unkindly about others, even when they deserved it. And she had certainly deserved it.

"Let's just say I never got over him. And I'm happy that he would consider giving me a second chance. So yes, I'm serious about him."

"These Scottish lads seem to be good at second chances," Andrea said, nudging her as she went back to the counter. Grace took that as tacit acceptance.

Serena studied her for a moment across the counter, then softened into a smile. "Well, I'm glad you're back. Ian's gotten too somber the last few years. Needs to be livened up a bit. It's hard to believe there was a time when he was the one out at all hours and Jamie was the workaholic."

"Jamie is still a workaholic," Andrea said. "The man

actually wants to open a seventh restaurant in Inverness. As if he doesn't have enough to do." But her smile held pride rather than censure. Yes, this woman was a good match.

"Well, I hope you have some time to explore the island while you're here. Lots of interesting spots for a photographer." Serena glanced at the wall clock, then threw her towel on the countertop. "Will you keep an eye on the timer? I need to go put Em and Max to bed. It's getting late."

"We'll watch the oven." Andrea plopped on the stool at one end of the island and crossed one long, slender leg over the other. Grace would have been tempted to hate her if she hadn't seemed so welcoming. Andrea waited until Serena was out of the room and then said, "It's a little overwhelming, isn't it?"

"What is?"

"Their sheer niceness. I was a hospitality consultant come here for the week, and by the time I left, they'd practically adopted me." There was something both appreciative and wistful in her tone.

"You have family of your own?" Grace asked.

"A sister, Becky, and her husband and kids. They're here for the wedding, but they turned in early tonight. Jet lag."

"No parents?"

"I haven't spoken to my dad in years." Andrea looked suddenly far younger and less confident than she had minutes before. "We had a falling-out after my mom died, and we just . . . drifted apart."

"Sounds familiar," Grace murmured. "My brother died when I was fourteen, and I've not seen my parents since I left home for university." She hadn't intended to deliver that personal information to a virtual stranger, but there was something about James's fiancée that made Grace think she was a kindred spirit. Andrea was clearly happy with her current life, but Grace knew all too well about the scars that even happiness couldn't erase.

Andrea didn't try to offer apologies or condolences, she just nodded and began wiping up the batter spills on the counter with a clean towel. "Jamie and I will be back in London after our honeymoon. We should try to have dinner together one night."

"That would be nice," Grace said, and she really meant it.

Serena returned not long after, the kids safely tucked into bed, and they swapped several other batches of breakfast breads into the oven. Just as Andrea began yawning into the back of her hand, the front door opened, followed by male voices. "The men are back. And just in time."

Ian and James came in through the dining room, laughing about something that they clearly had no intention of sharing. Jamie went straight to Andrea and wrapped his arms around her from behind. "Ready for me to take you back down? Big day tomorrow."

"Is it? I'd forgotten."

Ian nudged Grace. "Come on, they're going to start up again. We might as well head back to the hotel ourselves."

"You need a ride, remember?" James bent to kiss Andrea. "Serena, you need any more help here, or do you want me to come up in the morning to bring back all the pastries?"

"They still have to cool, so morning is best."

Despite the late hour, the sky was still light in the distance, a side effect of Skye's northern latitude. Ian ushered Grace out the door, bending to inquire, "So, did they interrogate you?"

"Not really," Grace whispered back. "They were pretty gentle, all things considered. You?"

"Grilled. Seems rather amused by the whole situation, Jamie does. He likes playing the wiser, married brother."

"Almost married."

"What are you two whispering about?" James came out with Andrea close behind.

"Just saying I hoped that marriage matures you some," Ian said.

"Not likely. Andrea is the adult here."

This time, both Ian and Grace climbed in the backseat of the car. As soon as the dome light went off inside, Grace found Ian's hand on the leather seat beside her and gripped it tightly. She hadn't even admitted to herself how nervous she was about seeing his family again, but they'd accepted her almost as if she'd never gone. She had Ian to thank for that, his maturity in keeping their business to himself.

James pulled up in front of the cottages on the opposite side of the hotel car park and switched off the engine. "I'm going to take Andrea to her cottage, and then I'll be up. I'm in six if you need anything. Your room keys will open the front door."

Ian and Grace retrieved their bags from the Healey's boot before returning to the hotel. Grace sighed as they climbed the stairs to their rooms. "It really is beautiful here. Do you ever think about moving back?"

"Never. Too many memories. Some good, some bad. It would be a nice place for a family, though."

Grace's steps slowed as they reared up on a topic they hadn't yet discussed. The night before James's wedding was hardly the right time to have this conversation, especially not in the hallway of the hotel, but she wouldn't be able to sleep if she didn't ask. "Does that mean you've changed your mind? About children?"

Ian paused, his expression as stricken as she imagined hers was. "Have I changed my mind about not wanting any? Grace . . . no. I've not changed my mind."

The energy went out of her in a rush. "Thank goodness."

Relief sparked in his eyes. "You weren't asking because—"

"Because I'd changed my mind about having them? No. Heavens no. I just . . . We were young when we discussed it. People reevaluate. And when I see how good you are with your niece and nephew, it almost seems a shame for you not to have any of your own."

"Our pasts haven't changed, Grace. Nor has my reasoning. I love children; I just can't do it. I like London. I like city life. And when I see how badly my parents balanced that—"

"You don't need to explain to me. I just didn't want to worry all weekend that I might disappoint you."

He slid his hand behind her neck to tilt her face to his. "As long as you're here with me, you could never disappoint me."

Their good-night kiss was sweet and slow and tender, but it still ignited a warmth in her that demanded an answer. She pulled back. "Tomorrow."

"Tomorrow. You in a dress."

"And you in a kilt."

"One will be more impressive than the other, for sure."

Grace winked at him. "You do have good knees."

"And now you're delusional. Good night, Grace."

She shut the door between them and retreated to her lovely hotel room, a different kind of warmth blooming in her chest. Here, surrounded by his family, she could finally envision their future together.

CHAPTER TWENTY-THREE

IAN WOKE TO THE SUMMONS OF daybreak through his hotel room curtains. He would have liked to believe it was just his body's internal clock waking him for his usual outing, but it was more likely the knowledge his sister would kill him if he wasn't up at the house first thing to help Jamie. Or perhaps it was the twist of anxiety over the idea of Marjorie and Grace being in close proximity. Despite the occasion, he wouldn't put it past his mother to throw a few jabs Grace's way.

After he dressed and set out his clothes for the ceremony, Ian found himself standing outside Grace's room, his fist poised to knock. But not a rustle or a thump came from inside to indicate she was awake. After yesterday's marathon drive, she'd probably not thank him for rousing her out of bed so early. Instead, he continued outside, digging his car keys from his pocket as he went.

He might be the only one awake inside the guesthouse, but preparations were well under way outside. A vast white tent had gone up in the meadow, with half a dozen workers setting out tables and chairs for the reception. Nearer, another group lined up chairs on either side of a carpeted aisle.

The scene up at the house was equally busy. Muriel stood in the center of her reception room, directing the activity with the steely aplomb of a field marshal while chaos spilled from every angle. Boxes of flowers and decorations. Baskets of cellophane-covered baked goods. And two overexcited children getting under the helpers' feet as much as possible.

"What's this?" Ian asked, stepping over Max, who was sprawled inexplicably in the middle of the rug.

"Ian!" Muriel made her way to him and squeezed him into a bone-breaking hug. "I'm so pleased you're here. Can you drive the flower arrangements down to the tent?"

"Of course." He looked her over carefully, but besides the slight shadows beneath her eyes, there was nothing to indicate cause for concern. Her silver hair was as impeccably coiffed as usual, her pantsuit pressed, if slightly looser than he remembered. "Why exactly is everything up here and not down at the hotel?"

"Paparazzi. 'Sullivan-MacDonald wedding' brings them out of the woodwork, but no one cares about a simple garden party at his unknown aunt's place." She waved a hand. "Malcolm, dear, help Ian with the arrangements?"

Malcolm? Ian frowned as an unfamiliar man straightened from where he was placing vases of flowers in boxes. He was shorter than Ian, with a muscular, stocky build. A leather jacket and scruffy beard gave him an almost-disreputable air. But when he fixed his attention on Ian, he offered a hand and a friendly smile.

"Malcolm Blake."

"Ian MacDonald." Ian shook his hand, noting the man's hard grip and the bruises on his knuckles. Boxer? Or brawler? And who was he to be standing in his aunt's living room?

Evidently, Malcolm caught Ian's confusion. "I'm the new hotel manager. And bartender. And handyman."

"The engineer?"

"So they tell me. Shall I give you a hand?"

Ian grinned suddenly. Leave it to Andrea to hire a bartender/handyman who looked like he belonged in a boxing ring but was actually an engineer. And no surprise that Muriel seemed to have adopted him like a son. That's what his aunt did.

"I'd appreciate it."

Malcolm hefted one of the heavy crates of flower arrangements, then waited for Ian to lead him out the door to the Healey. "I don't technically start until next week, but there have been some problems with the reservation system."

"And Muriel borrowed you for wedding duty."

He shrugged. "Glad to do it. Computer problem was a simple fix anyway. Just a script handling error."

So he really was an engineer, or at least somewhat technical. Ian opened the boot of the car to make room for the boxes. "These are all there are?"

Malcolm nodded and flashed an amused smile. "I'd offer to take them down with you, but I'm under strict instructions not to let Muriel overdo it."

Ian decided at that moment that he liked him. He held out a hand. "A pleasure."

"Same here. You need anything else, let me know." Malcolm gave Ian a nod, then greeted Jamie as he came out with baskets of baked goods in his arms.

Jamie looked past his brother to the hotel manager's departing figure. "You met Malcolm?"

"The engineer?"

Jamie laughed. "He dotes on Muriel. He's driving her a little crazy to hear her talk, but she likes him."

"Good enough for me. How about you? Nervous?"

Jamie strode across the gravel drive, releasing the boot of his car with his key fob. He deposited the baskets of baked goods inside. "What's there to be nervous about?"

"'I do. Till death do us part.' That sort of thing makes most men squirm."

"Would it make you nervous?" Jamie shot back with a smirk. Maybe he had a point.

They made several trips between Muriel's house and the hotel, Ian delivering flowers to the decorators while Jamie made sure there was coffee, tea, fruit, and pastries for the several dozen guests staying at the hotel. Ian was headed back to his room to change when he bumped into his uncle on the stairway.

"Rodney! I didn't know you were coming!"

"Came up with your mum last night." Rodney clapped Ian on the shoulder, then lowered his voice. "So you brought Grace, eh?"

"That was fast. How'd you know?"

"You just told me. Keep her away from Marjorie until later, though. They'll need fireworks as the grand finale."

Ian couldn't help but laugh. Rodney looked downright excited about the potential for an altercation. "I'll do my best."

"You can thank me later, by the way. I'm always right."

Grace still hadn't emerged by the time Serena came to summon him for photos of the groomsmen down in the meadow. Dressed in a sky-blue bridesmaid gown with a spray of flowers in her short hair, she looked younger and prettier than he'd seen her since her husband died two years earlier. He placed her hand in the crook of his elbow as they crossed the car park to the meadow.

"I feel like we haven't talked in months," Ian said. "Everything fine?"

"It's only been four weeks! Or have you been too busy to remember that?"

"Tell me what you really think, Sis."

She paused, then sighed and squeezed his arm hard. "It doesn't matter what I think. The only thing that matters is that you're happy. I've known for years that you still loved Grace. Why do you think I never pressed you about dating? Some people I guess you never get over."

"Is that how it is for you? You're young, you know. Edward has only been gone for two years, but—"

Serena waved a hand and inadvertently gave him a glimpse of her weariness. "I have two children. Not many men my age are looking for an instant family. Either they want their own or none at all. Not that I'm looking, mind you."

Ian leaned down and kissed the top of her head. "Someday. Don't give up too quickly, all right?"

"Well, look who's turned into a hopeless romantic?" Serena flashed a teasing smile before they got absorbed into the wedding party waiting for portraits.

"What are you smiling about?" Jamie came up between them, looking far more comfortable in his formal wear than Ian felt, his arms crossed over his chest.

"Nothing. You ready? In about an hour, you're going to be a married man."

"Can't wait," Jamie said easily. "Can you stay here and keep an eye on things? I'm going to go check on the food again—"

"Don't you dare." Serena glared at Jamie, then turned to Ian. "Your job is to make sure that he does *not* go bother Jeremy for the fourth time this morning. Today he is a groom, not a chef."

"I am always a chef," Jamie protested, but it was clearly more for their sister's benefit than any real desire to argue. "Plus, I'm an excellent host, and I want to make sure that our guests—"

"Will benefit from the only chef in whom you've ever invested, because you believe in his ability to turn out good food without your supervision."

"When did she get so bossy?" Jamie asked Ian.

"She's always been bossy. Granted, you gave her plenty of reasons growing up."

"All right, you two. That's enough of that. I'm going to make sure Em and Max haven't managed to destroy themselves before the ceremony. Don't go anywhere. The photographer may need you again."

Ian watched their sister go and slapped Jamie on the back, squeezing his shoulder hard enough to make him wince. "I'm happy for you, Jamie. I really am. Andrea is an amazing woman. And maybe the only one tough enough to keep you in line."

"Go ahead and have a laugh at my expense. I have a feeling I'll be the one laughing soon enough." Jamie glanced significantly over his shoulder.

Ian followed his brother's gaze and his mouth went dry. Grace picked her way across the gravel car park with a camera in hand, but he couldn't take his eyes off her long enough to determine which equipment she'd chosen. The clingy royal-blue dress skimmed over her curves, its color setting off her creamy Irish skin and blonde hair. When she spotted him and smiled, his gut twisted.

"I know that look," Jamie said, grinning. "You're done for."

Ian almost didn't register his brother moving away as Grace stepped up beside him. "Where's he going?"

Only then did he notice her dress was backless, the fabric plunging down to show a flowering tree tattooed across her back. He couldn't resist the chance to touch her, his thumb caressing her bare skin long enough to make her shiver. When he regained his ability to speak, he pitched his voice for her ears only. "It's a good thing we're in public. You in that dress may well be the sexiest thing I've seen in my entire life."

Her startled gaze found his while pink bloomed in her cheeks. "It's too much, isn't it?"

"No, it's most definitely not too much." His fingers tightened on her waist. "I just didn't know your cruel streak ran that deep."

The light pink deepened to crimson, but a secretive smile stretched her lips. Then he looked past her, and his heart sank. "Brace yourself, love."

Grace jerked her head up and stiffened when she glimpsed his mother crossing the meadow toward them, beautiful and icy cold in a gray silk suit more suited to London than Scotland. Grace tried to move away, but he held her fast. "No hiding. We're in this together, remember?"

Marjorie's perfectly groomed eyebrows went up when she saw Ian's possessive stance: his arm around Grace's waist, hand resting on her opposite hip. "There you are," she said with a practiced smile. "Am I late for photos?"

"Just in time, I'd say. Mum, you remember Grace Brennan?"

She shifted her focus to Grace and held out her hand. "Of course I remember Grace. Congratulations are in order, I think. It seems you've made quite a name for yourself since the last time we saw each other."

Ian let out his held breath. So his mum would be cordial for the sake of Jamie's wedding. That was something, even if the welcome she gave was not exactly warm.

Grace, for her part, put on a smile so convincing that Ian would have been fooled had he not still felt the tension in her stance. "Thank you, Mrs. MacDonald. How long will you be here in Scotland?"

"Just for the weekend. Seeing my younger son marry such a lovely and accomplished young woman is surely the highlight of the summer for me. Even if she is an American."

"Really, Mum." Ian sighed and inclined his head toward where the cluster of groomsmen had gathered for more photos. "If you want to take a photo with your sainted younger son, you'd better hurry."

Marjorie looked sharply at him, but she nodded to Grace. "I'm sure we'll have time to speak later, Grace."

"Don't count on it." Ian loaded warning into his voice. Marjorie's eyebrows lifted in surprise, but she said nothing else as she moved back toward the wedding party.

"That was considerably less painful than I expected," Grace said. "You didn't need to do that."

"Do what? Best she know I won't tolerate rudeness toward you. Now let's get you to your seat."

"I thought I'd snap some extra shots of the wedding. It could be a nice gift for Jamie and Andrea when they return to London."

"That would be lovely. I'll be doing my best man duties, but I expect you to save all your dances for me at the reception."

"That, you *should* count on." She smiled at him and then walked away with camera in hand, not even Jamie's amused attention able to distract him from the gentle sway of her hips in that dress.

"Get ahold of yourself, MacDonald," he murmured, wiping a hand across his face. Though he'd bet there wasn't a single man in the place who could blame him for his reaction. He strode across the meadow, giving his brother a sharp shake of the head as he passed. "Don't say it."

"Not a word." But Jamie's laugh followed him all the way to the aisle.

CHAPTER TWENTY-FOUR

THE GUESTS BEGAN TO FILL IN the chairs in the meadow, and Grace circled the hotel in search of the wedding party's approach. Considering James's high profile, it was a surprisingly low-key event, with under a hundred guests and none of the ostentatious touches that one would expect from a celebrity wedding. Of course, Andrea was shockingly down-to-earth, and it was pretty clear that James would give his fiancée anything she asked.

Grace found the staging area outside one of the three stone cottages that seemed to be serving as the preparation rooms for the wedding party. Serena stood in a blue gown that somehow managed to be the exact color of the island sky, two little girls in puffy white dresses giggling excitedly beside her. Another dark-haired woman, her petite, pretty looks suggesting she must be Andrea's sister, knelt beside a young boy who kept plucking at his clip-on bow tie.

Grace kept her distance, relying on the long lens to capture images without inserting herself into the scene. These would be the details that James and Andrea would want to remember later—the ones lost in the nerves of the pre-wedding moments. She couldn't help but admire Andrea's bravery in having not one, but five children as part of the wedding party.

Then the door to the middle cottage opened and Andrea stepped out. Somehow Grace had known she wouldn't choose a princess dress; instead, she wore a sleeveless white sheath with ruching that highlighted her figure, simple pleats in the back allowing her to walk. No train. No veil. Just a cluster of white flowers pinned into an elegant French knot at the back of her head. Grace shifted position to snap a few candids, knowing one of these would end up getting framed for James.

The prick of longing was so unfamiliar that it took Grace a few moments to recognize it. There was no fear in the eyes of the bride, only a smile that lit her entire face and seemed to illuminate the space around her. What would it be like to be so sure about her decisions? So in love and secure in that love that she could walk toward her future without a second thought?

They were sorting themselves into order for the processional, and Grace raised her camera again. At some point, Serena noticed her presence and shot her a rueful smile as she muscled her unruly toddler into line again. Andrea was right. The MacDonald family had a warmth about them that defied all expectations.

From the meadow, the strains of a bagpipe indicated the beginning of the processional, and Grace found a point on the edge of the seating where she could capture some shots of their arrival without getting in the way of the official photographer. First came the twin girl and boy she assumed belonged to Becky, strewing flower petals along the carpeted path to the altar, followed by Em and an older boy who had to be Andrea's other nephew. She noted Em's pink flush as she held the boy's arm—first crush in the making? Then came Max, toddling down the aisle with a pillow that held the rings. Grace held her breath as he tripped, but Serena set him on his feet again before he could hit the ground. Soft laughter rang out from the guests.

Everyone rose then as the bride appeared at the end of the aisle on her sister's arm. Andrea looked radiant and happy and so excited that Grace sighed along with the rest of the guests who had been caught up in the romantic setting.

James watched his bride's slow walk down the aisle, enthralled. Grace snapped a burst of shots and smiled to herself. One of these would surely be framed for Andrea's gift. What woman wouldn't want to remember the love in the face of her groom when he first saw her in her white dress? If there had been doubt in anyone's mind that the former playboy had found his soul mate, that single expression would erase it completely.

When she focused on the rest of the wedding party, however, she realized that not everyone's attention was on the bride. Ian was looking directly at her. Her breath caught. That look held so much emotion, she wondered if he was picturing them in James and Andrea's place.

Grace thrust herself into an empty seat before the strength

went out of her legs completely. Even after the piper stopped and the officiant began the greeting to the guests, she heard very little of what was said. She loved Ian. She'd known that from the second she'd set foot on the cement embankment outside his club, but the commitment he wanted, the promise of forever, had seemed too impossible to think about.

Now, watching James and Andrea hold hands and exchange their vows with love shining in their eyes, she couldn't suppress the wave of yearning. It took very little to imagine herself standing with Ian, exchanging their own vows. When she met his eyes again, he was still looking at her, a secretive smile on his lips.

She forced herself to listen to the rest of the ceremony, applauding with the other guests as James scooped Andrea into his arms for a tender and unhurried kiss, then escorted her back down the aisle with a foolish grin plastered on his face. Andrea was smiling and laughing, whispering things to her new husband as they went. Grace rose to get a picture of the recessional, both of the new Mr. and Mrs. MacDonald as well as Ian and Serena, who walked arm in arm behind them, his height dwarfing his petite sister beside him.

When he passed, she murmured in a voice just loud enough for him to hear, "Nice kilt, Scotsman."

He said nothing, just winked at her and gave her that half smile. And like that, her last bit of doubt vanished.

There were more pictures after the wedding with the bride and her attendants, but Ian kept an eye on the blonde in the blue dress who wove in and out of guests and caterers, her camera in hand. She had a knack for being in the right place at the right time to capture the candids the wedding photographer couldn't get to—her editorial skills at work. He had no doubt that by the end, she would have an album that told the alternate story of the wedding from a guest's point of view—probably one that would be more treasured than the formal shots of the wedding party.

"So, Brother dear," Serena said, "what do you plan to do about her?"

"What do you mean?"

"You couldn't take your eyes off her the entire time you were standing up there, and it was your brother's wedding. Did you even hear any of the vows?"

"There were vows?" Something about the whole event was making him punchy, and Serena's raised-eyebrow look said she knew it. He nodded toward the kids playing on the lawn. "Look, there's Em and Max. Go attend to your offspring. I'll survive without your supervision."

She stuck out her tongue before moving toward her two kids.

"It was a lovely wedding."

His smile formed before he even turned. "It was, wasn't it? They look truly happy."

Grace inclined her head to where the newly married couple was presiding over a receiving line, speaking to the guests beneath the expansive tent. "They really do. Of course, it's driving James absolutely mad not being able to oversee the food. Look."

Sure enough, Jamie cast a glance over his shoulder to where hors d'oeuvres were being circulated among the waiting guests.

"He never changes," Grace said with an affectionate smile.

"That's the thing. He has changed, and for the better. When they met, I didn't believe he could come to care for someone in such a short period of time. Or at all. But looking at them now . . ."

"Sometimes it takes the right person to bring out the best in another. Someone that makes you feel things you never thought possible." There was a new emotion shining in her eyes, and something in his chest gave a little tug in answer, as if recognizing what she left unsaid.

He took her hand. "Come, let's find our seats."

She didn't protest that she wasn't part of the wedding party, just interlaced her fingers with his and followed him through the crowd. He introduced her over and over, his hand resting on the small of her back, taking every chance he could to surreptitiously caress her exposed skin and thrilling to the occasional shiver that shot through her body.

"We're at my brother's wedding, and all I can think about is pulling you into a secluded corner and kissing you senseless," he murmured when they finally took their seats at the long head table beneath the tent. "Is that wrong?"

"Yes, it's completely wrong," she said, but the answering heat in her green eyes said something else entirely. That was all it took to ruin his concentration for the evening.

The food was impeccable. If this was any indication of Chef Davis's talent, it was no wonder that Jamie had decided to invest in the man's restaurant. Different from Jamie's elegant take on comfort food—more avant-garde, more international—it still had the care and precision Ian would expect from his brother's protégé. Still, he was glad when they progressed to the wedding cake, and then at last to dancing on the wooden floor set up in the meadow beneath the swiftly setting sun. It was a legitimate excuse to get Grace in his arms again.

"They really do look great together," she said. Jamie and Andrea swayed on the dance floor, wrapped in each other's arms, blissfully unaware of the existence of the other guests dancing around them. "They make me want to believe in happily-ever-afters."

"You make me want to believe in happily-ever-afters," he replied. "You also make me wish I were a better dancer. I didn't know you could dance."

"I'm multitalented." She grinned up at him with a naughty smile that made his heart seize again.

"Did I already say you'll be the death of me?"

"No, but you told me I had a cruel streak."

"The death part was implied."

She laughed, and then a few moments later, she sobered. "Thank you."

"What for?"

"For this. For making me feel like I belong. For making it clear to everyone that I'm with you."

It was so out of character for her that he stopped dancing and just held her in the middle of the other couples. "Grace, you do belong with me. And I promise you, no one will ever be allowed to make you feel otherwise when I'm around." Despite the fact that they were on display, or maybe because of it, he kissed her, long and slow and deliberately. Let them think what they wanted. Let them whisper about the shameful display—though he suspected he and Grace weren't the only ones affected by the romantic setting. Let his mother be horrified that he was kissing the woman he loved, who was not English, overeducated, or proper. She would have to get used to it, because in that moment Ian realized he could no longer imagine a future without Grace.

"There's something I want to do," he said suddenly, "but I have to go back to my room first. Will you come with me?"

"Is everything okay?"

"Everything's fine." And in a few moments, he hoped it would be better than fine.

Ian took the stairs two at a time and unlocked his room. It took only a moment to find what he was looking for in his suitcase—the gray velvet box he had picked up before they left London—and tuck it into the sporran at his waist. When he emerged back into the front foyer, however, movement in the dimly lit reception room caught his eye. His mother stood at the mantel with a glass of wine in her hand. From the look of her, it was not the first drink of the evening.

"Mum, what are you doing in here?"

"Looking for you." She turned slowly, taking in the renovated room. "They did a lovely job with this old place. I always did like this room."

Something in her voice told him this wasn't idle conversation. He moved closer and saw that her eyes were bleary, but not from alcohol. "Mum?"

"I haven't been back here since your father and I . . . Well, you're aware of that. I thought it would be easier after all these years."

Not for the first time, Ian wondered if the divorce and the move back to England had been harder than she'd let on. She'd never remarried or, until recently, even had gentlemen friends. But after the way she'd treated Grace, he wasn't inclined to feel sympathy for her.

"What's this all about, Mum?"

"You know very well what this is about. You had the audacity to bring her to a family affair—"

"No, that's not it. I had the audacity to love her. I don't understand. Do you refuse to accept her because she's Irish? Because of her tattoos? Or do you think she's beneath me?" He stared at his mother, willing a straight answer from her for once.

Marjorie's expression softened. She crossed the room and placed a hand on his chest. "I know you think I'm impossibly cruel, Son, and shallow. But I knew what kind of person she was from the first time I met her. I knew she would break your heart. And I was right."

She could not have said anything to surprise him more. He looked down into her face and saw genuine concern etched there. His mother was worried about him? He'd always assumed her matchmaking was out of consideration for her image and social status. But the slump of her shoulders held weariness. The set of her jaw revealed pain.

"You haven't been the same since she left you," Marjorie said quietly. "And I'm afraid this time when she leaves, it will break you. I love you, Ian. I don't want to see your love for this woman—as little as I can understand it—destroy you for good."

He put his hand on her shoulder. She looked up at him in surprise, and he gently put his arms around her. She might be meddling and sometimes cruel, but she was still his mother. She cared about him. She worried about him, even if she didn't manage to show it properly most of the time.

"Mum, you have to trust me. She's changed."

"I know you think so. But people like that don't change. You believe because they say you're the one, you'll come first in their lives."

"Are we talking about Dad?"

Marjorie pulled away and wandered over to a picture on one of the polished antique tables. It must have been either Jamie's or Serena's idea to include the family photo in the decor, this one showing the five of them in Scotland, before she and Duncan MacDonald had divorced. Before Marjorie had forced the children to choose between their parents.

"I know you think I did the wrong thing. But I loved your father. More than you could ever know. I thought I could give up everything for him, and maybe I could have." She turned toward him with a wry smile. "The problem was, he couldn't give up anything for me. Scotland and his music always came first. His students always came first. When I realized we had been married twenty years, and he had never once been willing to sacrifice anything to make us a family . . . I couldn't do it any longer."

Ian felt like he had been punched in the gut. He knew it was true. He had heard her say it before, and he had defended her to Jamie more than once. Hadn't he seen how the divorce had affected her? When they'd moved to London, she hadn't left her bedroom for a month. But somehow . . .

Somehow he had never made the connection between his father and Grace.

Would Grace's work always come between them? Would she really be able to sacrifice the thing that gave her life meaning?

Or would she leave him again?

"I'm sorry, Ian. I really wish I could give my blessing. But, Son, some people are not cut out for marriage. I would be willing to bet that Grace is one of them."

He looked out the window to where she waited, camera in hand, gazing out over the twilit water. Recalled how she had stopped him in the middle of Piccadilly Circus to say she loved him, dissipating for the first time the shadow of the past between them.

"I can't believe that, Mum. I appreciate your concern. But I love Grace. And I'm going to marry her."

"I respect that. But you will do it without me."

Ian pressed his lips together. It was what he had expected, but part of him had thought he could make her come around. "Very well, then. Jamie and Serena can represent my family. I hope someday you realize what a mistake you've made."

He strode from the foyer and joined Grace outside. "Come, sweetheart. Let's take a drive before anyone misses us."

She searched his face, her forehead creasing. "Is everything okay?"

"Fine. Better than fine. Let's go."

Grace climbed into the car, puzzled by the sudden frenetic energy in Ian's body. "Are we leaving?"

"Not for long. Besides, the party will go until the wee hours. No one will expect us to stick around now that Jamie and Andrea have retired for the night."

"That was your mother inside, wasn't it?" Grace chewed her bottom lip. "I shouldn't have come. I never meant to ruin what should have been a joyous family occasion."

"You didn't ruin anything. I wanted you here, and everyone but Mum understands that."

Grace soon realized he'd pointed the car toward Sleat's main road. "Where are we going?"

"A little spot I like here."

She flicked a glance at him. He'd never shown any particular desire to explore Skye, although he'd offered to show her around if she wanted to take photos. Her heart began to thud nervously against her rib cage when she sensed this was not merely a sightseeing trip.

When he finally pulled off the highway onto the verge, she drew in her breath. The sky was still light in the distance, showering the dark water with shades of orange and gold. He climbed out of the car, then helped her from the passenger side. When she shivered at the rush of cool air, he immediately draped his formal jacket over her shoulders. She nestled into his side beneath his arm and looked out onto the dark water of the sound.

"Something tells me you didn't bring me here to look at the scenery. And while I'd love to think this was just an elaborate way to get me alone, I rather doubt that as well."

He pressed a kiss to her temple, then fumbled with the clasp on his sporran. "I was going to wait to do this. I didn't want to take anything away from Jamie and Andrea, but now I simply can't wait."

She straightened when she saw the jewelry box in his hand. "Ian?"

For the first time in recent memory, he actually looked nervous. When he took her hand, his serious expression stole her breath. "I know this might seem sudden. But I fell in love with you when I was twenty-six and too stupid to know what

I had in front of me. I loved you when you walked away, and I loved you every minute thereafter."

Her hand drifted to her neck as if that would help loosen the lump in her throat. She couldn't manage a sound, but he didn't look to be done yet.

"Grace, the only thing that has ever mattered to me is you. And if you will let me, I will spend the rest of my life making up the time we lost." He sank down to one knee in the gravel and opened the box. "Will you marry me?"

She could barely process what was happening. He was wearing a kilt, a tuxedo shirt, and a very earnest expression, all the while holding a box that obviously contained a ring she couldn't see clearly in the dim light. When she opened her mouth to reply, the only thing that emerged was hysterical laughter.

His expression turned to dismay. "Grace?"

She forced herself to be serious. "I'm sorry. You caught me off guard, Ian. I don't need an elaborate setup or a fancy proposal. All I need is you."

The lines of his forehead smoothed. "Does that mean . . . ?"

"Yes. It means that I will marry you." Her smile stretched so wide it threatened to permanently cramp her face. "It also means you can get up now."

"Oh, thank you. The verge is gravel, and I'm not wearing trousers." He straightened, removed the ring, and slid it onto her finger. "I love you, Grace."

"And I love you." She lifted her face to him, waiting for his kiss. His lips moved over hers softly, tenderly, and she barely dared to breathe as she drank him in. When he drew back an inch, she held her hand up so the ring caught the light.

"It's different!" A delicate knotwork band cradled the diamond, which was surrounded by dozens of tiny ones.

"Same diamonds, same metal, just remade. With a little added to the band for strength."

Her vision swam in an unexpected wash of tears. He'd kept her engagement ring all these years and then had it remade into something new? Her heart felt too full to speak for several moments. "That might be the most romantic thing I've ever heard."

"That was the response I'd been hoping for." He pressed another series of kisses to her lips, her cheek, the spot beneath her ear, and she pressed into him while his fingertips grazed her back beneath the jacket.

"I'm sorry I laughed at you. I didn't take you for grand gestures and getting down on one knee and all that."

"What can I say? I was moved by the moment." His lips were brushing her neck in a deliciously slow path to her exposed collarbone. "You seem to bring out the unexpected in me."

"You mean I broke the curse of the suit?" Her voice came out shaky. It was getting harder to think by the second.

His laughter rumbled in his chest, and she felt him smile against her skin. "I'm not wearing a suit now."

"True. So perhaps we can thank the national menswear of Scotland."

"Never underestimate the power of tartan." His mouth found hers once more, conveying a level of need that mirrored her own, obliterating every last sensible thought. When he let her go, she almost moaned in frustration.

"We need to go back now, I think. While I can still act like a gentleman."

She wasn't quite sure she wanted him to be a gentleman, and that thought alone was enough to make her reach for the door handle. He waited until she gathered herself into the car, then shut the door behind her. She spent the time it took for him to reach the driver's side giving herself a stern mental lecture. The ring on her finger changed nothing.

Except it changed everything. A thrill of excitement shot through her, mixing with terror. Could she do this? Could she finally be the person he needed? The person he deserved?

Then he leaned over to kiss her, sweetly and carefully, and she shoved down the fear. No. She wouldn't let their past come between them. She wouldn't let her own failures ruin what should be the best night of her life.

"Ready? I imagine it's late enough we could avoid most of the questions."

"Until morning at least." She held her hand up to admire the sparkle of the impossibly large diamond, once more touched by the thought he'd put into it. It must have taken weeks. "Wait, how long ago did you have this made?"

"Over a month ago."

More than a month. Which meant just after she'd told him she loved him. Her heart clenched. So much faith in her, so much willingness to accept her back. It struck her with the deep conviction that she didn't deserve him.

And the deep determination to try.

CHAPTER TWENTY-FIVE

IAN WOKE EARLY, showered and changed, and then paced the perimeter of his room while waiting for the clock to show something approximating a reasonable hour. He could only guess what his family would say when they glimpsed the ring on Grace's finger. Muriel and Serena would be pleased. Mum, on the other hand . . .

Ian had made it clear that he intended to marry Grace, and Mum had made it equally clear she wouldn't support that decision. Whether she came around or not was irrelevant. He wasn't going to let anything else steal more of his time with Grace than he had lost already.

When the clock finally clicked over to 7 a.m., he gave up and knocked on Grace's door. It swung open immediately.

"Good morning," she said, bracing her shoulder against

the doorframe. She was already dressed, her hair tucked under her signature cap, though she actually wore a touch of makeup today.

"Sleep well?" he asked, moving in for a morning kiss.

"Not at all." She wrapped her arms around his neck and combed her fingers through the short hair at his nape, sending shivers down his spine. This woman was most definitely going to be the death of him. "It must have been the weight of this rock on my hand."

His heart lifted at her teasing tone. Part of him had worried that in the light of morning, she would regret accepting his proposal. Had she not been a captive here without a car or public transport, he might have questioned whether she'd be waiting for him at all.

"If we go down now, we might have some time to ourselves before the others wake." He nuzzled her neck, inhaling the scent of her skin and wishing he didn't have to share her so quickly. He wanted to keep the news of their engagement to himself for a little longer.

She pulled back with a smile. "I'm hungry. Let's go see what there is below."

Coffee, tea, and pastries awaited them, along with most of his family. Serena and Muriel already sat at one of the larger tables by the window, Em and Max positioned between them.

"Morning," Muriel greeted them brightly. She looked as cheery and healthy as always. Maybe they had been making too big of an issue over a little fatigue. "You two are up early."

Ian pulled out a chair for Grace at the table for two beside the others, just close enough to talk. "It's so bright here compared to London. I barely slept. I forget how it is up north."

"Mmm." Serena hid her smile in her teacup.

"What?"

"You didn't think we'd miss the ring, did you?" Serena shot a significant look at Grace's hand on top of the table.

Grace quickly whisked her hand into her lap. "Don't make a big fuss over it, please. We don't want to draw attention away from the newlyweds. And your mum—"

"You don't have to worry about that," Muriel said, her voice a touch stiff. "Marjorie left last night, and the happy couple started out at dawn. They have a flight out of Inverness this morning."

"Besides, you deserve to celebrate your news." Serena rose from her chair and pressed Grace into an awkward hug. "Congratulations. I'm so pleased for you two."

Grace's expression turned to surprise, and Ian suspected the fleeting glimmer in her eyes came from tears. At that moment, he'd never loved his sister more. He put his arms around Serena and kissed the top of her head. "Thanks, Sis."

Serena squeezed him back. "Be good to her, Ian. I want to see both of you happy."

Muriel replaced Serena and patted his cheek. "About time you two figured it out. Be happy and well. And don't tarry on your way to the altar."

He choked down his laugh, even as gratitude toward the women in his family filled him. No warnings, just sincere congratulations. And by Grace's expression, she was equally touched.

Other guests began to file into the room: family and

friends, some of whom Ian didn't know particularly well. The ones who noticed the ring on Grace's hand offered hearty congratulations, though there were as many surprised looks as smiles. After an hour of lingering over pastries and rapidly cooling tea, Ian couldn't take it any longer.

"Shall we go pack? We'll be driving through the night if we don't leave soon."

"Good idea." She stood and tossed her napkin on the table before shooting a look to Muriel and Serena. "Shall we come say good-bye at the house?"

"Please do." Something sympathetic surfaced in Serena's expression, but she said no more.

When they reached Grace's door, Ian asked, "Are you all right?"

"I'm fine. Why wouldn't I be? I can't blame anyone for being surprised you would marry someone like me."

He placed his hands on her waist to keep her from turning away. "You mean a talented, beautiful, sexy, smart, and witty woman? Frankly, the idea I wouldn't want you is an insult to my intelligence."

"Good one." She lifted her face for a kiss, which he was more than happy to supply. "Let me pack. I'll knock when I'm finished."

Ian had already hung his clothing from the day before in a garment bag, so now he folded his pajama bottoms and shaving kit into the suitcase and then sat on the edge of the bed to wait. After a moment's hesitation, he pulled out his mobile and texted Jamie.

Asked Grace to marry me. (She said yes.)

Anxiety churned in his stomach while he waited for the

return text. And then came a handful of messages, one after another.

Congratulations! About time! We love Grace.

Well, not all of us. Was Mother furious?

Andrea says you need to text a picture of the ring.

Ian laughed softly at the last one. Mum knows I was going to ask and refuses to attend the wedding. Thanks for the support. Tell Andrea I'll work on the pic.

When Grace knocked a few minutes later, he showed her the message thread, and she laughed too. "I adore your family. Even if Jamie and Andrea are so in love it hurts to be around them."

"Very true. I guess we need to start working on obnoxious levels of happiness."

"I'm getting there. Now let me have your mobile."

He handed over the phone and she snapped a picture of her left hand, then sent it back to Jamie. A few seconds went by before the reply came in. Well done, man. Andrea says it's perfect.

"It is," Grace murmured. "Now let's go before I feel the need to say it's perfect because you had it designed for me or because you gave it to me or some such nonsense."

"Nonsense?"

She stretched up and kissed him quickly. "Anything you gave me would be perfect. Just not *this* perfect."

His laughter rang out in the hall. He picked up his bag and one of hers and followed her down to the lobby below.

"Are you sorry to be leaving Scotland?" she asked.

"No. It was good to be back, but my life is in London. Our life together is in London."

A strange expression crossed her face. Then she smiled. "Let's get to it, then."

By silent agreement, they took a leisurely route home, even knowing it would get them back to the city in the wee hours of Monday morning. They stopped for lunch in Fort William, walking the cobblestone streets hand in hand, chatting about everything and nothing, kissing on a random street corner and getting asked if they were newlyweds.

"Newly engaged," Ian replied. Grace knew she should have been embarrassed, but she laughed. Nothing could dampen her happiness at the moment, especially after all the teasing she'd done about his aversion to public displays of affection.

When they finally arrived in London and Ian parked in front of her building, dawn had broken over the buildings, the light giving a bright crown to tops of dusky gray-and-white stone. In her sleepless, bleary-eyed state, that somehow seemed significant.

"Sure you can climb the stairs?" he asked as he carried her bags to the top of the interior landing. "You look asleep on your feet."

"My feet aren't touching the ground, yada yada, insert overblown romantic sentiment here." Grace grinned up at him. "I blame you for my newfound sappiness."

"For that, I will gladly take the blame. Call me when you wake up?"

"You might need to wake me for supper."

Outside the flat, he kissed her gently, and too briefly for her liking, then waited as she put her key into the lock. She whispered good-bye, then carefully tiptoed her way inside with her bags.

She needn't have worried. The lights were already on and the kettle bubbled in the kitchen. She dropped her luggage with a thud. "Ash? I'm back!"

Asha emerged from the bathroom, toweling her dark hair dry. "What are you doing here? I thought you didn't get in until later!"

"We ended up driving. How was your weekend?"

"Oh, no, don't try to divert me. How was *your* weekend?"

Grace couldn't help the grin that sprang to her face. "Good. The wedding was gorgeous, as you'd expect. Weather was surprisingly good for Scotland, which you wouldn't expect."

"And?"

"And this happened." Grace held up her left hand.

Asha's expression turned from surprise to shock to joy. She let out a squeal and launched herself at Grace. "Oh my, congratulations, Grace! That's amazing! Let me see it again." She grabbed Grace's hand and twisted it for a better view of each side of the ring. "Well. That is impressive. You're wearing the crown jewels on your ring finger."

Grace blushed. "It's rather showy, isn't it?"

"Oh, it's stunning. What a gorgeous setting. I never would have imagined you wearing a diamond that big, but somehow, it feels like you. He had it made, didn't he?"

"From my first engagement ring," Grace said.

"That may be the most romantic thing I've ever heard." Asha dragged her over to the sofa and pulled Grace down, tucking one leg up beneath herself like a little girl. "So how did he do it? When? Did he get down on one knee?"

"He did. He took me for a drive, but it was already getting

rather dark. Proposed overlooking the sound. And then I laughed at him."

"You did what?" Asha screeched. "Why do you do these things to the man?"

"I didn't mean to! He took me by surprise. He was telling me how much I meant to him, and then he got down on one knee, and I kind of panicked. I didn't take him for a down-on-one-knee sort of man."

"Oh, he is. Even I could tell you that. Grace, he's waited for you for *ten years*. He had your old engagement ring remade. You don't think he's going to make a statement of some sort?"

"Well, after I apologized for laughing at him, I said yes, and the rest is history."

Asha sighed happily. "Best story ever, with the exception of the fact it didn't happen to me. So, have you talked about a date?"

"Not yet."

"Didn't do a lot of talking after that, hmm?"

Grace laughed, but the heat returned to her cheeks. "Not really. I'm pretty sure he wants to get married as soon as we can. There are details to work out."

"Like what?"

"Like my job in London, wedding guests . . ."

Asha fell silent. "Do you think your parents would come?"

"I doubt it. The last time I called, they didn't pick up the phone and didn't return the message. It was never Mum, you know, but she'll go along with what Dad wants. She has no choice, really."

"I don't understand your dad. It wasn't enough to lose one child, so he had to drive the other away." Asha grimaced. "I'm sorry. I didn't mean to bring that up."

"No, it's okay. That's exactly what he did. He's never really gotten over the fact I ignored his ultimatum and ran off with my boyfriend, let alone followed in Aidan's footsteps. Stubborn Irish pride."

Asha grabbed Grace's hand and squeezed. "None of that now. Don't let them spoil your happiness."

Asha was right, but the doubt and the heaviness had crept in, stealing a little of her joy. She knew exactly what her father would say, if he bothered to talk to her. There were standards of behavior in the Brennan family, and she had never lived up to them. She'd always been too wild, too independent, too . . . unchristian. He'd say her current problems were the results of her rebelliousness. And he certainly wouldn't believe that she was settling down now.

He was wrong. Her father might never forgive her, but God was giving her a second chance of which she had barely dared to dream. She wouldn't start that second chance with negativity. She held tight to Asha's hand. "Of course this means you have to be my maid of honor."

"Well, of course I will. Who else would it be? I'm already picking out shoes in my head." Asha laughed and pulled her into a tight hug. The words she whispered into her ear were serious, though. "I love you, Grace. I'm so proud of you. You deserve your happiness. Now, go take it."

"I don't know what I would do without you, Ash." She hugged her one more time. "So now he and I need to set a date. Autumn or winter, I'd think. I get the impression neither of us are up for anything elaborate."

Asha's expression shifted. "I didn't mean to bring this up now, but I don't want you to be disappointed later. I certainly don't want you to change your plans for me."

"What is it, Ash?" Grace's stomach was getting more nervous by the second.

"I just got my leave approved. I'm going back to India in six weeks."

"What? That's great! So you'll be able to go for the opening of the Pune TB clinic at the end of September, yeah?" Asha had been invited by CAF months ago, but she'd almost given up on getting the requisite time away from work.

"It is great, but I won't be back until late January. Which means if you have an autumn wedding, I won't be there."

"I see." Grace thought through the possibilities. There wasn't any need to rush things. She'd only thought autumn because the weather was still nice . . .

Asha pushed herself off the sofa and wagged a finger. "Don't overthink this, Grace. And don't let me affect your decisions. You love him; he loves you. If you're sure you want to marry him, just do it. Don't give yourself the time to talk yourself out of what you really want."

Asha went to finish getting ready for work, leaving Grace alone with her swirling thoughts. Did Asha have so little faith in her that she thought she would run from the altar a second time? She'd made her decision. She loved Ian. She'd reconciled herself to leaving her other life behind, finding a new passion here in London. There was nothing that would make her throw that away.

Was there?

Asha came back from the bedroom, fastening tiny gold earrings into her earlobes. "I really hate the fact I have to work this morning. We should be shopping for wedding dresses or having a celebratory high tea."

"We can do that on your next day off. Besides, I need to

head over to the gallery this afternoon to check on Melvin's progress." And keep her mind off all the ways she might manage to muck this up.

But Melvin wouldn't be in the gallery for hours, and the enormous yawn that ripped from her convinced her she'd be asleep the minute she sat down on the train. Instead, Grace waited until Asha left, then took a long, hot bath—longer than necessary considering the time she spent admiring the sparkle of the diamonds in the bathroom's halogen lights. Then she put on her pajamas and curled up beneath a blanket on the sofa, too tired to bother pulling out the bed.

She woke to a shrill ring minutes or hours later and fumbled for her mobile phone while she wiped a trail of drool from her cheek. Had she actually slept through dinner? She answered and mumbled a sleepy "Hello?" into the handset.

It wasn't Ian's voice that came through. "Grace? It's Henry Symon."

Adrenaline flooded her system, instantly sweeping away the last cobwebs of sleep. "Hello, Henry. How are you?" It was an inane thing to say, but her synapses weren't firing as quickly as her pulse.

"Well, thanks. I wanted to let you know that our monthly board meeting has been moved to this Friday. Would you be available to speak at ten o'clock?"

"Of course. Do I need to prepare a presentation?" Her words were finally coming out semicoherently.

"I would. This is your chance to show them your vision and your passion. I'm confident you're the right person for the job. Now we just need to show them why."

And prove that a woman without a university degree could do the job.

Grace sat on the edge of the sofa, taming her stomach's backflips. It was all coming together so fast—first the engagement, now the job. Good things, but ones that drove home the truth: her career as a war photographer was well and truly over.

"Don't talk yourself out of what you really want."

Asha was right. What she really wanted was Ian, London, a second chance at life. It was right in front of her—all she had to do was reach out and grab it.

Second chances didn't come easy.

CHAPTER TWENTY-SIX

FOR THE FIRST TIME IN LONGER than he could remember, Ian woke up nervous.

It didn't make sense that he should be nervous when it was Grace's job that would be decided today, but in a sense it was also their future being decided. Settling into a desk job versus continuing to travel as a photographer. A new start together versus making their existing lives bend around their togetherness, their marriage.

Fortunately, he had his morning outing to take his mind off it, though which one was diverting him from the other was somewhat in question. Chris slanted him a curious look when they climbed the stairs to the locker room.

"What's going on with you? I haven't seen you this

distracted in the boat since Grace showed up. Everything all right?"

Ian smiled. He'd taken out his scull on Wednesday, so he hadn't had a chance to share his news. "Grace and I are getting married."

Chris ground to a stop. "Whoa. Really? That's ... quick."

"You don't approve?"

"I didn't say that. Given everything she's dealing with, I didn't expect you to jump into things so fast. Not giving her a chance to get away again?"

"We've been over this already," Ian said, his tone nearly a growl.

"Okay, okay, I didn't mean anything by it. Congratulations, mate."

Chris held out a hand, and Ian shook it, his irritation abating a degree. He couldn't blame Chris for his surprise. He'd already expressed his concern over Grace's mental state, and he'd seen what her leaving had done to Ian the first time. He didn't want to see him go through the same thing again.

"This time when she leaves, it will break you."

Ian shook off his mother's voice in his head. Grace was coping well; she was happy with him in London, making the effort to put down roots.

Except Grace had seemed happy with him the first time, right up until she left.

Curse his mother for putting the thought into his head. This time, it would be different. He knew that as surely as he knew anything. And today's board meeting would prove it.

The meeting had been scheduled at CAF's office to begin at half past nine, which meant he would be cutting his arrival close. He showered, shaved, and dressed in a dark suit—with a tie—and shoved his kit bag into his locker. Exactly forty-eight minutes later, he punched the up button on the lift in the posh Canada Square building and checked his watch. Three minutes to spare. At least no one could complain about his punctuality.

The office's efficient assistant, Alice, smiled at him warmly and held up a finger while she transferred a call. "Good morning, Mr. MacDonald. You can go straight through to the conference room. You're the last to arrive."

"Thank you, Alice." Maybe they wouldn't be as impressed by his punctuality as he'd thought.

At the end of the hallway on the exterior side of the office was the conference room, a small space with an oval-shaped table and an expansive view of the square below. Philip Vogel was engaged in an animated discussion with one of the other board members, but he gave Ian a nod of acknowledgment as he took his seat. In the corner, Vogel's assistant, Cecile, set up her laptop in preparation for recording the meeting minutes.

If Ian was asked later, he knew he wouldn't be able to recite any of the decisions made. Most of them had little to do with him anyway; while he kept generally informed of CAF's endeavors, the big topic of conversation had to do with donation shortfalls from the American branch of the charity, which had apparently taken a hit in the wake of a scandal. Americans tended to be far more critical of those involved in the organizations to which they donated than the English, so having a megachurch pastor step down from leadership because of accusations of impropriety had heavily impacted the bottom line.

Finally, Vogel tapped his pen against the page. "The matter of the new creative director. Cecile?"

Cecile leaned over to the intercom beside her and pushed a button. "Alice, has Ms. Brennan arrived?"

"Yes. Shall I send her in?"

"Please do. And send Henry down as well." Cecile clicked off and then rose to wait for them by the door.

Several minutes later, Ian glimpsed Henry Symon and Grace through the glass wall. Henry gestured for Grace to take a chair to the side while he pulled up a seat at the table and greeted the board.

"The position of creative director has been open for several months now," Henry said by way of introduction. "We've narrowed the position down to two candidates. I've asked my first choice, Grace Brennan, here to speak to you directly because I feel her vision for CAF's publications is best expressed in her own words. Even if you don't know her, you probably know her work. She's a renowned photojournalist who has worked for *Time* and *Newsweek* among others—including us. She has won numerous photography awards over the last ten years, and two years ago she was named NPPA's Photojournalist of the Year."

Henry took a stack of papers out of a folder and passed them around. When they circled to Ian, he saw it was her CV along with a selection of her more iconic photographs. His heart pricked with pride.

"Ms. Brennan, would you like to address the board?"

Grace rose smoothly and moved to the head of the table beside the whiteboard. Ian could tell from her slightly stiff expression that she was nervous, but anyone who didn't know her well would think she was merely serious.

"Gentlemen, thank you for the privilege of addressing you today. As you know, I've worked as a photographer for the past fifteen years. I've had the opportunity to visit some of CAF's missions in the field, from wholly sponsored feeding centers and medical missions to refugee camps where CAF was just one of many international aid organizations. I have seen firsthand the good this organization does. It is one of the few that puts the money on the ground where it is most needed.

"However, most of CAF's donors do not have the opportunities I have—they've not seen for themselves the faces of the people CAF serves. The only communication they have about where their money is being spent is through the monthly publications they receive in the post. And frankly, as I told Henry—Mr. Symon—in my initial interview, I believe CAF may be doing more harm than good with the current approach."

As Grace spoke, her voice grew more confident. She outlined how she believed CAF seemed to be doing *too well* from the glossy commercial nature of their publications, discouraging donors from making further donations. Ian couldn't resist a slight smile when she talked about her vision for a more editorial approach to their communications, a way to make people feel a part of the charity to which they contributed.

"I believe most people want to help. They just need to be given a reason to do so, and to feel that their direct contribution makes a difference in a child's life, even if they can't commit to individual sponsorships or monthly donations. You clearly have both the design and marketing talent to accomplish it, so I believe it's time for a new vision."

A quick glance around the table showed impressed expressions and favorable body language. His heart lifted further. They'd evidently picked up on her passion for the people and CAF's mission. If the impressed nods were any indication, she had this job locked up.

"Thank you, Ms. Brennan," Vogel said, rising to shake her hand. "We'll be making our decision soon. We'll be sure to contact you as soon as possible."

"Thank you, sir. Gentlemen." She hoisted her bag over her shoulder with a nod toward the table and excused herself quietly.

"I believe Ms. Brennan has expressed the reason we should hire her more clearly than I could have." Henry's smile said he anticipated as easy a decision as Ian did.

"Indeed, she's impressive," Vogel said. "She's pinpointed the problem with our current marketing approaches. Looking at her CV, however, I don't see a university degree."

"In this case, I believe that her experience more than makes up for her lack of formal education," Henry said.

"I'd have to agree with you." Vogel flipped through the paperwork. "Have we completed a background check yet?"

Henry faltered. "Sir?"

"A background check. It's required for every hire. Have we completed it?"

Hesitantly, Henry handed over a sheaf of papers and passed them down the table to Vogel. The chairman skimmed over it, his expression tightening with every page he flipped.

"I'm afraid this won't do." He passed the sheaf to Alvin Keller, the charity's general counsel. "A year ago, I would have dismissed it, and if this were a field position, I still might. But after the recent scandal, we simply can't afford to have any more scrutiny directed at our management staff."

Ian frowned. "I'm sorry. What are we talking about?"

Keller shoved the papers down the table. Ian frowned as he flipped the first page and then felt the blood drain from his face.

Grace had a police record.

He had known that she had done some things in her teen years that she wasn't proud of, and she'd alluded to trouble in Los Angeles, but this? Breaking and entering, a misdemeanor drug charge, a theft case that was later dismissed but apparently not expunged from her record.

He swallowed hard. "This is from fifteen years ago. Are you telling me that none of you have ever made a mistake?"

"Of course that's not what we're saying," Vogel said. "And we're making no judgment on her morality. Or even saying we believe she would ever commit another crime."

"In this case, the fact she has such a high profile as a photographer works against her," Keller said. "We can't guarantee that someone else couldn't dig this up. At this point, we can't afford any hint of impropriety."

Ian dropped the papers on the table and wiped a hand over his face. "I think you're making a big mistake."

Vogel cleared his throat. "MacDonald, I understand you're in a relationship with her."

That made him sit up straight. "Yes. And?"

"Henry could certainly call and tell her, but perhaps you'd rather give her the news."

Ian gave a sharp nod but said nothing as he gathered his papers and his mobile and shoved them into his briefcase.

"We've still a few matters to discuss," Keller said.

"I'm sure you'll manage fine without me. I'm finished. Excuse me, gentlemen." He pushed his chair up to the table, then strode from the conference room.

Only when he was riding the elevator down to the basement where Grace waited for him in the restaurant did he slump against the wall. This was going to crush her. She had made such an impassioned case for the job; how would she react when she knew she'd been turned down because of stupid teenage mistakes?

What would she do when the job she was banking on to keep her in London fell through?

He found her sitting at a small table for two in the warmly decorated restaurant, her hands wrapped around a cup of tea. She smiled when she saw him, but the expression faded when he didn't return it. He sat down across from her.

"You did wonderfully. They were incredibly impressed by your presentation."

"I sense a *but* in that statement."

"Why didn't you tell me about your police record?"

Her face paled, then flushed pink. "Why do you think, Ian? I was ashamed."

"But if I'd known about it, I could have done something—"

"Done what? You can't change my past. You knew there were things I didn't talk about. I just hoped they might see clear to overlook them, based on the fact that they were so long ago." She delivered the words flatly, dispassionately, as if it didn't matter to her.

"If it hadn't been for a recent scandal, they would have. I'm sorry, Grace. You are absolutely the right person for the job. We all agree on that. This makes me ill."

She set her cup down firmly on the table with a thud. "Go ahead and ask me."

"Ask you what?"

"What I did. I know you're curious. I know you're wondering what kind of woman you're marrying."

"I know exactly what kind of woman I'm marrying. A passionate woman who made some mistakes. I don't care what happened."

"Well, you might be the only one." Grace rose from the table and lifted her shoulder bag. "If you don't mind, I think I'd like to be alone. Go for a walk, maybe. I'll call you later."

Ian sighed and slumped back into his chair, watching her walk away from the restaurant with a decidedly defeated slope to her shoulders. Before she made it to the door, though, he leaped from his seat and followed her.

He grabbed her hand and pulled her to a stop. "No."

"Ian, please. I feel like being alone."

"I know you do. But you're not alone anymore. We're in this together, remember? You and me." He slid his hand down her arm and gripped her hand firmly. "So, the question is, what are we going to do?"

"You have to go to work."

He glanced at his watch. "Pretty certain I don't. It's lunchtime on a Friday, and everyone will be plotting an early escape."

Grace arched an eyebrow, but he could tell her spirits were lifting. "Change first, and then hit one of the street markets?"

"All right, then." He loosened his tie, tugged it over his head, and tucked it into his pocket. "I didn't get breakfast after my outing this morning. I'm famished."

"Then come on, Superman. Let me show you how to play hooky."

CHAPTER TWENTY-SEVEN

IT WAS ONE OF THOSE GLORIOUS, sunny August days that seemed to only come every five years or so, with fluffy clouds skittering across pale-blue skies. In honor of the occasion, Grace abandoned her usual trousers and boots in favor of cutoff jeans, sandals, and a tank top that showcased most of her ink and more of her curves than she was used to flaunting. The light in Ian's eyes when she emerged from the bathroom communicated his approval.

"I did mention that you had a cruel streak, didn't I?" He kissed her shoulder, then her neck, and finally her lips.

She leaned into him and twined her arms around his neck, encouraging him to continue. "You might have said it once or twice. But I can't turn down the opportunity to catch a little sunshine."

"Sure." His tone said he didn't believe her. Rightly so. Grace liked that look on his face, the way he managed to layer reverence with hunger when he touched her. Tempting fate, perhaps, but she knew Ian well enough to know that this side of him he reserved for her alone. He brushed his hands down her arms before he let her go, the longing clear on his face. "Where do you want to go?"

"I want to be a tourist."

"A tourist?"

"Right, like we're on holiday in London. I'll bring my camera, and we'll ooh and ahh over the sights and kiss in doorways and eat fabulous food from dodgy-looking street vendors."

"I like the kissing part."

"I thought you might. First question would be Portobello Road for paella or Brick Lane for Bangladeshi?"

In the end, they settled on sticky sweet jerk chicken and plantains bought from a Jamaican food van not too far from the famed Electric Avenue in Brixton, then wandered through the Friday market featuring offbeat crafts and food. Somehow, they made their way back to Westminster, where Grace talked Ian into jumping onto a double-decker bus for a tour, then back off to ride the London Eye. By that time, the sun was beginning to dip in the sky, and the jerk chicken had worn off enough for their stomachs to grumble. Ian stepped up behind Grace at their vantage spot on the Tower Bridge, watching water rush beneath it, and wrapped his arms around her. "Have you had a good holiday?"

She leaned against his chest and closed her eyes for a moment. "Lovely. So lovely I'm not ready to go home."

"Then what do you want to do now? It's going to get cold eventually, and you're not dressed for that."

"I'm sure you can keep me warm." She thought for a moment. "If we really were just visiting, I would want to stargaze on Hampstead Heath."

"Sunset picnic on the Heath it is, then."

That was how they found themselves sitting at one of London's iconic landmarks, eating Chinese food from paper takeaway containers, open fizzy drinks worked into the long grass beside them so they wouldn't tip. She fed him chow mein with expert motions of her chopsticks while he gave her tastes of his kung pao chicken with a plastic fork.

"What's the weirdest thing you've ever eaten?" he asked.

She didn't even have to think. "Bubble and squeak."

He'd probably been expecting her to say *deep-fried grasshopper* or the like and instead she'd picked an iconic British food. "Why is that?"

"It's odd, don't you think? Beans should be refried. Not vegetables."

"You spent too much time in America."

"Don't blame that on America. We have something similar in Ireland called colcannon, and I never liked that either."

"What else do you find mystifying about England?"

She set aside her empty container and stretched out on the grass. "I don't know. I don't think there's anything mystifying about England at all."

"And that's the problem with it, isn't it?"

"No. That's what makes it feel like home."

"Does it? Feel like home?"

She turned her head to look at him, taking in his profile in the dim light. There it was, that little twinge in her heart, the confirmation she had been waiting for. "It does. It really does."

Ian stretched out next to her and propped his head on his hand.

The way he was looking at her made her heart stutter. "What?"

"What do you want to do?"

"Now? I thought we were going to wait for the stars to come out."

"No, I mean in the future." He ran a finger across the little bit of skin that showed at her waistband where her top had lifted, then dropped his hand to the turf. "Are you going to look for another job? Or do you want to continue to travel?"

She shifted her gaze to his face. No judgment, no pressure. "I don't know. I want to stay here in London, but what's to say the same thing won't happen the next time I apply for a position?"

"Start your own business, maybe?"

"Doing what? Shooting weddings? No."

"Not necessarily weddings. Commercial, perhaps?"

She exhaled, the heaviness from this morning's failure returning. For a time she'd escaped reality, but it was time to face it again.

"I hesitate to mention this, Grace, but you don't have to work if you don't want to. Or you can do whatever you want, regardless of how much money it brings in."

"When we're married, you mean." Ian could more than support them, clearly, and she *did* have a sizable bit tucked away, but that wasn't what this was about. For so long her identity had been wrapped up in her career. She'd enjoyed a level of autonomy that came with having her own money.

Ian didn't understand what it would mean for her to give up her independence. She hadn't asked anything from anybody since she was nineteen, when she'd learned what happened if you pinned all your hopes on a man.

"It wasn't a stranger," she said suddenly.

Ian's brow furrowed at the change of subject. "What are you on about now?"

"The house I broke into. It wasn't a stranger's. I can't bear the thought of you thinking I'm a thief."

"Grace, sweetheart, I told you: I trust you. You don't have to tell me."

She pushed herself up on her elbows. "I want to. You know I left Europe to be a photographer's assistant when I was nineteen. That was my boyfriend. We got to LA and everything was fine for a few months. I suspected he was seeing someone else, but I had no proof. Then one day I came home and he'd changed the locks on me. Wouldn't even let me in to get my things. The landlord wouldn't help me because my name wasn't on the lease. So I broke a back window and climbed through."

"Hence the breaking and entering that was later dropped."

"Right. The judge saw my boyfriend was committing a crime by keeping my things."

"Why wasn't the theft charge dropped, then, if it was all your belongings? I assume that's what that was from."

Grace grimaced. "I had just given him an expensive camera lens for his birthday, so I took it back. Had I returned it, they would have dropped the charges, but I denied I ever took it. I would have rather had a misdemeanor conviction on my record than let him keep it." She peeked up at him, gauging his reaction. "So now you know. What are you thinking?"

He seemed very serious for a moment, then he chuckled. "This is why I love you, Grace."

"What?"

"That is so very you. Taking a theft charge rather than letting that prat get away with taking advantage of you."

"So you're not disappointed in me?"

"It's not really my place to be disappointed, is it? You were young. God knows we have all done things that were ill-advised when we were young."

"You're not going to ask about the other charge?"

"You never seemed like the type to take drugs."

"Not after I got caught smoking a joint some friends gave me. They ran; I didn't. There you have it. Never touched anything mind-altering again. Well, except for alcohol, but that's never held much interest for me anyway."

He stared into her eyes for a long moment, then trailed a finger down her cheek. "Marry me, Grace."

"Wasn't that the idea behind this enormous diamond?"

"I mean, marry me now. Soon. Let's go to the register office and sign the papers and run away from London for a month. We can go to Vienna or Prague or Florence and be tourists, just like this. Sightsee. Live off room service. Spend entire days in bed and venture out at sunset to the most romantic little cafés we can find."

Her heart gave a little hiccup at the earnestness in his expression, the way his eyes devoured her. "You make that sound so appealing. But you have responsibilities—"

"Hang my responsibilities. I've done everything anyone has asked of me my entire life. It's time I get to decide what I want to do. And now, the only thing I want is you. No responsibilities. No work or worries or concerns about the future."

Somehow he had moved closer to her on the grass without her noticing, and his arm was draped over her waist, while his lips lingered inches from hers. His lovely blue eyes, made dusky gray in the fading light, bored into hers. Her breath caught.

"What if I say I want a real wedding?"

"Do you?"

"I know it's stupid, but I've always thought that when I got married I'd have the white dress and flowers and all that."

He pulled back a little. "If that's what you really want, then that's what you shall have. Set a date and we'll do it."

"There's something else."

"Yes, love?"

"I want Jean-Auguste to walk me down the aisle. He's been more of a father to me than my own, and he's the only reason I made it this far. Somehow it only seems right for him to walk me from my old life into my new one."

"Then call him. If it's that important to you, we'll schedule it so he can be here."

She eased herself back down onto the grass and touched his face. "Thank you. But not now. Not tonight. Tonight we wait for the stars and talk about—"

"Room service?"

She laughed. "Room service. And then you kiss me—"

"In public—"

"In public, no matter how uncomfortable it makes you."

Ian dipped his head to the space between her neck and shoulder, brushing a light kiss there that made her shiver. "Oh no. I am a changed man. You before everything else."

CHAPTER TWENTY-EIGHT

GRACE DIALED JEAN-AUGUSTE first thing on Saturday morning, but the call went straight to voice mail. She wasn't surprised, even if she was a little disappointed. Who knew where he was right now? Half the time they worked in areas without reliable mobile signals, relying on crew and escorts' satellite phones for communication. He'd call her when he returned to the city.

Still, she couldn't resist leaving a cryptic message: "Jean-Auguste, it's Grace. Call me please? I have some news I want to share with you."

She hung up, then as a second thought, tapped out the same message via text. There. She'd done all she could for now. As soon as he called her back with his schedule, she and Ian would set a date.

It was a good nervousness, she told herself, but still she pulled out the ugly red-white-and-blue knitted socks so she wouldn't be tempted to manage her anxiety in other ways.

Fortunately the last-minute preparations for the showing—and Ian—distracted her from the future unknowns. She spent every day at the gallery, helping decide the placement of the newly framed photos, and every evening at Ian's flat, cooking to settle her nerves. He didn't seem to be complaining.

Friday night came almost as a surprise then, so focused had she been on ignoring it. She slipped on the new blouse Asha had badgered her into buying, then sat on the bed to let her roommate do her hair and makeup.

"You should let me do the makeup for your wedding," Asha said as she mixed eye shadow on the back of her hand. "I'm getting good at this."

"Did you have to mention the wedding? I'm already nervous."

"But not about the gallery showing."

Grace laughed. "That's true. Hurry up, will you? I'm supposed to make a grand entrance, but there's a difference between fashionably late and just plain late."

"Okay, okay," Asha muttered good-naturedly. "Stop moving, then."

Grace managed to keep her nerves at bay all the way to the gallery, her gaze focused on the lights flickering to life as the sun slid behind the buildings in a blush of pink and orange. Streetlights, neon, headlights. By the time the cab had navigated rush hour traffic and pulled up to the curb, full dusk had at last set in.

She froze with one leg out of the taxi, paralyzed. Bright light spilled out of the front of the space, illuminating elegantly dressed guests holding flutes of champagne while uniformed waiters circulated trays of hors d'oeuvres. It was far more refined and upmarket than Melvin had led her to believe, probably because he knew she would have this very reaction.

Asha gave her a little push from the cab, then linked arms with her as they entered the gallery. She steered Grace into the center of the room, where guests milled about, drinking champagne and discussing her photos like they were art.

"There's Ian," Asha said, nudging her.

Her eyes immediately tracked to the tallest man in the room, and involuntarily her breath caught. He was dressed in one of his beautifully cut suits, one of many similarly attired men, and yet he managed to stand out. The warm expression in his eyes when he spotted her melted the last bit of tension inside.

Asha squeezed her arm, then drifted away as Ian approached. He bent to kiss her cheek, but no more. "You look lovely. And the photos are magnificent. Such talent, Grace."

"You've been here long?"

"Long enough. But I was hoping you would show me around personally. Perks of being engaged to the artist."

"I suppose that does earn you a private tour." Before she could make good on the offer, though, she saw Melvin threading his way through the crowd toward her.

"Ah, there you are, Grace. There's someone I'd like you to meet." Melvin's attention shifted to Ian. He held out his hand. "Melvin Colville. I'm the gallery owner."

"Ian MacDonald. I'm the fiancé."

"So I assumed. You don't mind if I borrow her?"

Caught between the desire to say Ian didn't speak for her and the wish he would say he did mind, Grace said nothing.

Ian simply gave her another kiss on the cheek and made a gesture of acquiescence.

"Who are we meeting?"

"The editor-in-chief of *Beau Monde*."

"What?" Grace would have stopped had Melvin not taken hold of her arm. Based in Quebec, *Beau Monde* was a peculiar hybrid of art photography, high fashion, and social commentary. A controversial, often incongruous mix, it nevertheless garnered attention—and secured many a photographer's career. She'd heard from others that it was easier to score a spread in French *Vogue* than in *Beau Monde*. And its editor-in-chief was here?

"Relax. She is impressed. Wants to make your acquaintance personally."

Melvin led her to a tall, slender woman with her back to them, her blonde hair twisted up into an elegant knot. When she turned, Grace realized she was no stranger. "Monique."

"*Bonsoir*, Grace." She ignored Grace's outstretched hand and took her by the shoulders to kiss each cheek. "This is beyond what even I expected, and I've followed your work for some time."

Grace's brow furrowed. "You knew who I was when we met at the café?"

One elegant shoulder answered for her, very French. "When I saw your card. But of course, I did not know about the showing. I had no idea we would meet again."

"I suppose you're right. It's a pleasure to have you here."

"No, no, no, the pleasure is mine. Melvin tells me this is a personal project it has taken him over a decade to convince you to exhibit. Why now?"

"I don't know," Grace said honestly.

"Perhaps it was time to let go?" Monique asked, something sympathetic shining in her eyes. "The memories and the pain."

Grace stood there, frozen by the insight. Twenty years since her brother died. Twenty years of photography, even if those early teenaged attempts weren't represented here. Somehow she'd never noticed the significance of the dates, her return to London, her decision to let Melvin exhibit the photos. Maybe Monique was right. Maybe twenty years was long enough to let go of all of it.

"But I did not come to speak of such things. You're a rare photographer, Grace. You approach your subjects like a photojournalist, and yet you possess a painter's sensibility. Truly unique. Evocative, but not sentimental. Are you familiar with *Beau Monde*?"

"Of course."

"Then you know we only work with the best. I'd like you to do a feature for us."

Grace could barely force out an answer. "I'm flattered. But I'm not sure I could leave London right away."

"I respect that. And it won't be a problem. I wouldn't need you in Quebec until later this autumn."

"What's the project?"

Monique smiled mysteriously. "Portraits. But not just any portraits. Are you quite prepared to be the next Annie Leibovitz?"

"Not at all," Grace answered honestly. "But I'm intrigued by the idea."

"Good. My office will be in touch with the details."

"Thank you for the opportunity," Grace managed, somewhere between puzzled and stunned.

"You are more than welcome, *chérie*. And may I say, you

have fine taste in men." Her gaze dipped to Grace's left ring finger, then found Ian across the room, where he spoke with a small group of people. She winked and sauntered back into the crowd.

"*Beau Monde*," Melvin said approvingly. "A coup for any photographer. I'd trust her with your career, even if I wouldn't trust her with your fiancé."

"I'm not worried on either count," Grace said. The pride on Ian's face when he spotted her—his eyebrows lifting as if to question whether he could approach—did more to assure her of his devotion than any words could. This was her night, and he was here to support her in whatever way she needed. How could she not love the man?

When she nodded, he crossed to her side immediately. "Who was the VIP?"

"The editor of *Beau Monde*. She wants me to come to Quebec this autumn to shoot a feature for her."

"That's incredible. You always said *Beau Monde* was nearly impossible to land."

"It is. But it would mean more traveling. From the sound of it, I might be gone for a couple of weeks."

He didn't even hesitate. "Of course you should do it. It would be a huge boon to your career. If we time it right, we could honeymoon in Quebec. Maybe spend some time alone in Nova Scotia? I've always wanted to visit. Did you know there's a large Scottish community there?"

"There's a large Scottish community in *Scotland*, but you rarely go there." She grinned at him so he wouldn't see the sudden rush of panic that had occurred the second he mentioned the word *honeymoon*. This was all happening so fast. She could barely process the fact she was standing in the middle of her first gallery showing, let alone the leap from estranged to honeymoon in a mere two months.

Before they could discuss it any further, Melvin was at her side again. "Grace, are you ready to say a few words?"

Ian nudged her, then leaned down to give her a quick kiss. "Go. You'll be great."

Grace grimaced, but she let Melvin drag her off to the front of the gallery, where guests were beginning to gather. Her heart knocked painfully against her rib cage. They were here because of her. Yes, also because of the renown of Melvin's gallery and the charity angle, but she still would never have imagined her photographs would command the attention of London's art scene.

Grace cleared her throat and found Ian in the crowd. He gave her a confident nod that bolstered her courage. Even so, her voice sounded shaky to her ears. "The photos you see here are a collection I've worked on for over a decade, but they were never intended to be displayed. Such are Melvin's persuasive powers."

Soft laughter flowed through the gallery, and she relaxed a little. "You see, it shouldn't be me showing these photographs tonight. My brother, Aidan Brennan, was a talented photojournalist. He was the one who taught me the basics of photography when I was just a girl. Twenty years ago, he was killed in a nationalist riot while freelancing in Northern Ireland."

Murmurs of sympathy rippled through the crowd, but Grace hurried on. "My brother was a journalist and an artist, but most of all, he was a humanitarian. He believed that God had granted him his gift to give voice to the voiceless and to advocate for justice. With that goal, he began this project, but he never had the chance to complete it. I vowed that I would take the photos he never could with his prized camera. It seems appropriate to dedicate this collection to Aidan's memory."

Tears clogged her voice then, and she gave a decisive nod to indicate she was finished speaking. She focused on Ian's face to steady herself as she walked back through the applauding crowd. She'd never told him the story behind the photographs, even though he knew the part her brother played in her choice of careers. Would he understand that this was why it was doubly difficult to leave this life behind?

He put an arm around her shoulders and squeezed her briefly. "Aidan would be proud of you if he were here."

"I think he would. There's something of him in these. He was a traditionalist. He loved black-and-white portraiture."

"If it means anything, *I'm* proud of you."

She smiled up at him, grateful for his unwavering support. "That means more than anything, actually."

The rest of the evening passed in a blur. It was only when Asha caught up with her to offer her final congratulations and good-byes that Grace realized she'd lost track of Ian in the crowd. After Monique's open invitation to work with one of the world's most prestigious photography showcases and the uniformly positive response to her portraits, she had been too stunned to think of anything more than smiling and answering the guests' questions with something approaching thoughtfulness.

When the last attendee departed, Grace sank into a white leather sofa near the front of the gallery and kicked off her ballet flats.

Melvin flopped onto the sofa beside her and stretched out his long legs. "Long night?"

"Overwhelming." She glanced at him. "Thank you, Melvin. You did a lovely job on the exhibit. I hope by the end, we sell enough to cover the cost of production."

"You can't be serious, Grace." His sharp features twisted into incredulity. "You sold several pieces, and I expect we'll see more next week."

"How many?"

"Four tonight. Interest in three more. To move 30 percent of a showing as a result of a single event—that's almost unheard of."

"Even so, considering the prices we discussed—" She broke off at the look on his face. "What?"

"I might have revised the price list since you last looked at it." He handed her a printed white sheet.

Grace scanned it. Five thousand pounds? Eight thousand? Impossible. "Who in the world would pay that? It's mad!"

"Apparently, plenty of buyers disagreed. That's far below market rate for a one-off print by someone of your renown, simply because you wanted to raise money for the charity. Of course, it didn't hurt that your editor friend was talking you up. She's a better saleswoman than I could have been."

Grace put down the price list. If the other sales came through, even considering the cost of production and Melvin's cut, the exhibition would raise forty or fifty thousand pounds. It was hard to feel as if she wasn't doing enough, knowing the kind of good that money could do in a developing country. "Thank you for pushing me to do this, Melvin. It felt good. And Aidan would be happy to know the money is going to benefit those who truly need it."

"Go home, Grace. Have a glass of wine and savor the moment." Melvin stood and retrieved his keys to unlock the front door. "I'd offer to call you a cab, but I think someone might have beat me to it." He nodded his head toward the street, where Ian leaned casually against a waiting taxi.

Melvin practically propelled her out of the gallery, locking the glass door behind her. Ian straightened immediately and enfolded her in his arms. He buried his face into the side of her hair, his lips near her ear. "I'm so incredibly proud of you, Grace."

She soaked up his warmth and his compliment for a minute. "See me home, then?"

He took her face in his hands and kissed her, then opened the cab's door for her. Grace slid into the car, a strange feeling of contentment stealing over her. When Ian climbed in beside her, she sighed and leaned against him.

"Successful night?" he murmured.

"Very. It's what I needed, I think. To put the past to rest. To move on." She felt the sudden thread of tension winding through him, even though he said nothing. "I'm going to call Jean-Auguste again tomorrow."

The tension melted. "And then a wedding date?"

"And then a wedding date." She smiled up at him in the dark, her heart suddenly full. "Marry me?"

"Yes. Always yes."

CHAPTER TWENTY-NINE

JEAN-AUGUSTE DIDN'T ANSWER his mobile on Saturday.

Or Sunday.

Or Monday.

On Tuesday, Grace couldn't deny that her tiny niggle of concern had grown to full-blown worry. It wasn't unusual to be out of mobile coverage for a few days, but the workflow of modern photographers usually meant downloading and processing photos each night, then e-mailing them off to their editors. Even the photographers like Grace who preferred to linger over their work before culling their submissions never went more than a few days out of contact.

Grace sat down at her laptop and fired off a few quick e-mails to editors that both she and Jean-Auguste had worked with recently, men she'd be more inclined to call friends than colleagues. If they'd heard from him, she'd know by the end of the day.

"Are you ready?"

Grace looked up from the screen to where Asha stood, a trench coat over her blouse and trousers, her handbag over one shoulder. "What?"

"For your appointment at the bridal salon. You didn't forget, did you?"

"No, of course not." Grace closed the laptop with a snap and reached for her own bag, glad that she'd already dressed. "I'm ready to go."

But her mind wasn't on the parade of white dresses the consultant brought out in the posh Westminster shop; it was half a world away. When Asha caught Grace checking her e-mail on her mobile for the fourth time, she pulled her aside into one of the lushly upholstered changing cubicles.

"Grace, what's going on? Your mind is clearly not on wedding gowns. Are you having second thoughts?"

"About marrying Ian? No, of course not!" Grace sighed, then told Asha her worries about Jean-Auguste in barely more than a whisper. It was not exactly the kind of topic she wanted to voice around a handful of glowing, blissfully innocent brides.

"Surely you're just being paranoid," Asha said, but a note of concern had crept into her voice too. "Maybe he took a week off to sit on the beach in Bora-Bora."

"Maybe. Probably. You're right. I'm just anxious to set a wedding date. He's all we're waiting for now."

"Well, stop worrying. All will go off as planned—if we can

get you focused on the dress for a few minutes. You know it will be weeks before another slot opens up here."

So Grace wrestled her mind back to the dresses, all of which were too full or too sparkly or too . . . wedding-like. "I don't know, Ash. All these frills are the reason I don't wear dresses in the first place."

"Can we see something simpler?" Asha asked Madeline, the perfectly coiffed blonde bridal consultant. "Think along the lines of vintage Halston, not Marchesa. And stop trying to cover her tattoos. Her fiancé loves them."

"Ah! I know just the thing." The woman brightened and hurried off with renewed enthusiasm.

"Should I be scared?" Grace asked.

"Not at all. Have I ever been wrong?" Asha grinned at Grace's dubious look. "Don't answer that."

When the consultant came back with something that resembled nothing more than a white pleated sheet, Grace said, "I'm trusting you, Asha."

"Hey, it wasn't my pick. I'll wait out here."

Grace let Madeline help her into the dress, refusing to look in the changing room mirror, then walked to the dais amid a swish of fabric.

Asha gasped and covered her mouth. "Oh, Grace!"

"That bad?"

"Just look."

Grace stepped onto the round platform and froze. For the first time, her heart gave a little twist at the sight of herself in a white dress. "I look—"

"Stunning." Asha came up behind her and made her do a full turn. "This is the one."

Grace could only gape. It looked like 1970s couture

in white—all soft, draped chiffon that skimmed her body and made her look like some sort of ancient goddess. The gathered front was caught up in a high collar like a halter, the waist cinched by a plain satin ribbon. And the rest . . . simply didn't exist. The back, shoulders, most of the sides were left bare to show every last bit of her body art.

She felt daring and exposed and . . . like a bride.

"I'm really doing this," she whispered as the slow build of excitement welled up and spilled over.

Asha hugged her. "You really are."

And then Grace looked at the price tag. "It's *how* much?"

"Don't look at that. You can afford it. It's symbolic, Grace. A new life."

Asha was right. It was. She looked at the bridal consultant. "What now?"

"This dress takes approximately eight to ten weeks to arrive. When is your wedding date?"

Grace glanced at Asha again. "We haven't set one. And it might be sooner than that."

Madeline's smile fell, clearly seeing a sale slipping through her fingers. "You're sample size, so if it comes down to that—"

"Can you just write down all the details for her?" Asha asked quietly.

As soon as the consultant disappeared, Asha gave her another squeeze. "Okay, so we have just enough time for tea, and then I have to go meet Jake." Her eyes softened. "You're going to be a beautiful bride, Grace."

And oddly enough, Grace agreed.

———◦⟨☉⟩◦———

Grace floated through the next four hours, first her tea with Asha, then wandering Westminster streets with a freeness she'd not felt in years. Who knew that all it took to turn her into a puddle of mush was a couture wedding gown? But not just the gown, she admitted to herself. It was the image of walking down the aisle in that gown toward Ian, while he watched her with the same sort of awe James had displayed as Andrea approached him. The promise of forever.

She still wore a stupid grin when she knocked on Ian's door, a paper bag under her arm. "Did someone order Chinese?"

Ian swept the food out of her hands onto the foyer table and kissed her with a thoroughness that did nothing to mitigate her dreamy state. He pulled back and looked into her eyes. "Someone is in a very good mood."

"Someone found a wedding dress."

"Am I allowed to see it?"

"Of course not! It would be bad luck. But it is stunning. It would have to be—to get me daydreaming about an actual dress." She grabbed the food off the foyer table and took it to the dining room, where she began to unpack the little paper cartons. "I got us hot and sour soup, shrimp with lobster sauce, and . . . What? Why are you looking at me like that?"

He caught her around the waist and kissed her again. "Because I love you. And if you weren't so set on that gown, I would drag you down to the register office tomorrow."

"It's a good thing it's one amazing gown, or I might take you up on that."

"Are you sure I can't convince you otherwise?"

His convincing took the form of tiny, light kisses along her jaw. Just as she was about to tell him he was being a little too persuasive, her mobile buzzed in her jacket pocket.

"Hello?"

"Grace?" A man's American-accented voice came through.

Grace stiffened and Ian stopped what he was doing, his fingers tightening on her waist. She pulled the phone away to check the incoming number. "Jim. You got my e-mail. Do you have news about Jean-Auguste?"

"Grace—"

The hesitation in his voice amped up her heart rate and slammed her with a wall of dread. "He's okay, right? You've heard from him." Ian's arm slipped around her, but she barely noticed the support. "Jim, just tell me!"

"He went missing about three weeks ago in Kirkuk."

"But that doesn't mean—"

"There's a video, Grace."

Those three words—*there's a video*—knocked the remaining wind from her lungs. The mobile slipped from her hands and clattered to the floor. She lowered herself to a seat with trembling legs, vaguely aware of Ian picking up her phone and speaking quietly into it.

From across the room, the television drew her with an irresistible pull. She snatched up the remote, clicked on the first news channel she came to. The headline banner splashed bloodred across the screen, but before she could glean any information, Ian grabbed the remote from her hand. "No. You don't want that in your head. Trust me."

"But I have to know! There has to have been a mistake—"

"Grace, sweetheart, he's gone. I'm so sorry."

She stared at him for the longest moment before the

words sank in. And then came the grief, a crushing tidal wave dragging her under. "No, I don't . . . I can't . . ."

Numbly, she became aware of Ian's arms around her, his hands stroking her hair as she cried great gulping sobs, sounds far more animal than human. He murmured quiet words of reassurance and held her as her emotions poured out. Over and over she thought, *It can't be true. I don't believe it. It's a mistake.*

And for the third time in her life, because of this work they felt compelled to do, her world stopped spinning.

It must have been hours. It felt like hours because she couldn't remember how it had gotten this late, the bit of sky she could see through the windows a deep navy. Ian had turned on some soft music and covered her with a blanket and pressed a cup of tea into her hands, but for all that, she still trembled with a bone-deep cold.

She was in shock. She knew she had to be, because she was thinking slowly, reacting like she was underwater.

Ian sat down on the sofa beside her and rubbed her arms, his face concerned. "Grace, I'm so sorry." He slipped an arm around her.

She sank into him. "I can't believe he's gone. I knew something was wrong. I felt it. Why didn't I watch the news? He's been missing for three weeks and I didn't even know it." Three weeks in which she had been focused on herself and Ian and her own happiness while one of the people she loved most in the world was being held captive. Probably tortured. Brutally killed.

"You couldn't have done anything, Grace. It seems they weren't even sure he was missing."

He was right, but it didn't assuage the guilt. She closed her eyes, the grief falling heavily over her like a curtain.

Ian took her cup and set it on the table, then repositioned her on the sofa so she could lie against a stack of pillows with her feet in his lap. "Just try to sleep now, Grace. It's the best thing. I'll be here when you wake up."

She wanted to protest, but her eyes were too heavy and his hands on her feet were too relaxing, and despite her best efforts to put the words together, they got lost on the way to her lips. So she slept.

She woke with a gasp, clutching at her surroundings like a drowning man grasping for land.

Instantly, Ian was kneeling beside the sofa. "Are you all right?"

She blinked for a moment and then nodded. For a second, she wondered if she'd had another episode, but she remembered nothing of her dreams. No flashbacks, no nightmares. The nightmare was real.

"I'm okay," she whispered. "Thirsty. What time is it?"

"Near midnight. You've slept for almost two hours."

Only two hours? It felt like a decade.

Ian disappeared into the kitchen and reappeared with a glass of water and two aspirin. She took them gratefully and drained half the glass in one go. "I'm sorry."

"There's nothing to be sorry for." He transferred a book and his reading glasses to the table so he could sit again, and she automatically shifted into the shelter of his arms. "Just tell me what you want to do. Do you want me to take you back? Is Asha home?"

Asha. She couldn't think clearly enough to remember her work schedule. The hours before were all a blur. "I don't know. Can I just stay here for a while?"

"Of course you can." Ian didn't seem to know what to say. *She* didn't know what to say. It all seemed like a horrible dream, an ache in her chest that just wouldn't go away. It was like Jean-Auguste's death had left a hole in her universe, somewhere way out there. Even if she couldn't see the star, she felt the dark hole in the sky where it might have once been.

Ian pressed a kiss to her temple, a comforting touch, and it just seemed to widen that gaping spot in her middle. It felt like hunger and thirst and pain and longing and love, hollowing her out, pleading to be filled. She lifted her face to his, an unspoken invitation. When his lips brushed hers with such tenderness, she softened into him, breathing in the scent of his cologne and soap and skin, and sank deeper into that ache. In the furthest parts of her mind, she knew he offered comfort and understanding and love, and for the moment at least, it soothed the broken places.

Her hands were doing things of which she wasn't entirely conscious, sliding over the fabric of his shirt, trembling on the buttons. And then his soft voice in her ear: "Grace, love. Not now. Not tonight."

"Yes. Now. Tonight." She rose up again to capture his mouth, her heart fluttering in her throat like the fragile beat of bird's wings, unable to put voice to the desperation welling up inside her. A tear seeped from the corner of her eye, but she refused to brush it away, refused to break contact with him. In this whole broken, awful day, this was the only thing that felt right. His lips, his hands, his body—they were the only things holding the wildness at bay, that fearsome part of her she couldn't let consume her again.

He caught her wrists and tilted his head back to look at her. "Sweetheart, stop. You're not thinking clearly."

He was too principled to take advantage of her grief, but he underestimated how well she knew him, the strength of their shared memories. She kissed him softly and murmured the words she knew he wouldn't resist.

"I love you, Ian. I need you."

CHAPTER THIRTY

IAN STARTED AWAKE IN THE dim gray light, momentarily disoriented. He glanced at the clock by the bedside, getting another jolt from the glaring red numbers: 5:32. He should have been out of the flat thirty minutes ago if he were going to make his Saturday morning outing.

Then he turned his head and the events of the previous night came rushing back to him. Grace lay beside him, sleeping peacefully with the sheets twisted around her legs, clad only in her T-shirt and knickers. The enormity of last night hit him in the chest and sucked the air from the room.

Oh, God, what have I done? She had been the one to initiate it, true, but this hadn't been a reasoned, mutual decision. It had been born out of grief and pain and helplessness. It had been the only way he knew to fix anything for her in the moment.

He reached for his phone on the nightstand and realized it was still in the pocket of his trousers, which brought on another rush of regret. Had he taken advantage of her? He slid from beneath the covers, gathered up his clothing, and removed fresh kit from his drawer.

Then he halted. What was he thinking? He couldn't just slip out, as if this had been a one-night stand. This was his fiancée. He wanted her to wake in his arms, wanted to kiss her softly, to tell her he loved her. To apologize for his weakness. To assure himself he hadn't ruined their chances together.

He stood at the foot of the bed and watched her sleep, her colored tattoos stark against the white of the sheets in the dim dawn. She might not thank him for an early wake-up. She'd never been a morning person.

Ian slipped into the bathroom to dress, where he would be less likely to wake her. With a wash of shame, he realized he was a complete and total coward.

The sound of a door closing pulled Grace from sleep, an automatic warning that started her adrenaline pumping before her eyes even fully opened.

She was in bed. Ian's bed. Alone.

The memories of the night before rushed in, making her weak, sick.

What had she done?

No, she remembered everything they had done, in heart-pounding clarity. And then she remembered why.

Jean-Auguste. The call. The horrible reality she still didn't want to believe could be true.

Twin waves of shame and grief crashed over her, battling for the honor of being the one to destroy her first. Grace swung her legs over the side of the bed and propped her head in her hands, willing the nausea to pass, willing some sort of clarity from her thoughts.

It was her fault. Ian had known she was fragile, had been afraid of hurting her, of doing something they would regret. So she'd seduced him. Manipulated him. Used him. She knew this scene all too well. Run from the reality of the danger of her chosen profession. Seek comfort from a man—though it had always been a colleague or a friend or a fleeting romance. Wake to an empty bed and the knowledge that her grief wasn't a nightmare, all the more painful for the brief, illusory respite from it. And all it had taken was a single moment to send her running back to her old ways.

The truth was, Egypt or England, she hadn't changed at all.

The sound of running water from the bathroom made her jerk her head up and she checked the clock: 5:35. Ian would be getting ready for his morning outing. He hadn't left her after all. She let out a small, thready sigh of relief, which dissipated as soon as he entered his bedroom.

He gave her a sad smile and bent to kiss her. "Good morning, beautiful. How are you feeling?"

So he was going to pretend like nothing happened? Her blood echoed in her ears like the thrum of the ocean. "Well enough. Ian—"

"Don't." He sat down on the bed and took her hand.

"Grace, I owe you an apology. You had a shock last night.
I shouldn't have . . . It probably wasn't the right . . ."

"So you regret it too." Did that make her feel better or
worse?

"No! I don't. I mean, I do . . ." He sighed and wiped a hand
over his unshaven face. "Grace, this doesn't change anything.
We love each other. We're getting married."

She nodded, even though the words just hung in the air
without any real meaning. She forced a smile. "Right. We
just made a mistake. You should get going. You're going to
be late." She pushed herself off the bed and gathered up her
clothing on the floor.

"Is that all you're going to say?" Now his words carried a
hint of hurt, more than a little accusation.

"What do you want me to say, Ian? I forced you into it.
I seduced you. I take full responsibility."

He jumped up to block her escape. "In case you didn't
notice, there was nothing one-sided about what happened
between us last night."

"What do you want from me?"

"I want you to tell me what you're thinking!"

"What am I thinking?" Grace cried. "Let me see. I'm thinking I was a fool to believe I could leave my old life behind.
I'm thinking about how, when my dearest friend was being
kidnapped and tortured and killed half a world away, I was
trying on wedding gowns. And then rather than do the normal thing like cry and get drunk on cheap whiskey, I seduce
a man so I don't have to think about how absolutely screwed
up my life is."

"Just a man," Ian said, his voice strangled. "Strange,
I thought I ranked higher than that."

Grace blanched. "I didn't mean that the way it sounded."

"Grace, it's terrible what happened to Jean-Auguste. If I had any way to change that, I would. But I can't. Just like I can't change what happened last night. But could we please give ourselves a break? This is not the end of the world."

"Right. Not the end of the world. Go to the club. You're going to be late. I'm not going to feel like you're running out on me."

He nodded and dropped his hands, stepped back to give her some physical room even though that wasn't the kind of room she needed. Then he sucked in a breath. "Oh, no. Grace, we didn't use anything. What if—?"

She shook her head sharply. "I'm on the pill. Don't worry."

"How? You clearly didn't plan this."

She let out a harsh laugh. "Really, Ian, sometimes you can be incredibly naive. It's in case I get raped while on assignment. If you haven't noticed, bad things happen to journalists overseas."

He recoiled as if she'd struck him, and she took advantage of his stunned state to escape into the bathroom. After twisting the lock, she collapsed onto the toilet and buried her head in her hands. She ignored his light knock, his muffled apology through the door. Only once his footsteps receded did she flip on the shower and fill the small room with steam.

The hot water singed her skin, but even that minor pain couldn't numb the sick feeling of helplessness that ate through her middle. When she climbed out and toweled herself dry, she couldn't remember if she'd used soap or shampoo or if she'd just run out the water in the heater. She lifted her arm to her nose and sniffed. It was the familiar smell of Ian's soap on her skin that did what his words hadn't—doubled her over into racking sobs on the tile floor of the bathroom. At that moment, she didn't know which she was grieving more: the death of her friend, the wreck of her relationship, or the realization that her new start in London was simply a fantasy.

When she had nothing left inside to cry, she pushed herself up from the floor, pulled on her clothes, and went in search of her mobile, which had fallen beneath the reception room sofa. Only then did she notice the message from Asha that had vibrated it off the coffee table. Grace, where are you? I'm worried. Call me.

She quickly texted back I'm fine, then shoved the phone into her pocket.

Now she could add lying to the list of her failures.

CHAPTER THIRTY-ONE

"YOU'RE LATE."

"I know, I know." Ian didn't meet Chris's eye as he opened his locker and dragged off his coat. Street clothes came off, Lycra shorts and formfitting T-shirt went on, then waterproofs. He thrust his feet into his wellies, knowing that he'd blown his chance for a proper warm-up this morning.

"That's interesting, Mr. 'I Always Wake Up Alone.'"

He shot Chris a warning look. "Don't."

"Don't what?" Chris asked innocently, though his smile grew broader with Ian's discomfort.

Ian ignored him. The last thing he needed was the typical "good going, man" thump on his back. As if he really wanted congratulations for breaking his fiancée's trust and putting their relationship at risk. He rolled the kink out of his neck, shoved his clothes in the locker, and slammed the door shut.

"So, are we going to row or are we going to talk?"

"You gonna warm up?"

"You my mother?"

Chris raised his hands. "Fine. If you pull a hamstring or throw out your back because you're an idiot, don't cry to me."

Ian slowed. Chris was right. He couldn't let his bad mood get the better of him. He had always prided himself on his focus in the boat. His crewmates depended on him to have his head together, especially considering their lack of a coxswain on the weekday outings.

Still, by the time he took his place at the stern, marginally warmer and only slightly less likely to injure himself, he couldn't shake the knot of dread in his middle. He shouldn't have left things the way he had, even if Grace had purposely pushed him away. There was nothing about this outing that was more important than her. But it was too late now. He pulled his wellies into the boat and shrugged off his jacket beside him in the hull.

The Tideway was crowded this morning, the clubs and university crews out in full force, pleasure craft glutting the center lanes. Ian forced his mind off of Grace and onto Chris's voice as the bowman guided them out into the Middlesex lanes, rowing with the tide. He started them with some easy strokes, warming them up, before he kicked up the pace. Ian focused on the effort of his muscles, the sweep of the oar, the angle of entry into the water. Unaccountably, his heart lifted with the growing burn in his lungs and the increasing strain on his body. It was hard not to believe that everything would work out when he was out on the river.

"Heads up, Oxburn!" Chris shouted, flicking the rudder to avoid collision with an overtaking crew that had drifted into their lane. Ian winced as he caught sight of the blue hull out of the corner of his eye. Too close. A junior squad out for a turn on the Tideway.

The farther they moved up the river, the worse the chop became. Chris's flawless technique in the bow was keeping them on course, but Ian felt the instability of the boat when they started their second piece.

Ian never saw the boat; he only heard the thrum of its motor and felt the chop of its wake against the shell. From the bow end, Chris shouted, "Hold her hard!" and immediately the crew squared their blades into the water for a rapid stop.

Too late. A sickening crack rang out behind him. The impact shuddered up through the boat, jerking Ian's hand off the oar and throwing him aside at an odd angle. Before he could fully comprehend what had happened, the shell tipped strokeside into the murky water.

Ian sucked in a breath just before he went under. It wasn't his first time capsizing on the Thames. He stayed calm, twisting and lifting his feet to release the shoes from the foot stretcher. His right foot came out easily, but the left stuck in place. He tried again. Jammed.

His lungs burned as he bent double, reaching for the laces. Just as his breath was about to give out and his calm turned to concern, he managed to slide his foot free of the shoe and kick upward.

He broke the surface to chaos. Pieces of the shattered shell floated around them with lost oars, other members of the crew bobbing in the water.

"Oi there!" someone yelled. He twisted his head toward

a man leaning over the edge of a coaching launch, his hand outstretched. As Ian took his first overhand stroke toward him, however, he knew something was wrong, and not just because of the pain in his shoulder.

He couldn't move his arm.

CHAPTER THIRTY-TWO

GRACE FIT HER KEY IN THE DOOR, dry-eyed and numb. *Please let Asha already be at hospital,* she prayed.

No such luck. As soon as she pushed through the door, Asha rushed out of the kitchen, still in her pajamas. "Thank God, Grace. I was so worried!"

"I texted you."

"*I'm fine* doesn't really cut it after you don't come home, you know." She looked Grace over, settling on her tearstained face. "What happened? Are you okay?"

Grace opened her mouth to say something casual. Instead, she started to cry.

"What happened?" Asha put an arm around her and guided her to the sofa. Even through her tears, Grace noticed her looking for the ring on her left hand. "Grace, sweetie, you can tell me. Is it about Ian?"

Grace wiped her eyes, but it did no good since the tears were still falling. "Jean-Auguste is dead. He was killed in Iraq."

"Oh, Grace." Asha put her arms around Grace again, cradling her like a child. "What can I do?"

"I don't know," she whispered. "I'm just numb. I can't believe it. Aidan, then Brian, now Jean-Auguste. It's all so surreal."

"Where's Ian? I know he wouldn't want you to be alone."

"Rowing. We argued and I made him go. I messed this all up, Asha. It was supposed to be different this time. *I* was supposed to be different."

"Grace, nothing is ever going to be perfect. You're going to make mistakes. And you've experienced things that no one should ever have to see, let alone live. So give yourself a break, will you?"

"That's exactly what Ian said."

Asha took her by the shoulders. "Grace, he loves you. And you love him. There's a reason why he's the one you want with you in your worst moments. Don't push him away."

Grace twisted the engagement ring on her left hand, watching the diamond glint in the setting. Asha was right. She loved Ian. She was letting her grief and her helplessness spill over into the one good thing she had found in her life, pushing him away rather than letting him walk beside her.

Her phone rang in her pocket, and she drew it out, her chest involuntarily constricting when she saw the unfamiliar number. Was it more news about Jean-Auguste?

"Grace?"

"Who is this?"

"Chris. Chris Campbell. Ian's friend?"

Grace's gaze flew to Asha's in alarm. "How did you get this number?"

"From Ian's phone."

A sick feeling crept into her middle. "Chris, what's going on? Where's Ian?"

"There was an accident on the Tideway. He's at Princess Grace. He's okay—mostly. But I think he would like you here."

Awful scenarios flashed through her head. The Tideway was crowded, not just with oared craft, but with motorboats, tugboats, pleasure vessels. What on earth had happened?

"I'll be right there." She ended the call, too stunned to even ask where she should go or what kind of condition he was in.

"Grace?" Panic tinged Asha's voice.

"Accident on the Tideway. Ian's at Princess Grace. I've got to go."

"Do you want me to come with you?"

"No. I'll be okay. I need to go now."

She stood, but her trembling legs wouldn't hold her, and the room swam around her. From a distance, she heard Asha calling her name, telling her to breathe. She sucked in a lungful of air, and it yanked her back from the edge of unconsciousness. The fact Ian was at a private facility and not the nearest A&E should have reassured her. But it still didn't cut through the sudden, overwhelming feeling of panic.

She couldn't lose him. He was all she had left.

Grace held her breath the entire cab ride to hospital. It was impossible not to think the worst. Most people were so far

removed from tragedy that they automatically denied anything so terrible could rip their lives apart. But Grace knew
better. Terrible things lurked just around every corner, and it
was a miracle that they didn't collide more often.

*Aidan. Brian. Jean-Auguste. Please, God. Please don't add
Ian to the list.*

"He'll be fine." Asha found her hand on the seat next to
her and squeezed. Grace held on hard and said nothing.

The taxi dropped them off outside the hospital's urgent
care entrance, and while Asha paid the driver, Grace stared
at the glass entry enclosure. It didn't help that she knew this
was not the type of place at which one arrived by ambulance.
The sick, helpless feeling was all too familiar.

"Come on," Asha said quietly, taking her arm. "It's better
that we go inside and find out for ourselves."

The waiting room was clean, bright, and nearly empty,
without the usual queue of emergency department patients.
The advantages of having money, Grace supposed. She
let Asha do the talking with the nurse at the glass-topped
reception desk, unable to do more than concentrate on her
breathing and stare at the hospital logo on the wall behind
the woman's head. Asha had to nudge her before she realized
that the older woman was talking to her.

"You're family?" the receptionist asked again, not unkindly.

"I'm his fiancée." Grace held up her left hand, as if her
ring proved she was telling the truth.

"If you'll have a seat, I can check for you."

Grace nodded numbly and walked toward one of the
banks of chairs, but she heard her name before she managed
to sit. She spun to find a nurse pushing Ian in a wheelchair,
Chris several steps behind.

In a flash, Grace was at Ian's side, searching him for any sign of his injuries. He was fully dressed with his right arm in a sling, but otherwise he looked no worse for the wear. "What happened? I feared the worst when Chris called!"

Ian's startled expression said it all.

"He didn't tell you he called, did he? You didn't want me here."

"No, no." Ian reached for her hand. "I just didn't want you to worry. I'm fine. We were hit by another boat and I dislocated my shoulder. Minor rotator cuff tear. Nothing to be concerned about." He worded his answer carefully and precisely, but his accent softened around the edges and let some of the Scottish slip in.

"Why are you in a wheelchair, then?"

"Mite unsteady on his feet from the drugs," Chris said, amused. "Thought it best he didn't walk under his own power at the moment. Do you want to see him home?"

"Will you be with him then?" the nurse inquired. "He shouldn't be alone tonight. There could still be a minor concussion."

"Grace and I don't live together—" Ian began.

"It'll be fine," Grace said quickly. "Does he need to be woken in the night?"

"No, but he'll likely need another painkiller in four to six hours."

A few more brief instructions and they were allowed out on the street to hail a taxi in front of the urgent care entrance. Grace checked her watch. Only ten o'clock. The miracles of private medicine. When at last a black cab pulled up to the curb, Grace held the door open for Ian, then turned to Asha and Chris. "Thank you, both of you. Are you sure you don't want to be dropped somewhere?"

"We can find our way home," Asha said. "Phone me later."

Grace climbed in beside Ian and gave the driver his address. After a moment, Ian scooted close to her and put his good arm around her.

"I'm sorry, Grace."

The conflict within her was too deep to form words. He was fine. There was no reason to think this was a bad omen, that the accident was more than mere chance. She looked up at him and saw his eyes were already closed, no doubt a result of the medication. Perhaps the injury was worse than he'd let on.

When the cab stopped in front of his building, she shook him gently. "Feeling unwell?"

"No, just tired." Still, he didn't object when she confiscated his key ring and opened doors for him. She tossed the keys onto the hall table and led him directly to his bedroom. The rumpled sheets made her stomach toss.

"Grace, you don't have to do this. I'll be fine. I was never unconscious. I didn't inhale water. I'll have Chris check in on me later if you want to go back to Asha's."

"Nonsense," she said briskly. "Now take off your shoes and have a kip. I'll make you some lunch when you wake up."

"Grace, come here."

She moved closer to the bed, and he put his good arm around her waist, looking expectantly into her face. "Are we okay?"

She gave him a quick smile. "We're okay. Now get some sleep. We'll talk later."

He kicked off his shoes and stretched out on the bed.

Grace helped him remove the sling and propped a pillow under his arm, then pulled up the duvet. Even she was aware of how cold and mechanical her movements seemed. His eyes closed immediately, and she shut the door behind her as she slipped from the room, her chest tight.

Thank You, Jesus, for keeping him safe. God had answered her desperate prayers, had saved Ian from something that could have been far worse.

And yet she could not deny that in two days, her faith had been shaken. She had naively thought that London could be a haven from trouble. But in reality, there was nowhere far enough to outrun it.

CHAPTER THIRTY-THREE

WHEN IAN WOKE, the light through the bedroom window had deepened and the scent of curry drifted from the kitchen. Unfortunately, the pain in his shoulder had escalated from a twinge to a dull throb. He turned onto his good side and found the amber bottle and a glass of water waiting for him. He tossed back a pill and drained the glass.

"Thank you, Grace," he murmured before a sick ache overtook gratitude.

She was angry at him and trying not to show it, out of consideration for his injury. Slowly, he pushed himself to an upright position, grateful that his headache was dimmer than the shoulder pain, and struggled back into the sling.

When he emerged, Grace stood at the range, humming to

herself while she stirred something in a pot. The image was so cheerily domestic that he hesitated to interrupt it with his presence.

But she sensed him anyhow. When she turned, her expression immediately shuttered. "How are you feeling?"

"Not terrible considering. You let me sleep?"

"It's about time for another pill. They're on your nightstand."

"I took one, thank you."

"Then you should probably eat. You never did well with painkillers on an empty stomach."

Something about the way she delivered the words, brusque and unemotional, broke through his fuzziness. "Grace, we need to talk."

"No, we don't."

Ian pulled her to him with his left hand, ignoring her sound of protest, and rested his cheek against her head. "Talk to me, Grace."

She was quiet for so long, he thought she might refuse. "When Chris called and said you were at hospital, I thought I was going to lose you."

He swore softly under his breath. "That's why I didn't want him to call you."

"But you should have." She finally looked up at him. "Had *you* called, I wouldn't have panicked. I wouldn't have nearly fainted in Asha's reception room."

"Grace, sweetheart, I'm so sorry. I didn't think it was that big of a thing. Just a minor injury. I've had worse in capsizes. The doctor says with a little physical therapy, I'll be back to rowing in six weeks."

"That's not the point. The point is you didn't trust me to

handle the news. You didn't think this was something you should immediately phone me about."

She was right. Once more he'd taken the cowardly way out, not because he didn't want her to be part of his life, but because he thought she was angry with him. "I'm sorry. You're absolutely right. I didn't want to pile anything more on you, and I only made it worse. But that's not why you're angry."

"I'm not—"

"You are."

"No, Ian, I'm upset with myself. I'm ashamed of myself. And I really don't want to talk about it."

"I think it's a little late for that. We made love, Grace. Did you think it wasn't going to happen after we got married?"

"That's different."

"It's not that different. We'll be married in a matter of weeks."

"It's just . . . I get this terrible news about Jean-Auguste—" she choked up for a moment and blinked away tears—"and I immediately went back to my old ways of dealing with it. I can't stand the thought of my old life following me into my new one. I can't stand thinking of you like . . ."

"All of the other men." There was the root of his failure. He'd acted just like the others, taking advantage of a grieving woman with a traumatic past. It didn't matter what his intentions had been, didn't matter that he'd tried to dissuade her, didn't even matter that what they shared went far beyond the physical. In her eyes, he was just another man who had failed her.

But no, he couldn't accept that, wouldn't. He placed his hands on her arms and looked her in the eye. "Grace, I am deeply sorry that I hurt you. But it's not as if you went home with a stranger from a bar. I *love* you. I'm going to be your husband. Will you please stop treating me like I'm just some bloke you picked up on holiday?"

She recoiled, a sick look washing over her features. "Don't say that."

"Then don't think that. Marry me."

She held up her left hand. "I think we've already covered this."

"Marry me now."

"You're insane!"

"How is wanting to be with you forever insane?"

"For one, you just got home from hospital and you're drugged up on painkillers."

"Then no more pills. We can do it tomorrow."

Grace pulled away from him, and this time he let her go. She stirred the curry in the pot, purposely not looking at him. "I'm not marrying you on a whim."

"This is not a whim! Do you think it's an accident that I've waited for you for ten years? Do you think it's an accident that I've not brought anyone home to meet my family in a *decade*?"

She didn't say anything, and the temper Ian hadn't even known was building snapped. He pushed away from the countertop. "I'm going to lie down for a bit."

He didn't storm across the reception room to the bedroom, nor did he slam the door, though it would have suited his mood. Instead, he pushed it closed with a soft click, sealing her out. Less than a day ago, they'd shared something that should have been special. Instead, it had driven a wedge between them as surely as time and distance ever had.

When he woke some time later, more clearheaded, he expected the flat to be empty. Instead, Grace was curled on the sofa beneath a blanket, the television turned down low, knitting something in hideous multicolored wool.

"I didn't think you'd be here," he said.

"The nurse said you shouldn't be alone tonight so I had Asha bring over some things. I'll sleep on the sofa." She swung her legs down and pushed her blanket and knitting aside. "Can I warm up some curry for you?"

Even though his stomach rumbled, he didn't much feel like eating. But he sensed this was her way of making peace, so he nodded. She went to the kitchen and scooped out rice and curry into the bowl. His heart gave a little clench at the sight of her barefoot and in her pajamas. Was he wishing for things that in the end, he couldn't have?

She sat beside him while he ate, stealing glances at him when she thought he wasn't looking. Finally she said softly, "Just give me some time. It's all too much to take in at once. I need to get it sorted for myself."

He didn't know if she meant Jean-Auguste's death or their relationship or her past traumas, but he nodded anyway. "I won't push you. Just . . . tell me I'm not losing you again."

She forced a smile and picked up her knitting. "You're not losing me again."

Somehow, taken with the angry movement of the knitting needles in her hand, the words were less than reassuring.

Grace's presence in his flat over the next four days felt not like a relationship but like a business arrangement. She cooked for him and helped him pull his arm through T-shirts, made sure he took his medication on time and fielded phone calls while he was sleeping, but anything approaching personal contact had vanished, along with the easy rapport they had shared.

No matter what she said, she slipped a little further away from him each day.

Ian quit the painkillers on the second day. The throb was just this side of bearable without them, and the medication made his memories and perceptions go soft around the edges. There might also have been a bit of masochism involved. The drugs didn't dull only his physical pain, and if he were going to lose Grace, he wanted to experience every agonizing minute of it.

He woke up on Monday morning to find her cooking breakfast. "I'm going back to work."

"Already? You're sure?"

"I'm sure. And if I'm well enough to go to work, I'm well enough to be here on my own without help."

For a second, something like hurt flashed through her eyes, though that made no sense. She'd made it clear she was here out of duty, nothing more. "Just eggs and toast this morning. If you're not going to be rowing for a while, I figured you would want to cut back your calories. It will make it easier to go back if you don't gain weight."

"I'm touched that you're so concerned about my girlish figure."

She didn't seem amused as she slid the poached eggs from a spoon to his plate. "I know how you get."

"Have I been that horrible already?"

"That's not what I meant." She retrieved the toast, which she'd fried in the pan, and placed it next to the eggs. "Here. Are you going to need help with your suit?"

"No. But I would really like help finding my fiancée. Someone replaced her with a home health aide."

She grimaced and fell back against the counter, rubbing a hand through her hair. "That's not what I'm doing."

"Isn't it? Because I don't know what else to think."

"Maybe . . . maybe we need some distance. It's been a difficult few days."

"No, distance is what we have now. I would like to see some feeling from you."

She swallowed, but she didn't look up at him again. "I can't right now, Ian. Either you understand that or you don't."

Disappointment arced through him, sharp and biting. He pushed the untouched plate away from him. "Thank you for breakfast. I find I'm not all that hungry." He strode to the bathroom and flipped the water on in the shower. He ripped the sling over his head with too much force and had to bite down on his cheek to avoid a cry of pain. So maybe his shoulder wasn't healing as fast as he'd implied. But he couldn't sit imprisoned with Grace and her vacant stare any longer.

Once more he assumed she would be gone, but when he got out of the shower, he heard the water running in the kitchen along with the clank of stoneware. That made no sense. If she was so miserable here, why did she stay? Was her sense of obligation that strong?

He struggled into his trousers and shirt, buttoning them one-handed, but the tie proved to be too much for him. He pushed down his pride and walked out into the reception room. Grace was in front of him in an instant, taking the tie from his hands and looping it around his neck. Even the brush of her fingers as she flipped up his starched collar ignited a yearning in him that he barely tamped down in time.

She tied a full Windsor with surprising ease and smoothed down the two ends against the front of his shirt. Then she took his cuff links from his pocket and fastened them into the holes without asking. When she at last looked into his face, he saw the reflection of his own longing there.

He couldn't help himself. He bent to kiss her, and to his surprise, she returned the sentiment as good as he gave.

"Oh, Grace, I've missed you." He kissed her again, not willing to let her slip away from him again, not even an inch. When she slid her arms around him beneath his jacket, he nearly sighed with relief. "Now I hate the fact I'm going to work. Meet me for lunch?"

Slowly, she nodded, even managed a smile. Though it contained underlying sadness, a glimmer of his Grace emerged.

"Do you want me to pick up something on my way?" she asked. "You'll be busy after being out of the office most of the week."

"That would be nice. I love you, Grace. Don't forget that, please?"

She stretched on her tiptoes for a farewell kiss. "I know. I love you too. Just give me time."

"Okay. I'll see you around noon."

His light mood lasted as long as the cab ride to the Westminster office—he hadn't wanted to risk the press of the morning commute on the Tube with his injury. Dread hit him as he punched the lift's Up button in the foyer. What would await him when he arrived? He'd never taken more than two days off from the office the entire time he had worked for Jamie's company. Would he be spending the next month catching up on whatever disasters had managed to occur in his absence?

No one waited for him outside his office, though, which was a miracle, considering he'd left word with Bridget that he'd expect an update from various employees when he came in. Ms. Grey sat at her desk in front of her computer screen as she had every day since he hired her. She looked up and smiled pleasantly. "Welcome back, Mr. MacDonald. I trust you're feeling better?"

"I am, thank you, Ms. Grey. Give me a moment to get settled and then I'll want an update."

"Yes, sir."

Ian moved into his office, expecting to find a pile of paperwork on his desk. It looked as neat as it had when he left on Tuesday afternoon. He popped open his briefcase on the surface, then realized that he hadn't taken any work home. He'd just stowed the case under his desk when Ms. Grey reappeared in the doorway, a stack of files in her hands. She settled in the chair opposite his desk, then arranged the files neatly in stair-step fashion on the polished surface. "We need to discuss budget, contracts, and some vendor changes for the restaurants in England."

"Vendor changes? That's James's department."

"Yes, but I noticed the Knightsbridge and Notting Hill locations have incurred a 20 percent increase from their seafood vendor that doesn't correlate to menu changes or receipts."

Surprised, Ian nodded. "I'll speak with the chefs in James's absence. What's next?"

"Budget, sir." She flipped open the second file. "The other employees have submitted their budget requests for next fiscal year as you requested. I've flagged areas that I thought could be a problem." She paused, uncertainty crossing her face. "I'm sorry. Have I crossed a line? I just thought—"

"No, no. Your thoroughness is very admirable. I'll take a look at your notes. Thank you."

"Of course. The next matter is the network contract. It looks like Mr. MacDonald's—" she paused, apparently unsure how to distinguish the two Mr. MacDonalds and still maintain her formality—"your brother's show is going into syndication. Since you haven't replaced Mr. Barrett yet, I thought you'd want to look over the contracts yourself."

"Yes, thank you, Ms. Grey."

"I'll leave you to it, then. Please let me know if you need anything."

Ian watched her go, then looked down at the stack of files on his desk. Each had been annotated with sticky notes in her precise handwriting, pointing out areas of concern, even on the network contract. His eyebrows flew up when he saw the specificity of the comments. Ms. Grey had contract knowledge as well?

Perhaps there wouldn't be as much to catch up on as he thought. She was clearly the perfect assistant for him. For once, he had done well in his hiring.

Except just as he'd feared, she was far too capable to remain an assistant. How long before she wearied of the tedium of a support job, when clearly she belonged at the head of a department, maybe the head of a corporation?

Even with Ms. Grey's efficiency, his e-mail in-box was filled to bursting. He sorted through the messages, tagging those that needed his immediate attention, forwarding those that could be delegated to Ms. Grey, shooting quick replies back on those that were easily solved. He was so absorbed in clearing his backlog that he didn't notice the time creeping past noon until he looked at the clock. Good enough. Grace would be here in a few minutes with lunch anyway. If he could take care of this final list, he might even make it out of the office before 5 p.m. today.

The clock inched past one o'clock. Then one thirty. Unease crept into Ian's gut. He pulled his mobile from his jacket pocket on the back of his chair. No messages.

Quickly, he tapped out a text message: Still having lunch today? Everything okay?

He set the phone on the edge of his desk, where he would notice if her reply came through.

By three thirty, it was obvious that she wasn't coming and she didn't intend to reply to his message. He couldn't breathe through his tight chest.

"Ms. Grey, my shoulder is bothering me. I'm going to leave early. You can reach me on my mobile if you need me."

"Of course, sir. Tomorrow?"

"Bright and early." He shrugged his jacket onto his shoulders without putting his arms through. "Thank you for all your hard work. I've never been able to take time off and not come back to a disaster."

"It's my pleasure, sir. Rest up."

Ian held on to his composure until he stepped onto the lift and punched the button for the ground floor. Then he slumped against the wall and let the feeling of panic that had been clenched in his stomach rise up.

When he got back to his flat, would he find a ring on the counter?

CHAPTER THIRTY-FOUR

As soon as Ian left the flat, Grace began straightening up and found herself circling her laptop on the dining room table like a satellite around a planet in an ever-tightening orbit. Ian had insisted she stay away from the news so her memories of Jean-Auguste would remain untainted, and she'd hunkered into a fog of shock and disbelief, embracing the numbness so she wouldn't think about him. But that morbid need to know the truth gnawed at her, a dull ache that harried the edges of her consciousness, the only relief from which was to shut down completely. As long as that fear and dread remained, she would never be able to move on. She would never be able to move forward in her life with Ian.

On her third circuit, she sat down at the table and lifted the lid of the laptop. She hesitated only a moment before typing in *Jean-Auguste Cassin*. A long line of news stories materialized on the page. Grace clicked one after another, scanning the text with helpless fascination, absorbing fragments that only added to the horror without explaining a thing.

Ambush. Kidnapping. Murder.

She'd worked in the Middle East long enough to read between the lines. Jean-Auguste had trusted the wrong person and been betrayed. Maybe for idealism; more likely for money or out of self-preservation. It was a risk they all took, working with fixers whose alliances were uncertain at best and ever-shifting at worst. Most of the time it worked out. Jean-Auguste proved how badly things went when it didn't.

She was on the second page before she came up with a link to a video on an unfamiliar, sketchy-sounding site. Her hands trembled over the touchpad for several seconds before she could manage to click it.

Nothing. The video had been taken down.

Gripped with dark determination, her whole body shaking, she changed to the search page's video tab and clicked link after link until she found one that worked.

Five seconds. That's all it was. Grace pressed play, steeling herself for what she was about to see. But at the last moment, she lost her courage and closed her eyes, her entire body rocking with the pounding of her heart.

Watch it, Grace.

She forced her eyes open and braced herself to click it again, even though her very soul recoiled at the thought of what she would see. But she owed Jean-Auguste that much. He had died among strangers, without anyone who loved him. He deserved to have a witness who would mark and mourn his passing.

She clicked the button. And she watched all five seconds.

Sat there for five more, her breath frozen in her lungs, until the horror sank in and she had to dart for the washroom. She hung over the toilet, her stomach heaving, and yet the tears she'd felt sure would come remained locked behind a veil of horror and grief. There was only one thing she could do.

She pulled out her mobile and sent a message to a number she hadn't used in years. Just as she had expected, she got an answering text within minutes.

Come over at 10. I'll open the shop early. Bring coffee.

A few minutes after ten, Grace climbed a dirty, dingy stairwell to the first floor of a disreputable-looking building near Camden Market. She juggled her two paper cups while she tried the door—unlocked, even though the sign clearly stated Closed—and pushed through into a space that looked far more like the Putney art gallery than a tattoo studio. Bright-white walls bounced light within the open area, with blond wood floors and sleek, Scandinavian-style furniture in the reception room. The front desk, which would have looked at home in one of London's expensive boutique hotels, stood empty.

"Hello?" she called out. "Mika?"

A door opened in the back, and a man strode toward her. "Grace!"

She smiled. Anyone expecting a biker-looking bloke with a beard and more ink than an art store would have been sorely disappointed. Mika Havonen was almost painfully good-looking, in that brilliant blond Scandinavian way that brought to mind tales of Viking gods: hair cropped short, model-perfect muscles shown off by a tight white T-shirt and artfully whiskered blue jeans. His only body modifications were a small, discreet diamond in each ear, and he wore a plain brown leather cuff on one wrist. The overall effect was much more like the heartthrob lead singer of a Finnish boy band than one of London's most renowned tattoo artists.

She accepted his kiss on both cheeks, then handed him one of the coffee cups. "It's been a while, Mika."

"Indeed. There are exactly two people I'd open early for, and you're the one who doesn't wear a crown."

"Somehow I don't see the queen getting inked."

"The queen didn't lend me rent for my first year either." He leaned casually against the desk while he sipped his coffee. "So, this was a nice surprise. What are we doing? A new project?"

He never called them tattoos. Only projects. And he was booked four months out, unless you were Grace Brennan or a handful of other close friends.

"A new one. Left arm."

"Come to my office, and we'll take a look."

Mika led her to a room in the back that reminded her of a university professor's office, overflowing with books from every nook and corner. Only the drafting table, with its computer and light box, were clear of literary debris, and a small leather sofa sat against the opposite wall. He gestured for her to take a seat and pulled up a stool opposite her. "So what have you been up to, Grace?"

Grace held out her right arm, knowing what he was really asking. He slid on a pair of black-framed glasses and gripped her wrist in strong fingers, turning it to examine her last "projects."

"Good work. Who did it?"

"Olivier."

"Very nice. He still in that little place in the eleventh arrondissement?"

Grace nodded.

"You starting a new sleeve?"

The question took Grace aback. She'd said the dragon on her right wrist would be her last, but that was before Jean-Auguste. It wasn't right to leave him uncommemorated, and she wouldn't rework an existing design for him. He deserved more than that.

"I don't know," she said finally. "For now, just a cross with a fleur-de-lis element."

His forehead furrowed. "With dates?"

She nodded, not trusting her voice.

"I'm sorry, Grace. I'd hoped never to do another one of these for you."

Grace chewed her lip and forced back tears. Mika had done her very first tattoo, the one on her right shoulder that memorialized Aidan. In fact, it had been his idea to drape a replica of Aidan's camera over the cross. "I'm thinking iconography . . . French heraldry, maybe."

Mika's expression changed, and she knew he was putting the details together. She'd already proven that the latest murder of a Western journalist was all over the news. "Maybe you shouldn't rush this. I can draw up some designs, e-mail them later."

"Can we just . . . get it over with?"

Mika sighed. "Whatever you want, *kulta*. You look tired,

though. Why don't you lie back here while I work up the design? I'll wake you when I'm done."

Grace stretched out on the sofa, only intending to close her eyes for a few minutes, but the next thing she knew, he was shaking her awake. "I'm finished. Take a look."

She rubbed sleep from her eyes and moved to the drafting table, where a piece of paper lay among a scatter of open art books. He'd drawn a small stone cross with fleurs-de-lis at the end of each arm, his fine-arts background evident in each stroke of the pen. "It's perfect."

"Good. Let's go out front, then."

Grace dragged her sweater over her head, then stretched out in the adjustable chair at one of the studio's six work spaces, chewing the inside of her cheek to keep from focusing on the hollow feeling in her middle. Mika scrubbed up and pulled on a pair of nitrile gloves, then began to set up his station with surgical precision.

When he'd finished his prep, he took his seat silently beside her. He knew she didn't like him to talk while he worked. She closed her eyes, felt the swab of alcohol wipes, the scrape of a razor, the press of the transfer as he positioned the design on top of her left arm. Only the buzz of the machine warned her that he was about to begin. The first sharp stabs of the needle took her breath away before she remembered to relax into the pain.

And at last, the tears that had remained locked away for days slid down her face, one after another in an endless stream. At that moment, she didn't know what she was grieving more: the death of her friend or the realization that no matter how far she ran, she would never be completely free of her past.

CHAPTER THIRTY-FIVE

IAN PUSHED THE BUZZER on the front stoop of Asha's building, his heart thudding in his ears. He'd started here first,
trying to convince himself that Grace had simply moved her
things back to Asha's flat this morning as planned and fallen
asleep. After a minute, a speaker crackled to life. "Hello?"

Asha. "It's Ian. Is Grace there?"

"No. I thought she was at your place."

"Has she been home today?"

"Not that I know. Is something wrong? Do you want to
come up?"

"No, we just probably got our plans crossed." He let go of
the button and stepped off the stoop, rubbing his shoulder
as if that were what actually pained him. He chose to walk

the mile or so to his flat, steeling himself for the sight of her things gone, her ring on the counter. She had run away again. He should have known this was going to happen as soon as she began distancing herself.

But when he entered his flat, her duffel bag still sat in the foyer, her camera case on the table. The air rushed out of his lungs in a wave of relief, but a pang of concern followed just as quickly.

If she hadn't missed their lunch date because she was leaving him, where was she? Had something happened to her? London was a relatively safe city, and Grace certainly knew how to take care of herself, but accidents still happened. He took out his mobile and dialed her number. It rang several times, then went to voice mail.

Grace, call me, he texted. Worried about you.

He sat there for a few more minutes, then rose. He should go grab something to eat for supper and wait for her. He took a moment to change from his suit and hang the pieces neatly in his wardrobe, then slipped into a pair of jeans and a loose pullover that didn't require too much contortion to get into.

Thirty minutes later, he was back with a paper bag containing two paper-wrapped Reuben sandwiches from a nearby Jewish deli. He could only assume Grace would come here instead of Asha's flat. She might not care about her clothes, but she wouldn't leave her camera behind. He flopped onto his sofa and flicked on the television, keeping one eye on the minute hand of his watch. Fifteen minutes passed, then twenty. Just as he was about to gather their uneaten meal, a key scraped in the lock and the door handle rattled.

He was on his feet instantly as Grace walked into the hallway, cap pulled low over her eyes and her cardigan wrapped tightly around herself as if it were winter. Something in the way she moved sent up an alarm in the back of his mind. Was she hurt? Ill?

She looked up at him and blinked slowly. "Ian? What are you doing here? Is it your shoulder?"

"I left work early. You missed our lunch date. I was worried." He tried for casual, but even he could hear the undercurrent of tension in his voice.

"I'm fine. Are those sandwiches?" She nodded toward the bag on the coffee table and set down her rucksack. She wasn't meeting his eye, and she still hadn't acknowledged the fact that she'd stood him up today.

"Grace. Tell me what happened."

"Nothing happened."

"Then why didn't you come today?"

She blinked, seeming legitimately surprised. "I'm so sorry, Ian. I completely . . . I got sidetracked and then I forgot."

"You're holding something back. What is it?"

She slipped out of his grasp and went to the kitchen. She got a glass from the cabinet, filled it with orange juice, and replaced the carafe in the refrigerator before she said anything. She didn't look him in the eye. Her voice shook as she said, "If you were smart, Ian, you would just let me go."

Another spike of fear impaled him. "What are you saying? What's going on?"

"I'm saying that I'm beyond help. No matter what I do, I fail. I failed myself. I'm going to fail you." Tears gathered on her lower lashes and spilled over onto her cheek.

"Ah, sweetheart . . ." He reached for her and rubbed her arms in what he meant to be a soothing gesture. She winced and squirmed away from his touch.

"Grace," he said in a low voice. "What did you do?"

She pulled down the wide neckline of her sweater to reveal the large rectangular dressing that covered the upper part of her left arm and peeled it away to show the newly inked cross, the skin beneath it pink and puffy.

"Oh, Grace . . ."

Her spine stiffened immediately at his tone. "Lots of people have tattoos. More than me."

"You know I would love you if you were covered in them from head to toe. I don't care about what. I want to know why."

"Why? You never wanted to know before, Ian. You never asked."

Guilt added to the queasy feeling in his stomach. "I'm asking now."

She pulled her sweater off over her head and stood before him in her tank top. "Take a good look, Ian. It's all there. All my hang-ups, all my trauma." She pointed to a tattoo of a cross and an old-fashioned camera on her upper arm. "Right there is the first one I got for my brother." She pointed to a shaded key. "There is the one I got when my parents kicked me out of the house. And these, all the crosses for the colleagues I've lost in the field."

He crouched down to pick up the sweater and paused, giving himself time before he handed it to her. She pulled it on over her head, her eyes glistening with unshed tears. "Grace, I'm sorry I never asked. I thought I was protecting your privacy. Tell me why. Make me understand."

The fight left her abruptly. She slumped against the counter and rubbed her hand across her forehead. "When I got my first, it was to make my parents angry. They thought if they pretended Aidan had never lived, it would be like he never died. All the photographs, put away. But I had to remember. I wanted proof that he had existed. After that, it was a way to show the things I'd experienced really happened. Bad things. Good things. Everyone I'd loved and lost."

Her voice dropped even lower. "Sometimes the pain of the needle was the only thing I actually felt. Other times, it was the only thing that could relieve the pressure." She lifted her eyes to his. "You don't know what it's like to feel like you're suffocating, to never draw an easy breath. Or to go around in a fog, detached.

"So I kept going back. Looking for some kind of relief. I'd been okay recently, since I rededicated my life to Christ. He'd taken that compulsion, I thought. Then Brian died on the anniversary of Aidan's death, and I had to do something to honor them both." She fingered the green dragon that finished the sleeve around her right wrist. "I said once the sleeve was done, I was done. No more holding on to the memories. But today I panicked. I was afraid I wouldn't ever be able to feel anything again. So I did this."

Ian didn't know what to say, gripped by guilt and pain and sorrow. That the woman he loved had struggled so much and he'd never known . . . he'd thought he was respecting her space, but in reality, he hadn't wanted to know. He'd been content with the way things had been years ago, perhaps even smug about her insatiable appetite for him. But that hadn't been about him. It hadn't even been about love, and he'd been too dumb or selfish to realize it.

Just like her giving herself to him a few days ago had far less to do with love than her need to forget.

He gathered her to him, carefully avoiding the new tattoo,

and buried his face in her hair. "I'm sorry, Grace. Forgive me. I should have known. Maybe if I'd pushed you to get help back then—"

She jerked away from him. "Don't talk to me like that."

"Like what?"

"Like I'm broken. Like I'm something that needs to be fixed. I told you I don't want to be defined by my issues."

"That's not what I'm saying." He kept his voice gentle despite the dread in his chest, squeezing with each heartbeat. "I'm just saying that ignoring it isn't making things any better. If anything, it's getting worse."

"I tried!" she shouted. It was so out of character, so out of the blue, he stepped back. Tears brimmed on her lower lashes. "Don't you think I've tried? It. Didn't. Work."

"One therapist, Grace. That doesn't mean it didn't work; it just means you had the wrong one." He sighed. "I just want to see you get better."

"That's just it." Her tears spilled over. "There might not be a better me. You want the version of me who can tell your friends brilliant stories about firefights and exotic locations. But you don't want to know about the dead children and the raped women and the death squads."

He reached for her with his good arm, but she twisted away. "I know I can't fully understand," he said. "And I'm sorry if I haven't been as supportive as I should have been. But that's why I want you to talk to me. And to get help. Will it make it go away? No. Nothing will ever change the past. But it could at least be bearable."

"Bearable," she said with a laugh. "Do you really want to be saddled with a wife for whom life is just bearable?"

"Good, then. Life can be good. You've seen it yourself.

You've been happy with me up until now. It's just been too much, one thing on top of another. It won't always be this hard."

"Ian, you're being naive again. Whatever you think you see in me—I'm not that woman. We've been fooling ourselves to think otherwise." She rubbed her eyes with the back of her hand, weariness evident in every movement. "I think I'm going to go now."

"Grace, please, don't do this." He grabbed her by the elbow, but this time she didn't flinch. Her gaze was back to that distant, numb look again. "Just wait a bit. Don't make any decisions now."

Slowly, she nodded. She opened her mouth to say something, but her mobile phone rang in her pocket before the words could emerge.

He let her go.

"Grace Brennan," she said quietly, flicking a glance in his direction. "Yes, Monique. How are you?"

He leaned back against the counter, knowing he should give her privacy but unable to make himself move.

"No, I can't, I'm sorry. I'm still finishing up some things here in London. I couldn't possibly come this month." Her voice was still flat, emotionless, but when she glanced at him, he almost thought he saw disappointment in her face.

"Sure. If something changes, I'll let you know." She clicked off the line and stared at the phone in her hand, silently.

"She wants you to go to Montreal."

"Yes. But I promised you. No decisions right now."

He searched her face for some sign of peace, something to spark hope in the suddenly dark space in his chest. But he found nothing.

CHAPTER THIRTY-SIX

GRACE STARED THROUGH THE viewfinder of her camera, snapping pictures of the muddy waters of the Thames as it slid silently beneath Westminster Bridge. She scarcely saw her subjects, too conflicted to concentrate on her work. She had barely eaten, hardly slept in the week since she'd faced off with Ian. It was as if pouring out the whole truth had opened the floodgates. She scarcely passed a night without waking in a cold sweat from another reenactment of the horrors in her past. She lost parts of her day without explanation, sometimes minutes, other times hours.

She said nothing to Ian, though. She had promised him she would stay, and she was staying. They ate supper together, watched films at his flat, kissed good night, but it was nothing more than routine. She wasn't a good enough actress to sell emotions she couldn't feel.

Except when she found the business card for a therapist on his dining room table. That she'd felt—a fury disproportionate to the offense. She'd ripped it up into tiny pieces in front of him and then burst out crying. To his credit, he'd simply held her, and for the first time in days, she felt a flicker of love stir in her.

And yet she could still see the pain in Ian's face. He knew she was pulling away from him, knew she was considering leaving him again, and he wasn't going to hold her here if she didn't want to stay. Not just because he had too much self-respect to cling to a woman who didn't want him, but because he loved her too much to force her into something she didn't want.

Except she did want him.

The thought broke through the numbness that had been her constant companion like a ray of light through the clouds. She loved Ian. She knew she loved him, because even when she was broken and miserable, he was the only thing that felt safe. When she wanted to run away, she didn't, because she couldn't bear to think what that would do to him.

When she thought about leaving, it was like the whole world was falling to pieces again.

She was shattered, make no mistake. But he had stood by her even when she pushed him away. Why was she so determined to face her problems alone when he had told her over and over they were in it together?

If she didn't marry him, it would be the stupidest thing she'd done in her life, and she had a long list already.

For the first time in days, a smile touched her lips.

Yes, she would marry him. As soon as they could manage it.

Grace considered going straight to Ian's flat, but she didn't want to show up in a wrinkled T-shirt and faded black trousers. When she asked him to elope with her, and soon, she wanted to look decent. More than that, pretty. Years from now he should remember the way she looked in that moment and smile.

She chose her clothes with care and took a few extra minutes to put on her makeup. Before she left for Ian's flat, she sent a text message: I need to talk to you. Are you home?

I'm home. Need to talk to you too.

The trip seemed to take forever, and she slowed as she approached the historic building. Ian sat on the steps, his right arm cradled to his body in the sling, his jacket thrown loosely around his shoulders. He said nothing, just patted the step beside him.

Her stomach lurched. She sank down and pressed her clasped hands between her knees to keep them from trembling.

Silence stretched. Then he said, "When we were children, my parents used to take us to the Edinburgh Zoo. Jamie loved it. He would've sat and watched the big cats for hours if they'd let him.

"I hated it, though. The way they paced their enclosures made me sad, as if they were just looking for a way to escape. But no matter how they paced, day after day, they would die behind those barriers." His voice lowered, roughened. "Some creatures aren't meant to be caged, Grace."

Her heart swelled into her throat, choking off her air as she realized what he was saying. "Ian—"

"Don't." He reached into the inner pocket of his jacket and

pulled out a long, slender folder. She recognized the British Airways logo as he tapped it on his knee. "I want to be here for you, Grace. I do. But I can't watch you pace the boundaries of our life together any longer."

She took the plane ticket from his hand and flipped open the folder. First class for Grace Margaret Brennan, London to Montreal. One way. "Why?"

"Because you need to decide what you really want, and I can't be the person standing in your way." Pain shone in his eyes as he leaned over and pressed his lips to her forehead, lingering long enough that she felt the hitch in his breath. Tears rose in her eyes, threatening to spill over. "Take care of yourself, Grace."

He stood and walked up the steps. Before he stepped inside, she called, "Wait!"

He turned. She'd hoped to see some hint of hope in his expression, some indication that his mind was not made up, but she saw only resolve. "That's it? You're letting me go? Without even asking me?"

"Don't make this any harder than it needs to be. It's what you want."

"What if it isn't?" Panic built in her chest. He couldn't be doing this. Not now. Not when she saw her future clear for the first time in her life.

"Then maybe it's what I want." He let himself in the door of his building, pain evident in the way he held himself, though she didn't know whether it was his body or his heart.

Grace stared down at the ticket, choking back sobs until she could force herself to her feet. So there were limits to what he could endure after all. She had discovered the edge a day too late.

CHAPTER THIRTY-SEVEN

IAN WOKE BEFORE HIS ALARM the next morning and glanced at the clock. Five thirty. Late for his outing. He jerked upright in bed before the pain knifed through his shoulder and pushed him back down on the pillow.

He didn't have an outing this morning. He'd be lucky to get back into a boat anytime in the next month. The only thing that could help him deal with the knowledge that Grace was gone had been taken away from him as cruelly as his hopes for his future.

He willed the sick feeling in his center to go away. It had been the right thing to do. They would have just continued on in this pattern: Grace refusing to admit there was anything wrong while she went through the motions of their relationship. But always he would be waiting for that day when he would come home to an empty flat. The first time had nearly broken him. He couldn't survive a second.

He breathed in and out for several minutes until he summoned the will to swing his legs over the side of the bed. He moved his shoulder experimentally and winced. As tempting as it would be to swallow one of the narcotics in the bathroom, he needed to be alert, wanted to feel the pain. Some grief was too deep to numb. Sometimes it had to be embraced so it didn't tear you apart from the inside.

A quick glance at his reflection in the bathroom mirror convinced him that it would take more than a couple of painkillers to get him ready for work today anyhow.

A long, hot shower eased a bit of the ache in his shoulder, though it did nothing for the feeling in his chest. He wrapped a towel around his waist and leaned over the sink, running a hand along his scratchy jaw. He had his face lathered and the razor in his hand when he caught his reflection again.

Strange that he should look exactly the same when his whole life had crumbled around him.

He set the razor down and washed the shaving foam from his face. What was the point? He could keep on with the way he'd been going, but for what? He was turning forty years old next month. All the things he possessed were just empty reflections of wealth that couldn't buy him what he really wanted. A partner. A life. A sense of purpose.

You had ten years to get a life and you didn't. That's not Grace's fault; that's yours. What does it say about you that she's the only meaningful part of your existence?

Wherever the words came from, they struck with the sting of truth. He ignored the gray flannel suit hanging on the back of the door and instead yanked on a pair of blue jeans and yesterday's pullover. Then he picked up his mobile phone, found his brother's number in the contacts list, and dialed. He knew Jamie was still in London, even though he hadn't seen him since he returned from the honeymoon.

"If someone isn't dying or a restaurant isn't burning down, I'm hanging up on you." Jamie's sleepy voice didn't sound annoyed, just matter-of-fact.

"I need to talk to you."

He could practically hear Jamie snap to alertness on the other end of the line. "What's wrong?"

"Not over the phone." He cut himself off before his voice could break.

"Meet me at the Regency Café at eight. And for heaven's sake, next time wait until it's light outside, would you?"

Ian hung up without saying good-bye and tossed his mobile onto the bed. He walked automatically to the kitchen, filled the electric kettle, and flipped it on without thinking. Then the memory of Grace standing there doing the same thing just days before knifed through him and he couldn't breathe.

He was the worst kind of idiot. He'd known what he was risking when he got involved with Grace, knew what it would do to him when she left, and he'd done it anyway. The fact his mother had been right about her was almost worse than the heartbreak. Almost.

He arrived at the Regency a few minutes before eight, but Jamie had already claimed a corner table, looking as put-together and self-satisfied as he always did. "You look terrible."

"Thanks. I feel even worse."

"I'm sorry to hear about your accident. You're in that much pain?"

Ian just stared at him, and the truth seemed to seep into Jamie without words. "Oh no. Grace. You two—"

"Are no more. She left. Or rather, I told her to leave."

"Why?"

Ian stared out the window at the busy pedestrian traffic. He'd been asking himself the same thing all morning. "She needs more help than I can give her. And until she comes to that conclusion on her own, we're doomed to failure."

Jamie just studied him from across the table. "I can't decide whether you need sympathy or a swift kick in the rear."

"You think I shouldn't have done it?"

"It's really not my place to say. I'm just surprised. When Grace came back, you seemed—"

"Like my old self. I know."

"Right. But maybe that's the whole problem."

Ian frowned and searched his brother's expression. "What do you mean?"

"Come, Ian. Your family cares about you. You think no one noticed that you just stopped . . . living . . . after Grace left?"

"I didn't stop living. I realized that it was time to be responsible. You haven't seemed too upset about it while it worked in your favor."

"No, I'll admit, it's worked out quite nicely for me. But when you got your law degree, I figured you'd finally go join some human rights group like you'd planned. Instead you did corporate contracts for a few years and then came to work for me."

Ian's first impulse was to deny it, but he couldn't. Not

anymore. He'd known that to his family, it must have looked like Grace's departure had turned him bitter, shattered his idealism. And there was some truth to that.

But the full story was far more pathetic.

He'd been waiting. Somewhere inside him, he'd always believed Grace would come back to him. If he was off in the Netherlands working at the International Criminal Court as he'd once dreamed, she wouldn't be able to find him. And the longer he'd waited, the more he'd had at stake. His pride. His future.

Then when Grace had reappeared, it was like he was being rewarded for his patience—or his refusal to move on. That's why he'd rushed things with her, proposed when he knew there were still obstacles to their life together. If she left again, it would make him a fool. Worse, it would prove he'd wasted the last decade of his life on a futile dream.

But he was done with that. He wasn't going to waste another second. "That's why we're here. I came here to tell you I quit. I'm happy that I was able to help you when your business started growing, but you don't need me anymore. In fact, I think I've already found my replacement." He proceeded to tell his brother about Ms. Grey and her capabilities, his belief that she was far more qualified for the position than he was.

"She sounds very qualified, and I'm happy to interview her. But first . . . have you prayed about this?"

Ian jerked his head up. Jamie was the last one he would expect to get spiritual. But his brother had changed. Andrea had made him think of things, including his faith, in a completely different way. Not just something for church holidays, but to live every day.

When was the last time Ian had thought of God in more than the most superficial light?

He'd been raised to have faith. He went to church. He'd lived a temperate, celibate life for a decade, because that's what Christians did.

Or maybe that's just because you had no other temptations. No greater priorities.

Had church or God or his faith even crossed his mind since Grace came back into his life? He'd loved her with a fervor that he could only call religious. When was the last time he'd served Jesus with that same level of passion? Had he ever?

Jamie must have sensed the tumult inside him because he leaned across the table to clap Ian on the shoulder. "Seems like you've got a lot to think about. I won't consider the resignation final until I've got it in writing." He smiled down at him, seeming to enjoy the role of older, wiser brother. "Take your time. You've waited this long; the future isn't going anywhere."

Ian watched his brother stride from the café, even more unsettled than he'd been when he arrived. He'd come in ready to take charge of his life, and now all he could think about was what a mess he'd made of it on his own. Was that the point of all this? That it was time to get over his self-centeredness and start listening?

For better or for worse, God had used Grace to get his attention. He couldn't go back to the way it was before she'd come. He could never look at the world—and his life—in the same way again.

CHAPTER THIRTY-EIGHT

"ABOUT THREE INCHES TO YOUR LEFT," Grace said in French, peering through the viewfinder. She made a quick focus adjustment and snapped the picture. "Perfect. *C'est fini. Merci, mademoiselle.*"

Her subject, a lovely Québécoise woman in her thirties, unfolded herself from her perch on the lushly upholstered stool and flashed Grace a pretty smile. *"Et vous aussi."*

"If you'll give us a few moments, we'll be out of your home so you can continue with your evening." Grace dipped her head and unscrewed her lens from the camera body, then placed them in their respective cases as a man approached from behind her.

"Should I take down the reflectors and lighting now?" he asked quietly in French.

Grace nodded, and her assistant turned to the studio lighting they'd brought in to illuminate the tiny space. René was young and capable, and he more than earned his keep, with both his efficiency and his knowledge of Montreal. She would never have survived the last month in the bustling city if it had not been for her young Québécois companion.

The project Monique had promised would make her the next Annie Leibovitz hadn't quite panned out as she expected. It was a magazine feature on the ten most influential people in Montreal. Among others, she had shot a fashion designer, a software programmer, a chef, the owner of a minor league hockey team, and today, the French-speaking movie star Alicia du Longue. Pretty standard fare, except they had been chosen not for their career accomplishments, but for their dedication to philanthropy. Grace's job had been to capture the essence of their personalities, their public personas, and their charitable activities, which explained why she was currently shooting in a walk-in closet filled not with designer clothes but with hundreds of pairs of plastic clogs—shoes for children in Ethiopia.

Not for the first time, Grace wondered what she was doing here, cataloging the efforts of others when she should be out there herself.

When she and René had all the gear packed and loaded into Grace's rental wagon, René paused with his hand atop the roof. "That was our last shoot together. You have time for a drink to celebrate?"

Grace considered for a moment. René was nearly a decade younger than she was, but so far he'd shown nothing but the general friendliness she would expect from a coworker. She gave a nod. "Have any suggestions?"

He threw her a grin. "There's a decent Irish pub in Ville-Marie we could try."

"Sounds good. You navigate. I still can't find my way around Old Montreal."

Grace pulled the car out onto the narrow street, following her assistant's confident directions through increasingly heavy traffic. Ville-Marie was a centrally located borough containing downtown and most of the cultural happenings in Montreal, which also meant that it was the most heavily traveled area of the city. "We should have left the car at my hotel and taken the bus," she said as she stopped at yet another traffic light.

"Not much farther. You'll need to look for a metered space on the street."

Grace tried not to grumble beneath her breath. Miraculously, another car pulled away just as she paused for a light, and she swooped into the empty space. René hopped out of the car, dropped several coins into the meter, and then pointed to their destination: a neon harp in the window of the upper floor of a small brick building.

"That is not a proper Irish pub," Grace muttered to herself.

"We're in Quebec. What do you expect?" René threw back in perfect English.

"You never told me you spoke English!"

He shrugged and stepped off the curb. "You never asked."

Young professionals and college students crowded the interior of the pub, well on their way to inebriation at five o'clock on a weekend. Grace wound her way through the throng and snagged a tiny table with two chairs in the corner.

She picked up a plastic menu. "You hungry? What's good here?"

"The Guinness," he replied, flashing that charming grin. Grace wondered suddenly if she had misread him. Was he flirting with her after all? Or was four weeks away from London merely reminding her how much she missed having Ian in her life?

She studied René across the table. She had hired him because he seemed like a kindred spirit. Spiky black hair stood away from a passably handsome face, and as he always did when he was working, he wore a conservative button-down shirt and jeans. Right now he had his sleeves rolled up, showing off the tattoos that marked his forearms, and there was no hiding the gauge piercings in his ears. He was the type of guy that, once upon a time, she would have taken up with without a thought. But those had been in her dark days, and attractive as he might be, she had no interest in going back.

A waitress sauntered over to her table, and Grace's ears perked up at the Irish accent, discernible even in her French. They each ordered a Guinness, and then Grace decided to ask for fish-and-chips as well. René leaned back in his chair and studied her in a way that made her slightly uncomfortable.

"Tell me the truth, René. Are you trying to take me home?"

He leaned forward again, his smile fading. "Not with that ring on your finger."

The way he said it made Grace flush with shame. She automatically hid her hand in her lap to conceal the engagement ring she still wore. It made her ill to look at it. Funny thing, it made her feel even more ill to take it off.

"You're clearly attached, ring or no ring," he continued. "What I want to know is, where's the guy who bought you that flashy rock?"

"London."

"Are you going back there?"

His tone was soft, sympathetic even, and that surprised her. "I don't think so. He made it pretty clear we were over."

"So clear you're still wearing his ring?"

Grace ran a hand through her cropped hair as the waitress set their glasses down before them. She ignored hers. A headache had just begun pulsing behind her eyes, and alcohol would only make it worse. "He let me go."

"So it was your choice to leave."

"Not really. I was ready to get married, and instead he gave me a plane ticket to Montreal." She twisted her glass around on the table, watching it make rings on the scarred and polished surface.

"That doesn't sound like someone who was trying to get rid of you. That sounds like someone who thought you wanted to go. So why did you?"

How many times had she asked herself that same question?

The answer was simple. Because she was hurt. Because he reminded her that she was damaged. And because just when she had finally thought she could give all of herself to someone, he had decided she wasn't worth the pain.

But had she really given him any indication that there was a payoff on the other side? She'd refused to go to therapy, thrown all his efforts to help in his face. What man would want the dysfunctional life she offered? Hadn't she told him he didn't care enough to understand what she was going through? She twisted the ring around her finger, so lost in thought that she didn't realize René had switched seats to the one beside her.

"Will you just answer one question?"

She looked at him quizzically, and before she could do anything, his lips were against hers, his hand holding her head lightly. Grace waited to feel . . . something . . . but all she could think about was how quickly she could pull away without completely destroying his feelings.

In the end she didn't have to. He broke first and gave her a rueful smile. "Nothing?"

"I'm sorry."

"Go back to your Londoner, Grace." He took his Guinness and sauntered off toward the bar, where a group of girls immediately made room for him.

Grace shook her head in amusement, suddenly feeling old and staid. *"Go back to your Londoner."*

Even René knew she didn't belong here.

Forty-eight hours and one sickeningly expensive plane ticket later, Grace stood in front of Ian's building, wrapped in a trench coat against the fine October rain. She hadn't thought this through, not wanting to give herself time to talk herself out of it, but it meant finding herself on his street with absolutely no idea what to do.

Who was to say their four weeks apart hadn't made him realize their relationship was too much work, that she had too much baggage? She wouldn't blame him if he slammed the door in her face. It was nothing less than she deserved.

But she wouldn't know if she stood here all day. *Please,* she prayed, unable to put together words with any more eloquence. She took a deep breath and climbed the stairs, where she stood with her finger over the intercom button.

"Just do it," she whispered. She pressed the button. Silence.

She pushed the button again, even though her hopes had already crashed somewhere around her feet. Still no answer.

The front door of the building opened, and a gray-haired woman stepped out, covered in a faded raincoat and holding an umbrella.

"Sorry, ma'am. Do you know the man who lives on the first floor? In number six?"

The woman stopped and looked her up and down. Grace must have looked at least somewhat trustworthy, because she finally gave a nod. "The Scottish lad, you mean?"

Grace's heart thumped against her ribs. "Yes, that's the one. He's a friend of mine."

"Haven't seen him in weeks now." She frowned. "Come to think of it, I saw him put a fair bit of luggage and some boxes into the boot of that flashy car of his."

"How long ago was that?"

"A month, maybe? I didn't pay it much mind."

"Thank you," Grace said faintly. A chill started at the top of her head and crept downward to her toes. She sank down onto the steps. Gone, with what sounded like a good portion of his possessions. What could that possibly mean? Had he moved? Taken a long vacation?

She dug for her mobile in her pocket with trembling hands and dialed his office number. A woman's voice answered. She racked her brain for his assistant's name. "Ms. Grey?"

"May I say who is calling?"

"Grace Brennan. I'm actually calling for Ian MacDonald."

"Just a moment, please. I'll connect you with Ms. Grey."

The line went quiet for a moment; then a professional,

Scottish-accented voice answered. "Ms. Brennan? This is Abigail Grey."

"Um, hi, Ms. Grey. I was looking for Ian."

Another long pause. Her stomach took another dip.

"Mr. MacDonald resigned his position a month ago. I'm the new COO. Is there something I might help you with?"

Grace felt as if she'd been slugged. All the air rushed out of her lungs in a whoosh.

"Ms. Brennan? Grace?"

"Thank you, Ms. Grey," she whispered. She ended the call and clutched her mobile like it was her last connection with Ian.

Whatever had happened after Ian let her go, he didn't seem to want to be found. For the first time since she had left her parents' house, she sat on the front steps of a place she'd thought of as home and cried.

Grace was halfway down to the Underground platform before she remembered Asha was already in India. She stood there, unable to move from her sudden paralysis, while she watched train after train stop and then speed on, crowds of travelers moving about her like water around a rock.

London had begun to seem like home, but she now knew that had more to do with the people who lived there than the city itself.

She managed to break free of her indecision and boarded the eastbound train with the next wave of passengers. Almost without thinking, she disembarked at Westminster and found herself at the same spot along the Thames where she had come to the conclusion that she should marry Ian.

This wasn't how it was supposed to work. In all the romantic books and films, the girl would be standing out in the rain, thinking that nothing would ever work out again, and here came the hero, ready to take her back with open arms. They'd run to each other and kiss and vow to never be apart again.

She'd been deluding herself to think that kind of thing happened to people like her.

Or maybe it had, and she'd been too scared and blind to see it. She'd hurt the one person she had always loved completely, hurt him so badly that he felt the need to drastically alter his life. God had given her a second chance for a new life in London with Ian, and she'd wasted it.

Why would either of them give her a third?

She climbed atop the stone platform and sank into one of the wet benches, her arm curving over the wrought-iron curlicue support. The cold of the metal bit into her skin, but she didn't take her hand away. That required some feeling, some reaction. And right now, she wasn't sure there was anything left inside but emptiness. She slumped against the backrest, watching the colors trace across the London sky.

Elsewhere in the city, where the shadows fell early between buildings, streetlights winked on in clusters, little bright spots in the steadily darkening evening. The river churned around a handful of sightseeing boats and pleasure vessels, the tide about to ebb again. She imagined the vessels that were floating leisurely with the tide now having to rev their engines, put more power into just staying at the same speed. It was a fine metaphor for her life. Just when she thought things were flowing in her direction, the tide changed, and she had to work harder and harder just to stay still.

She might be able to bear the knowledge that she had ruined her chance with Ian if there were anything else left for her. Her career hadn't simply been a job to her; it had been a calling. Shining light into the dark places of the world that had been forgotten, illuminating the people whose tragedies were somehow deemed less important, simply because of a quirk of birth and geography. Even when it seemed like the world didn't care, she cared. She bore witness to their lives through her photographs, commemorated their place in the world through the marks on her skin. It might not have made her happy, but it had given her a purpose, a reason for her existence.

Grace stood and stumbled off the bench, made her way to the stone railing. All that was conceit, anyway, something to make her feel better about how she'd spent her last decade. She'd been gone from the field for almost four months, and the world hadn't stopped turning. In fact, were she to jump from the Westminster Bridge, but for the momentary horror of passersby, no one would know or care. Her eyes lifted to the structure that arched over the swift-moving river, and for a brief moment, she let herself fantasize about what it would be like to hit the water, wondered how long it would take before she stopped struggling against the current.

The buzz in her pocket made her jump guiltily back from the rail. She dug for her mobile and pressed it to her ear in a daze. "Hello?"

"May I speak with Grace Brennan?"

"Speaking," she said, her thoughts slowly catching up to the present.

"This is Henry Symon. I've been trying to reach you."

"I'm sorry, I've been traveling. I just got back to London."

"Oh, you've already heard, then?"

Grace squeezed her eyes shut, trying to make sense of the conversation. "Heard what?"

"We hired our second-choice candidate for the creative director position, and quite honestly, it was a disaster. The board is willing to give you a chance. That is, if you're still interested?"

"I—" She swallowed and gathered her wits together. "Yes, I'm still interested."

"Wonderful, Grace. I can't tell you how pleased I am that this will work out after all. If you can come by the office tomorrow, there's some hiring paperwork to be completed. You can start officially next week."

"Thank you, Henry. You have no idea—"

"You will be fantastic. I'll see you tomorrow."

Grace stared at the phone in her hand, still in disbelief. What had just happened? Moments before, she'd been toying with the unthinkable, feeling as if she had nothing left to offer the world. And Henry had called at that exact moment?

"Are not two sparrows sold for a penny? And not one of them will fall to the ground apart from your Father."

The words from a long-ago sermon in Ireland came into her mind, as clear as the first time she'd heard them aloud. And in that moment, she saw it all plainly. Yes, she had been called to be a witness. But there was a greater witness beyond her and the rest of humanity, standing beyond the constraints of time and borders and self-interest. God saw the pain of the world, even when no one else did. The lives of all those to whom Grace felt an obligation did not go unseen. Just as the life of one insignificant woman standing on the bank of the Thames, doubting her worth, did not go unnoticed.

Tears welled in her eyes and spilled down her cheeks. She may have known God was with her, in the vaguest sense of the word, but this felt like His very hand pulling her back from the precipice. He was saving her life just as he'd done before on the streets of Damascus. She wiped her face with the back of her sleeve, a new, unfamiliar feeling growing in her chest amid the cold.

Hope.

The grief was still there, a constant ache that might never fade completely, but hope left no room for despair. She shoved away from the railing and strode back down the pavement just as the lights of the Houses of Parliament clicked on.

CHAPTER THIRTY-NINE

THE PLANE TOUCHED DOWN at Chhatrapati Shivaji International Airport—Mumbai Airport for short—thirty-six minutes ahead of schedule and amid a brown cloud that surpassed anything Grace had seen in the time she'd lived in Los Angeles. Her stomach fluttered—not in fear, but in anticipation. It had been two years since she'd been in India, and she'd purposely planned Mumbai as the final stop in her monthlong journey visiting CAF's Asian offices.

To say she was coming back to India a changed person would have been overstating the facts, but the last two months had brought her a measure of peace she hadn't felt in years— maybe decades. Ian was always on her mind, but after her second week in London, she'd stopped trying to locate him.

Perhaps God was telling her that they really weren't meant to be. Perhaps they had been given those few months together to teach each of them a lesson. She hoped if that were the case, Ian's had not been nearly as painful as hers.

Lord, give me peace, she prayed as she stood in the aisle and retrieved her bag from the overhead compartment. She was getting better at arresting and cataloging her intrusive thoughts, and she had to admit prayer was much better than the alternatives.

Her new London therapist believed the combination of Aidan's death, the trauma of her job, and losing two friends in close succession through violence had left her with a complex presentation of post-traumatic stress disorder. Once, Grace would have resisted the diagnosis, but it was comforting to have a plan, to know she could start mending those broken pieces, even if she wasn't there yet. Connecting with her faith in a personal way was an important part of that plan.

She managed her bags on her own from the carousel: just one duffel and a small case containing her most necessary camera equipment. Still, she was pleased to see a uniformed driver standing at the exit of the airport, holding a sign in English and Marathi that read *Brennan.* That probably meant she was to go directly to the office without getting distracted by all the sightseeing and photo opportunities.

The driver gave her a little bow as she approached. *"Namaste."*

"Namaste," she repeated with a smile.

"May I help you with your bags?"

Grace stepped aside and let him take her cart, then followed him out the doors to the car park and a waiting Toyota sedan that was significantly bigger than the tiny Indian cars to which Grace was accustomed.

"You have been to Mumbai before?" the driver asked as he navigated the roads onto the airport return.

"A couple of years ago." She settled back against the seat to take in the sights as they left the airport property. Even after all her years in Asia and Africa, the contrast between the modern and the traditional, the wealth and the poverty, struck her. And the traffic! She had forgotten the congestion: lorries, tiny passenger cars, motorbikes, scooters that looked barely big enough for one holding two or even three passengers. She smiled as they passed one of the bright-yellow-painted rickshaws—a cross between a car and a three-wheeled motorcycle—that acted as taxis throughout Mumbai.

It was good to be back.

She rethought that feeling when the driver slammed on his brakes and swerved to avoid a family that darted into the road, horns blaring around them. She'd often thought one needed to be mad to drive in London, but five minutes on the road in Mumbai made her remember how orderly the English drivers were in comparison. No wonder Ian had been suspicious of her driving skills.

Her enjoyment faded a little bit as the small, squat—and poor-looking, by Western standards—shops transitioned into high-rises and then into one of Mumbai's major slums, homes constructed of scrap metal and wood, covered in bright-blue plastic tarps. All the time she had spent feeling sorry for herself, and there were people who lived on less money each year than she had in her wallet, while she transported thousands of quid worth of camera equipment in the boot of the sedan.

After several more minutes, the driver let her off in front of a grimy-windowed building in an older business district and unloaded her baggage from the back of the car. She declined his offer of assistance and tipped him for his help before he pulled back onto the busy street.

Before she could even hoist a bag, however, the door opened, and a tall, athletic-looking man stood in the doorway. He took one look at her camera hanging around her neck and said, "You must be Grace Brennan. You have some timing."

"And you must be Mitchell."

He shook her hand enthusiastically. "I am. Come on up and I'll introduce you to the Mumbai staff."

Grace slung her rucksack over her shoulder and lifted her camera case while Mitchell took her duffel. As she followed him up the narrow staircase, he detailed the status on the projects and outreaches Grace was here to shoot. "We've arranged a driver to take you and some other support staff to the various locations this week."

"Do you think three days in Mumbai will be enough time? I'd planned on going to the TB clinic in Pune on Friday." It was the clinic in which Asha was spending her three-month sabbatical, and she secretly couldn't wait to see her friend. She had purposely held back the fact she would be visiting.

"It should be. But you'll be the best judge of that."

He stopped in front of a door with a crisscrossed 1970s safety glass insert and pushed it open for her. "Welcome to CAF's Mumbai office."

It was tiny and just as outdated as she expected from the building's exterior, with metal desks and chipped linoleum tiles. A young Indian woman smiled and stood at her approach.

"Grace, this is our office manager, Kalyani. Kalyani, this is Grace Brennan, our creative director at headquarters."

"A pleasure, Ms. Brennan." Kalyani shook her hand with enthusiasm. "Welcome to India."

Mitchell nudged her toward the back office. "Come meet the program coordinator you'll be going around with. He's here meeting with the Maharashtra program director."

"Oh, I met Bakul before I left London. Nice man."

"Bakul left CAF nearly a month ago," Mitchell said with a frown. "This is his replacement. No one told you?"

"No, I hadn't heard. It must have happened right after I left London. I'm surprised they found someone to fill the position so quickly."

"It was an internal hire, as I understand it."

Grace sucked in a breath when Mitchell opened the office door. Surely she had to be hallucinating. This couldn't be possible. But she didn't need the man to turn around to know it was Ian standing by the window, his mobile pressed to his ear. Every molecule of her body seemed to recognize his presence even from a dozen feet away.

Then Mitchell was smiling and making introductions, saying something about administrative positions and donations and project timelines. She couldn't keep any of it straight in her head, her eyes fixed on Ian, looking as devastating draped in tropical linen as he ever had in his Western suit and tie. More devastating because she knew now that he didn't belong to her.

"Grace." The one word rippled through her from head to toe, making her momentarily forget how to breathe.

"Ian."

Mitchell looked between them. "So you do know each other."

Ian tossed a wry smile in the man's direction. "We're acquainted, yes."

Grace wanted to sink into the floor.

Apparently, Mitchell sensed there was far more going on beneath the surface and made a hasty exit. Ian gestured to the chair across the desk. "Sit. You look like you're about to faint."

"I feel like I'm about to faint." She'd never been the type of woman to be overcome, but now her mind whirled far too fast to make any sense of what was going on. "What are you doing here?"

"Besides the obvious, you mean?" He regarded her with a cool expression. She recognized that look. It was the same one he had used on her when they had bumped into each other at the benefit at the Savoy. Polished. In control. And just a hint of bitter.

"I mean, what are you doing in India with CAF? What—why—?" She sucked in a shaky breath. "I finished the job in Montreal, and when I came back, you were gone. I thought you'd taken a long holiday."

The cool facade never budged. "I did. But I really should thank you, Grace. You made me reevaluate my life. I realized that I'd been living for everyone but myself and consulting everyone but God. I'd done all I said I never would, just to please my mother, who will never be pleased with anything. Seems international law and operational experience made me a good candidate for a regional program coordinator."

"In India."

"Well, technically, it's in London, but it's hard to coordinate resources for something you've never seen." He softened. "That's something else I should thank you for. You've always loved India, always talked about the needs here. When CAF needed someone to fill the position quickly, it was an easy choice."

"And James's company? All the zeros?"

The corner of his mouth twisted up. "You seem to forget that money isn't a necessary component of my career choices."

"You said you would never touch your trust fund."

"Things change. You should know that better than anyone. Listen, Grace, I don't mean to make this any more difficult than it needs to be. I know you've been hired as the London creative director. Even though I'm not returning until Christmas, I'll be coming back and forth for the foreseeable future. It might be difficult to stay out of each other's way."

The steel in his voice pierced her heart. She'd been hoping the fact that he was here, in India of all places, might be a sign they could still mend what she had broken, but he seemed to want nothing to do with her. There were still things that needed to be said, though, whether or not he'd be receptive to them. Grace briefly closed her eyes, trying to get control over her emotions, trying to figure out what to do next. *God, give me peace.*

"I want you to know you were right," she said at last. "I was denying how bad things had gotten for me. I didn't want to believe that I was messed up enough to need therapy. But I found someone in London. And she . . . understands. It's helping."

"Good. I'm glad to hear that, Grace. I really am."

She pushed herself out of her chair and reached for the door handle. "I'll get out of your way, then."

"Wait."

She turned and realized his gaze was fixed firmly on her hand.

"You're still wearing my ring."

She dared a look into his eyes. "I couldn't bring myself to take it off."

Before she could comprehend what was happening, he was at her side, bracing the door shut, blocking her way.

"You're wearing my ring." This time a hint of hope colored his voice. "Why did you come back to London?"

Tell him.

Her heart rose into her throat, but she managed to whisper, "I came back for you."

He searched her face, as if trying to verify the truth of her words. She stood transfixed beneath his gaze, not daring to even breathe.

"Why?" he whispered. "Why did you come back?"

"Because I was scared and stupid and selfish for leaving. I was afraid if I admitted I had real problems, you would only see me as damaged. And instead I just drove you away. You are the best thing that has ever happened to me. Both times."

"True." A hint of humor colored his words, but his expression remained serious. "But that's not why you came back."

He wanted her to say it. She took a deep breath and spilled it all out in one sentence. "I love you, Ian. I always have. I always will. I want to marry you and spend the rest of our lives together. I won't blame you if—"

Before she could get the rest of the sentence out, his lips were on hers, the fervor of the kiss destroying the rest of the thought as if it had never existed. She clung to him, awash in relief and love and desire so intense, it left her gasping and weak.

"Wait." She disentangled herself enough to speak. "Does this mean you forgive me? After all I've put you through? You still want to marry me?"

"Yes, yes, and yes." He punctuated each word with a kiss. "Be my wife, Grace Brennan."

Her brain spun like a whirlpool, tossing her thoughts to and fro like a piece of driftwood in the current. "But how will we make this work? You left your job, and now we'll both be traveling . . ."

He flashed that tiny, heart-stopping smile. "Does it matter as long as we have each other?"

In that moment, the tide shifted in her soul. She'd thought that God was pulling her away, but she'd forgotten that at the end of the day, the tide always turned, bringing her back. To the man she'd always loved, to the life she'd always wanted.

Home.

Discussion Questions

1. Grace has a hard time leaving behind her career because of her deep need to draw attention to the overlooked and oppressed. Ian tells her he feels he has an obligation to those who haven't had his opportunities. What kind of responsibility do we have as both world citizens and people of faith to recognize and meet the needs of others?

2. The search for home and safety are two central themes in *London Tides*. How are those two related in Grace's mind? How does the idea of purpose intersect with those themes?

3. How are the ideas of unveiling and revealing used symbolically throughout the book?

4. Why do you think Grace relates so strongly to the oppressed, displaced, and forgotten?

5. Grace quotes Nietzsche when she talks about why she is leaving her career: she fears the darkness she has witnessed is changing her. What do you think she's running from?

6. Grace's identity is wrapped up so tightly in her career, and then later in her relationship with Ian, that she feels hopeless when it seems like she's lost both. What is the danger in placing our self-worth in the changeable? In what other things should we find our value?

7. At the beginning of the story, Grace hides her tattoos from Ian because they're a reminder of all the things she wants to forget but can't allow herself to forget. Near the end, she chooses a wedding dress that shows every last tattoo. How might this be symbolic of their relationship?

8. Both Ian and Grace come away changed from their short reunion without knowing if they will get a chance at forever. Can you think of instances when other people have been used as instruments of change in your life, even if you didn't see the reason behind it at the time?

9. Ian realizes that he'd loved Grace with a fervor that surpassed his passion for God. What happens to our priorities and our relationships when we allow things—even good things like love—to become idols?

10. *London Tides* uses the familiar "traumatized veteran" story as a framework for a romance, but in this story, the woman is the returning hero and the man has been waiting for her at home. How does flipping the gender roles in the story affect how you view the characters and the trope itself?

About the Author

CARLA LAUREANO is the RITA Award–winning author of contemporary inspirational romance and Celtic fantasy (as C. E. Laureano). A graduate of Pepperdine University, she worked as a sales and marketing executive for nearly a decade before leaving corporate life behind to write fiction full-time. She currently lives in Denver with her husband and two sons, where she writes during the day and cooks things at night.

Chapter One

THREE HOURS into Saturday night dinner service and she was already running on fumes.

Rachel Bishop rubbed her forehead with the back of her sleeve and grabbed the newest round of tickets clattering through on the printer. Normally orders came in waves, enough time in between to take a deep breath, work the kinks out of her neck, and move on to the next pick. Tonight they had come fast and furious, one after another, tables filling as quickly as they were cleared. They were expecting two and a half turns of the dining room tonight, 205 covers.

It would be Paisley's biggest night in the six months since opening in January, and one they desperately needed. As part-owner of the restaurant, Rachel knew all too well how far away they still were from profitability. There were as many casual fine dining places in Denver as there were foodies, with new ones opening and closing every day, and she was determined that Paisley would be one of the ones that made it.

But that meant turning out every plate as perfectly as the last, no matter how slammed they were. She placed the new tickets on the board on the dining room side of the pass-through. "Ordering. Four-top. Two lobster, one spring roll, one dumpling. Followed by one roulade, two sea bass, one steak m.r."

"Yes, Chef," the staff answered in unison, setting timers, firing dishes. Over at *entremet*, Johnny had not stopped moving all night, preparing sides as fast as they came through on the duplicate printer. It was a station best suited to a young and ambitious cook, and tonight he was proving his worth.

"Johnny, how are we coming on the chard for table four?"

"Two minutes, Chef." Normally that could mean anything from one minute to five—it was an automatic response that meant *I'm working on it, so leave me alone*—but at exactly two minutes on the dot, he slid the pan of wilted and seasoned greens onto the pass in front of Rachel and got back to work in the same motion. She plated the last of table four's entrées as quickly as she could, called for service, surveyed the board.

A muffled oath from her left drew her attention. She looked up as her sauté cook, Gabrielle, dumped burnt bass straight into the trash can.

"Doing okay, Gabs?"

"Yes, Chef. Four minutes out on the bass for nineteen."

Rachel rubbed her forehead with the back of her sleeve again, rearranged some tickets, called for the grill to hold the steak. On slow nights, she liked to work the line while her sous-chef, Andrew, practiced his plating, but tonight it was all she could do to expedite the orders and keep things running smoothly.

"Rachel."

She jerked her head up at the familiar male voice and found herself looking at Daniel Kearn, one of her two business partners. She wasn't a short woman, but he towered above even her. Her gut twisted, a niggling warning of trouble that had never steered her wrong.

"Hey, Dan," she said cautiously, her attention going straight back to her work. "What's up?"

"Can I talk to you for a minute?"

"Now's not a great time." Dan might be the rarest of breeds these days—a restaurateur who wasn't a chef—but considering he owned four other restaurants, he should be able to recognize when they were in the weeds. The energy level in the kitchen right now hovered somewhere between high tension and barely restrained panic.

"Carlton Espy is here."

Rachel dropped her spoon and bit her lip to prevent any unflattering words from slipping out. "Here? Now? Where is he?" She turned and squinted into the dim expanse of the dining room, looking for the familiar comb-over and self-satisfied smirk of the city's most hated food critic.

"No, he left. Stopped by my table before he went and told me to tell you, 'You're welcome.' Does that make any sense to you?"

"Not unless he considers questioning both my cooking and my professional ethics a favor." She looked back at the tickets and then called, "Picking up nine, fourteen!"

"You really need to issue a statement to the press."

She'd already forgotten Dan was there. One by one, pans made their way to the pass beneath the heat lamps and she began swiftly plating the orders for the pair of four-tops. "I'm not going to dignify that troll with a response."

"Rachel—"

"Can we talk about this later? I'm busy."

She barely noticed when he slipped out of the kitchen, concentrating on getting table nine to one of the back waiters, then table fourteen. For a few blissful moments, the printer was quiet and all the current tickets were several minutes out. She took a deep breath, the only sounds around her the clatter of pans, the hiss of cooking food, the ever-present hum of the vent hoods. After five hours in the heart of the house, they vibrated in her bones, through her blood, the bass notes to the kitchen's symphony.

Her peace was short-lived. Carlton Espy had been here, the troll. Of all the legitimate restaurant reviewers in Denver, a scale on which he could barely register, he was both the most controversial and the least likable. Most people called him the Howard Stern of food writing with his crass, but apparently entertaining, take on the food, the staff, and the diners. Rachel supposed she should be happy that he'd only questioned her James Beard Award rather than criticizing the looks and the sexual orientation of every member of her staff, as he'd done with another local restaurant last week.

The thing Dan didn't seem to understand was that slights and backhanded compliments from critics came with the territory. Some seemed surprised that a pretty woman could actually cook; others criticized her for being unfriendly because she didn't want to capitalize on her looks and her gender to promote her restaurant. She had never met a woman in this business who wanted to be identified as "the best female chef in the city." Either your food was worthy of note or it wasn't. The chromosomal makeup of the person putting it on the plate was irrelevant. End of story. Tell that to channel seven.

As the clock ticked past nine, the orders started to slow down and they finally dug themselves out of the hole they'd been in since seven o'clock. The post-theater crowds were coming in now, packing the bar on the far side of the room, a few groups on the main floor who ordered wine, appetizers, desserts. The last pick left the kitchen at a quarter past eleven, and Rachel let her head fall forward for a second before she looked out at her staff with a grin. "Good job, everyone. Shut it down."

Ovens, grills, and burners were switched off. Leftover *mise en place* was transferred to the walk-ins for tomorrow morning. Each station got scrubbed and disinfected with the careless precision of people who had done this every night of their adult lives, the last chore standing between them and freedom. She had no illusions about where they were headed next, exactly where she would have been headed as a young cook—out to the bars to drain the adrenaline from their systems, then home to catch precious little sleep before they showed up early for brunch service tomorrow. By contrast, Rachel's only plans were her soft bed, a cup of hot tea, and a rerun on Netflix until she fell into an exhausted stupor. At work, she might feel as energetic as she had as a nineteen-year-old line cook, but the minute she stumbled out of the restaurant, her years on the planet seemed to double.

Rachel changed out of her whites into jeans and a sweatshirt in her office, only to run into Gabrielle in the back corridor.

"Can I talk to you for a minute, Chef?"

Rachel's radar immediately picked up the nervousness beneath the woman's usual brusque demeanor. Changed out of her work clothes and into a soft blue T-shirt that made her red hair look even fierier, Gabby suddenly seemed very young and insecure, even though she was several years older than Rachel.

"Of course. Do you want to come in?" Rachel gestured to the open door of her office.

"No, um, that's okay. I wanted to let you know . . . before someone figures it out and tells you." Gabby took a deep breath and squared her shoulders. "I'm pregnant."

Rachel stared at the woman, sure her heart froze for a split second. "Pregnant?"

"Four months." Gabby hurried on, "I won't let it interfere with my work, I swear. But at some point . . ."

"You're going to need to take maternity leave." In an office setting, that was hard enough, but in a restaurant kitchen, where there were a limited number of cooks to fill in and new additions disrupted the flow they'd established, it was far more complicated.

Gabby nodded.

"We'll figure it out," Rachel said finally. "And congratulations. You're going to make a wonderful mother. I bet Luke is thrilled."

Gabby's words rushed out in relief. "He is."

"Now go get some sleep." Rachel's instincts said to give her a hug, congratulate her again, but that damaged the level of authority she needed to maintain, made it harder to demand the best from Gabby when she should probably be focusing more on her baby than her job. Instead, Rachel settled for a squeeze of her shoulder.

Andrew was the last to head for the back hallway, leaving Rachel alone in the kitchen to survey her domain. Once again, it gleamed with stainless-steel sterility, silent without the drone of vents and whoosh of burners. It should probably bother her more that she had no one to go home to, no one waiting on the other side of the door. But Rachel had known what she was giving up when she set off down this career path, knew the choice was even starker for female chefs who had to decide between running their own kitchens and having a family. Most days, it was more than a fair trade. She'd promised herself long ago she wouldn't let any man stand between her and her dreams.

Camille, Paisley's front-of-house manager, slipped into the kitchen quietly, somehow looking as fresh and put together as she had at the beginning of the night. "Ana's waiting for you at the bar. I'm going to go now unless you need me."

"No, go ahead. Good work as always."

"Thanks, Chef. See you tomorrow."

Rachel pretended not to notice Camille slip out with Andrew, their arms going around each other the minute they hit the back door. The food service industry was incestuous, as it must be— civilians didn't tend to put up with the long hours, late nights, and always-on mentality. There had been plenty of hookups in her kitchen among waitstaff and cooks in various and constantly changing combinations, but they never involved Rachel. On some points at least, she was still a traditionalist—one-night stands and casual affairs held no appeal. Besides, she was an owner and the chef, the big boss. Getting involved with anyone on her staff would be the quickest way to compromise her authority.

Rachel pushed around the post to the dining room and crossed the empty space to the bar. A pretty Filipina sat there, nursing a drink and chatting with the bartender, Luis.

"Ana! What are you doing here? Did Dan call you?"

Ana greeted Rachel with a one-armed hug. "I worked late and thought I'd drop by to say hi. Luis said it was a good night."

"Very good night: 215."

Ana's eyebrows lifted. "That's great, Rachel. Way to go. I'm not going to say I told you so, but . . ."

"Yeah, yeah, you told me so." Rachel grinned at her longtime friend. Analyn Sanchez had been one of her staunchest supporters when she'd decided to open a restaurant with two Denver industry veterans, even though it meant leaving the lucrative, high-profile executive chef job that had won her a coveted James Beard Award. And she had to give part of the credit to the woman next to her, who had agreed to take on Paisley as a client of the publicity firm for which she worked, even though the restaurant was small potatoes compared to her usual clients.

Luis wiped down an already-clean bar top for the third time. "You want anything, Chef?"

"No, thank you. You can go. I'll see you on Tuesday."

"Thank you, Chef." Luis put away his rag, grabbed his cell phone from beneath the bar, and quickly slipped out from behind his station. Not before one last surreptitious look at Ana, Rachel noticed.

"Do I need to tell him to stop hitting on you?"

"Nah, he's harmless. So, Rachel . . ."

Once more that gut instinct fired away, flooding her with dread. "You're not here for a social visit."

Ana shook her head. "Have you seen the article yet?"

"The Carlton Espy review? Who hasn't? Can you believe the guy had the nerve to come in here tonight and say, 'You're welcome'? As if he'd done me some huge favor?"

Ana's expression flickered a degree before settling back into an unreadable mask.

Uh-oh.

"What is it? You're not talking about the review, are you?"

Ana reached into her leather tote and pulled out a tablet, then switched it on before passing it to Rachel.

Rachel blinked, confused by the header on the web page. "The *New Yorker*? What does this have to do with me?" The title of the piece, an essay by a man named Alexander Kanin, was "The Uncivil War."

"Just read it."

She began to skim the article, the growing knot in her stomach preventing her from enjoying what was actually a very well-written piece. The writer talked about how social media had destroyed civility and social graces, not only online but in person; how marketing and publicity had given an always-available impression of public figures, as if their mere existence gave consumers the right to full access to their lives. Essentially, nothing was sacred or private or off-limits. He started by citing the cruel remarks made on CNN about the mentally disabled child of an actress-activist, and then the story of a novelist who had committed suicide after being bullied relentlessly on Twitter. And then she got to the part that nearly made her heart stop.

Nowhere is this inherent cruelty more apparent than with women succeeding in male-dominated worlds like auto racing and cooking. The recent review of an award-winning Denver chef suggesting that she had traded sexual favors in return for industry acclaim reveals that there no longer needs to be any truth in the speculations, only a cutting sense of humor and an eager tribe of consumers waiting for their next target. When the mere act of cooking good food or giving birth to an "imperfect" child or daring to create controversial art becomes an invitation to character assassination, we have to accept that we have become a deeply flawed and morally bankrupt society. The new fascism does not come from the government, but from the self-policing nature of the mob—a mob that demands all conform or suffer the consequences.

Rachel set the tablet down carefully, her pounding pulse leaving a watery ocean sound in her ears and blurring her vision. "This is bad."

"He didn't mention you by name," Ana said. "And he *was* defending you. You have to appreciate a guy who would call Espy out on his disgusting sexism."

Rachel pressed a hand to her forehead, which now felt feverish. "Anyone with a couple of free minutes and a basic understanding of Google could figure out who he's talking about." A sick sense of certainty washed over her. "Espy knows it, too. Without this article, his review would have died a natural death. He should have been thanking *me*."

Cautiously, Ana took back her tablet. "I'm hoping people will overlook the details based on the message, but just in case, you should inform your staff to direct media requests to me."

"Media." Rachel covered her face with her hands, as if that could do something to stave off the flood that was to come.

"Take a deep breath," Ana said, her no-nonsense tone firmly in place. "This could be a good thing. You've told me about the difficulty women have in this business, the kind of harassment you've put up with to get here. Maybe this is your chance to speak out against it. You'd certainly get wider attention for the restaurant, not that it looks like you're having any trouble filling seats."

Rachel dropped her head into her folded arms. What Ana

said was right. It would be publicity. But despite the old saying, it wasn't the right kind of publicity. She wanted attention for her food, not for her personal beliefs. To give this any kind of attention would be a distraction. And worst of all, it would make her a hypocrite. Playing the gender card for any reason—even a well-meaning one—went against everything she stood for.

"No," she said finally, lifting her head. "I won't. I'll turn down all the interviews with 'no comment' and get back to doing what I do best. Cooking."

"I thought you'd say that. I'll issue a statement to that effect. Just be prepared. Reporters can be relentless when they smell an interesting story." Ana hopped off the stool. "I'm beat. Call me if you need me."

"I will." She hugged Ana and watched her friend stride out the door, five-inch heels clicking smartly on the dining room's polished concrete floors. Rachel didn't move from her perch at the bar, though she was glad that Luis was already gone for the night. He would take one look at her and pronounce her in desperate need of a drink. The last thing she needed to do was send herself down that unwitting spiral again.

Instead, she would head to her office in the back as she always did, look over the pars that Andrew had calculated for her that morning, and pay the stack of invoices waiting in her in-box. Work was always the medicine for what ailed her, even if she was hoping that for once, her gut feeling was wrong.

Because right now, her gut told her everything was about to go sideways.